Praise for *The Underwriting*

A *Huffington Post*, *New York Post*, *Redbook*,
and *Metro* Summer Reading Pick

"Miller is a master at pacing—this tour de force gathers speed as it heats up. Adrenaline junkies, take note: You're in for a wild ride." —*Glamour*

"A Silicon Valley/Wall Street crew is living proof that more money = more problems." —*Cosmopolitan*

"You'd think it would be hard to write a rip-roaring novel that actually elicited our sympathy towards investment bankers—but Michelle Miller has managed it. Miller not only gets the reader to care about [their] anxieties and secret desires . . . she also spins an exciting piece of intrigue." —*The Guardian* (US)

"I'm going to be honest: it's been a long time since I've sat down and read a book. That ended after I picked up *The Underwriting*. From the very first paragraph, I was hooked. It's sharp, sexy, smart, and everything else you need for a perfect summer thriller. I wouldn't be surprised if this was the next book to land a huge movie deal." —Lindsey Sirera, *E! News Online*

"Miller's debut novel reads like a salacious, ripped-from-the headlines tell-all of Manhattan's young, wealthy, and uber-successful. From the very first page, I felt like I'd met these characters in real life: Todd, the hot, rich, d-bag banker; Tara, the striver perfectionist who can't quite please everyone; Kelly, the good girl with a secret; and Josh, the creepy savant genius who just might change the world. What do they all have in common? A certain location-based hookup app that alters each of their lives in shocking ways. Get ready to settle in—you won't be able to put down this book." —Lauren Weisberger, *New York Times*–bestselling author of *The Devil Wears Prada*

"A more intricate *Devil Wears Prada* for the tech generation." —*Kirkus Reviews*

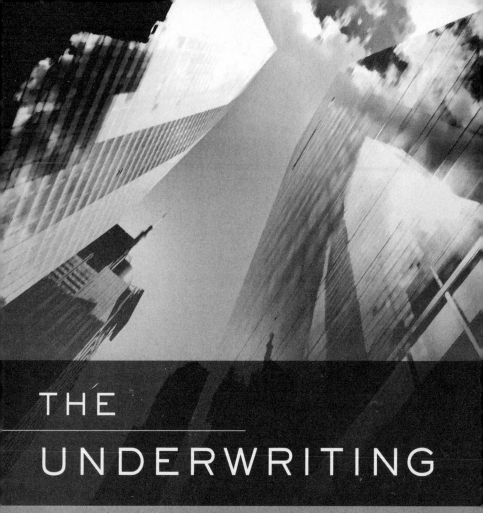

THE
UNDERWRITING

MICHELLE MILLER

G. P. PUTNAM'S SONS   NEW YORK

G. P. PUTNAM'S SONS
Publishers Since 1838
An imprint of Penguin Random House LLC
375 Hudson Street
New York, New York 10014

The Library of Congress has catalogued the G. P. Putnam's Sons hardcover edition as follows:

Miller, Michelle, date.
The underwriting / Michelle Miller.
    p.   cm.
  ISBN 9780399174858
1. Single women—Fiction. 2. Investment bankers—Fiction. I. Title.
PS3613.I54555U64   2015   2014049771
813'.6—dc23

International edition ISBN: 9780399176524

First G. P. Putnam's Sons hardcover edition / May 2015
First G. P. Putnam's Sons international edition / May 2015
First G. P. Putnam's Sons trade paperback edition / December 2016
G. P. Putnam's Sons trade paperback ISBN: 9780143108238

Printed in the United States of America
1   3   5   7   9   10   8   6   4   2

Book design by Meighan Cavanaugh

This is a work of fiction. Names, characters, places, and incidents either are the product
of the author's imagination or are used fictitiously, and any resemblance to actual persons,
living or dead, businesses, companies, events, or locales is entirely coincidental.

For the Muppies

Whenever you feel like criticizing any one . . . just remember that all the people in this world haven't had the advantages that you've had.

—F. Scott Fitzgerald, *The Great Gatsby*

THE

UNDERWRITING

1

TODD

"You are such an asshole." Her face had gone from red to white as she pulled her naked legs from under the sheets. Retracing last night's steps from the living room to the bed, she collected the trail of discarded clothing in her arms.

Todd reached for the remote and turned on MSNBC, hoping the sound would drown out the awkwardness. He hated morning awkwardness.

The girl came back into the room and started rummaging through the sheets for her underwear.

"I just don't . . ." she started, looking at him. "I just don't understand why you're so afraid of commitment."

"I'm not afraid of commitment," he said simply, pretending to be absorbed in the television, where two commentators were discussing the latest scandal at L.Cecil, involving traders who allegedly peddled two hundred million dollars of shares they knew were overvalued to unwitting investors. Todd made a face at the television: that better not affect his bonus.

The girl pulled her skirt over her thin hips and refastened her push-up bra; she had a nice rack, but her thighs were too big and she looked like the type who was going to balloon when she hit thirty-five. She was an 8 out of 10 on an attractiveness scale, which was where Todd liked to play: eights were hot, but insecure about not being tens, so they worked hard to please.

Right now, though, she was barely scraping by as a six with her smudged eyeliner and greasy blonde hair.

"Then what's so wrong with taking me to dinner?" she said softly, still for the first time since she'd left the bed.

"Because that's not what you are to me," he answered honestly.

"Then what am I?" Her voice was even softer. Her fingers clenched the sheets as she waited for the answer she didn't want to hear.

"Listen: we've had a really good time. Why ruin it?" Todd said, meaning it.

Her jaw set and her watery eyes shimmered. "You mean I'm the girl you fuck."

Todd didn't respond. He needed to get to work.

"Do you know I went to Penn? Like, I'm not some bimbo idiot. I work at a top-tier law firm. I'm the girl you date, not the girl you fuck."

"I'm sure you're right."

"So let's go to dinner!" she said, exasperated.

"I don't want a girlfriend."

"Then why did you—"

"You." Todd cut her off, his patience exhausted. "*You* contacted *me*, drunk, at a bar at two a.m. after you put your profile on a location-based dating app. What did you expect?"

She didn't break her gaze. "Hook is a tool for meeting people. You're on it, and you're presumably normal. Why does my being on it make me a slut?"

"I didn't say you're a slut. I said you sought me out in the context of a late-night booty call, and that's the implicit arrangement we've got."

"But that was four times ago," the girl protested.

Todd didn't want to hurt her, but he also really didn't have time for this kind of drama. All of his focus needed to be on his career. Having just celebrated his thirty-second birthday, Todd was all too aware that he had twelve months to make a serious deal happen at L.Cecil's investment bank if he still wanted to reach his goal of being the youngest-ever managing director in the prestigious Wall Street firm.

"We've gotten to know each other since then." She kept talking, refusing to let it go. "We talked about your job and I told you about my family and I was late to work last week because I know you like morning sex." Her lip was trembling.

"I didn't ask you to do that."

Her cheeks went red, knowing it was true. "I can't believe this is happening." She turned and finished dressing, abandoning the search for her thong.

Todd continued watching the television, where it was agreed that, while not illegal, the fact that L.Cecil traders knew that what they were selling was crap made it unethical and worthy of fines. It was a bullshit argument—the role of a trader was to facilitate trades; it was up to the investor to determine whether or not the trade was worth putting his money behind.

Todd waited for the front door to slam and got out of bed, stepping his six-foot-three-inch, former-Division-One-water-polo-player frame under the waterfall showerhead.

The question of whether to bring a girl back to his place or go to her apartment was a perpetual conundrum for Todd. On the one hand, the expensive minimalism of his spacious one-bedroom guaranteed that any girl he brought back would have sex with him, even if she'd been committed to prudishness up to that point; on the other hand, away games had the advantage that he could leave on his own terms. He should have gone to her place last night, given he knew she'd fuck him, but he'd had one too many tequila sodas at Monkey Bar and wasn't thinking clearly when he'd written her a message on Hook.

Todd shaved and put on his standard uniform—bespoke suit, Hermès tie, Armani socks, Gucci loafers. He used the Uber app on his phone to order a car and glanced approvingly in the mirror before heading downstairs.

When he exited the front door of his apartment building the girl was standing by the door, blowing into her hands to ward off the March breeze. "Jesus Christ," he whispered under his breath.

She saw him and bit her lip apologetically.

"I'm sorry," she said. "I really didn't mean to be dramatic, it's just I think this could be more. I mean, I could be more—I *am* more—than that girl in the Hook profile."

He put his hand gently on her hip and kissed her cheek gently. "It's okay," he said, "but I've got a lot going on, and what we've got now is the most I can do. If you want more, I respect that, but I can't give it to you."

She nodded and looked at the ground.

"Will I see you again?" she asked softly, without looking up.

"I'm not going anywhere," he said, dodging the question. "Can I help you find a cab?"

She shook her head. "No, I'll walk."

"Okay. Have a good day, all right?" he coaxed, making his blue eyes smile.

"Okay." She headed down the street, her four-inch stilettos and tangled hair a scarlet letter on the Wednesday morning sidewalk.

Todd climbed into the black car and navigated to his list of "Favorites" on Hook. What was her name again? A-something. Amy? Allison? Amanda. Right. He found her, and promptly deleted her profile.

Block user? the app asked. He tapped *Yes*.

Leave a review? *No*. She wasn't worth any more of his time.

The BlackBerry he used for work buzzed in his pocket and he exchanged it with his iPhone, scrolling through the twenty-six new e-mails he'd received overnight. There were the normal morning blasts: the Asian market update, the FX daily forecast, an e-mail from Catherine Wiley, the president of the investment bank, providing a compliance-approved stock statement to feed to clients who asked about the L.Cecil trading scandal.

And then: an e-mail from Josh@hook.com.

Todd—Have decided to go public. Want you to do it. JH

Todd almost choked; he read it again. He looked up at the driver, as if the man might understand the significance of what Todd was holding in his hand. Todd could feel his heart racing: Josh Hart was CEO of Hook, the app that had not only made his sex life considerably more efficient, but which was also the hottest company in Silicon Valley. An IPO on that app wouldn't just make a lot of people a lot of money, bringing it into L.Cecil would solidify Todd's promotion. Fuck managing director—a deal this big might propel him to group head status.

Todd scrolled to the e-mail signature and dialed Josh's number.

The phone rang and he glanced at his watch, realizing it was only six fifteen in San Francisco, but Josh Hart picked up on the third ring. "Hello?"

"Josh!" Todd exclaimed a bit too enthusiastically. "Josh, it's Todd. Todd Kent. I just got your e-mail and—I'm sorry, is this a good time?"

"It's fine." Josh's voice was like a robot's.

"Listen, I'm . . ." Todd struggled to find his composure.

He raced to remember the last time he'd actually talked to Josh Hart: it was two years ago in Las Vegas, at the Consumer Electronics Show, when they'd met at a strip club. Josh was a pasty-white computer dork with dark circles under his eyes and boyish curls that clung to his head. He'd been wearing a hoodie and pleated khakis. Todd had spotted him across the room and beelined for him—for a guy to get into the club looking like that, he had to be important—and invited him to his table. Josh had sat studying the dancers as if they were aliens, twitching every time Todd tried to talk to him about his financing strategy, as he angled to get L.Cecil involved.

At the end of the night, Todd had given Josh his card and never heard from him again. But he must have said something right, Todd assured himself, for Josh to contact him, two years later, with the biggest deal of either of their lives.

"I just wanted to see what you were thinking, in regards to us working together on financing Hook," Todd finally said.

"I told you in my e-mail." Josh sounded irritated, as if his one-liner were more than sufficient to set an IPO in motion. "I've decided to take Hook public and I've decided you should underwrite it. I'd like to raise 1.8 billion dollars at a 14-billion-dollar valuation."

Todd blinked. Hook still hadn't turned a profit, and Wall Street was starting to question the value of social media apps. Then again, Wall Street had doubted Facebook and its share price was soaring. Now that he thought about it, if Facebook was worth one hundred fifty billion, Hook was probably worth *more* than fourteen billion.

"Those numbers seem right. So the typical process is to do a bake-off, where different banks pitch you and—"

"I don't want a bake-off. I want you to do it."

Todd's brain whirred: there was always a bake-off. Was skipping it even allowed? "That's great, I mean, that saves us a lot of time," he said.

"So I'll talk to my boss, Larry, he's the one who will be in charge of the—"

"No," Josh corrected. "I said I want you to do it. You."

"What? Me?"

"Yes," Josh said. "Isn't this what you do? Oversee deals?"

"Well, yes, I've worked on dozens of deals, but this is really huge, Josh, and there are a lot of more senior people who—" Todd stopped himself. Larry had been at the bank longer, but did that really mean he knew more than Todd? Larry was also forty-five and married: what did he know about a location-based dating app whose primary users were millennials? And if Josh, who was thirty, could create a company like Hook, Todd could surely lead its IPO.

"Yeah," Todd corrected himself to the phone, "I can absolutely lead this deal for you."

"Good," Josh said. "We can meet here tomorrow to finalize."

"Tomorrow?" Todd sat forward. "I still need to get the contract together and—" He thought quickly: what else did he need? "And I've got to determine the right team."

"Team?"

"Well, yeah, we'll need to loop in a couple analysts and an associate from my group, plus someone from Equity Capital Markets to advise on market conditions and the road show, and we probably—"

"Three. You can have three more people, max."

Todd laughed. "Josh, for a deal this size, you're going to want—"

"Let me be very clear about something, Todd." Josh cut him off. "I hate Wall Street. You are all morons who do nothing but insert yourself into processes in order to profit from the inefficiency you create. If I could raise 1.8 billion dollars without you, I would, but I don't have time in the midst of creating a company to also fix the financial services industry."

Todd's jaw unhinged. He knew from growing up in Northern California that tech guys didn't like Wall Street, but it took a lot of nerve to buck a system that had been thriving for hundreds of years.

"So you can have three people on your team," Josh continued, "but any slick dicks and the deal is off. Is that clear?"

"Yeah, sure."

"Fine. See you on Friday, then."

"Friday." Todd nodded. That at least gave him a day. "We'll see you on Friday. Really excited to—"

He heard the phone click off and looked at it. Had that really just happened?

"We're here," the driver said from the front seat as Todd hung up the phone.

Todd looked up, coming back to the moment, then looked out the window and saw L.Cecil's Park Avenue headquarters. He'd spent every weekday and most weekends of the last ten years there, save the annual two weeks' vacation regulators forced bankers to take in a worthless effort to curb insider dealing. The glass building stretched forty-three floors into the sky, reflecting the morning light in its mirrored-glass windows. The brass letters L.CECIL hung above the revolving door entrance, set back from the street by a wall topped with flowers meant to make it look friendly, but not so friendly that people missed the fact that they weren't invited in.

Suits flashed their security badges as they streamed into the building, all of them hoping that today would be the day a deal would come that would take them from being a cog to designing their own wheel. Today, Todd realized, was his day. Josh might be an arrogant prick, but he was going to make Todd one of the most powerful investment bankers in history. Holy shit, this was huge.

NICK

"I know you don't like talking about money, but as the chief financial officer of this company, it's my responsibility to tell you that we have no choice but to raise more capital if you want to keep this vision alive," Nick Winthrop said determinedly into the mirror. "I want to very firmly recommend we pursue a public offering."

He stared at his bare-chested reflection and tried to visualize Josh's reaction.

"Now, I know you hate Wall Street," he said, preempting the CEO's imaginary protests, "which is why I've gone ahead and prepared this PowerPoint deck outlining each firm's track record and filtering the top ten who ought to be invited to the bake-off."

He couldn't say no to that. Even Josh Hart, the computer science wunderkind who had created Hook and seemed to take pride in his lack of business acumen, couldn't argue with Nick on this point. Which meant Nick just had to get Josh's sign-off on the IPO, and then Nick could quietly call the top investment bankers in the world and have them suck up to him for weeks, all for the right to have their name in the deal that would turn Nick's equity stake into eighty-five million dollars in cash and, more important, put him in a position to have the kind of global impact he deserved.

Nick had been reluctant to take the position at Hook. He had graduated from Stanford in 2004 and started his career at McKinsey & Company, the number-one-ranked management consulting firm in the world, where he'd excelled. He'd left after three years to join Dalton Henley Venture Partners, where he became the mentee of Phil Dalton, one of the most respected venture capitalists in Silicon Valley; Phil had written his recommendation to Harvard Business School, where Nick was a Baker Scholar, i.e., the cream of the cream of the crop in the business leadership community.

While at HBS, Nick wrote the business plan for ApplyYourself, which would completely disrupt the university application market by forecasting a user's likelihood to get into the various top programs around the country. The company would start with the Ivy League + Stanford, like Facebook had, then grow to all universities and, eventually, create prediction algorithms for the job market, too.

When Nick had shown the business plan to Phil Dalton, however, Phil had suggested Nick should instead apply to the open chief financial officer position at Hook. Nick had been devastated: he was ready to be an entrepreneur, not the CFO of a company started by someone younger than him who hadn't even gone to business school.

But when Nick had had his first success in failing (all good entrepreneurs had at least one failure) by not raising his one and a half million, he'd remembered that adaptability was another core component of entrepreneurial success, and so adjusted his definition of prestige to confidently accept the CFO role, along with a 0.5 percent equity stake in Hook.

When Hook had started to take off last spring, growing to over five hundred million users and capturing international media attention, Nick had had a profound moment of faith in the universe's plan for him.

That plan, he knew, would make him a person who had real impact on a global scale, and he could feel in his veins that he was on the precipice of becoming one of the world's great leaders.

Nick took a deep breath and collected himself, glancing down at his pecs admiringly. The CrossFit package he'd bought on Groupon last month was really paying off, equipping him to be at his best when magazines started photographing him for covers. He traced the line forming around his shoulder muscle with satisfaction and plopped to the ground to do ten push-ups, just for good measure.

It was six thirty in the morning, but Nick was wide awake as he punched the button on his Nespresso machine to make a *forte*, sprinkling organic cassia cinnamon into it in order to regulate his glucose levels, a trick he'd learned from *The 4-Hour Body*. He checked his iPhone to see if Grace had texted since he had last checked ten minutes ago, and told himself to relax when he saw she still hadn't: she was a hot girl and had a right to play it cool, and he was a cool guy who could roll with that.

Still, he wished he could tell her what a big deal he was about to make happen—to see her face when she realized what kind of guy she was dating. But the deal would have to stay strictly confidential until the S-1, a hundred-page legal document detailing the investment opportunity, was filed with the Securities and Exchange Commission, and that would take months. He made a note to book a table at Gary Danko every Friday in May to celebrate.

He finished the espresso and put the mug in the dishwasher, wiping the handle of the machine with a Lysol cleansing pad to remove his finger smudge from its stainless steel finish. He checked his iPhone one more time—nothing—and zipped his Dalton Henley–branded fleece vest as he headed out the door to make the short walk to Hook's headquarters.

This was his favorite hour of the workday: the engineers didn't clear out of the office until the early morning hours, and the HR staff didn't get in until around ten, so for now the pristine, just-constructed glass office on San Francisco's Embarcadero was all his own.

He held his hand to the state-of-the-art security sensor outside the building's entrance and took the elevator to the sixth floor. He crossed the main floor where the computer programmers sat; it was cluttered with stuffed animals and colorful plastic balls that had spilled from the ball pit in the corner. Next to it, a life-sized gorilla doubled for a helium machine, which the engineers used to fill managers' offices with balloons on their birthdays, and, more often, to get high.

Everything about this space made Nick anxious. Converting it into an acceptably professional workspace was the first thing he was going to do with the IPO proceeds. He didn't care what the engineers had to say about it.

He reached his corner office and relaxed, embracing the purity of his pristine personal space.

"Hey."

Nick looked up, startled, at Josh's form in the doorway. "Oh, hi." He took a moment to process. "What are you doing here?"

"I was coding," Josh said. The bags under his eyes were dark and heavy and his head twitched, tilting ever so slightly to the right and straight again. "Lost track of time."

"Nice." Nick smiled affirmatively. Another lesson he'd learned from Phil Dalton was to always encourage engineers when they got lost in their coding. *You may not understand what they're doing, but great things come out of those late nights*, Phil had said, and Nick had written it in the Moleskine notebook he carried with him to write down wise advice.

"I need you for a meeting at eleven on Friday," Josh announced, turning to leave.

"What for?"

Josh turned back and his head twitched again.

Nick had never figured out what set off the Hook founder's twitch, but he'd learned to ignore it. If anything, Josh's quirks just meant Hook would need a different face for all the press that was going to happen when the company went public, and Nick was humbly willing to accept that role. There was a tradition at HBS where all the MBAs put ten dollars in a pot to give to the first person in the class who got his pencil drawing on the cover of the *Wall Street Journal*, and Nick realized with confidence that it was going to be him. Take that, Stephen Hartley. Who's the coolest guy in school now?

"L.Cecil is coming in," Josh said without further explanation.

"What?" Nick sat forward. "Why is L.Cecil—"

"They're taking us public," Josh said. "And they're coming in Friday."

"What are you talking ab—" Nick started, shaking his head. "You don't make those decisions, Josh. I'm Hook's chief financial officer and that is a financial decision."

Josh stared at him. "It's my company."

"It's *partly* your company." They had talked about this before. "You have a responsibility to your invest—" He stopped himself, remembering that the IPO was what he wanted, and feeling like this was one of those times when he was fighting for the sake of winning, something he'd gotten negative feedback for in business school. He said slowly, calmly, "There's a process, Josh. And, as CFO, I should be in charge of that process."

"I know," Josh said, "I don't want anything more to do with it."

"I mean, there is a process for *picking* a bank," Nick said. "You have to do a bake-off and then banks pitch you and you select based on—"

"Why?" Josh's eyes bored into Nick's. Nick felt his face flush.

"Because—" he started. They couldn't just skip the bake-off. Banks had to suck up to them. "Even if you could, L.Cecil is a terrible choice. Have you seen the news? They're under investigation for trading—"

"I know," Josh cut him off, his head twitching. "That's what makes them a good choice."

"What?" Nick squinted. L.Cecil hadn't even made his list of bake-off participants. "How can you possibly think that?"

"They're desperate for business. They need us." Josh stared at Nick; he was irritated that he had to explain his decision. "Always put yourself in the power seat, Nick. Don't they teach you that in business school?"

Nick's blood boiled. It was bad enough when Josh was arrogant about computer things, but business decisions were Nick's domain.

"Actually, at HBS we—" Nick protested.

"The guy I've hired has nothing to do with the scandal anyway."

"What do you mean 'the guy' you hired? You don't just—"

"Todd Kent. I met him two years ago at CES," Josh said. "He's running the whole thing."

Nick's voice caught in his throat. "Todd Kent? Todd Kent is the coverage banker you picked?"

"Do you know him?" Josh studied Nick's face.

"We went to school together." Nick's head started to pound. "Undergrad, not business school. He didn't go to business school. I'm sure he couldn't have gotten in." He said it automatically, spitefully.

Josh smirked. "Good. You can catch up at the meeting."

Nick watched a ball from the mess outside roll into his office as Josh left. He picked it up and crushed it in his hand before hurling it back at the empty room.

TODD

WEDNESDAY, MARCH 5; NEW YORK, NEW YORK

"You screw this up and we're fucked." Larry's neck was pulsing like a pit bull's.

"I know, man. I totally get it."

"I'm not talking *you* fucked. I could give a shit about your year-end." Larry's voice loosened a tiny bit at the power he had over Todd's bonus, but then wound up again when he remembered getting cut out of a deal in favor of his junior employee. "I'm talking about *me* getting fucked—about this group—about this division—fuck, this whole fuck-ing bank." Larry paused to take a breath before starting in again. "Jesus fucking Christ. These fucking Silicon Valley fucking idiots." Todd was silent. "Get out of my office before I cut off your cock."

Todd concealed a laugh as he shut the door. Poor guy.

By the time Todd had gotten to the twenty-seventh floor this morn-ing, where he sat with the rest of the Technology, Media & Telecom group, he was confident that Larry had to be cut out of the Hook IPO. Josh was right: Todd Kent was the man to lead this underwriting, not just because he was a great banker, but because he carried the cachet the app company needed to really convince the markets of its fourteen-billion-dollar valuation. No matter how much experience Larry had leading deals, he was old and going through a divorce resulting from his wife's discovery of his porn addiction. Definitely not the brand Hook was going for.

Todd walked proudly across the floor, carrying a confident smirk so that everyone who turned—and everyone did turn—knew that Todd had come out on top of whatever was behind the muffled shouting they'd just overheard in Larry's office.

"What'd you do to set him off?" Kal Taggar, the other senior VP in the group, asked without looking up as Todd took a seat at his cubicle in the block of six.

"You know Hook?"

"Obviously. Why?" he said to his computer screen, where he was fill-ing in his NCAA tournament bracket.

"They're going public." Todd paused, anticipating Kal's reaction to the punch line. "And Josh Hart wants me to lead the deal."

Kal turned in his seat, his jaw hanging. "What do you mean, Josh Hart wants you to 'lead the deal'?"

"I mean he wants me to be in charge of it—no bake-off, I pick the team. Only caveat is no 'slick dicks,'" Todd said in air quotes.

"You mean no Larry?" Kal laughed. Todd nodded. "Holy shit," Kal said with a mix of resentment and respect. "You fucking bastard."

Todd grinned. His phone rang and he picked it up merrily. "Todd Kent."

He sat up a little straighter when he heard the voice on the other end.

"Todd, it's Harvey." There was only one Harvey in L.Cecil: Harvey Tate. The seventy-year-old executive had once led the most important investment banking deals on Wall Street. *Had once led* being the operative words. Under the banner of a senior vice chairman title, he now spent his time dispensing clichéd wisdom and taking credit for deals he had nothing to do with from his massive corner office on the forty-second floor.

"Harvey, it's great to hear from you." Todd rolled his eyes and mouthed *Harvey Tate* to Kal, who watched eagerly.

"I heard about the deal and wanted to congratulate you," Harvey said.

"Thank you, sir." Todd was surprised but impressed that senior management agreed it was a good thing for a young guy to be leading this IPO.

"I've got a few ideas. Why don't you come up to my office and we can discuss?"

Todd hesitated. He had less than thirty-six hours to pull together a team, a work plan and contract; he didn't have time to pander to Harvey Tate. "Sure," he said, "I'll reach out to your assistant to find a time next week." Harvey was old: maybe he'd forget.

"Ten o'clock work for you?"

Todd's jaw set in irritation. He was also supposed to meet his trainer, Morgan, at eleven, for a workout he desperately needed to clear his brain for all of said work. "Sure," he heard himself say, wishing for the thousandth time his mother hadn't instilled him with such good etiquette. Life would be so much easier if he were an asshole.

"Great. See you in an hour."

"Looking forward to it." Todd hung up the phone. "Fuck."

"What?" Kal leaned in. When a man worked sixteen hours a day, six days a week, in a cubicle that smelled like the revolving ethnicity of last night's takeout, gossip was like Vicodin. And Todd had just become the best dealer in the firm.

"Fucking Harvey Tate wants to be my mentor."

"Ha! The perks of being a big deal, man," Kal said sarcastically.

Neha Patel, the group's overly eager second-year analyst, appeared at his desk, looking down at a stack of papers in her hands, speaking with her standard Adderall-amped speed. "Here's the deck you asked for. I put in an extra section showing historical earnings reports for similar media companies, and I printed out all my assumptions. The only thing I think we need to discuss is this part about—"

"Whoa, whoa, whoa." Todd blinked. "Slow down, hot rod. I haven't had my coffee yet."

"Do you want me to go get you one?" she asked automatically, looking up over her glasses. She had a line of dried spittle on her chin, evidently unnoticed since she returned to her desk from the nap room. Most analysts pulled two all-nighters a week, but Neha averaged two *non*-all-nighters a week in her unbridled drive to be the best analyst in L.Cecil's history.

"No, Neha," he said, "it's fine. What is this for?"

"It's the Viacom pitch you asked me to put together." Her voice sounded like a tape on perpetual fast-forward.

He looked at the deck: he didn't need this for another three weeks, if ever.

"Were you up all night working on this?"

"I took two forty-eight-minute naps," she said. "As long as you don't hit fifty-five minutes you don't go into REM sleep so you don't actually get that tired."

"When was the last time you slept at home?"

"Last Friday." Neha said it without any hint it was odd. This was exactly the attitude one wanted in an analyst.

"Do you want to come to California?" he asked the girl.

"What?"

"I'm taking Hook—the dating app company—public. Do you have the bandwidth to be the analyst?"

Neha's spittle-flecked jaw dropped. Her face was round and dotted with acne; she definitely didn't wear makeup and had never been introduced to a pair of tweezers. "You mean the biggest privately owned company in Silicon Valley? The one backed by Dalton Henley Venture Partners with five hundred million users and a two hundred fifty percent quarterly growth rate?"

Todd looked at her: all she cared about was the financials—she probably had never even used the app. This was also exactly what one wanted in an analyst. "That's the one," Todd said.

"Are you kidding? Of course I want to work on it!" The thought sank in and she got more animated. "I mean, I'll work my butt off. I mean, thank you. Thank you so much for the opportunity."

"Sure thing." Todd smiled, her enthusiasm making him feel benevolent. "I need you to drop everything else and pull together as much information as you can tonight, as well as an outline for a work plan. We fly Friday morning."

"Yes, done! I'll get going right now!" She scrambled back to her desk, like a three-year-old who'd just been given a new Lego set.

Todd turned back to his computer, and noticed Kal still looking at him. "What?"

"You dick," Kal said. "You're taking our best analyst, too?"

"Sorry, bud." Todd grinned. "You bring in a 1.8-billion-dollar deal and I promise we can draw straws for her."

"Whatever."

"Hey, what's an eight percent fee on 1.8 billion?" Todd mused aloud at what the firm was going to make on the deal. "And what's-his-face that brought in Catalyst last year made, what, a five-mil bonus? His deal was only half that—"

Kal threw a pen at him. Todd laughed. He could already feel the five million in his bank account.

"Here," he said, handing Kal his Equinox card as he stood to go to his meeting with Harvey. "Take my training session. Morgan's boobs'll cheer you up." Todd patted Kal's shoulder as he moved past.

The twenty-seventh floor was crowded with loud-talking investment bankers. Analysts and associates, the lowest-ranking employees, sat crammed at three long tables in the center of the room, each appointed a double-monitor computer and a Bloomberg terminal. On either side of the analyst desks were stacks of six cubicles, where VPs sat. Managing directors were rewarded for decades of servitude to the firm with small, glass-enclosed offices on the building's perimeter, hogging all the sunlight.

As he walked to the elevator, Todd played the game where he counted the number of people who blushed when he passed: men got half a point, hot women got two. From desk-to-elevator, Todd collected eight points, which was a 72 percent hit rate. Or maybe it was 81 percent. Sonja was a maybe—it was hard to tell when Indian people were blushing.

The elevator doors opened onto Chad Horton, a fat, pink-shirted trader, and Tara Taylor, a VP in Equity Capital Markets, looking down at her BlackBerry.

"Hey, buddy! Heard the big news," Chad said and punched Todd's shoulder. Tara didn't say anything, engrossed in whatever she was reading on the device in her hands.

"Shh . . . not too loud. Don't want Tara's people to start fighting over which of them gets to be on the team," Todd said.

The girl's head snapped up. Wait for it . . . Yes. There was the blush.

Ten points for the day. Or maybe nine and a half—Tara was attractive, but not quite a two-pointer. Definitely borderline. When you broke down her attributes, she wasn't that hot: great legs and a tight little waist, but no curves; her ass was flat and she couldn't be more than a B-cup. And her brown eyes were a little too close together, though whatever she was doing with her makeup helped. But her chin was still too sharp—nothing you could do about that. Still, there was something about it all together that was attractive. What the hell, give her two points. He was feeling generous.

Tara smirked and said nothing, returning to her BlackBerry.

Chad kept talking: "Heard you guys had a big night last night, eh? Just ran into Lou downstairs. Boy, did he look like hell. Said he didn't go to bed till sunrise."

Every other month Lou Reynolds organized drinks for the 2004 analyst class, of whom twelve of the eighty were still at the bank. The guys weren't nearly as cool as Todd's outside-of-work crew, but he knew his presence meant a lot to Lou and that Lou would pay it back with loyalty someday when Todd was running things. "Ha. I left early."

Chad elbowed him knowingly. "I heard you bailed, but wasn't exactly to go to sleep. Old girlfriend?"

"Yes," Todd lied, weirded out, but also flattered, that these guys paid so much attention to his sex life.

Todd tried to catch Tara's reaction in his periphery and was grateful when Chad stepped off on the next floor and he could turn to her and laugh. *"Men."*

"Yep!" Tara smiled closed-lipped before returning to her e-mail.

They'd slept together twice during his senior spring at Stanford, when she was a freshman. The first time was at a Pi Phi–SAE Redneck Racing pledge event. It was a frat favorite because all the girls showed up in their best Jessica Simpson–in–*Dukes of Hazzard* short-shorts, spray-tanned and made-up to the hilt. Except Tara, who arrived in overalls with fake teeth that would have made Gisele Bündchen ugly. Todd was manning the bar and joked with Tara about the teeth, but she, pretty drunk by that point, insisted they were real and feigned offense. They bantered for a bit and he spent his next half hour on keg duty devising something clever to say, which he delivered when he found her on the dance floor with SAE's token gay pledge, Corey.

"Excuse me, Tara, but I still think those teeth are fake, and I'd like to prove it by removing them for you, preferably with my tongue."

She'd laughed and turned to Corey, saying in a voice loud enough that Todd could hear, "The very popular Todd Kent wants to hook up with me, Corey. I guess I should probably go with him, right?" and, with Corey's overwhelming approval (who said gays weren't good for the frat?), turned back to Todd: "Oh, fine. Let's go. But I'm leaving the teeth in."

And she had, the whole time they drunkenly fumbled through sex while the music pounded outside his frat room. When he woke up she was gone, but had left the teeth on his desk, with a note that said: *Souvenir.*

He'd expected to hear from her, but didn't. He stopped by Pi Phi for lunch with his friend Nicole the next week, but when he saw her she pretended not to notice him. Finally he got a casual "Hi there!" when he followed her to the soda fountain. "Diet Coke, eh?" He'd gestured to the glass she was filling at the tap. "Original, huh?" she'd offered, returning to her seat.

That night he'd gotten drunk and showed up at her dorm room.

She'd opened the door in checkered pajamas, but Todd didn't remember much beyond that. He'd woken up in her twin bed, her long, naked body squeezed between his own and the wall. There was a condom wrapper on the side table. His head had pounded as he gently sat up to take a sip of water, knocking a worn teddy bear off the bed as he did so.

"Morning," Tara had said, sitting up and pulling a T-shirt from under the covers over her head.

He'd thrown the stuffed animal at her playfully. "Nice teddy bear, freshman."

"Ha. Thanks. It was my sister's."

"She give it to you as a going-to-college present?" he'd teased.

"Nah. She's dead."

His heart had dropped. "Fuck, I'm sorry."

"Not your fault," she'd said simply, pulling her long legs out from the covers to step over him and re-dress her lower half. She'd noticed his concern and added, for his benefit, "I've still got one."

She'd grabbed her shower caddy and a towel and headed for the door, told him she had to study but didn't mind if he kept sleeping. He hadn't known what to do, unaccustomed to being left in bed and under the impression that all girls liked cuddling. So he'd left before she got back from the shower, and that was it. The next week he'd graduated and moved to New York and five years later they'd been reintroduced by Lillian Dumas, an MD in Equity Capital Markets who'd had it out for him ever since he'd rejected her advances at a holiday party in favor of Suzie Tebow from Investor Relations. He'd hardly recognized Tara in a fitted suit and Longchamp bag and makeup to match the New York working-girl uniform, and he'd felt a pinch of sadness that she, too, had become a cliché.

"After you." Todd held the elevator door open, wondering whether she still slept with the teddy bear.

"Thanks." She swept past, heading right as he turned left.

Harvey's assistant had Todd wait for twenty minutes outside the plush office where the senior vice chairman was laughing into his phone's earpiece. The forty-second floor was only fifteen up from where Todd sat, but it felt like a different universe, with expensive art on the walls and massive offices that wrapped around the perimeter, looking out over the bustling city below.

"Sorry for the wait," Harvey said when Todd was finally permitted entry into the spacious corner office. His handshake was stronger than his five-foot-seven frame might have led a person to expect. "My real estate broker." Harvey shook his head with a congenial *I-know-you-don't-know-but-trust-me-on-this-one* look. "I'm buying a new place in East Hampton. Southampton's gotten overrun. You wouldn't believe the kind of people they're letting into the Meadow Club."

"Sounds like a wise decision," Todd said neutrally.

"Please, sit," Harvey offered, and Todd followed the instruction. Harvey leaned back in his chair, tapping his thumbs together in his lap and staring into Todd's eyes, studying. Todd could feel the muscles in his neck tense down through his shoulders, the way they used to before a water polo match when he saw the opposing team.

"Hmph," Harvey finally grunted, shifting his weight in his chair, setting his arms on the desk between them, as if he'd uncovered all he needed to know about Todd.

"When I was your age," he started, "I was in the navy. I was stationed in the Pacific, in command of a crew of a hundred twenty, most of whom were older than me. It was right after the war and we were there to reingratiate ourselves with the Vietnamese."

Todd held his breath. He hated when old guys talked about their military days.

"A lot of the guys liked going into town to visit the whorehouses. It was cheap entertainment and helped them relax, so I didn't mind."

Harvey's silver-blond hair was combed over his always-tanned skin; he wore an Ermenegildo Zegna suit over a starched white shirt and Cartier cuff links. Old school slick dick.

"But then this one guy, Pete, started getting tired of going into town.

He picked his favorite whore and had her come back to the barracks." Harvey shook his head, laughing as he thought about it.

"He was from Princeton and thought he was pretty smart, and she was just a dumb whore who didn't speak much English. But then one night I came into my office and she was there, rifling through my files."

Todd glanced out the window. The slightest bit of snow was starting to fall from the gray clouds.

"So I killed her," Harvey said. Todd's eyes snapped back and Harvey pressed his lips into a calm, amused smile. "The authorities arrested Pete for it and, given it was his fault the whole thing had happened in the first place, I let justice take its course."

Todd shifted uncomfortably in his chair.

"You see, Todd, what Pete didn't understand is that there are things you can't see. There are systems you can't see, but they're there, and they're bigger than you."

Todd held his breath, his irritation returning: what was the point of all this?

"And to the system"—Harvey sat forward—"you are nothing." He paused, like a self-important prick, then sat back. "Now, who's going to be on your team?"

Todd willed his eyes not to roll. "Neha Patel will be the analyst, she's the best in the group and—"

"I'll let you have Beau as your associate," Harvey interrupted.

"What?" Beau Buckley was Harvey's business manager, a notoriously useless associate who owed his ironclad employment to the fact that his billionaire father was one of the firm's largest clients. Everyone knew he was being groomed for an executive role at the firm, which meant he spent all his time networking without touching any actual work.

"I've talked to Beau. He knows the application well and has an interest in technology. It'll be good experience for him to get exposure to a deal of this magnitude," Harvey said, not leaving any room for discussion.

"All due respect, Beau has no experience and, with Josh wanting to keep the team small—"

"Lillian Dumas will be your point for Equity Capital Markets," Harvey continued, ignoring Todd's protest. "She's been helping me with our Silicon Valley strategy."

"Absolutely not." Todd put his hands up. Not only did Lillian hate him for blowing off her advances three years ago, she was as high maintenance as women came: she was a female slick dick.

"Why not?" Harvey said calmly but firmly.

"Because she's a bitch—" Todd started, then corrected. "She'll make Josh uncomfortable."

"You're selling the value of an online-dating site to a mostly male sales force. You need a girl on the team."

"We've got Neha."

"Is she pretty?" Harvey asked bluntly.

Todd paused. "Tara," he heard himself say. "Tara Taylor can do it."

Harvey studied Todd's face. "Fine. That's the team, then."

"Fine," Todd said, processing what he'd just said. Tara was a good idea, right?

"We need this to go out in time for second quarter earnings."

Todd lifted a brow. "It's March. To make it into Q2 earnings it would have to be out by mid-May. You know this will take at least three and a half—"

"L.Cecil goes before the federal court the last week in May. I need this deal before then to counteract negative press."

"You can't decide an IPO based on press reports."

Harvey calmly crossed his hands on the desk, waiting.

"Fine," Todd said. "We'll move as fast as we can."

"When do you meet with the team?"

"Friday."

"I'll look forward to your status report."

"I don't have time for—" Todd stopped, knowing this wasn't worth his anger—he could have Neha do it. "Sure," he finally said.

"Good," Harvey said, picking up his phone as an indication the meeting was finished.

Todd stood, feeling like he'd won more points than Harvey but somehow still lost the game. Harvey was such a dick; he couldn't wait to blow this deal out of the park and put the old man in his place.

TARA

WEDNESDAY, MARCH 5; NEW YORK, NEW YORK

"Oh my god, can you believe George E is dating that, like, total peasant? Like, on the one hand it's totally awesome that he, you know, is worth a gazillion dollars and dates normal people? But on the other hand, oh my god she's like totally busted. I mean, like, le-gi-ti-mate-ly not attractive." Meagan talked like someone addicted to the sensation of vocalizing.

Tara stopped typing and waited, helplessly, for her colleague's voice to stop.

"Let me see." She heard Julian, the eager-to-please associate, roll his chair over to see Meagan's screen, fulfilling his duty as a junior colleague of making VPs feel good about themselves.

"Right?" Meagan asked.

"Do you think his stuff is really that good?"

"Of course it's that good: his last piece sold for seventeen million dollars."

"But is it, like, good art?" Julian asked.

"Julian, the value of art cannot be measured objectively—it's like what I taught you about public equity markets: perception creates reality. Is Facebook worth fifty dollars a share? What does that even *mean*? The market says it is, and therefore it must be so. And the market says George E should be with someone *way* hotter than this girl."

Tara sighed. What she wouldn't give for a scandal. The firm's current trading violations were news, but all they led to was an excuse for senior management to cut associate bonuses. What she needed was a bankruptcy or a Ponzi scheme or a massive round of layoffs to make life more interesting. She'd been at L.Cecil since she graduated from Stanford in 2007, back when markets were good and everyone with a 3.9 GPA from a top-tier university fought to get into investment banking or management consulting.

But that was seven years ago. The financial crisis had drained the adrenaline from Wall Street, as well as promotions and retire-at-thirty bonuses. Now the path that was supposed to be the right one felt . . . static. Tara did everything right: she worked out every morning; she showed up to the office on time and was never the first to leave; she avoided gluten, limited her dairy and didn't eat after nine p.m.; she called her parents once a week and contributed to her 401(k); she exfoliated her skin but not too often, cut her cuticles but not too close, waxed down there but not all the way; she read *The New Yorker* and supported NPR; and she always remembered to drink a glass of water for every glass of wine. So why did she still feel unfulfilled? What self-help book had she missed?

Maybe she should call her doctor to up her Celexa prescription.

The office mail clerk arrived with a box, and Tara looked up hopefully for she-wasn't-sure-what, and sighed when the package was for Meagan.

"Oh, perfect," Meagan said, taking the box.

Tara refocused on the status report she'd spent the last hour typing, taking her shoes off under her desk and spreading her toes on the carpet to ease her mind from existential crisis. She wondered what had happened to that girl Lori Pratt—the one who had left L.Cecil to become a writer—was she any happier?

"What's that?" Julian asked Meagan.

"It's my cleanse," Meagan said, clearly pleased that he'd asked. "I'm juicing for five days starting tomorrow. I've *got* to lose six pounds before my Miami trip next weekend."

"Yeah, totally," Julian said.

"What?" Meagan's jaw dropped. Tara turned just enough to see. Meagan had wanted Julian to tell her she didn't need to lose weight, even though she really *did* need to drop a few pounds. Already prone to jelly bean binges, being on the same floor as the on-average-15-percent-below-healthy-body-weight public relations team had caused Meagan to pack two dress sizes onto her five-foot-four frame in fits of Luna Bar gorges. "Are you calling me fat?"

Julian's hands jumped in front of him to backpedal. "No, no, no—I just meant—those girls in Miami are just, like, so *ridiculously* skinny that I could understand why—"

"Please go get me a coffee," Meagan interrupted, assigning the associate his punishment. "Two-pump sugar-free vanilla skinny latte, three Splendas. Tara, you want anything?"

"No, thanks." Tara turned in her chair and smiled politely.

"Hey, by the way, do you know whether Kelly Jacobson accepted her offer?"

"I'm actually talking to her tonight," Tara explained. Kelly was their top pick from last summer's intern class—a cheerful and bright Stanford senior whom Tara had been assigned to "convince to accept her offer" on account of their shared alma mater.

"Who is she deciding between?"

"Us and Google, I think."

"Ugh." Meagan made a face. "Why would you work at Google? Everyone gets totally fat there."

"I'll be sure to mention that," Tara said.

"I'm serious, Tara." Meagan didn't appreciate the sarcasm. "You know I'm in charge of the summer intern recruiting committee. If she doesn't accept the position I'm going to look totally retarded."

"Of course," Tara demurred, turning back to her computer, pleased to find an instant message on her screen.

TERRENCE: OMG I can hear her from here.

Tara looked over to Terrence, who sat three cubicle-blocks away. He was the best-looking and most intelligent person Tara knew at L.Cecil but, as a half-black gay man, was a perpetual outsider. He had landed in Investor Relations because the firm felt the best way he could serve the company was by showing his face to the press and investors who might, seeing it, believe the company was committed to diversity.

He was also one of Tara's closest friends. They would have been friends under any circumstances, but being depressed in their jobs had helped to solidify the deal.

Tara smiled at Terrence across the room and typed back.

TARA: Will I go to hell if I tell this Kelly girl she should come work here over Google?
TERRENCE: At least the men are better looking here.
TERRENCE: Even if they are douchebags.
TARA: Speaking of . . . Todd Kent encounter in the elevator this morning.
TERRENCE: Didn't you used to sleep with him?

Tara blushed . . . Had she told him that?

TARA: No.

Best to deny these things.

TARA: Once.

She could trust Terrence.

TARA: Fine, twice. But it was college. It didn't mean anything.

It had, of course, meant something then, when she'd lost her virgin-
ity to him at SAE and then he'd never called. But it didn't matter now—
not ten years later when they were both adult professionals.

TERRENCE: Right.

"Tara, my office. Now."

Tara looked up from her screen at Lillian Dumas, who swept by in
knee-high boots that gapped around her hyper-skinny legs, a bold test
of business formal attire that senior management let slide because the
boots were clearly expensive.

Tara slipped her shoes back on, suddenly self-conscious of their last-
seasonness, and followed Lillian to the glass-enclosed office. They reported to the same group head, but Lillian was a managing director five
years Tara's senior in the Equity Capital Markets Group, and so liked to
consider herself Tara's boss.

"Close the door." Lillian's voice was shaking. Tara did as told and
moved toward a chair. "Don't sit down."

Lillian's skeletal collarbone heaved as she breathed heavily through her firmly set jaw. She crossed her arms in a stance she'd lately adopted to show off the four-and-a-half-carat diamond the hedge fund manager she'd been dating for three years had finally conceded to give her.

"I don't know who you slept with," Lillian spat, "but I hope you realize who you're stealing from."

Tara felt her stomach knot in instinctive dislike of being in trouble. "Wha—"

"Hook has decided to go public and they want you to be the ECM."

"What?" Tara's brain and heart raced. "Who—" she started, but Lillian wasn't listening.

"I'm a managing director at this firm and you *just* got promoted to VP. And you *know* I've been working on a Silicon Valley strategy. Josh Hart has been in the system under my name for the past year." One of Lillian's favorite pastimes was putting every executive or potential executive in the business universe in the internal database as someone she knew so that she could get credit if and when they became clients of the firm. "I was supposed to meet him next month," she lied. "This deal should be mine."

"Lillian, I—"

"You must have slept with someone. Who was it?"

"Lillian, how do you even know—"

"Steve got a call from Harvey Tate saying you're supposed to be one hundred percent on this and I have to pick up your other work." She made a face. "How does Harvey Tate even know who you are? Eww, did you seduce him? He's like seventy." Lillian's face went white and her painted lips parted. "Oh my god, did you fuck Todd?"

Lillian had infamously thrown herself at Todd Kent at a holiday party three years ago, only to be rejected in favor of a girl in IR, whom Lillian had been instrumental in edging out of the firm six months later. Despite filling her present calendar with wedding planning, Lillian still felt Todd was her territory.

"No, Lillian." Tara shook her head. "I don't know what you're talking about. This is the first I've heard of any of this."

Lillian's green eyes lasered into Tara's. Lillian was legitimately gorgeous: silky chestnut hair framed her perfectly symmetrical face, and her petite features looked handcrafted. Tara could feel Lillian thinking about whether Todd, the man who had rejected her in all her physical perfection, would actually be seduced by Tara's plain frame and last-season shoes. Lillian squinted her eyes at her junior colleague's imperfections until she regained her cool and turned to her computer, apparently satisfied that it was out of the question.

"Well," she said to Tara flippantly, looking at the screen, "whatever happened, you're not getting any help from me on this. And you haven't made any friends." She turned to face Tara one last time. "And everyone is going to think you slept your way into it. There's no other explanation."

Tara ignored the remark. "So is Todd Kent the—"

"I said no help from me," Lillian snapped.

"Okay." Tara put her hands up defensively and turned to leave the office.

As she closed the door behind her, anxiety gave way to adrenaline. She was going to be on Hook's IPO deal team? Flying solo, with no one else from ECM? Was that really possible?

The thought made her brain clear, as if she were waking up after a groggy nap, as if that thing that might make the static routine more exciting wasn't just happening—it was happening to *her*.

But what did Todd Kent have to do with it?

She turned the corner and saw Todd himself sitting at her desk.

"Hello again," he said merrily, swiveling the chair. He gestured to the desk drawer where she kept her vitamins; he'd opened it. "You're quite the pill popper, Miss Taylor."

She moved to shut the drawer, but he held it open. "Gingko, vitamin B, biotin, milk thistle." He lifted one of the bottles. "What is milk thistle for?"

"It helps with hangovers." Tara grabbed the bottle and shut the drawer before he found the Celexa. She wasn't ashamed of being on the antidepressant—she'd been on it since she was fourteen—but she didn't need Todd Kent to know and get the wrong idea.

"Really? See? I knew you were going to come in handy on this deal."

"Glad I'm already adding value," she said. "Now, can you explain what's going on?"

"I'd be delighted. Have a seat," he said, forgetting he had taken her chair. She turned her hips to face him and propped back against the desk.

"So Josh Hart e-mailed me this morning"—he started the story with the familiarity of having told it many times already—"and told me he wants to take Hook public. He wants a 14-billion-dollar valuation and a 1.8-billion-dollar raise. Doesn't want to do a bake-off, and insisted on a small team with no douchebags."

"And he picked you?"

"Yep," he said proudly, missing her sarcasm. "And I, in turn, picked you."

Her cheeks flushed: it *was* because of Todd that she was on the deal. "Why?" she blurted. "I mean, I'm thrilled—you know this is huge for me—but I've never done one of these deals solo, and Lillian thinks—"

"Screw Lillian. You're smart and unintimidating and you know how to deal with nerds. And it's not like your piece is rocket science anyway."

She paused, not sure which part of his analysis of the situation was most insulting.

"Plus it'll be fun to work together," he said. "Like a little Stanford reunion. Did you know Nick Winthrop?"

"Student body president Nick Winthrop?" she asked. Nick had been three years ahead of her at Stanford and had once shown up at Pi Phi drunk, with a bunch of flowers he'd plucked from the sorority's rose garden, to serenade Tara with a song he'd written, asking her to be his date for a Sigma Nu formal. She'd declined.

"Yeah, super dweeb. We cut him day one of rush."

"Yeah, I remember him." She didn't mention how.

"He's Hook's CFO." Todd laughed at the thought. "The last time I saw him he was trying to get SAE on alcohol probation because we planned a kegger the same night as his a cappella concert and no one was there to listen to his cover of 'Brown Eyed Girl.'"

"I hope he doesn't still hold a grudge," Tara said.

"Nah." Todd brushed it off. "Who holds on to things from college?"

She studied him for a moment to make sure he wasn't implying anything. Todd was right. There was no need to hang on to the fact that they'd slept together in college. She'd slept with lots of guys since then. Well, seven. Eight if you counted that one time with . . . Whatever. Sleeping with Todd didn't mean anything, and it wouldn't happen again, and it had nothing to do with why Todd had picked her to be on the deal.

"Anyway," he said, finally moving to stand, "we fly Friday morning to meet with Josh, Nick and Phil Dalton, their big VC."

"Who else is on our team?"

"You, me, Beau Buckley and Neha Patel."

"Beau Buckley?" She'd worked with Beau last summer on a recruiting event—he was great company, but worthless when it came to actual work. "Did you need a party buddy?"

"It was Harvey Tate's idea." He rolled his eyes. "Don't worry. Neha's got enough horsepower for both of them."

He turned to leave and Tara pulled her legs out of the way, standing to let him pass. Their bodies were close in the cubicle and she could feel his heat meet her own. He paused for a moment, letting it linger.

"I'll have Neha send the deck and meet you in the lobby at seven on Friday," he said, breaking the moment and moving past her to the elevator bank.

"Hey, Todd." He turned back. "Thanks," she said.

"My pleasure." He winked, heading out the door.

Tara felt her skin tingling, like the atmosphere had shifted to something intoxicating to breathe. Her phone rang, interrupting her reverie.

"Shit," Tara said, looking at the clock on her computer and realizing she was late for her call.

"Kelly!" she said, picking up the phone. "How are you?"

"I'm good! Do you still have time to talk?"

"Yes, of course," Tara said, sitting back down. "How is the decision coming? I know the deadline is approaching, so I just wanted to see how you're feeling."

"I'm like ninety-nine percent there," Kelly launched in, more honest than she probably should be. "I loved the summer and I know I'd learn a lot but I just—well, honestly, people keep saying that investment banks are really hierarchical and I know I have a lot to learn but I also want to, you know, feel like I'm contributing and not have to wait until I'm forty or whatever to be empowered."

Terrence approached Tara's cubicle and she put up a finger to tell him to hold on.

"I definitely know what you mean, Kelly. But it really isn't true that young people don't get opportunities." She felt the statement's personal truth as she said it. "You have to be patient, but there are amazing opportunities here if you work hard. In fact, I just got appointed to be the ECM point person on a major IPO . . . and I'm twenty-eight."

"Are you serious?"

Tara looked up at Terrence, who was making a face at her. She batted him away, laughing, feeling spirited for the first time in a year.

"Yeah," Tara said. "And I promise that's more impact than you'll get as a non-engineer at Google."

"That's awesome!" Kelly sounded more excited than Tara. "You're totally going to be the next Catherine Wiley."

"I wish!" Tara laughed, but let the thought linger all the same, thinking about the investment bank's wildly successful female president. "But if you come here, I want to help you however I can, okay? I'm excited to have another Stanford girl around."

She looked at Terrence's gagging face and threw a pen at him.

"You mean you'd be my mentor?"

Tara paused: she'd never thought of herself that way before. Was she old enough to be a mentor?

"Well, yeah," she said. "If that's what you want to call it."

"I think that just made my decision."

"Amazing, Kelly. I can't wait to see you here this fall."

"You are so going to hell," Terrence said as she hung up the phone.

"What?" She looked up innocently at Terrence's cocked eyebrow. "She thinks I'm going to be the next Catherine Wiley. Maybe she's right?"

"I'm just glad you're going to get laid."

"I am not getting laid. Todd is so not interested," she said, then added, "And neither, for the record, am I."

"Right."

Tara scoffed: she wasn't. Todd was a player. Thinking about how many girls he'd probably slept with since her made her nauseous.

"Not like there's going to be time anyway—you know how intense these deals are, and there are only four of us on the team."

"I'll give it till the road show."

"Thank you for your confidence in me," she said.

His eyes softened and he smiled. "You know I'm so proud of you."

"Thanks, T."

"Now get to work." He came around the cube and kissed her on the cheek. "I'm already late to SoulCycle."

Tara watched him leave, followed shortly by the rest of the floor clearing out for the evening. She turned back to her computer, her workday just beginning, but not at all upset by that fact.

KELLY

Kelly hung up the phone and looked at the two letters on her dorm room desk one last time: the first, an offer letter from L.Cecil investment bank; the other, an offer letter from Google.

The L.Cecil letter was beige with an embossed, traditional font. It felt heavy and important. The Google letter was bright white with the company's multicolored logo across the top. It had been hand-signed by the recruiting manager, who inserted a smiley face next to his note. It was playful and not at all intimidating.

"Okay," she said, picking up a pen. "Moment of truth."

Kelly bit her lip, taking a minute to observe the significance of the fact that she was even here, in this dorm room on Stanford's campus, making this decision. She'd grown up in the not-cool part of Brooklyn, the accidental (but well-loved) second child of a public school teacher mother and an accountant father whose professional promise was tempered by his on-again, off-again alcoholism. Kelly was the product of one stroke of luck after another—the right third-grade teacher who encouraged her to skip a grade; the right seventh-grade teacher who encouraged her to apply to Stuyvesant High School in Manhattan; the right college counselor who told her a school like Stanford wasn't out of her reach; the right freshman RA who encouraged her to rush Pi Phi, where she met her best friend, Renee, whose Wall Street executive father helped Kelly get last summer's internship at L.Cecil.

Yes, Kelly knew, she was so lucky it was almost unfair. Which is why she couldn't treat the opportunities life had given her lightly.

She moved the pen to the L.Cecil letter and signed her name.

Kelly went down the stairs of Xanadu, the old three-story house on Mayfield Avenue that Stanford had converted into a student residence. She took a deep breath before slipping the envelope into the mail slot at the bottom of the stairs.

"What're you mailing?"

Kelly turned to see Robby Goodman, her RA, coming in through the main door with a case of Bud Light under either arm. Robby was tall and big but in an athletic way, equal parts rugby player and teddy bear. She was glad Robby was the first person she could tell the news to because she knew he'd be happy for her.

"My offer letter for L.Cecil," she said. "I just accepted."

"Whoa, seriously?" Robby's shoulders dropped. "Does that mean you're moving to New York?"

"Yeah!" Kelly said. "I can't wait."

He was quiet. She indicated the beer in his hands. "Big party tonight?"

"Yeah," he said. "The new rugby recruits are in. We're going to get schmammered. Actually, there's an after-party at Theta Delt if you want to come? I'll be blacked out, but it should be fun."

"I'm going to this concert at Shoreline, but maybe we'll swing by when we're back?" she offered, knowing Renee wouldn't be caught dead at a rugby party at Theta Delt.

"Cool," he said, but didn't make any effort to move, like there was something else. "Hey, do you—"

The sound of a Skype ring interrupted him and Kelly looked at her watch. "Oh crap—that's my brother"—she ran up the stairs to catch the call—"Have fun tonight!"

She got to her room just in time to open the laptop and see Charlie's face on the screen. Charlie was eleven years older and an international correspondent for the Associated Press. She knew that his rugged tan skin, shaggy hair and green eyes that captured the intensity of his intellect must be attractive but intimidating to other girls. She assumed that, along with his constant movement, was why he'd never had a serious girlfriend. But she saw through his serious demeanor. To her, Charlie was the goofy older brother who let her put makeup on him when she was seven, the one who taught her how to raise just one eyebrow and, when she got older, sneak down the fire escape at night without anyone hearing.

He was her best friend, her number-one confidant and fan. Which is what made it so hard to know she was about to let him down.

"What did you decide?" he asked as soon as she came on the screen.

"Hey," she said. "Where are you?"

"Istanbul," he said. "What did you decide?"

"I'm going with L.Cecil," she said. "I just signed my offer letter."

Charlie didn't say anything. He hated Wall Street.

"And I'm happy with my decision."

"Why?" he asked.

They'd already been through this when she accepted the banking internship last summer: was he really going to make her do it again? "Because I'll learn a lot. And I'll be around smart people. And it'll open a lot of doors. And I'll do things that matter."

As soon as the words came out of her mouth she regretted them.

"Do things that *matter*?" His eyes flared up on the screen. "Helping rich corporations get richer? That *matters* to you?"

"I don't want to go work in Syria, Charlie. I'm sorry if you think that makes me a bad person."

"I don't want you to work in Syria, either. I just want you to do something that's meaningful."

"It can be meaningful," she said. "Corporations need money to—" She stopped herself, knowing she'd never win that argument. "It's not like I'm doing it forever," she said instead. "A lot of people only stay for a couple of years, then go do other things. And at L.Cecil I'll get good training, and meet influential people, and then if I don't feel like I'm

making a difference, I can go to Africa or whatever and have more impact than I could now anyway."

"Do you know how many people say that? They suck you in, Kelly,
and then all of a sudden you're fifty and you've given your entire life to
some firm that—"

"I'm sick of being poor, Charlie," she interrupted.

Charlie stopped. They'd both gone to school on scholarship, and she
knew he'd been as self-conscious about it as she was.

"Well at least now you're being honest," he finally said.

"I'm not going to change, Charlie, or get sucked in. You don't have to
worry about me."

"I'm your brother. It's my job to worry about you."

"Maybe you should find a girlfriend to worry about."

"There aren't exactly a lot of eligible ladies for atheist American men
here."

"Why don't you come back, then?" she asked carefully. He'd been in
the Middle East permanently since 2010. She'd understood at first, but
not anymore.

"They need me here, Kelly," he said.

She nodded at the camera, letting go of the hope that he'd come to
California for her graduation.

"I better get going," she said, checking the time.

"Hot date?"

"Going to a concert."

"Be safe."

"Speak for yourself, dear-brother-who-works-in-Syria."

SHE TOOK OUT her journal—it was a big day and felt like it deserved
to be recorded. Later she pulled up a dance playlist on Spotify and got
ready for the night. Her phone buzzed with a text and she hurried to

finish glossing her lips, taking one last look at herself in the mirror before grabbing her purse and heading downstairs.

"Don't you look lovely," Renee said as Kelly got into the passenger seat of her friend's BMW. "Perfect for Kyla, and for your first night with Molly."

"Are you sure I should do it?" Kelly asked.

"Yes." Renee didn't hesitate. "Why wouldn't you?"

"It's just—" Kelly started. "I guess I'm just worried something might go wrong."

"Nothing's going to go wrong," Renee assured her. "You're going to be surrounded by friends and I'm staying sober all night, so if you get nervous just say the word and we'll leave, okay?"

"Okay," Kelly said, convincing herself again. "Just promise you'll make me go to bed by two? I'm supposed to speak on a recruiting panel tomorrow about banking internships."

"Did you decide on your offers?"

"I just signed with L.Cecil."

"What?!" Renee stopped the car abruptly. "OMG, Kelly. That is *such* great news."

Renee's excitement was like a salve on the burn from Charlie's disappointment.

"We are going to have *so* much fun in New York after graduation."

"I know," Kelly said, "I can't wait."

Renee pulled the car onto the 280 freeway, heading south toward Mountain View. The sun was setting over the Santa Cruz mountains and the warm air blasted through the windows, making Kelly feel like she was flying.

"Will you get my phone and text Luis to tell him we're on our way?" Renee asked, indicating her tote in the backseat.

"Two new matches on Hook," Kelly noticed out loud on the phone's screen as she pulled it out of the bag.

"Who?" Renee asked, curious.

Kelly opened the app. Hook was a permanent fixture in her and her friends' lives. The app let you set parameters for guys—age, height, distance from you—then used the GPS in your phone to alert you when guys who met your critera were close by. It showed you a guy's picture and you swiped left to "reject" or right to "approve." If you approved a guy and he approved you, then you got a notice saying you'd been matched, allowing you to communicate but also to see the guy's reviews from users and the cumulative Hook score based on the reviews.

"Francois is the first one." Kelly turned the phone so Renee could see the photo, then opened his profile to read it aloud. "Eww, Renee, he's like thirty-four and in the business school—that's so sketchy."

"Whatever," she said. "We're seniors now, it's time to start dating older. What's his score?"

"5.3," Kelly said.

"Okay, that's bad," Renee admitted. "Who's the other guy?"

Kelly navigated to the next match. "Ah! You matched with Robby!"

"Who's Robby?"

"My RA," Kelly said. "He's awesome. Totally sweet. I actually just ran into him and he invited us to a rugby party tonight if we want to go after the concert."

"Oh god." Renee made a face and Kelly laughed. "I knew you'd say that."

Renee pulled the car into the Shoreline parking lot and they joined their group of friends.

"Now the party can get started," Luis said loudly when he spotted the pair, causing everyone else in the group to turn in their usual agreement with whatever the suave international had to say. Luis was Mexican—the kind of Mexican whose father ran the country and who occasionally disappeared with no explanation other than that he had to "take care of some family business." He pulled Renee into a side-hug, her small frame disappearing into his sturdy height, but kept his dark eyes on Kelly.

"Did you decide to join us on Wall Street next year, Kelly?" he asked.

"Yeah," she said, blushing, "I just signed today."

"Rock on." He smiled. "I'll be around the corner at BlackRock."

"My parents just bought a place in Soho," Renee said. "Me, Kelly and Steph are all going to live there. It'll be sick," she said, then spotted a friend. "Hey, Jess!" She waved her arm at the girl, then left to find her, leaving Kelly and Luis alone.

"You ready?" he asked, bending in close.

"Yeah," she said, willing herself to be cool before she overthought it.

Luis pulled a small piece of paper out of his wallet and unfolded it, revealing a bright white powder.

"What do I do?" she asked.

"Wet your finger and dip it in, then lick it off," he said without judging her ignorance.

She did as told, squinting at the bitter taste as he refolded the paper and put it back in his pocket.

"Now what?" she asked.

"Just wait."

They went to join the rest of the group as Kyla La Grange came onto the stage.

"Do you feel anything yet?" Renee came up beside her, handing her a bottle of water.

She looked at the lights on the stage below and shook her head, then turned to Renee, suddenly worried that meant something was wrong. "What does that mean?"

"Nothing."

Kelly turned to the stage, then back to Renee: had she said something? No. She'd said nothing. But not nothing as in she'd said nothing, nothing as in she'd said "nothing," which was something that meant it meant nothing that Kelly felt nothing. Right. She turned back to the stage, convinced.

But this time the stage was moving. Kyla was singing and her voice was reverberating through the grass and a rush of heat spread out from Kelly's chest through her body and she giggled helplessly as the warmth made her shiver. They were outside and the clouds were crossing the moon and she could see the man tucked in the blue shadows and she waved to him and grinned and beckoned him to come play. She looked up: she'd like to find someone to tell.

"Anything yet?" Luis asked from her side.

"Luis!" She didn't realize that's who she was looking for, but here he was.

He smiled and laughed. "There it is!"

KELLY HEARD KNOCKING and squeezed her eyes tighter shut, her brain slowly coming alive. She felt her pillow first, then her body stretched out in sheets that were familiarly her own. She opened her eyes and saw next to her the L.Cecil water bottle Renee had filled up when she put her to bed last night. Beyond it, she saw her desk and remembered the L.Cecil offer letter and Charlie being mad and the Molly.

The knocking kept going and she stood carefully to answer the door. She blinked when she saw him, confused. "What are you doing here?"

"I was in the neighborhood. I thought I'd stop by," he said. He looked drunk.

"What time is it?"

"Almost three. Were you sleeping?"

She looked at her bed, then back at him. "Yeah."

"Get up—come party with me."

"I'm—" She looked back at her bed. "Can we just see each other tomorrow?"

"No," he said. "Let's hang out now." He handed her a bottle of water. "Here—have some."

She looked at the water and realized she was desperately thirsty and took the bottle and drank it in gulps. It tasted sour.

He laughed. "Whoa there."

"I need to go to the bathroom," she said, pushing past him down the hall. She heard music next door and a bunch of guys shouting in the lobby and tried to keep her eyes half-closed against the fluorescent hall lights.

But when she got back to her room, he was sitting on her bed, leafing through a Henry James novel he'd picked up from the shelf.

"I forgot you were an English major," he said. "Why are you working at L.Cecil?"

"I—" she started, but something in her stomach lurched. "I wanted—" A burp came up into her throat and she swallowed it back down. She felt like she was going to fall over. "I don't feel very well." She reached for the bed and sat down.

He stroked her face. "It's okay," he said. "Just lay down."

She did, letting her head fall back on the pillow. She felt his body next to hers, and turned, searching his eyes. He kissed her and she pulled away. But he kissed her again and it felt too hard to resist and she let his tongue enter her mouth. Her stomach lurched again, but her brain was racing now, alive and spinning as he kept his lips pressed against hers and reached down to pull off her shirt.

But his lips didn't move, and she started to realize they were melting into her own, melding together and cutting off her airway. She coughed but she couldn't shake his suffocating lips off. There's another way to breathe, she thought, but she couldn't remember what it was, and her heart panicked in her chest as she felt him press himself inside her, and then everything went dark.

2

AMANDA

Amanda Pfeffer wasn't an idiot.

She'd given herself forty-eight hours to be upset about Todd Kent, during which period she'd had a mani-pedi, eaten sixteen dollars' worth of pay-by-the-ounce FroYo, watched eight episodes of *Suits* and taken an Ambien at seven thirty last night so that she could be up, fresh and ready for a new start this morning.

And that fresh start included confronting the facts, which she did as she rode the escalator up from the subway and stepped back out into the cold.

Fact A: Todd was super-hot, incredibly smart and more manly than any guy she'd ever hooked up with at Penn or since. He was also sweet when he wanted to be (Evidence: she'd heard him call his aunt on the phone, twice) and he found her attractive enough to sleep with multiple times.

Fact B: Todd could be an asshole.

Fact C: Fact B was not Todd's fault. Society conditioned men to want to be James Bond as much as it primed women to be Barbie: in the same way it told girls the path to happiness was a flat stomach and clear complexion, it told men that satisfaction came from wealth, power and no-strings-attached sex. As a rich, attractive white man, Todd Kent was born with a leg up on actually getting the life that most men only dreamed of. She couldn't really blame him for pursuing it. In other words, Todd could be an asshole because Todd *could get away with being* an asshole. It was New York City: he didn't have to call, and he didn't have to take her to dinner, and he didn't have to commit to her as a girl-friend, and he'd still have plenty of women to satisfy the noncommittal sex he thought he wanted.

Thought he wanted.

Fact D: All men eventually realized there was more to life than sex on tap, and Todd would, too.

But it would take the right girl. One who understood, like she did, that being an attractive, rich white man wasn't all fun and games. Sure, Todd had advantages, but those advantages came with the pressure to live up to an impossible bar, and constant temptations that those who were less well-endowed didn't experience. Most of all, though, Todd's privilege allowed him to be blind to others' feelings, but also to his own. He needed a girl who wouldn't judge him for that, and who had the patience to show him that there was a better, deeper happiness to be had as soon as he dropped the magazine fantasies and committed to a real woman.

A real woman like Amanda.

Which is why she wasn't giving up on Todd Kent. He may have said he didn't want a girlfriend, and he may not have called since their fight, but eventually he'd see her for all that she really was, and all that they, together, could be.

Amanda straightened her spine as she walked past L.Cecil's office building. It would have been faster to transfer at Grand Central to the 7 train, but she liked the walk. She scanned the suits streaming into the building from behind her Jackie-O sunglasses, but didn't see him amongst them today. Not to worry, she reminded her calm, confident brain: he'd told her he wasn't going anywhere, and neither was she.

TODD

Friday, March 7; New York, New York
→ San Francisco, California

"Who's Tara Taylor?" Neha asked as they stepped onto the elevator, dragging her enormous suitcase behind her.

"Are you bringing a body with you?" Todd asked, indicating the bag. They were only going to California for two days.

The girl's face flushed. "I wasn't sure what to bring."

"Tara's a senior VP in Equity Capital Markets," Todd explained. "She follows the broader markets so she can advise on comps and will help coordinate the road show and the sales syndicate."

"I've never heard of her," Neha said, a hint of arrogance in her voice.

"She's good," Todd said. "She started in our side of the bank, so she knows how to work hard," he explained. Equity Capital Markets was known for being where pretty, but not pretty enough for Investor Relations, girls and guys who couldn't cut it in other groups landed.

The elevator stopped and Todd spotted Tara across the lobby talking on her cell, her brown hair glossy against her ivory coat, standing out amongst the men in black suits.

"Mom, I promise people are not going to think I'm a lesbian," Tara was saying. "I have a career, Mom—a career that happens to be going very well right now. They will understand that I don't have a date."

Tara saw Todd and blushed. "I've gotta go, Mom. Yes, I promise I'll book my flight this week." She hung up the phone. "Sorry."

"Everything okay?"

"My Southern mother believes her friends will think I'm a lesbian if I don't bring a date to my sister's wedding."

"You're single?" he asked, confirming his suspicions.

"To my mother's dismay," she said.

"When is the wedding?"

"May tenth," she said. "It's in Maine so I'll just need the one day to slip away."

"Should be fine," Todd said, realizing she was asking for his permission and feeling powerful.

"You must be Neha." Tara noticed the analyst behind him and stuck out her hand. "I've heard so many good things about you."

Neha took Tara's hand, her chin lifted proudly. The two could not be more different: Neha with her zits and baggy suit, Tara with her silky hair and structured coat.

"I haven't heard anything about you," Neha said, "but I'm sure that's fine."

Tara forced a closed-lipped smile. "Better nothing than negative, I suppose."

"The car's outside," Todd said, indicating the door. "Shall we go?"

"Is Beau not coming?"

"He's already out there—was working some summer intern recruiting event," Todd explained.

They got to JFK and, at Tara's insistence, waited for Neha to check her bag.

Todd had asked his assistant to book Tara's seat next to his in business class. Per company policy, analysts traveled coach, leaving Tara and Todd alone.

Tara took off her coat and reached to put it in the overhead bin, giving Todd an opportunity to check out her physique. The jeans she'd worn clung to her hips and showed off her long legs, made even longer by her heels. Her sweater was equally tight, accentuating her waist and downplaying the flatness of her chest. She was a seven overall, but she was so close to having a nine body—he really didn't understand why she didn't just get a boob job.

"Whew!" she said, plopping into the seat.

"Get any sleep last night?"

"Not really," she said. "You?"

He shook his head. "Too much adrenaline."

"Do you make it back to California much? You're from out there, right?"

"Yeah," Todd said, pleased that she knew. "Marin. I try to go back once a year, but it's not really home anymore."

"Understand the feeling."

Todd was still deciding how to play Tara. They were obviously going to sleep together at some point during the deal, but he wanted to make sure it didn't happen too soon. The last thing he needed was her getting emotional and causing drama in the deal.

"Seat belts, please," the flight attendant instructed as the cabin door shut. She was hot and Todd winked at her as he followed her instruction. She smiled back.

Tara waited for the flight attendant to finish, then pulled out a printed copy of the deck Neha had sent around yesterday with a summary of Hook's public financials, turning her attention to the company's revenue streams. He watched her, surprised she didn't want to chat more, then pulled out his copy of the *Wall Street Journal*: two could play at that game.

TARA

"Holy shit." Beau Buckley broke the silence as the car pulled up to a massive glass building on the Embarcadero.

"They used to be in Palo Alto, but San Francisco gave them a tax break to entice the company to move here," Neha explained. "And it helps them, too, because all the good engineers want to live in San Francisco, not the South Bay. Plus Hook has the best food of any of the tech companies, so they pretty much get whoever they want."

Tara stared at the girl. She was like a walking encyclopedia, one of the hard-charging, chip-on-her-shoulder analysts whom the firm would work to the bone building models but never give any actual power because they were socially inept.

Of course Todd would get an analyst like that, she thought to herself. It was true that she'd allowed herself to think the deal might be the start of a serendipitous romance. She'd let her mind wander to the narrative wherein Todd wasn't actually a douchebag—he was a really good guy who just hadn't found the right girl, just like she hadn't found the right guy—and the deal would be the start of what they hadn't finished in college and . . .

She'd been wrong. He was a douchebag. She'd stopped by his desk yesterday to ask a question about the schedule, and he'd been across the room flirting with a receptionist. During a fifteen-minute meeting to hammer out the target syndicate list, he'd checked his text messages four times, and she'd caught him looking at his own stats on his Hook profile. Then this morning he'd been flirting with a flight attendant . . . at eight forty-five in the morning. Now Neha? He wasn't just not what she'd hoped, he was worse than she'd feared.

But that was better, Tara told herself as she got out of the car. Her big break was just starting to happen—it was the worst possible time to finally fall in love. In fact, if Todd *had* been the one, it would have been the cruelest kind of trick by fate, to force her to choose between love and career opportunities when she'd been waiting for either/or for so long. With Todd out of the way and the romance option quashed, though, she could focus on the deal and see what opportunities—professional and personal—a 1.8-billion-dollar deal under her belt would net her.

She'd woken up this morning at four a.m. with that resolve. The gym wasn't open yet, so she'd done her six-mile run on the West Side Highway—it was dark and cold, but invigorating, and gave her time to prepare her mind for today. She'd followed it up with a green juice, a coffee and an extra tablet of Celexa. She'd called her doctor and he'd agreed she should double the dose as a precautionary measure, and given her a Xanax prescription for emergencies. For the next three months she needed to stay focused—she couldn't risk her anxiety causing an emotional spell like had happened when she was fourteen. Then, she'd been paralyzed with sadness for weeks, unable to rationalize herself out of the funk. She couldn't afford that now—not now that things were happening.

The foursome walked into Hook's headquarters, where they were meeting Josh Hart, Nick Winthrop, Phil Dalton and a PR girl named Rachel Liu.

"You must be the bankers!" a young blonde in a tank top and cut-off shorts greeted them as they walked through the front door into the atrium lobby.

"Are we that obvious?" Todd gave the girl his politician smile. Neha had worn a terrible boxy suit, but the rest of them had dressed down: still, their haircuts, postures and lower body fat percentages screamed *New York* in the office's sea of hoodies, flip-flops and muffin tops that showed the consequences of the office's endless free food supply.

"You can take the man out of New York but it's hard to take the New York out of the man." The girl grinned.

"I'm Todd." He reached out his hand.

"I'm Julie!" she said, smiling at the group. "I'll get Josh's assistant for you."

"That's okay, Julie," Nick Winthrop said as he emerged through the side door.

He was pudgier than in college, and his reddish hair was thinning. His eyes were big and round behind his plastic-framed glasses and matched the round tip of his nose. If it was true every person looked like an animal, Nick definitely fell into the bug phylum.

"Todd." Nick stuck his hand out to the investment banker, but Tara could sense his awareness of her. "Nice to see you."

"Nick." Todd took his hand. "Been a long time, man. How are you?"

"I'm great," Nick said proudly. "Things have really just kept getting better for me since college."

"It sounds like it." Todd smiled jovially. Tara wondered if he knew Nick was set to make eighty-five million dollars on the deal. It had to hurt Todd, the cool kid in college, to know that Nick, the social wannabe who'd been dismissed from SAE rush, was going to make more in a year than Todd would make in twenty, and that it was Todd's responsibility to ensure it happened.

"Nick, it's great to see you." Tara stuck out her hand, smiling warmly.

Nick tilted his head. "I'm sorry, do I know you?"

Was he joking? "Tara," she reminded him. "Tara Taylor. I was a few years behind you at Stanford?"

"Oh, Tara . . ." Did he seriously think she'd forget the drunken sere-nade? "I didn't recognize you. You've gotten . . . older."

Tara forced a smile. "Haven't we all?"

"Tara's in Equity Capital Markets." Todd stepped in.

"Huh," Nick said. "I wouldn't have pinned you for such a job."

Tara's chest burned. How dare he suggest she wasn't smart enough to work on Wall Street. Did he think she was just some dumb sorority girl whose usefulness expired after she rejected him?

"Shall we go to the meeting?" Nick continued, turning on his heel.

He held his badge to a door at the side of the room and a woman's voice came through a speaker: *"What is the square root of 1,764?"*

"Forty-two," Nick said back to the speaker, and the door opened.

"Is that the secret code or something?" Todd asked.

"Gamefication," Nick explained. "It's big in Silicon Valley right now. Basically, turning regular tasks, like taking taxis or grocery shopping or walking through your office, into games where you collect points." He checked his phone. "I just got two points for that one." He lifted the device to show Todd his score. "People love it!"

"What happens if you're bad at math?" Tara asked.

Nick smirked. "We don't really have that problem here."

Tara gave Todd a *did-he-seriously-just-say-that* look as they followed Nick to the conference room, and Todd lifted his eyebrows in agreement, holding the door open for her to proceed. She could smell Todd's aftershave as she passed and felt her skin prickle. What was it about aftershave? She turned to look at him, but he was winking at Julie. Tara rolled her eyes.

Todd's version of Nick's gamefication was, evidently, flirting; both of them seemed like grown-up children.

The hallway was a round glass tube that stretched down a pier, like the inside of an aquarium, flanked by the Bay Bridge to the right and Alcatraz to the left as it funneled into a glass bubble that constituted the conference room.

"Are these by George E?" Beau piped up from the back of the group, pointing to graffiti-style mermen that looked like painted photographs on the glass. Beau was twenty-six, but he seemed older because he was old-school, the preppy product of the Upper East Side. He wore pink chinos and a white polo shirt with his monogram on the collar. His skin was tan from winter weekends in Palm Beach and his brow was eerily smooth, like it had never had a cause to furrow.

"How'd you know?" Nick asked suspiciously.

"I have one of his early pieces," Beau explained casually, as if it weren't odd that someone his age would collect million-dollar art. "I'm on the Young Fellow board of the Frick and people started talking about him a couple years ago so I figured I'd get in the mix, even though the stuff is totally pervy."

"I'm sorry?" Nick seemed offended by the remark.

"Dude: Mermen? There's some Freudian shit going on in that, don't you think?" Beau was cool, unintimidated. He was confident, but without the inflated ego, and Tara got the feeling he might end up being her favorite person on the team.

"He's one of Phil Dalton's favorites," Nick said, his voice infused with condescension. "Actually, Phil invested in him as a human capital deal. That's the new trend in art, you know. Successful venture capitalists like Phil give guys like George E seed funding in exchange for equity in their future work, and then help promote them by securing commissions like these mermen. Phil's like a modern Medici, and Hook's like the new Sistine Chapel."

Yikes, Tara mouthed to Beau, who grinned in agreement. Computer nerds determining the future of art didn't feel good for anyone.

They entered the conference room, where a glass table sat in the center of the glass-encaged room.

"This is the fishbowl," Nick explained. "Josh designed it." He glanced behind them, and Tara turned back to look in the direction from which they'd come. The main Hook building stood tall at the shore, and six stories of employees were gathered at the windows looking down on them.

"We have a very open culture here," Nick went on. "We built this conference room so that everyone in the company could see what meetings are going on, but they'd be blocked from public view."

"That must make visitors nervous," Todd said.

"It does."

Josh Hart walked through the door, followed by an attractive Asian woman in a tight pencil skirt and patent pumps. Josh looked at the foursome and his face twitched before he walked to the far side of the conference room table and said, "You brought a crew."

"Promise this is the full team," Todd said. Josh ignored his extended hand, so he shifted it to the woman instead. "I'm Todd," he said with a dazzling smile. Did he ever stop?

"Rachel Liu," the woman's precisely lined red lips spoke. Her hair was done in a thick bun and she looked decidedly not San Francisco. "I handle PR for Josh and Phil."

"Phil likes to keep Rachel in the loop on most things," Nick explained.

"I think I'd feel the same way," Todd said, grinning. She offered a thin smile in return.

With the sexual tension established, they all sat down, the New Yorkers across from the Californians, all of them under the age of thirty-five, to discuss the fourteen-billion-dollar valuation of the dating app company.

"So I printed an agenda," Nick said, passing around a sheet of paper. The first item was "Presentation of L.Cecil's capabilities."

Tara looked at Todd: Hadn't they already won the deal? Why did they need to present a pitch?

Todd looked at the sheet, equally confused, then looked back up at Nick. "We didn't bring a pitch," he said carefully. "I thought it was decided that we were working togeth—"

"It has been," Josh interrupted. "I signed the contract this morning."

Now Todd was confused. "Who gave you a contract? I've got the papers right here for us to review." He indicated the stack in front of him.

"Harvey Tate and I worked it out yesterday. I faxed over the agreement this morning," Josh said without interest in where the confusion had occurred.

"What?" Todd said. "What did you agree to?"

"Firm commitment. One percent fee. Target date May eighth."

"One percent?" Todd voiced Tara's own reaction. These deals usually went for six to seven percent, a point or two higher when there was a firm commitment, which meant the bank was responsible for buying any shares that didn't sell in the initial float. How had Harvey agreed to those terms, and how had Todd not known?

May 8 was also just two months away—she'd never heard of a deal ever happening that fast.

"I—" Todd started, but he was interrupted by Phil Dalton, who entered the room jovially. He was six-foot-three and looked like a cross between Ronald McDonald and Chris Noth.

"What'd I miss?" Phil asked the room, taking a seat next to Rachel and leaning in enthusiastically. In addition to making over two billion dollars on his investments in Silicon Valley's most preeminent social media companies, Phil Dalton had established himself as a "mentor capitalist" in Silicon Valley, the self-appointed advisor to entrepreneur-wannabes, whom he was happy to advise in exchange for a significant cut of anything they ever produced. Tara found the whole construct bizarre and hard to take seriously.

"We were just going through the deal terms," Nick said, straightening in his chair. Tara looked between them. Nick was, evidently, one of Dalton's aspiring protégés.

"Did we discuss how much we're going to sell in?" Phil asked. Founders and early investors like Phil used IPOs to sell their shares into the deal in exchange for cash. They had to disclose how many shares they sold, however, and selling too many made it look like they didn't have confidence in the company's continued growth.

"How much do you want to take out?" Tara asked.

Phil seemed to notice her for the first time. "Sorry, who are you?"

"I'm Tara Taylor, I'll be your point from the Equity Capital Markets side of things."

"Ah, yes. I was told to keep an eye on you," Phil said. Tara blushed, not sure who would have given such an instruction. "I'd like to do a third of our holdings. Will that raise any eyebrows?"

"That should be fine," Tara said.

"Can I talk to Tara alone, please?" Josh cut the conversation short.

Tara's head snapped to the CEO. Josh was nondescriptly white: a distinctly American blend of European heritage that resulted in medium-toned skin, an average-sized body, and facial features that were neither too prominent nor too proportionate. Light brown curls gripped his head, which was a little too narrow, as if someone had put metal plates on his ears and squeezed them together. What kind of animal was Josh?

"What do you need to talk to Tara abo—" Todd started.

"You are not interesting to me," Josh interrupted bluntly. "She is."

Tara looked at Todd, who looked at Rachel, who was consumed in a side conversation with Phil and didn't notice.

"Probably better for us to talk through everything off-line anyway," Nick said, standing. "Since I'm the one who's going to be running the show on this."

"I—" Todd struggled, but finally stood. "Yeah, sure."

Tara felt her palms start to sweat as her colleagues left the room, her skin hot as her brain raced for what about her was "interesting" to Josh Hart. She sat forward in her chair.

"Get the shade, please," Josh commanded Nick, who hit a button on the wall that caused a screen to drop, blocking the view of the room from the employees in the building back on the mainland, before leaving Josh and Tara alone in the room.

Josh sat back in his chair, his hands folded in his lap, and studied Tara with the apathetic diligence of a dermatologist scanning a patient for signs of disease. For the first time in her life, Tara wished she were less attractive.

His tongue shot out from the corner of his mouth and moistened his lips. A lizard, she thought: he looked like a lizard.

"Why are you here?" he finally asked.

She glanced around. "You asked me to—"

"I mean, why are you *here*," he said. "What is your purpose?" His words were pointed, with a tinge of spite.

"I work in Equity Capital Markets," she said, "which means I coordinate—"

"Wrong," he interrupted, like a game show buzzer.

She looked at him for an indication of what he was looking for, but found nothing. "The price you can get is only as good as the price you can sell," she said carefully, "and I'm here to provide data on the markets so that—"

"Still wrong," he said, tapping his thumbs in his lap.

"I've worked at L.Cecil for seven years, so I have a solid understanding of how the bank and these deals are supposed to run, and will use that to be sure—"

"Wrong." He slammed his open palm on the table, his irritation breaking. "Are you actually this stupid?"

Tara's breath caught in her throat. "I—" she started. "I'm sorry, but I really don't know what you're looking for."

"You're here to distract, Tara," he said.

She looked at him but didn't say anything.

"You are an attractive woman, and you are here to use that attractiveness to blur objective thinking so that investors will be more likely to do what you want them to do."

"I take great pride in ensuring my reports present the—"

"Which you know," he ignored her protest, "because you're wearing tight jeans and heels and makeup."

She stopped, sitting straight in her chair.

"I like to look nice," she said, "for myself."

"No," he said, "you thrive on external validation. 'For yourself' simply means men turning their heads makes you feel better about yourself. How small are women's brains that you actually convince yourself of these things?"

"Excuse me, but I went to Stanford," she said, feeling her voice get stronger. "I was one of the top analysts at L.Cecil, and am one of the youngest vice presidents. My brain is—"

"Trying to validate your intelligence by success within a stupid system only makes it worse," he said.

"Wh—" she exhaled, but didn't know what to say.

"Let me spell it out for you," Josh said. "You're here on the assumption that I'll want to sleep with you, and will, therefore, be more likely to do what you say. What you say, in turn, will be dictated to you by one of your bosses. And you will listen to that boss because he tells you that you're smart, even though he's only using you because you're pretty."

"You can believe what you want," Tara said firmly, "but I know that I am objectively good at my job."

"You see, that's why people are so drawn to Hook," he said. "We cut out all the bullshit and give people the freedom to embrace their core instincts. There's no 'packaging,' no 'selling,' no obstruction of the truth: just a photo and rating, and a simple yes/no decision about whether or not a user wants to engage. We cut out all these stupid manipulations people engineer to convince themselves their motives are more profound than they actually are."

"I'm going to strongly suggest we don't say that to investors."

"But you do understand that is why Hook is the most intelligent social media platform, right? Because we actually get to the core of how human beings work?"

"I disagree with your evaluation of humanity," she said.

"Which is why you work for a bank pushing paper and I have built a platform used by five hundred million people."

"I think people want something deeper," she said, feeling an old part of herself awaken—that part that used to sit around the dinner table in college debating the meaning of life. "They want meaningful relationships, but apps like yours are easy and fun and instantly gratifying in a way that distracts them."

"Is that why you don't use it?"

"How do you know I don't use it?"

Josh sighed and ignored the question. "What you just said will not get me a good price, so let's just agree to use your looks instead of your brain."

Tara searched for the right thing to say. "My job is to evaluate the market value," she finally said, "and be truthful about that. Not to get into the complexities of human interaction."

"Good girl," Josh said. "Smile a little more when you say it and you should be ready."

"I don't have to take this," she said, snapping out of the hypnosis she didn't realize she'd been under, and moving to stand.

"You're going to be great with Callum," Josh said, unbothered by her movement. "He loves girls with control issues."

"I do not have control—"

"He's going to try to fix you, though, which you can use as leverage."

"I'm not playing my sexuality with anyone, Josh," she said, standing. "Callum," she knew, was Callum Rees—one of Hook's earliest investors. "I'm going to do my job objectively and fairly."

"Just don't sleep with him," Josh said. "That's the one way you know you've lost all your power."

"You know I could sue you for sexual harassment?" she said, looking down at him across the table.

Josh's nostrils flared and he smiled. "You wouldn't do that."

"Is that a challenge?" she asked, lifting a brow. "Do you have any idea how much money I could make on a suit against you?"

"But then you'd be that girl who made her money filing a sexual harassment suit," he said. "You don't want that."

She paused, knowing he was right.

She watched him from across the table, part of her wanting to get out of the room as quickly as possible, the other part feeling like she couldn't leave on this note. "Was there anything else you wanted to talk about?"

"No."

"Okay," she said, turning to leave. When she reached the door, she turned back. "Why did you put down the shades?"

"So people won't know what we talked about," Josh said. "Or did."

"We didn't *do* anything," she said carefully.

"They don't know that."

"What the—"

"Careful how you manage power, Tara." He finally looked up and smiled a lizard smile.

She felt her chest tighten. Who was this guy?

"I'll be in touch," she finally said, pushing the door out into the glass tube hallway. When she looked up she saw dozens of Hook employees in the main office, peering down at her like hyenas. She looked straight ahead and willed herself to ignore them. She felt like she'd just been assaulted.

"Hey!" Todd called after her as she pushed through the atrium, past the receptionist desk and toward the main door. She could hear Todd end the call he was on and start to follow her. "Hey, Tara, wait."

She got out onto the sidewalk and stopped, closing her eyes and letting the warm air resettle her emotions in the few seconds she had before she felt Todd grab her arm to turn her toward him.

"How'd it go?" Todd asked, his voice concerned. "What'd he want to talk about?"

Tara felt her face form into a calm, polite smile. "Fine," she said normally. "He just wanted me to explain some market basics. I guess he was embarrassed to ask in front of you."

"Huh." Todd looked back at the room, satisfied that Josh wanted to impress him. "That's good to know." He turned back to her, pleased with that nugget.

"I've got a killer headache," Tara said. "If it's all right with you I'm going to go to the hotel and work from there."

"Sure," Todd said. "I e-mailed you the break-out for who's on what for the filing, so let me know if you have any questions about your pieces."

"Sounds good," she said, grateful when he turned to wave and she could let her shoulders drop.

JUAN

Friday, March 7; San Francisco, California

"What's going on?" Juan Ramirez asked as Brad returned from the window where a dozen or so programmers were gathered.

"Dude, we're totally going public." Brad's big blue eyes were wide, like a little kid's in front of a stocked Christmas tree.

"What?" Juan swiveled his roller chair from his computer to face Brad. "Going public? How do you know?" Juan didn't pay much attention to the business side of Hook. He preferred to concentrate on the programming, and on organizing the company social calendar.

"Check it, bro." Brad nodded his wide chin to the window. "There are these four cats here—real New Yorky types, all done up and serious. Down in the fishbowl meeting with Josh and Nick and that hot PR chick. Or at least they *were* all meeting, but now it's just Josh and the hot girl New Yorker in there with the shade down. You know what that means: *Josh is getting a blow job!*" He sang the last bit, pumping his chest in celebration of his CEO's manly conquests. "Celebratory BJ for the newly minted billionaire. Rock on."

Ever since someone had suggested that Brad was Hook's resident "brogrammer," the Santa Cruz–bred beach volleyball player turned computer scientist had taken the title up like a mantle, exaggerating his surfer stereotype to the point where Juan sometimes didn't know whether the words he was speaking had any actual meaning.

"What does that mean?" Juan asked.

"A blow job? It's when a girl—"

"No, the bankers being here." Juan put his hand out to stop Brad's pantomime.

"Dude. Means we're gonna be friggin' loaded. Siiiicck."

Juan laughed at his friend and turned back to his computer screen, where he was coding an update for Hook's Android app. Juan had stopped looking at his share statement three years ago, when Josh said his ownership was worth four hundred thousand. He knew an IPO was the only reason Josh would be talking to New Yorkers in suits, and he knew that an IPO would mean that the $400K—or whatever it was worth now—would become cash, but he didn't want to think about it any more than that. Because he also knew, having grown up in Silicon Valley, that as much as money from an IPO could be real, it could be gone. The 2002 crash was still fresh in Juan's mind, along with all the multimillionaires in Atherton who went broke and told his mother they couldn't pay her for the time she'd spent cleaning the houses they could no longer afford. Of all the things Juan knew, the thing he knew most of all was that he was never, ever going to be like them.

And so Juan didn't pay attention to the money, just the app and his colleagues and making the most of the opportunities he'd been given.

"Juan, can I borrow you?" Nick Winthrop's voice interrupted his drifting.

"Sure." Juan stood up and followed Nick to his office.

"Teacher's pet," Brogrammer Brad whispered mockingly as he clipped away at his keyboard. Brad was an idiot, but he made work not feel like work.

Nick, however, was the epitome of work that felt like work. He'd joined Hook two years ago, and he acted like he owned the place, talking about his Harvard MBA as though it made him the expert on everything. As far as Juan could tell, the only thing Nick had done since his arrival was put hand sanitizer on every desk and replace the M&M's in the bulk candy stations with the generic kind. He'd threatened to scale back the hours Joey, the company bartender, served cocktails in the tiki bar on the second floor, but Juan and Brad had led an office-wide sit-in, drinking frozen margaritas on a Tuesday in solidarity for Joey and his right to health benefits that would be lost if his hours were cut to part-time. By noon everyone in the office was drunk, and at seven p.m., Nick finally relented, letting Joey keep his schedule without ever mentioning it again.

"What's up?" Juan asked as he entered Nick's office, acknowledging a girl and guy who Juan assumed were from the investment bank.

"Shut the door, please, Juan," Nick directed, his brow serious. Juan did as told, and introduced himself to the bankers.

"Juan," he said, shaking each of their hands.

"Beau." The guy's teeth were unnaturally bright.

"Neha." The girl's palms were alarmingly clammy.

"Beau and Neha are from L.Cecil," Nick said, "an investment bank in New York that Josh and I have selected to take Hook public."

Nick paused, waiting for Juan to be impressed. Juan remained silent, waiting for the secret information.

Juan didn't not like anyone, but he didn't actively like Nick Winthrop. He knew the M&M's were just the start: Nick wanted to change the company, and Juan was worried Josh was going to let him do it, not because Josh agreed, but because Nick was just so annoying that Josh might not have the stamina to protest.

And so that was something else Nick had done: he'd driven distance between Josh and Juan, and Juan resented that even more than the M&M's.

Juan had started working with Josh Hart when he was in college and joined full-time after he graduated from UC Berkeley in 2009. Juan had gone to school on scholarship from the Lipmann Foundation, which provided college tuition to children of immigrants and helped them become naturalized citizens. Phil Dalton was a board member of the foundation and the one who introduced Juan to Josh as a good programming mentor.

And that he was. Josh Hart was the best programmer Juan had ever encountered. He was one of those coders whose whole brain thought in code: everything was a binary, a node, a decision point that did what you told it to. The thinking was so much a part of him that he could see coding problems before others did. He knew that by making X decision at node 1, you'd have to make Y decision at node 50. His foresight allowed him to fix things at node 1 and avoid inefficiencies, creating programs that functioned more smoothly and identified more closely with human intuition than other apps.

So when Josh asked Juan to come help him build an app he thought would crush all other dating apps, Juan didn't hesitate. For eighteen months it was just the two of them, staying up all night most nights in a dingy basement office in Mountain View eating cheap Chinese takeout and programming what would, eventually, become Hook. It was before funding and users and a fancy office in San Francisco that gave some stability to the notion that their effort would lead to something. There was nothing glamorous about it—it was just really hard, uncertain work—but it was raw and real and Josh became a much-needed companion when Juan's college friends were working their normal day jobs and his high school friends back in East Palo Alto were working minimum wage. Josh could be rude and demanding, but he understood and didn't apologize for the isolation of being different. And, as someone who had always struggled to fit into a system where he felt like a perpetual outsider, Juan admired that.

Nick didn't get it. He'd always been part of the system, and he'd always followed the crowd to do what was comfortable and secure. Now that Hook was getting huge he was trying to take credit for things, but all he'd really done was hitch on to a rising tide.

"By going public, I mean we'll be offering a portion of our shares on the NASDAQ stock exchange, where the general public will be allowed to buy them, like they can shares of GE and Google and Facebook. This will allow us to raise money to grow the company," Nick explained, his voice dripping with condescension. "It's very important that you not talk to anyone else about this—not even Brad."

"Oh, everyone already—" Juan started to tell him they all knew, then changed his mind. "Sure," he said. "Lips sealed."

"There's going to be a lot of work to do, getting the documents ready to file with the Securities and Exchange Commission, and I need you to help Beau and Neha get the information they need for their analysis. Can you do that?"

Juan glanced around the room. He needed to program, not entertain bankers, and Nick's patronizing tone made his skin bristle. "Sure," he said, "if you tell me what you need."

"I'll be upping your security clearances," Nick said, "so you have access to all the information in the database in order to help the bankers calculate user statistics." He pulled out a piece of paper from his perfectly pristine file cabinet. "I'll just need you to sign this NDA verifying that you won't share any of the information."

Juan stepped forward to sign the sheet. As if Juan couldn't access the databases if he wanted to: he'd built the entire program. How dumb did Nick think he was? "What kind of information will you need?"

"Just basic demographic information about our users—all anonymous, of course. Just things to help prove our market penetration and user engagement."

"Sure," Juan said, handing the signed sheet back to Nick.

Nick checked his watch. "Okay, then. I'll let you all get to it."

Juan glanced at the other two, hoping they knew what they were supposed to get to, and the three left Nick's office.

"I say we check out the bar," Beau suggested. "I heard it's hip."

"I think we should get to work," Neha corrected.

Juan glanced between them, trying to decipher the relationship. "How about I find you both desks, and then I'll give you the tour."

There were two open computer stations on the long desk where Juan and Brad sat, formerly occupied by a financial analyst who had quit six months in and the general counsel, Glen Fanning, whom Josh had unceremoniously fired three months ago. Glen, who was a fat fifty-year-old with two kids, had been the only thing close to adult supervision at Hook, and no one had been sorry to see him go.

Juan moved a stack of costumes he and Brad had been deciding between for the upcoming company broomball tournament out of one of the chairs. "Will these work?"

The bankers nodded, and Neha took a seat, opening her laptop and burying her nose in some Excel model. Beau lifted an eyebrow, then turned back to Juan. "How about that bar?"

Juan led him across the hall, past the basketball court, and down the stairs to the cafeteria, where the former executive chef for the White House prepared three meals a day for Hook's staff, all free to employees and guests. They proceeded through the game room, full of beanbag chairs, every variety of video game console on the market hooked to large flat-screens, and a custom-designed foosball table. The tiki bar was a long open room that extended to a deck that looked out over the Bay and had, as its centerpiece, a fully stocked, surfboard-shaped bar.

"My man Joey." Juan fist-bumped the bartender.

"What's happenin'?" Joey returned the friendliness, reaching his tattoo-sleeved arm out to Beau. "I'm Joey."

"Nice to meet you," Beau said. "Think I could get a bourbon?"

"Coming up." Joey turned to his craft.

"So what information is in the database?" Beau asked.

"Oh, we track everything," Juan said. "Comments, when and where people log in, who they meet up with. All apps do. You can't make your program better if you don't know how people are using it."

"Is that all in your privacy policy?" Beau asked.

"I guess?" Juan didn't get into that stuff. "We keep information users provide—like names and e-mail addresses—separate from the information we collect about behavior so that none of it's identifiable," Juan said, then shrugged. "So it doesn't really matter, does it?"

"Bourbon straight up." Joey returned with Beau's drink.

"God, you all live the life," he said, looking around the bar and taking it in. "Maybe I should come out here."

"Do you not like working on Wall Street?" Juan asked.

"I'd have preferred to do what you do." Beau shrugged. His blue eyes were friendly. "But I didn't exactly have a lot of options, given my family."

Juan didn't follow. Beau looked really rich, like he came from the kind of family that had nothing but options. "Have you ever coded?" he asked.

"I was a CS minor in undergrad," he said. "I was decent."

"Juan!" He turned at the voice and saw Julie walking toward him. "Oh, hi," she said, noticing Juan's companion. "You're Beau, right?"

"You two met already?" Juan asked. Julie was the Hook receptionist and one of Juan's roommates.

"Yeah, I checked them in this morning."

"Good to see you again." Beau lifted his drink to toast her. She blushed and Juan lifted an eyebrow, recognizing Julie's shift into flirtatious mode. Of course Julie would go for a Wall Street guy like Beau.

"So Carey just e-mailed that she got the job in LA so she's definitely moving out at the end of the month, which means we have to have a party ASAP and find a new roommate."

"I'll post something on Craigslist tonight," Juan said, "but for now, I've got to get back to work." He looked at Beau and indicated the guy's half-finished drink. "Feel free to bring that with you."

"Or Julie can finish showing me around?" Beau said.

"Don't you have work to do, for this deal?"

"Nah—I'm more the sales guy than the executor. My part comes later," Beau said, turning back to Julie.

Juan rolled his eyes, but neither noticed. "I'll see you back at home then, Jules. Beau, let me know if you need anything."

CHARLIE

FRIDAY, MARCH 7; ISTANBUL, TURKEY

Charlie threw a pen at the laptop when he saw the e-mail.

"Idiots!" he yelled at the screen, standing from his chair and pushing it back to the desk angrily.

He pulled on a T-shirt and laced up his running shoes, letting the door to the tiny apartment slam as he made his way down the six flights of stairs to the street.

He ran on the road, finding it easier to dodge honking cars and bicy-cles than beggars and broken sidewalks, and ignored the locals who stared at his unabashed Westernness. It was one thing for a white man like Charlie to set up residence in one of their apartment buildings, but to exercise in public, wearing a dry-fit T-shirt and performance running shoes that cost more than most here made in a month, was an offense that warranted a glare.

He waited until he got to the water to let his mind go back to the e-mail, taking in the meaning of its content while he took out his frustration on the pavement.

Charlie had joined the Associated Press after graduating from Columbia, where he'd finished his undergraduate degree in three years and spent the fourth getting his M.A. at the journalism school. He'd started college with the vague notion of going into academia, but when 9/11 happened his sophomore year, everything had changed. He'd come back uptown from Ground Zero different, then gone back day after day to volunteer. When he finally had to resettle into university life, he'd enrolled in an Arabic class and never looked back.

He got his first break in 2008, when he was sent on assignment to Tunisia to cover protests. When the Arab Spring began two years later, he was perfectly positioned, and now, at thirty-two, he was one of the AP's top Middle East reporters. He wasn't the smartest, or the best writer, and he lacked the native knowledge of his colleagues, but his willingness to go where the action was and, once there, understand the viewpoint of the Arab-who-resented-the-Western-world had won him trust and respect amongst authorities who now fed him stories before anyone else.

Which is why he'd asked to go back to Talmenes, to investigate rumors of a chemical attack government officials were said to be plotting. He'd sent an impassioned e-mail to his editor, Raj, yesterday, insisting he approve Charlie's return to Syria. He asserted that it was time the AP started reporting *before* things happened so that they might prevent them, instead of writing more pieces about dead bodies after the fact.

And Raj had responded that Charlie should "go home and take a break"? What the hell?

The thought made Charlie run harder. Was Raj trying to push him out? He knew his e-mail had been forward, but he had a right to voice his opinion. He'd given his life to the AP—he'd sacrificed any semblance of a social life, risked his safety and damaged his health in who knew how many ways to get the story. And now they were going to send him home, right in the middle of a civil war that was the culmination of everything Charlie had dedicated his life to understanding? Fuck that.

His phone rang in his headphones and he stopped on the side of the pavement.

"Hello?"

"It's Raj."

"What the hell was that e-mail?" Charlie snapped.

"I'm just calling to see how you're doing."

"How I'm doing?" Charlie guffawed. "I'm pissed. I want to go back to Syria."

"Charlie, what are you doing?" Raj's voice was soft.

"My job!" he said. "Have you forgotten we're in the middle of a civil war?"

"You need a break."

"Syrians need a break," Charlie said. "I'll take mine when the violence has stopped."

"The violence isn't going away whether you're there or not," Raj said. "Go home and be with your family."

"I'll see my family at Christmas, like I always do."

"Jesus, Charlie. How hard has this place made you?"

"Hard enough to go back to Talmenes and figure out what the fuck is going on there before another hundred civilians die. I know my e-mail was forward, but we have to—"

"Are you seriously not even going back for the service?"

"What service?"

Raj was quiet.

"What service?" Charlie repeated.

"Fuck," Raj said, "I thought you—"

"What?"

"Your sister," Raj said. "Your sister's dead."

Charlie's arm dropped from his ear, letting the phone fall to the grass as the call to prayer rang from the mosque behind him, stretching out across the Bosphorus to the sun setting on the horizon beyond, deafening him like an explosion detonating in his brain.

3

AMANDA

Amanda refreshed her browser.

Nothing.

She stared at the message icon. *Just one more time then back to work.* Her finger hovered above the mouse, willing a red box to appear. A simple *Todd Kent has accepted your friend request* was all she needed.

Click.

Refresh.

Red box!

Her heart beat heavily in her throat. Who said positive imagery didn't work? She opened the message, feeling the sweat in her palms.

Harold Hammonds has invited you to the event I WON A FREE HAPPY HOUR AT MAGGIE'S!!! MARCH 26, 5-7PM!!!!

"Ugh," she said out loud, turning back to the printout of the shareholder agreement she was proofreading.

She was at her cubicle on the fifty-eighth floor of Crowley Brown. She read two pages of the document, willing herself to concentrate on the activity that made up the majority of her time at the bottom ladder rung of a top-tier New York City law firm. She found a misplaced comma and circled it with satisfaction: "Gotcha!"

The key to being a successful attorney, Amanda had discovered in her two years as a paralegal here, was to not dwell on the lack of importance of anything you did. Rather, you had to focus on creating more complication to breed more unimportant work so you had so many unimportant things to do you didn't have time to think about their unimportance.

Maybe she should go to the party, she thought. Harold Hammonds was one of the least cool guys she knew from Penn undergrad, but she was pretty sure he'd gone to work at a hedge fund, so maybe he'd have cool coworkers?

She looked up Maggie's: it was on Forty-seventh Street, three blocks from L.Cecil. Her throat tightened again: maybe Todd would be there. Maybe that was his local bar, his after-work spot. Maybe he'd walk in and she'd be at a table, looking professional but sexy, with her jacket off and her head back, laughing at something Harold had said. And Todd would see her, having fun with all of Harold's hedge fund colleagues, and then he'd be jealous and finally see what he hadn't seen before.

Are you done yet?

An internal instant message appeared from the second-year associate on the case, Kerry. Amanda looked up: Kerry was sitting in the cubicle next to her, literally an arm's length away, staring at her screen with her earphones in.

"No," she said out loud to Kerry.

"I'm sorry?" Kerry took an earbud out, bothered. "What did you say?"

Amanda glared at her. "I said no, I'm not done with the document."

Kerry lifted her eyebrow disapprovingly and turned back to her screen.

That was what Amanda had to avoid. Kerry might have a JD from Harvard Law, but she was still single. And twenty-nine. In New York. It was a death sentence.

Amanda saw the way things shifted when women reached a certain age in this city. As girls crept toward thirty, their dying eggs seemed to excrete desperation, and men could smell it a mile away. Before they knew it, they were Amanda's mother: living alone in Florida dating losers, spending their money on creams and fad diets in a futile attempt to recoup the youth they squandered on men they'd failed to fix.

And so, as important as the work in front of her might be, it was more important that Amanda lock something down before she turned twenty-seven and everything started going to hell. That gave her a year and five months.

Plenty of time, she assured herself, turning back to the document.

Or was it? She'd already been in New York for two and a half years and Todd was the only close-to-a-boyfriend she'd had. Her roommate Cindy was probably marrying her boyfriend from college, and her other roommate, Claudia, didn't need to worry because she was from the Upper East Side and always had a string of attractive, eligible bachelors ready to procreate with her blue blood.

What did Amanda have? Great boobs, she knew that. And a killer metabolism that kept her skinny without exercising, which meant she also didn't have man-arms like a lot of the women in New York. She was ambitious, but not so career-obsessed that she wouldn't quit working to raise her kids, to whom she would contribute Ivy League–worthy intelligence.

She rolled her eyes in frustration: there was no reason she didn't deserve Todd. She was the right girl for him, she just had to show him that. And to show him that, she had to see him, and she couldn't leave that up to chance in a city as busy as New York.

She opened Facebook again and sent him a message:

Hey—totally random, but I've got a happy hour at Maggie's the Wednesday after next, March 26. You should stop by if you're free. Will be fun. A.

She read it again. And again.

Send.

TODD

WEDNESDAY, MARCH 12; NEW YORK, NEW YORK

"We've got to work on your Hook profile, T Two."

Todd glanced up from his laptop at Beau, who was shaking his head at his iPhone, then across at Tara, who had stopped typing.

"Are you talking to me?" she asked.

Todd had had his assistant reserve a conference room on the twenty-seventh floor for the team so they could work together and Todd could keep track of what everyone was doing. They'd gotten back to New York on Sunday and the room hadn't been empty since: they were all working around the clock to get things ready for the IPO, fueled by Harvey's demand that the deal be done by May 8.

Todd was still furious with Harvey for going behind his back to negotiate the fee. And 1 percent? It was a fucking joke. It only affirmed Harvey's diminishing power and his desperation to maintain some sense of significance by undermining the real talent in the firm. It made Todd sick, and more motivated than ever to nail the deal so that he could take all the credit and neutralize any senior manager who tried to stand in his way.

Todd rolled his neck to release the tension. He couldn't get worked up over Harvey—there was too much else to think about. He needed to get the S-1 together and send it to the SEC. From there, the deal would be announced publicly and attention would start to flood in; then the road show, the pricing call, and the big day when they'd ring the opening bell on NASDAQ and all make millions.

"Yeah." Beau squinted at his iPhone without looking up. "T Two. Tara Taylor. Get it?" He waited for her to be impressed with his cleverness. "Anyway," he went on, "you've only got eighteen reviews. Twelve hundred eighty-three views, but only eighteen reviews. What gives?"

Tara shrugged. She seemed to genuinely not know her stats. "I don't really use it," she said, going back to her computer.

"Boyfriend?" Beau asked.

"No." She looked up and gave him a polite *Please shut up* smile.

"Aren't you, like, thirty?" Beau pressed. "Better get on it."

"I'm twenty-eight." She finally looked up. When she saw the playfulness in Beau's smile, she laughed, cracking.

Beau grinned, pleased with himself for lightening the seriousness in the room.

"How many views have you got, Todd?" Beau asked.

"Me?" Todd cocked a brow. He'd last checked Hook this morning, on the way into the office. He'd had eight new messages and 432 new views since last night. "I don't know, seventy thousand or so?" Not true: it was 83,612, but he could afford to be modest.

"Okay, big shot." Tara pretended not to be impressed with Todd's stats and turned back to Beau, her long brown hair falling over her shoulder as she tilted her head. She looked particularly pretty today, which Todd assumed was for his benefit. "What do I need to do?"

"Well . . ." Beau adjusted himself in his seat and sat up seriously. Neha glanced up from her computer long enough to show she wished they would shut up.

"For starters, you have to rate more guys," Beau instructed. "Here, let me see your phone." He grabbed it before she could protest and clicked open the app.

"Hey!" she said.

"Password?" he asked.

"Jetgirls two thousand three," she said.

Beau lifted an eyebrow.

West Side Story." Todd didn't realize he'd said it out loud until he saw them looking at him. "She was in *West Side Story* in college," he explained to Beau. "My buddy Tom was in it, so I had to go see." Then he turned to Tara. "And you were very good. That dance number." He gestured with his hands.

She laughed again.

"Whatever," he said and went back to his computer.

Beau was into Tara's Hook app now, flipping through and tapping like a pro.

"What are you doing?" She reached across the table for the phone.

"I rated Todd and me each as tens, hope that's okay." He pulled the phone out of her reach. "The only way you're going to get more people to see you is if you rate more people," he said. "I'm helping you out here, T Two!" His voice was comical and easygoing, the voice of a guy bred to be the charismatic life of the party.

"But I don't need help," she insisted. "I promise, I don't use it."

"You're twenty-eight and single! You have two years left before you go crazy and men don't date you anymore," Beau said energetically. "The time is now, T Two!"

"Not through Hook," Tara said, making a face. "It's gross."

"Why?"

"I don't want to meet up with some stranger just because he's close by," Tara said.

"And also liked your profile," Beau corrected.

"A guy liking my profile has more to do with how desperate he is to get laid at that moment than anything to do with me."

"No different from real life," Beau said.

"Don't tell me that," Tara said.

"It's true. Right, Todd?" Beau asked him.

"I'm going to pass on this one."

"At least in real life you can get a sense of a person's energy," Tara said. "It's not just about a photo that's probably doctored anyway."

"Don't worry, I'm fixing your photos, too." Beau ignored her philosophy, refocused on her phone. "What's this one?" He rotated the screen to face them.

"Do *not* put that on there," she said.

Beau handed the phone to Todd. It was a black-and-white photo of a girl's naked back, one arm pulling a sheet across her bare chest as she looked at the sunlight streaming through the window.

He felt his jaw drop. Was that Tara?

Tara leaned over and grabbed the phone from Todd's hand, their eyes meeting as he looked from photo to model before she blushed and put the phone facedown on the table without saying anything.

"Really? No explanation?" Beau's blue eyes were smiling.

Todd was no longer pretending to work, his mind racing to understand the side of Stanford grad–turned–L.Cecil banker Tara Taylor that posed for nude photos.

"I took a photography class once and a classmate of mine needed models to practice on," she said defensively, putting the phone back in her bag.

"Sure," Beau said.

"Anyway," Tara said, closing her laptop, "I have to go."

"Another photo shoot?" Todd grinned. He was definitely sleeping with her now.

Tara straightened her skirt. "I've got a meeting."

"With who?" Beau asked.

"Callum Rees."

"What?" Todd's face lost its smile. Callum Rees was the billionaire serial entrepreneur who had given Josh Hart a hundred thousand dollars when Hook was just getting started, making him the company's largest non-employee individual shareholder. He was also a notorious international playboy. "Why are you meeting with Callum Rees?"

"He e-mailed me to set up a meeting," Tara said. "I'm not sure why."

"Where?" Todd asked.

"Downtown," she said.

He started to stand. "I'll come with you."

Tara put up a hand. "I'm sorry, why?"

"I'm the coverage banker on this deal," Todd said. "I should be meeting him as much as you should."

"He e-mailed me," she said firmly. "I'll handle it."

"Why?" he said a bit too angrily, realizing Callum, not him, was the impetus for her looking pretty today. "Are you trying to get a date out of it?"

"No," she said.

"Then why are you dressed up, meeting an unmarried man downtown at eight o'clock?"

"I am meeting a *client* with a huge stake in our deal, when and where he was available to meet," she corrected without apology.

"Tara, I think you need to seriously consider what this could look like," Todd said, meaning it.

"And I think you need to seriously consider why you perceive it as looking like anything other than me doing my job."

"Perceptions matter," Todd said. "You're representing the firm, you know."

"Thank you, Todd Kent, master of perception management." She rolled her eyes, turning out the door.

"Knock him dead, T Two!" Beau called after her cheerfully.

TARA

WEDNESDAY, MARCH 12; NEW YORK, NEW YORK

Tara could feel her pulse hammering as she rode the elevator down to the lobby.

How *dare* Todd imply that there was anything inappropriate about her meeting with Callum, as if half of Todd's job wasn't getting drunk with clients late at night. Hadn't L.Cecil only gotten the Hook deal because Todd had met Josh Hart at a strip club? And he had the nerve to criticize her for meeting the largest independent shareholder of the company, at his request, for a single drink.

Then again, she knew part of the reason she was so defensive was because she was nervous: Josh's words "You're going to be great with Callum" were still lingering, and she wasn't sure what to make of them.

But Josh wasn't worth getting upset about, she reminded herself for the seventeenth time. He was clearly a sociopath—one of those tech geniuses whose brains were so consumed by coding that they never developed the ability to relate to human beings. Still, it bothered her, the way he had diagnosed her person so bluntly. It felt visceral, like he had violated her. Even if she'd felt like she could tell someone, she didn't want to. As though repeating Josh's argument would give it some validity and leave her powerless.

She noticed the flashing light on her BlackBerry and looked down at the new e-mail.

FROM: Catherine Wiley

CC: Catherine Wiley assistant two

SUBJECT: Frick

heard good things from Phil Dalton. firm has a table at the frick event nxt Weds. Can you make it? Leslie will send you details.

sent from my blackberry

The elevator stopped, but Tara didn't notice, her eyes frozen on the e-mail in front of her.

Catherine Wiley was president of L.Cecil's investment banking division. She was the highest-ranking woman in the firm, one of the highest-ranking women on Wall Street, and probably one of the most successful women in the world. Had she seriously meant to e-mail Tara Taylor?

Another e-mail came through:

FROM: Catherine Wiley assistant two (Leslie Cowper)

SUBJECT: Re: Frick

Tara,

See attached for invitation to Gala for George E's art exhibit at the Frick Wednesday, March 26, as well as bios of the clients who will be in attendance. John Lewis from L.Cecil Asset Management will also be in attendance. Please arrive no later than 6:30 PM. Dress code is Black Tie.

Let me know if you have any questions.

Leslie

The elevator arrived on the ground floor and others moved past her to exit while Tara read the note again, finally looking up and smiling at the empty lobby.

Oh my god.

Tara laughed out loud, her mind whirring as she went down to the street. Catherine Wiley was known for handpicking female protégés, giving them opportunities and grooming them for leadership positions within the firm. And now she was asking Tara Taylor to represent the firm at an art gala? Was she seriously considering Tara as one of her mentees? Because of a ten-minute meeting she'd had with Phil Dalton last week? Had she even said anything while he was in the room?

Her brain froze: was he just saying she was pretty, like Josh had implied was all that mattered?

Whatever, she shook the thought away. *Why* it happened wasn't as important as the fact that it was happening. She was getting her break. This was what it meant to be on your way, climbing up the corporate ladder, finally recognized for the potential she'd always known she had, even if she'd started to doubt it. How quickly things could change.

Tara climbed into one of the black cars outside L.Cecil and directed the driver to the Crosby Street Hotel, her aggravation with Josh and Todd replaced by gratitude to Catherine and Leslie.

The Crosby Bar was full of the downtown business crowd. Unlike the midtown business crowd, who hung out at places like the Peninsula, frequenters of the Crosby owed their personal fortunes to exploits outside the financial services industry. Same twenty-dollar martini, but served with trendier pretension.

Tara was fifteen minutes early. The hostess showed her to a table, and she pulled out her iPhone in order to look occupied and important when Callum arrived, trying not to get carried away thinking about all that Catherine's e-mail implied.

She blinked with surprise when she saw thirty-two new notifications from her Hook app, still open from when Beau had been "fixing her profile." She went back to the main screen, where the app showed her photos of guys within a one-mile radius and instructed her to swipe left if she didn't like them and swipe right if she did.

She looked at the first photo:

Mark stood on a beach, the wind blowing on his perfectly bronzed skin. He peered flirtatiously into the camera. *No personality*, she thought, and swiped left.

Jordan flexed his tattoo-covered bicep. *Yikes.* Tara swiped left quickly.

Timmy grinned open-mouthed at the camera, his cheeks pudgy and inviting. He looked funny and kind. She clicked to his profile. Height: five feet seven inches. *Swipe left.*

Frank lifted his hand in a fist pump to the camera, standing behind a beer pong table wearing fluorescent orange sweatbands, short shorts and a custom jersey. *Stuck in college. Swipe left.*

Harry held a glass of champagne in one hand and positioned the other in his tuxedo pocket. His closed-lipped grin smiled sardonically at the camera. She clicked to his profile. Trinity College. *Trustafarian with a drug problem. Swipe left.*

Tarik flashed a smile that was warm and inviting. She opened his profile. Harvard Business School, Morehouse undergrad. She hesitated. She'd seen *Save the Last Dance*. Even if he was perfect, she couldn't be that white girl who took a good black man. *Swipe left.*

"How's the selection around here?" a British accent said from above her. She looked up at Callum Rees and blushed furiously, suddenly realizing how engrossed she'd become in the app.

"Oh, I—" she started, then stood, offering her hand. "I'm Tara."

He took it. "I figured."

"Sorry, I was just—"

"Doing exactly what Hook hopes you'll do," he interrupted. "Get Hooked."

"I don't think I like it." She shook her head, looking down at the phone. "I feel like a total jerk."

He laughed. "I hope you've got better user testimonials for the road show than that."

Callum was in his late forties and not particularly good-looking. He had an average height and build, and was classically English: his face was long and rectangular, and his brown hair receded at the corners atop a high forehead and watery eyes. But there was something about him—his deep accented voice or his smile or the confident way he now sat across from her, leaning his elbows forward on his knees—that was undeniably sexy.

The waitress approached the table. "What can I bring you?"

"Sparkling water for me," she told the waitress, "with lime."

Callum made a face. "You're going to make me drink alone?"

"I have to go back to the office." She smiled. "And I assume you'd rather I be sober getting things ready for your company's IPO?"

He pursed his lips, considering, then shook his head. "No." He looked back at the waitress. "We'll have two vodka martinis," he said. "Extra olives."

"But—" Tara started.

He gave her a look.

"Fine," she said. She did love martinis.

The waitress left and Tara turned back to him, reminding herself this was a business meeting. "So what can I do for you?"

"I want to cash out," he said.

"What?" Her mouth opened and she sat forward. "You can't cash out. You're the largest non-employee shareholder."

"So?"

"We have to disclose what you sell in the IPO. When people see you're cashing out, they'll assume you think the company's overvalued, that you know something they don't," she said, knowing he knew this. "It'll kill demand for the offering and the price we're able to get for the shares."

Callum shrugged. "I want out."

"You can't," she insisted.

"I can, and I am, and you're not going to change my mind, so we might as well enjoy a drink and talk about more interesting things," he said, plucking an almond from the bowl the waitress had delivered. "How long have you been at L.Cecil?"

"The price—it'll drop twenty-five percent, if not more." Her mind raced back to the price calculation model, then raced forward to Catherine Wiley. That Frick event was history: the minute Catherine heard the deal was running off track she'd replace Tara with someone else, setting Tara back even further than if Catherine didn't know about her at all. "Which also means your holdings will lose twenty-five percent in value, which means that to make this economical for you, you have to believe the price is going to drop more than twenty-five percent after the IPO. Can't you just hold it through May?"

"Do you like it?" He ignored her question. "Working on Wall Street?"

"You can't do this, Callum," she repeated, undeterred. "Have you talked to Josh?"

"I'd hate it." Callum shifted back in his chair, thinking aloud. "All those insecure suits running around acting like they create value, when all they do is make money off of money, like money is the most important thing."

"Says the billionaire," she said, catching his bait.

"I never did anything for the money, which is probably why I made so much of it."

"Why are you so desperate to get out of Hook?" She wasn't going to let him distract her.

"I don't believe in it anymore."

"Why not?"

"Intuition."

"You must have a better reason than that."

"What better reason is there than intuition?"

"Facts?" she suggested. "There's nothing wrong with the company. I've been neck-deep in their data."

"Is fact synonymous with truth?"

"I'm sorry?"

"Philosophical question. I think if you equate facts to truth, you miss just about everything in life."

"I think philosophical musings are better left out of investment decisions."

"Then how about the fact that you don't like the app?"

"I'm not the target demographic."

"Twenty-eight-year-old single woman? I'd say you are."

She blushed. How did he know she was twenty-eight and single?

The waitress brought their drinks and Callum clinked his glass to Tara's. "To truth," he said.

She took a sip of her martini, re-pooling her argument.

"Okay," she started. "Truthfully, I think it's incredibly selfish of you to risk upsetting the success of the IPO because you have an intuition."

"And why is that?"

"Because money might not matter to you, but that's because you have a lot to fall back on. But it's not just your shares that lose twenty-five percent if you do this, it's everyone's, including people who need it."

"Point A." He lifted a finger. "My not caring about money is not because I have a lot to fall back on. They are unrelated. And Point B, anyone who thinks they need money that's based on something so intangible it can float twenty-five percent in value based on one man's decision needs to seriously consider his principles."

"What about Juan Ramirez?"

"Who's Juan?"

"The first employee," she said, proud of herself for thinking of this argument. "Juan immigrated to California when he was eight with his widowed mother, after his father was shot in Juárez. He grew up in the projects while his mother cleaned houses for wealthy VCs in Atherton.

He stayed out of gangs and got a scholarship to Berkeley and now, because of his Hook shares, he's going to have money for the first time in his life."

"How much?"

"If we go out at twenty-six dollars a share? Over two hundred million." She smiled as she said it. "It's the American dream."

"And if I, as the bad old Englishman, cash out my position, he'll only get a hundred and fifty million," he said, then corrected, "Or seventy-five after taxes."

"Right."

Callum lifted his eyebrows, considering. She sipped her martini, pleased that she'd won.

Callum didn't say anything, just studied her, sipping his drink.

"What?" she finally asked.

"A twenty-something-year-old kid is going to have seventy-five million dollars and you're telling me I'm a bad guy because he doesn't have twenty-five more?"

"You have two billion!"

"Who gives a shit? That kid's life is fucked."

"No." Tara shook her head and sat forward in her chair. "That kid is finally getting what he deserves."

"You know what he gets for seventy-five million? An in-box full of e-mails from wealth managers and real estate agents and people from college pretending to be his friend. And when he doesn't respond— because how can you respond to five hundred e-mails a day?—they say he's an arrogant ass who's gotten too big for his britches. Meanwhile, he buys his Escalade and retires, only to discover three years from now that he has no real friends, no purpose in life, no edge over the programmers who have kept in the game, and he's spent half his money on shit that doesn't make him happy."

"You don't know that."

"I do, though: I've seen it a hundred times in Silicon Valley. Look at the early Googlers, or Facebook's TNR250."

"Even if that's a possibility, it's not your decision to make."

"You're correct," he said. "I can only do what I think is right for me based on the information I have at my disposal, and I no longer wish to be associated with Hook."

Tara's blood was boiling. "But there are other people—"

"No buts," he said. "I know this space better than you."

"I've been in the space my entire career."

"Then you know that, as the company's first employee, Juan should have gotten founder's shares, but was, instead, given options."

Tara shrugged. "What difference does it make?"

"A lot, if you're Juan. And it says a lot about how Josh Hart makes decisions," Callum said. "I'm getting out."

"What about me?" she heard herself say quietly.

"What about you?"

"I need this deal to go well," she said, "for me."

He was still, watching her. She wasn't sure if the concern was fatherly or friendly or sexually inspired. "You think this deal is going to be your break." He said it as a confirmation, not a question.

"Yes," she admitted. "I've worked at this firm for almost seven years, and for the first time in my life I feel like I'm getting somewhere, like it might not all have been a waste."

"Where are you getting?"

"Catherine Wiley just e-mailed me." She looked down, laughing at how insignificant it must seem to a man like Callum. "The president of the entire investment bank wants me to represent the firm at an event in two weeks. I know that doesn't sound like much, but that's what this firm does when it wants to fast-track someone like me." She looked up at him. "It's my chance, but if this deal goes badly, it's gone."

"Do you want to be Catherine Wiley?"

"Sure," she said automatically.

"Really?" he pushed.

"A gorgeous, successful woman with a high-powered career and a husband and two kids and a penthouse on the Upper East Side?" Tara laughed. "Yes, I would take that."

Callum took a sip of his martini.

"You're not what I expected," he finally said.

Tara's spine straightened, not sure what that meant.

"How much is Phil Dalton taking off?" he asked.

"A third."

"I'll do a third, too, then," Callum said.

"Really?" Tara asked hopefully.

"Yes," Callum confirmed. "On the condition we have another martini to celebrate."

Tara's caution returned and she said, carefully, "What are we celebrating?"

"That's to be determined." He clinked her glass and took a long sip, his hazel eyes steady on hers, making her toes tingle with an unfamiliar feeling she couldn't quite describe.

TODD

WEDNESDAY, MARCH 12; NEW YORK, NEW YORK

Todd tried to concentrate but couldn't. How could Tara possibly think it was appropriate to meet a male client known for being a womanizer for drinks, downtown, at eight o'clock, in that outfit? And why was Callum requesting a meeting with Tara instead of Todd if not for sex? For all girls bitched about being objectified, they certainly didn't complain when it worked to their advantage.

An analyst arrived in the conference room with their Seamless Web order. It was way too much food for three people, but it felt like a waste to order anything less than L.Cecil's forty-dollar dinner allowance.

Todd took a break to eat his chicken parmesan and read the day's news. Bloomberg's top headline read *Stanford Student's Death Fuels New Drug War.* He opened the story.

PALO ALTO, Ca.—*Kelly Jacobson, a senior at Stanford University, was found dead in her dorm room last Thursday morning by her RA, campus officials said in a press release issued Saturday. The official cause of death was ruled to be a heart attack caused by an overdose of MDMA, or "Molly," a drug popular amongst concert-going twenty-somethings. The girl's death has shocked the Stanford community, and is now fueling a debate in Washington over drug use in the millennial generation.*

"This is exactly what happens when you start legalizing marijuana and lightening sentences for drug dealers," insisted Congressman Carl Camp (R–NE). "Our most promising students are getting corrupted by the liberal brigade. We've got to go back to harsher penalties for dealers. Lifetime sentences for dealing, period."

Sean Robinson, president of the Congress of Racial Equality, disagreed: "The only reason this is getting any attention at all is because Kelly was a privileged white girl and Molly is a privileged white kid drug. If you want to talk tragedy, go to the projects, where dozens of poor kids die unnoticed every week."

"Have you ever done Molly?" Todd asked Beau, ignoring Neha, who clearly hadn't.

"Sure, man," Beau said. "Why?"

"Was just reading about this Kelly Jacobson girl."

Beau took a sharp breath in. "Yeah. Sucks."

"What's it like?" Todd had never done drugs. Random testing by the NCAA had kept him from ever trying in college, and booze had always suited his needs since.

"It's just a purer form of ecstasy," Beau said, rubbing his eye. When he realized Todd hadn't done ecstasy, either, he went on, "It makes you euphorically happy, and all your senses and emotions are a little sharper. And you get really, really affectionate—not in a sexual way, just in a really see-the-best-in-everybody-and-feel-really-close-to-them kind of way."

"Does it give you a hangover?"

Beau shook his head. "You come down like two days later, when all the serotonin leaves your brain. That can be pretty rough," he said, then shrugged. "But better than a booze hangover."

"Interesting," Todd said.

He went back to outlining the risk factor section of the Hook S-1 filing. This section was always such a joke, especially for technology companies like Hook that weren't even profitable. Everything about the proposition was risky to investors: the company had no revenue model and was run by a sociopath of a CEO and a socially incompetent CFO. As far as Todd could tell, the only thing that made Hook worth anything was that sexually desirable men like him were on it.

He typed:

+ *If attractive people find a better alternative*
+ *If monogamy becomes popular*

"Did you and T Two ever bone at Stanford?"

Todd looked up. "What?"

"You and T Two. Did you ever hook up in college?"

Todd shook his head and looked back at his computer. "Not my type."

"You think she's Callum's type?"

Todd shrugged, trying to play it cool. "I don't really give a shit."

"You know they're at the Crosby Street Hotel."

"What?" Todd's head snapped up. Pretending a downtown meeting was innocent was one thing, but drinks at the man's hotel?

"Ugh," Neha said judgmentally from her corner. Todd had forgotten she was there.

Beau slid his phone across the table to show Todd a map with a blue dot floating over the Crosby Street Hotel.

"How do you know that's where she is?"

"Tracking her on Hook." He grinned, pleased with himself.

"You can't do that." Todd shook his head. He used Hook all the time: you could find out what girls were within a quarter mile of you, but not their exact locations.

"You can if you change a user's settings." Beau shrugged, looking back at the phone. So that's what Beau had been doing when he took Tara's phone.

"How did you figure that out?"

"I was a computer science minor at Georgetown," he said. "Anyway, Harvey's going to be so pissed if she runs off with him."

"What?"

"He gets cranky when the firm invests all this money to train smart girls, and then they quit and go be wives before they generate any real value for the firm."

"Why would she do that?"

Beau looked around. "Wouldn't you rather be the wife of a billionaire than a VP in ECM?"

"Callum's like fifty."

Beau shrugged.

"I wish she would leave," Neha said without looking up. "She doesn't do anything anyway."

"I'm sorry?" Todd turned, not sure what to make of the analyst's outburst.

"Sorry," she said, "I know you picked her for the team and all, but she doesn't know how to do anything. She just asked me to reformat an entire PowerPoint deck, as if I don't have better things to do."

"You are an analyst," Beau pointed out.

"I'm *Todd's* analyst. If I'd wanted to be an ECM analyst, I would have been," Neha said. "Maybe if she spent less time curling her hair she could do the work herself."

Todd laughed. "What's got you so wound up?"

"Tara!" she said. "I was supposed to work on my statement for my promotion tonight, and now I've got to do this because she wanted to go have drinks." Neha pushed her glasses up on her nose, staring back at her computer.

"What promotion?" Todd asked. "Aren't you a second-year?" Analysts didn't move on to the associate role until year three.

"Yeah, but they're promoting two of us early since Matt and Rohit quit."

Todd considered that. If Neha was gunning for a promotion, she'd work even harder on this deal. *Score.*

"She's on the move," Beau said, noticing the phone on the table, watching the blue dot move across town, stopping on Greenwich Avenue. "Does she live in the West Village?"

Todd shrugged.

"I think we're safe," Beau said. "If I were going to bone an old-balls billionaire, I'd stay at the hotel. I hear the suites at the Crosby are sick."

Now Todd was annoyed. She *was* trying to hook up with Callum. And going home at ten forty-five when they had a deal to get done. Maybe Lillian would have been a better choice. Or one of those gay guys from ECM who Todd knew had a crush on him.

"Hey, do you—" Todd started to address Beau, but then remembered Neha panicking beside him and sent Beau an instant message instead:

TODD: Drink?
BEAU: Thought you'd never ask.
TODD: Campbell Apartment?
BEAU: I'll go first.
TODD: Be right behind you.

Beau took a deep exhale, and closed his computer. "I am beat," he said. "I'm going to go take a little power nap and get back to it at home, if it's all right with you."

Neha's jaw dropped. "You're joking," she said. "We're not even half-way through, and we're supposed to—"

Beau lifted a hand. "I know my limits, Neha. I'll be more productive if I can just get a quick snooze in, do a little midnight workout, get back to it."

Neha looked at Todd, expecting him to do something about it. "Perks of being an associate," Todd explained. "Work hard on this deal and I really think you'll get that promotion, though, and then you can do the same."

Her chest rose and fell and she went back to her computer, looking irritated but motivated. Good girl. Beau packed up his stuff and left the room.

Ten minutes later, Todd shut down his computer. "So I've done all I can do until you finish that model. I'm going to go get some shut-eye. When do you think you'll be done?"

Neha looked at her computer, concerned. "I'll have it to you by six, I think. Six thirty at the latest. Is that okay?"

"Yeah," Todd said. "Should be fine."

"Okay," she said, refocusing on the screen.

"I'll talk to Tara about all the work she's throwing at you," Todd said as he stood up, "but for now, finish what I sent you, then work on your app, okay? Her stuff can wait."

"Thanks." Neha looked up at him, grateful.

"Sure thing," Todd said.

Todd headed downstairs. A break would do more good than sitting there getting riled up over Tara. He braced himself for the cold as he powered against the wind and the snow that had just started to fall on Park Avenue. When he got to Campbell Apartment, the swanky bar in Grand Central Terminal, he found Beau already chatting up two girls.

There were two great things about Campbell Apartment: (1) it was a known banker hang, and therefore attracted a crop of women primed to fuck anyone with an L.Cecil business card; and (2) it closed at midnight, creating a natural opportunity to invite a girl back for sex and still get six hours of sleep, as opposed to a club or two a.m. bar where girls always wanted to stay for one more song. Todd checked his watch: eleven fifteen, just enough time to close the deal with one of these girls. He hadn't had sex since the weekend and could use a midweek boost.

"I see you've met the second biggest deal at L.Cecil," Todd told the girls as he strolled up to the bar.

A petite blonde wearing a short black skirt and four-inch patent heels turned her enormous breasts to him. "And who's the first biggest deal?" She pursed her lips around her straw.

"Me." He grinned, turning casually to the bar to get a drink. He could feel her eyes lusting after him. This wouldn't even take forty-five minutes. They had mindless conversation for ten minutes, while Todd continued to think about Tara and Callum and get more and more irritated.

"I have to be honest with you," Todd said, interrupting something the girl was saying about fashion week. He'd already forgotten her name. "I had the longest day and am seriously so beat. I was just going to come for a quick drink with Beau and then go hit the sack."

Her chest fell, disappointed.

"But then I met you," he said, "and I'm having such a conflict right now, because I'm so tired, but I don't want this to end."

Her eyebrows lifted as her confidence rebounded. "Well, I could give you my number and we could go out some time and—"

"The thing is, I'm on this insane deal. I wish I could tell you about it, but it's all confidential. And I am literally working around the clock for the next two months. And I just know by then you'll be taken." He shook his head. "Girls like you never stay on the market long."

She hesitated, thinking. "Tonight, then?" she said.

"Oh, I—" He looked down, falsely sheepish, then back up. "Are you serious? I don't usually—"

"Me, either," she interrupted, giggling but committing to the idea. "But there's a first time for everything, right?"

A cab ride, an hour, and a mediocre blow job later, Todd passed out on his pillow, no longer thinking about Tara.

CHARLIE

WEDNESDAY, MARCH 12; PALO ALTO, CALIFORNIA

Charlie parked the car behind Memorial Church, and a woman in black robes ushered him into the church's alcove. He felt his eyes get hot when he saw his mother, hunched in a chair, her little body folded into itself as his father stood, helpless, beside her.

"Hey," he said, gently touching her shoulder. The sight of him made her sobs start anew, and he wrapped her in his arms.

He'd arrived from Istanbul this morning and come straight to

Stanford's campus for Kelly's memorial service. Raj had told him to leave on Friday when he got the news, but Charlie had insisted on staying to hand off his work. He just wasn't ready to face the truth.

He'd learned that Kelly died of a drug overdose. She'd taken Molly at the concert she'd told him about last Wednesday when they Skyped, then come home and passed out in her bed. Charlie didn't even know you could die from Molly, but Kelly's RA had found her unconscious the next morning. He'd taken her to the hospital, but it was too late: she was pronounced dead of a heart attack from heatstroke caused by the Molly that saturated her lifeless veins.

He'd accepted the story but he still didn't believe it. He and Kelly were as close as anyone: he'd have known if she were getting into drugs. Wouldn't he?

Or had he pushed her away with his disapproval? He'd been furious last year when she told him she was interning at L.Cecil, but he'd been certain the summer would dispel any fascination she had with it. She'd meet the worthless guys he'd hated in college—the ones who thought wearing a suit made you a man—and she'd understand what a waste it would be to give her talent to them. She hadn't seen that, though, and he'd felt sick when she'd told him she'd decided to return after graduation.

And so his last experience of the sister he loved more than anyone else in the world had been one of disappointment. He collected that failure and focused on it, knowing anger with himself was easier to manage than the thought that she was really gone.

The church bells rang and the chaplain opened the doors to the sanctuary, overflowing with people. The sound of the organ mixed with murmured weeping, and he felt his mother start to shake into tears, covering her face with her hands. Charlie and his father kept her from falling and led her to the front pew.

The service was a two-hour parade of classmates tearfully recounting stories of Kelly's energy and warmth as her framed portrait smiled out into the congregation.

The chaplain said the final prayer, one of the campus's a cappella groups sang "Amazing Grace," and the crowd slowly emptied the church to go to various support groups that had been organized around campus.

"Come this way," the woman who had read the scripture said quietly but firmly to Charlie, leading the family through a side door.

"What's going on?" Charlie whispered.

"The press is here," she said apologetically. "We tried to keep them out, but Stanford is an open campus."

"Why is the press here?" he asked.

"The Carl Camp thing?" she said, then bit her lip, realizing he didn't know. "Carl Camp—the congressman—he's using Kelly's story as a reason to clamp back down on drug policies."

"I haven't been watching the news," he admitted. It hadn't even occurred to him anyone would cover Kelly: weren't they all more worried about Syria?

"I'm sure it'll all blow over," she said unconvincingly, "but for now drive up Serra Street. They won't see you."

His parents climbed into the backseat, too overcome with grief to realize what was going on, and Charlie edged the car out onto the road. He heard someone pounding on the trunk and slammed on the brakes as a girl came around to his window, tears streaming down her face.

He rolled down the window.

"I'm so sorry," the girl bellowed. Her chest was heaving. "I'm so, so, so, so sorry."

Charlie put the car in park and got out. "I'll be right back," he told his father.

The girl's thin shoulders were hunched over, shaking with the damp cold and her sobbing. He led her under the cover of the walkway that circled the quad and gripped her arms, her distress causing him to temporarily shut down his own. "What's going on? Are you okay?"

"No." She shook her head, sniffling. "No. It's all my fault."

"What's all your fault?" He shifted into reporting mode.

"Kelly. I killed her." She coughed out sobs as she said it, her pretty face contorting as mascara streamed down her cheeks.

"I don't think that's true," Charlie said as calmly as he could. "Tell me what happened."

"I told her it was okay," the girl said. "She asked me if she should try it and I told her she deserved to have a little fun. And she wasn't sure, but I said I'd watch out for her. And I did." She looked up, her blue eyes big and innocent. "I promise I did. I was with her the whole time and she only took one hit. Really, she only did a little." She looked hopefully at Charlie, like he could make it go away. He recognized her now: she was Kelly's friend Renee, the rich sorority sister whose father had gotten Kelly the internship at L.Cecil.

"Then what happened?" Charlie asked steadily. "After she took the hit?"

"She was definitely high—I mean, she was being even more sweet and energetic than she usually was, just telling everyone how much she loved them and talking about how happy she was and how excited she was about New York and L.Cecil. Literally, all the way home, she was totally with it. And I gave her some water—but not too much, I swear! And she put on her pajamas and brushed her teeth and I put her to bed and waited until she fell asleep and then locked the door behind me and she was fine, I promise she was. But I should have." Another sob burst through the girl's open mouth. "I should have stayed with her."

"It's not your fault," Charlie said, knowing it wasn't. "You couldn't have known."

"But how . . . I just don't understand how it happened. It took us an hour and a half to get back—if she'd taken more when we were at the concert it would have kicked in before I left her alone." Her eyebrows were squeezed together. "Right?"

"Charlie, can we please go home?" His father opened the car door. "Your mother needs to—"

"You're Renee, right?" Charlie said.

"Yeah. Renee Schultz. We were in the same pledge class. We were going to live together in New York."

"Thank you, Renee, for telling me."

"I'm so sorry," she sniffed.

He drove back to the hotel and dropped his parents off before checking in himself. The student dean had delivered a box of Kelly's belongings, and he looked at it cautiously as he sat on the bed, not sure he wanted to know what was inside.

Kelly hadn't told him she would live with Renee in New York. What else hadn't she told him?

He picked up the keys and went back out to the car, following the signs to Stanford Hospital.

"SHE WAS DEAD when she got here," the doctor, a short, round woman with frizzy red hair, said without looking up from a patient's chart as she headed to her next appointment.

Charlie followed, offended by her tone. "But her RA said she still had a pulse."

"Her RA should have gotten a DUI for driving her here," the doctor said impatiently. "You could smell the booze on his breath. I assure you, by the time that girl got to me she was gone. There was nothing I could do." The doctor turned to the door.

"I'm not accusing you of anything," Charlie said, "I'm just trying to figure out what happened."

"What happened?" The woman turned back and lifted her eyebrows as if he were stupid. "She took a huge amount of drugs, she had sex, and she died. Don't overthink it."

"She'd had sex?"

"Yes. We could tell from the autopsy."

"Did they run the DNA?"

"No. She didn't die of sex, she died of drugs."

"I just don't understand how she could have overdosed," he pressed the doctor.

"By taking a gram of Molly and a punch of dextromethorphan, on top of a diet pill, an Adderall and six Advil. No heart could have survived that."

"A gram? Her friend said she took one hit," Charlie said. Why was she taking diet pills?

"Then her friend is lying," the doctor said, then finally paused and said, more softly, "Why do you care so much?"

"I'm her brother."

The woman sighed heavily, adopting the sympathetic voice her med school hadn't done a good enough job teaching her. "Listen, I get that it's hard to accept the truth about people you're close to, but don't make this more complicated than it is."

"You don't know a damn thing about my sister," he snapped.

HIS HEART was still racing when he got back to the hotel. None of this made sense. If it had been a massacre in the Middle East he'd be thinking clearly, looking at the facts and uncovering the story. But it wasn't. It was *Kelly*, and all his brain could see was a deep, dark hole.

He looked at the box the dean had delivered again.

He drank a little bottle of whiskey from the hotel's minibar in one gulp as he tried to decide whether he was ready to go through it. He drank the vodka, too, then started in.

He removed her books—copies of Henry James and Virginia Woolf and Jane Austen and, at the bottom of the pile, the worn copy of *Man's Search for Meaning*, the book she knew was his favorite. The spine was broken and the pages covered in highlights. He felt a lump in his throat, realizing how much time she'd spent with it, and another when he saw a picture fall out.

He knew the photo before he turned it over: it showed the two of them together on the day of her high school graduation. She was wearing her cap and gown, her enormous grin matched only by his beaming next to it. He'd just been staffed permanently in Tunisia and she'd written him a long e-mail saying she understood that he couldn't make it back for her big day. He remembered how he'd laughed when he got it—the AP could have offered him a Nobel Prize–worthy assignment and he wouldn't have taken it—there was no way he was missing his little sister as valedictorian. He'd booked a ticket without telling her, and she'd spotted him at the end of her speech, laughing on stage, and running down into the auditorium to give him a hug, ignoring the administrator's horror at the interruption to the ceremony. He couldn't remember the last time he'd been so happy.

He put the book down and looked through the photos she'd framed of herself with her sorority sisters—he was biased, but she was the prettiest one. He flipped through her binders, full of old tests and papers organized by semester. He found her laptop and her iPhone and two water bottles with the L.Cecil logo, which made Charlie roll his eyes: was one not enough?

He saw a yellow book at the bottom of the box, and his chest clenched again when he recognized the journal he'd sent her the day she left for college. He gently undid the string and read the first entry:

Thursday, September 16, 2010

How to begin this journal? I feel like I need to write something really significant, like I need to say something profound to mark this

moment. I'm on a plane from JFK to SFO. How cool to write that?
S-F-O. And to know it's just the first of lots of flights to SFO. Oh!
It gives me chills just thinking about it. I can't believe this is
happening. I can't believe I'm going to California and to Stanford
and that everything is about to change. Charlie gave me this journal.
The only problem with California is that it's so far from Tunisia, but
he swears we'll Skype all the time. We better—the only thing that
makes me not nervous about college is knowing I can talk to him
about anything. I love that he gave me a journal. Like, a real
journal. I think it's harder to write the truth when you're typing. I
think you need a pen and paper sometimes, to get to the underneath
of things. Is that profound? Or will I look back on this in four years
and laugh at my now-self and think how silly I was thinking I was
intellectual at seventeen. Sigh! Who am I going to be four years from
now? What will I know? Will I have a boyfriend? I hope so. Will
I have a job? Don't think about that. I wonder who my roommate
will be? I hope I don't embarrass her. I hope I'm not the stupidest
person there.

Charlie looked up at the ceiling to ward off the unfamiliar feeling of tears forming.

"I can't do this," he said aloud.

He turned on the television and flipped to CNN, grateful to find a report about another roadside bombing that put his tragedy back into perspective. But then the reporter cut to new coverage from California. Charlie's throat burned when he saw Kelly's photo.

"Students gathered today for the memorial service of Kelly Jacobson, the Stanford senior found dead of a drug overdose last week, just three months before the girl was scheduled to graduate and go work for the investment bank, L.Cecil. The conservative pundit Rush Limbaugh was quick to opine, criticizing the university for honoring a girl he says represents the irresponsibility of the millennial generation and the moral decline of the nation—"

Charlie shut off the television. "Fuck," he said out loud.

He reached for his bottle of Ambien and picked up one of the L.Cecil water bottles and went to the sink to fill it. But when he took off the lid he noticed a white film at the mouth. He licked his finger and touched it: it tasted sour, like a crushed-up pill. He went back to the other water bottle: it was clean. Was this . . . ? He tasted more of the white residue: it was Molly. It had to be. But how had it ended up in her water bottle?

4

TODD

"Boom!" Todd turned his laptop to Tara.

The note was from Hook's lawyer at Crowley Brown, announcing that the S-1 had been officially submitted to the Securities and Exchange Commission, the culmination of three weeks of around-the-clock work. S-1 filings normally took twice that time to pull off. Take that, Harvey Tate: just try giving Todd Kent a challenge he can't overcome.

Tara smiled thinly. She looked exhausted, and that made her look pretty, in a vulnerable way that almost compensated for the glasses and pinned-back hair.

"Everything okay?" Todd asked.

"Yeah," Tara said. "Just tired."

He could tell something was wrong, and guessed it had to do with Callum Rees. Apparently he'd just wanted to get her advice about market conditions and how much of his position he should sell. Tara said they hadn't even had drinks, just soda water, and that he'd spent the whole time checking out other women. That had to have sucked for Tara—comparing herself to all those hot girls at the Crosby—and Todd felt a little bad for having been so hard on her.

He liked Tara. She worked hard and didn't get stressed out and occasionally said things that were funny. She didn't get upset when he and Beau talked about sex or sports, and she didn't inundate them with questions about men. She was still neurotic—she only ate salads without dressing—and overly serious—she never took part when they ordered beers into the office—but he liked working with her more than he had any other woman, and would still sleep with her if the opportunity arose.

"I'm going to go home before the honeybees land." Tara stood up and straightened her dress, wrinkled from a day and a half of wear. Honeybees were the employees who filled their days doing internal networking, picking up gossip and pollinating it elsewhere in the office. They scoured firm-wide announcements for employees who looked like they were on the rise, then e-mailed congratulatory notes and scheduled coffee chats to "get in front of" them in hopes of being remembered someday, once the rising colleagues were in charge.

"Congratulations, guys." Lou Reynolds popped his head into the room as Tara slipped her heels back on and smiled knowingly at Todd. "Heard the big news!"

"Thank you," Tara said, reaching out to squeeze the honeybee's hand. Lou blushed at Tara's warmth; he was used to buttoned-up, professional Tara, not the exhausted, tender Tara whom Todd had gotten to know over the past three weeks.

"Will you be back later?" Todd asked her, ignoring Lou.

"No, I've got this event at the Frick," she said, shaking her hair from the clip that secured it and refastening it more tightly as she spoke.

"Since when do you rub shoulders on the Upper East Side?"

"It's work," she said. "L.Cecil's got a table and Catherine asked me to go."

"Catherine Wiley?" Lou's jaw dropped.

Todd's throat constricted: why was Tara on a first-name basis with the president of the investment bank?

"I guess a couple of important clients are going to be there and Catherine wants me to get some exposure," she said innocently, as if she weren't aware of what that meant.

"Why didn't you say anything?"

"I didn't think you'd care," she lied.

"Of course I care," Todd said, dumbfounded. Senior management wasn't teeing up introductions for him, and he'd brought in this deal. Tara was only on it because he'd chosen her.

"Good luck tonight," Lou told her. "And let's grab a coffee later this week. Would be great to catch up."

"Sure thing," Tara said, winking at Todd. "See you guys later."

"Dude, what are you going to do to celebrate?" Lou sat down where Tara had been, anxious for whatever manly adventures his hero was plotting for the evening.

Todd was in fact going to PH-D, the nightclub in the Meatpacking District, but no way he was telling Lou that. His face was still on the door. How the hell could the firm give Tara such a leg up like that? Because she was a girl? That wasn't gender equality, that was reverse discrimination.

He glanced at his watch. "Right now, I'm going to the gym," Todd said to Lou, not lying. "It's been too long."

Lou stood, embarrassed he'd just sat, as Todd picked up his gym bag. "Yeah, totally. I hate it when I've got a big deal and can't work out."

Todd tried not to laugh. "Well, thanks for the congrats."

———

HE FELT HIS ANNOYANCE subside as he opened the doors to Equinox and breathed in the over-oxygenated, eucalyptus-infused air.

"Long time no see," Morgan, his super-hot personal trainer, teased when he came out of the locker room. Her spandex capris made no attempt to hide her sculpted legs and ass. Todd's friends had all written off personal trainers, insisting P90X was the way forward, but Todd couldn't imagine giving up Morgan or sessions of her undivided attention focused on perfecting his body. "I hope you have a good excuse," she said.

He swatted her ponytail playfully. "I do, in fact," he said, leading her to the gym floor, where he reached up to turn one of the flat-screen TVs to CNBC. She pointed him to the bike below it and he climbed on, watching the screen.

"A group of Stanford students today announced their intention to create a nonprofit investment fund honoring Kelly Jacobson, the Stanford senior found dead of a drug overdose in her campus dorm room earlier this month," the anchor said. "The students struck a deal with the crowd-funding site Kickstarter to use the site to raise the two-million-dollar fund, which will be managed by the university's Student Finance Club, and donate five percent of annual proceeds to programs supporting women's rights, a cause Jacobson was passionate about when she was alive."

"We're creating the fund to continue the work Kelly wanted to do, both in her finance career and in her passion for helping women around the world," a pretty brunette told the camera. "Kelly was an amazing girl, and we want to make sure the world remembers her that way."

"That was Renee Schultz, a sorority sister of Kelly's. We contacted Sean Robinson, a vocal critic of the fanfare surrounding Jacobson's death, for his comment."

"I'm not saying I don't commend the students' efforts," Sean Robinson said, raising his hands to the camera. "All I'm pointing out is that a black kid ODs and no one pays attention, and a white girl ODs and she gets a televised funeral and a memorial fund."

"You're working on Kelly Jacobson's memorial fund?" Morgan turned her attention from the screen, punching up the resistance on Todd's bike.

"Wait for it," he said, feeling his heartbeat rise with the movement of his legs and anticipation of the moment to come.

"In business news," the anchor continued, "the location-based dating app company, Hook, filed an S-1 with the SEC today, indicating its intention to offer its shares on the NASDAQ stock exchange. The deal, which is speculated to value the company around fourteen billion dollars, is being underwritten by L.Cecil. It's a piece of good news for the global investment bank that has, otherwise, only been making headlines for SEC investigations. The announcement comes as a surprise to many analysts, but is already generating speculation that it will be the hottest issue since Twitter went public last November."

Todd grinned at Morgan. She looked back from the TV, pursing her lips in approval. "Not bad."

Bam, Todd thought. *That* was the moment that mattered: the moment when a hot girl was impressed by his power and authority and involvement in things that got reported on CNBC.

"Come on," Morgan instructed him off the bike to the weights. "Let's see if you've got any muscle left in those manly, important arms of yours." He let her flattery spread across him like a steroid.

"So, do you have a big celebration lined up?" Morgan asked as she adjusted the weights on the lateral pulldown. He could see a girl on the mat checking him out in the mirror. *This one's for you*, he silently told her, pulling down on the bar.

"Going to PH-D tonight. Come as my date?" He smiled slyly.

"Afraid I don't date clients." She sighed but grinned in a way that made him know it wasn't off the table.

"I'll fire you, then," he countered. The idea suddenly seemed very smart: Morgan must be incredible in bed, with all that core strength and endurance. "Come on, it'll be fun."

She laughed. "I've got plans."

"Who's the lucky guy?"

"Girl," she corrected. "Her name's Rosie. And it's our anniversary."

Todd let go of the metal bar and it clanked back up. "You're gay?" It came out with more disgust than he intended.

"You thought I was straight?" Morgan laughed, unbothered.

"How?" was all he could muster.

"Well, when a girl—"

"No, I—" He grabbed the bar again. "I just didn't realize." She *hadn't* been wanting to sleep with him this whole time? "Is your girlfriend hot, too?" he finally asked, consoling his masculinity with the vision of Morgan having sex with an equally attractive girl.

"I think so."

"Are you into threesomes?"

"Get on the bench." She pushed him over to the chest press with a smile.

NICK

The Rosewood Hotel, a subtly designed sprawl of five-hundred-dollar-a-night suites tucked at the top of Sand Hill Road, was *where it all happened*. The venture capitalists who ruled Silicon Valley, and by extension anything interesting happening in the world, came here for their power lunches and after-work drinks. It was the only place in Northern California where you could order a proper twenty-three-dollar martini and be surrounded by women who'd made an effort to look great.

Sure, there had been some scandal around a prostitution ring, and some older VCs claimed the excess was out of character for the Valley, but they were behind the times. Not like Nick. He was the new wave, a ruler of Silicon Valley *3.0*. His phone buzzed and he checked the text message.

> Grace: Call me when you have a second?

To celebrate Hook's S-1 filing, Nick had scheduled this meeting at the Rosewood with Darrell Greene, the esteemed wealth manager, to discuss his finances, followed by dinner with his girlfriend, Grace. He hadn't told her, but he'd also reserved a suite at the Rosewood for after dinner. He had a feeling tonight was the night they were finally going to sleep together, and he didn't want to have to go back to San Francisco or, worse, her sorority house.

He checked his watch and dialed her number.

"Hey," she answered. Grace's parents were Chinese immigrants, but you'd never know: she was pure American Sorority Girl, a hot Pi Phi who also happened to be smart, though not as smart as Nick, which was the way it should be.

They'd met last fall at an entrepreneurship conference where Grace had been helping with registration. He'd asked her to dinner at Evvia (girls never turned down dinner at Evvia), and it had been easy to win her over from there.

"What's up?" he asked the phone, scanning the lobby for important people. He rolled his eyes when he saw Ashton Kutcher on the sofa, talking to some guy who was probably a second-tier venture capitalist. He hated the celebrity infiltration of Silicon Valley and the implicit assumption that a decent Twitter following made a person capable of evaluating a start-up's potential. Had Ashton Kutcher even gone to college?

"I don't think I can make it tonight," Grace said.

"What'd you say?" Nick turned his attention to the phone.

"I'm sorry, I'm just really upset about the news."

"What news?" Nick tried to control his voice. The only news that had happened today was that his company had filed for an IPO, which was going to make her boyfriend famous, a fact she had yet to acknowledge.

"That congressman is protesting the fund we're raising for Kelly," she said. "And now Kickstarter's saying they might cancel our partnership because they don't want to get involved."

Kelly Jacobson, the girl who had died at Stanford, had been in Grace's sorority. But Nick had never heard Grace mention Kelly until the girl died. He didn't understand why she was so upset.

"What fund?" Nick didn't try to hide his irritation.

"The investment fund we're starting to raise money to help women's rights," she said.

"How big is the fund?"

"We're aiming for two million dollars, with a five percent distribution to charities."

"A hundred thousand a year?" Nick scoffed at the amount.

"It should grow over time." Grace tried to defend it.

"Are you the one negotiating with Kickstarter?" he asked.

"No, I'm just helping raise awareness for the project," she said, then was quiet, realizing that meant she didn't have any excuse for canceling dinner. "I'm just having a hard time with it all," she said softly. "Like, it's really hard to process, especially with everything else going on."

What else was going on? She was a twenty-one-year-old sorority girl. He was CFO of a major company about to go public, and *he* still found time and energy for the relationship.

"You're joking, right?"

"I'm sorry, Nick. I just want to be with my friends right now."

"Fine," Nick said. "I have to go." He could feel his blood pressure rising as he watched Ashton Kutcher laugh from the couch. *Screw you!* he wanted to scream. *Airbnb is a fluke!*

"Can I help you?" a hostess in a low-cut black dress asked.

Nick turned, pushing his anger away. He wasn't going to let Grace ruin this for him. "I'm meeting Darrell Greene here." He articulated the name carefully, hoping she caught the significance of it. Darrell Greene was Silicon Valley's premier wealth manager, overseeing the fortunes of Mark Zuckerberg and the other under-thirty-five masters of the new universe.

"Of course, right this way." She smiled. Her hips moved as she walked and calmed Nick. She was hotter than Grace, and she recognized how important he was.

"Nick." The wealth manager stood and offered his hand. "Great to see you, man," he said in a thick Australian accent. He was pudgy, with ruddy cheeks and curly hair, wearing pleated khakis and a polo shirt tucked in.

"You, too." Nick felt his anger at Grace dissipate.

They sat at the corner table in the bar, an intimate L-shaped room that looked out glass doors to the Santa Cruz Mountains, and Darrell ordered a bottle of champagne.

"Now, what can I do for you?" Darrell asked.

"Well," Nick started, glad someone recognized the significance of this day, and of him. He pulled out the file that summarized his personal finances. "I brought my current portfolio, and thought we could start by—"

"Let me stop you," Darrell interrupted. "What do you want?"

"Well, right now I'm feeling bullish on U.S. midcap, but I obviously want to stay diversified and—"

Darrell cut him off again, smiling as he closed the folder. "Let's not get into the nitty-gritty. Big picture: what do you want?"

"What do you mean?"

"You've got eighty-five million dollars now. What does Nick Winthrop *want*? A house? Seven houses? A private foundation, Gates-style? A private island, Ellison-style?"

Nick blushed. He wasn't sure how Darrell knew his number, but loved the feeling of hearing it out loud, and his name alongside Larry Ellison's.

The waitress returned with a bottle of Dom Pérignon, popped the cork, and filled their glasses.

Nick leaned forward and confided, "I want to be big, you know? Like, I want to be that guy who touches things and they turn to gold. The guy who sets the bar for what's smart in business and cool in life."

"I love it, man." Darrell congratulated him, clinking his glass.

Nick took a sip, pleased with the validation.

"I take it you've exercised your options?"

"Only a hundred thousand," Nick said, pointing to the sheet where he had it laid out.

"What?" Darrell sat forward. "Why?"

Nick shrugged. "I haven't got the money. It would cost two million to exercise them all."

"And save you tens of millions in taxes if you plan to sell anything before 2016."

This wasn't news to Nick: the clock for long-term capital gains treatment, which meant a shareholder paid 15 percent instead of 40 percent in tax in exchange for holding the shares for more than a year, started when the shares were purchased. Right now Nick only had stock options, which meant he didn't actually own the shares yet, just had the right to purchase them at the value they'd had when they were given to him, an amount that totaled two million dollars. If he'd had two million dollars, he would have already purchased the shares so he could start the long-term capital gains clock, but as it was, he'd have to wait until after the IPO, so he could simultaneously purchase and sell enough shares to cover the cost of buying the rest.

"I know," Nick said. "It's not ideal, from a tax perspective, but I haven't really got any choice."

"Nonsense. Why don't you get a loan?"

"From who? The only assets I have are my Hook options. No bank will go for that."

Darrell lifted an eyebrow. "What do you think I'm here for?"

"You're not a bank," Nick said.

"Banks are antiquated. I've got other clients who have the cash to front a loan, and they understand your situation. I'll have your two million tomorrow, guaranteed."

"You can do that?" Nick had thought he'd have to wait two years to actually get any cash from the IPO. But if he could get the loan and purchase his shares now, he could sell a year from now at a 15 percent tax rate and be on his way.

"Consider it done." Darrell smiled. "Assuming, of course, you want to work with me?"

"Yes." Nick nodded. "Definitely."

"Good." Darrell refilled Nick's glass and toasted him again.

The bar was starting to fill up and Nick was feeling good. A woman in high heels and a tight silver dress at the bar was smiling at him, and he felt his cheeks burn.

"So, have you got a girlfriend?" Darrell asked.

"Yes, Grace," Nick said, looking away from the woman.

"You think she's the one?"

"I—" The woman at the bar was still looking at him. "I don't know."

He'd thought he liked Grace, but maybe he didn't. Maybe he needed something more.

"Can I be honest?" Darrell lowered his voice. "And I'm not saying anything bad about Grace, but if I were you, I'd ditch her. You have no idea what's about to come your way. Why limit yourself right as you're getting going?"

The waitress refilled Nick's glass, leaning forward to provide an even better view of her cleavage. Nick felt the pulse in his veins.

"You know she canceled dinner on me?" he confessed, shaking his head. "I had this whole evening planned to celebrate today's filing and she just called—right as I was walking in here—and canceled."

Darrell shook his head. "Dude, some guys have to deal with that shit, but you don't. The world's your oyster now."

"Should we go talk to them?" Nick tilted his head to the bar, where the woman in the silver dress had been joined by a friend.

Darrell followed his gaze. "That's the spirit." He turned back and clinked Nick's glass as they stood. "Welcome to your new world."

AMANDA

WEDNESDAY, MARCH 26; NEW YORK, NEW YORK

Amanda was wearing her favorite work outfit: a tight but still professional black Theory pencil skirt and a purple silk camisole from Club Monaco under a black wrap sweater by a designer she didn't know, but assumed was expensive because her rich roommate Claudia had given it to her as a hand-me-down.

Amanda wanted to hate Claudia, but she'd been Amanda's best

friend ever since they were randomly assigned as roommates freshman year at Penn. They'd had a blast together in college—they worked hard but played hard, too—a notorious duo who could get any guy in undergrad and most in the business school, too.

But when they'd moved to New York, things had changed. Claudia grew up in the city and, with her grade school connections, fancy clothes, and ample free time—owing to the fact she worked forty hours a week, if that, at Sotheby's—thrived on a whole new level. She traded Penn reunion parties for fashion week soirees and their old reliable hookups for older guys with their own investment funds. Meanwhile, Amanda worked ninety hours a week at a job she despised, and tried to fit in at the swank events she went to with Claudia, but always seemed to get caught when someone asked where she "summered" and her lack of a Nantucket/Hamptons/Newport/the Vineyard answer gave her away as a fraud who grew up in not-Palm-Beach Florida.

Two months ago, Claudia had started dating a guy she met in St. Barts over New Year's and now Amanda barely saw her at all.

Which Amanda couldn't get mad about because Amanda knew she'd have done the same if the roles were reversed. That was the problem with being friends with girls: you could only count on them until they found a boyfriend, and then there was an implicit *You can't get mad* understanding that he would take priority and the single girl would be left alone.

Which is why you couldn't be the last one.

Which is why Amanda was wearing her favorite work outfit and had curled her stick-straight blonde hair in the Crowley Brown bathroom and said she had a doctor's appointment so that she could leave work in time to show up to Harold Hammonds's happy hour precisely fifteen minutes late.

Todd hadn't responded to her Facebook message, but that hadn't kept her from planning out how the night could go if he did come. She'd imagined the scene to its every last detail: he'd come in and she'd watch him look around the room for her, then smile casually when he spotted her at the bar with two hot men; he'd interrupt them to tell her she looked beautiful, she'd accept a drink, he'd say he was sorry, she'd say she understood, he'd say let's get out of here, she'd say okay. They'd go to a restaurant in the West Village, he'd order for them both, she'd say let's get it to go, he'd smile in agreement, and they'd go back to his apartment and make love and laugh about how silly it was that people didn't believe in soul mates, or that those who did thought soulmating was always easy. Amanda smiled at the vision, buoyed with the energy of possibility as she walked into the bar.

It was empty. She went upstairs and found Harold with two equally unattractive guys. *Don't panic*, she told herself, but she could already feel her vision collapse into a vacuum of disappointment.

"Amanda!" Harold called. "Amanda, hey!"

She forced a smile, pushing the black hole away. She kissed Harold on the cheek, careful to maintain as much distance as possible between their bodies. He introduced her to the friends he was with, a scrawny kid who barely spoke English and a short, overly aggressive guy who tapped his foot and kept talking about how he was about to go hit on the girls who had materialized in the corner. She didn't pay attention to their names.

"Can I get you a drink?" Harold asked.

"Sure," she said, kicking her heart to readjust its expectations. She could make this work; she just needed to get very drunk. "I'll have a Grey Goose greyhound," she said to the bartender. It was the first drink Todd had ever ordered her, when they'd met for the first time at The Standard.

"Sorry, what's that?" the bartender asked.

"Grapefruit juice," she said with a fake smile, "with Grey Goose."

"All I got's cranberry," the bartender seemed to take pleasure in telling her, "and only well drinks are included in the happy hour."

Amanda wanted to cry. "Vodka soda, then," she said. "Double, please."

"Sure you don't want cranberry?" Harold asked.

As if she would waste an extra sixty calories on this. "That's what I drank in college," she explained. "Unfortunately, pledge quarter ruined them for me."

"Oh, yeah, sure," Harold said. "You were a Chi O, right?"

"Theta," she corrected, wondering if he had any idea how insulting it was that he'd just asked her whether she was a Chi O. Theta was the cool sorority at Penn. Chi O was for leftovers.

She downed her drink and immediately ordered another.

The bar slowly filled with bankers who got more attractive as she got more drunk, and she perched at the bar waiting for someone to talk to her. A cute boy looked her way and she turned to find Harold so she could pretend like she was laughing at something he said, knowing she looked prettiest when her neck was arched back.

She glanced at the cute guy and laughed, letting herself lean into Harold. "That's so funny," she said.

He blinked, not sure what he'd said, but willing to take the attention.

The guy across the room came toward them and Amanda braced herself. *Finally.*

He walked beside her and she could feel the warmth of his body on her bare arm. He touched her elbow and she turned, opening her eyes wide to show off her enviably long eyelashes.

"Could you hand me a menu?" he asked, lifting his chin to indicate the menu on the counter in front of her.

That's a new line, she thought, reaching to get the menu and handing it to him.

"Thanks," he said, turning to leave.

What the hell?

She turned back to the bar and ordered another double vodka soda, ignoring Harold. The bartender brought it back and placed it on the counter. "Thirteen," he said.

"What?" she snapped.

"It's thirteen," he said, and she realized he was telling her the price.

"Oh, no, I'm with the happy hour."

"Ended at seven."

She looked at her watch: it was 7:02.

"Crap." She smiled at Harold, waiting for him to pay.

"That sucks!" he said, missing his cue.

She scoffed in disbelief and put fourteen dollars on the counter, chugging the cocktail before standing up from the stool.

"Hey, I know it's last minute, but do you have plans Friday night?" Harold asked, realizing she was leaving. "My friend is having this—"

She stared down at him. Was he serious? Anger was the last stage before the disappointment took over, and she clung to it with all she had.

"Yeah," she cut him off, turning on her heel to leave, "I do."

IT WAS SNOWING OUTSIDE and the wind hit her face hard. It was almost April: there was no reason it should still be this cold. She pulled her coat tight around her and tiptoed on the accumulating snow to keep her feet from slipping out of her heels, feeling the physical discomfort creep up through her toes and spread across her chest and into her heart. *Don't cry*, she willed herself.

She put her arm out for a cab, knowing it was futile as the yellow cars rushed by, lights off and already occupied, like physical signs of her rejection. This city was mean, and for no good reason: What was so wrong with her? Why couldn't New York just give her a light and let her in?

She stood on the corner of Forty-seventh and Park and looked north, noticing L.Cecil looming and, for the first time in the past three months, not hoping to run into Todd. She wanted to go back to college, where she knew what to do, or to Florida, where she'd been bored but at least had been in control. But she knew she couldn't go back, and the heaviness of that thought made her hope sink down into her stomach where she hardly noticed it anymore.

But then a cab stopped to let someone off. She felt her legs move to rush for it, the will to survive surging through her veins with animalistic instinct that didn't care when her foot submerged in a puddle of gray slush at the curb, ruining her shoes.

She gave the driver her address. Traffic was slow and she stared out at the lights in the windows, trying to remember what it was like to think this city was cool. She hated it. Hated the men and the snow and her numb limbs and the shitty thirteen-dollar cocktails at shitty midtown bars. Why did she even want its approval? The thought of another weekend here, alone, made her heart swell with the claustrophobic panic of being trapped on an island.

She reached into her purse to fish out her BlackBerry.

She found the e-mail she'd seen earlier from Crowley Brown's HR department titled "Transfers."

For paralegals interested in transferring to other offices on a temporary or permanent basis, please contact your HR manager.
The following offices presently have openings for first and second year paralegals:
Dubai
Shanghai (Mandarin required)
San Francisco

She forwarded the e-mail to her HR manager and typed in the body of the e-mail:

I'd like to be considered for San Francisco, please. Ready to leave immediately.

CHARLIE

WEDNESDAY, MARCH 26; NEW YORK, NEW YORK

"We'll take another round," Johnny Walker told the bartender, without asking Charlie whether he wanted it.

Johnny, a slender, fashionable native New Yorker who did not find his name as amusing as his parents had thirty-three years earlier, worked at the *New York Times*, where he and Charlie had met as college interns. Johnny was the closest thing Charlie had to a best friend, though they normally only saw each other once a year, for drinks at the Distinguished Wakamba, a kitschy cocktail lounge in the Garment District that had become a journalist hang after an undercover cop killed an unarmed security guard on its doorstep and made it feel edgy.

"So are we going to talk about it?" Johnny finally asked, checking his watch as Charlie passed the second empty beer bottle back to the bartender and asked for another. It was the first evening he'd gotten out of his parents' Brooklyn apartment since he'd flown back with them after Kelly's services and he wanted it to last.

"It's just strange to be on the other side," Charlie confided.

"I'm sure."

The press wouldn't let go of Kelly's overdose, or the platform it provided to argue over drugs in America. And the memorial fund Renee had started, despite all its good intentions, was just making it all worse, fueling a national debate over whether Kelly was a victim or a spoiled girl who'd squandered her opportunity.

Charlie sipped the fresh beer. "Do you think Sean Robinson's right? About the white girl thing?"

As one of the few black reporters at the *Times*, Johnny was the go-to "racial issues" coverage person, a position he despised.

"I think they're right that no one would be so concerned if it were a poor black kid that had died, but I doubt they'd care as much if she'd been an ugly white girl, either." He studied Charlie's face. "Come on, man, you know everyone is going to make this a platform for whatever they want. You can't take it personally, you know that."

"I just don't get it," he said. "She was a girl in college, not a public figure."

"Welcome back to America."

He was right: Charlie had forgotten how the American press worked. Amongst the many things he was struggling to readjust to, the prioritization of public interest in his sister's death over the thousands that were happening in the Middle East was at the top of his list.

"How's your mom doing?" Johnny asked.

"Terribly." Charlie shook his head. "You know they talked every single day? Kelly called my mother *every single day*. I think I called my parents once a semester when I was in college."

Johnny sipped his beer. He was one of the most talented guys Charlie knew, but had never gotten the recognition he deserved. It would have been so easy to break through by playing the race angle, but Johnny wouldn't do it. He refused to let an agenda drive his work, or be tempted by the salability of sensationalism.

"I think she was murdered," Charlie said quietly.

Johnny's eyes snapped up. "What?"

Charlie took another sip of his beer before he delivered the facts he'd carefully collected to form the narrative he now believed.

"Her friends only saw her take one hit of Molly. All of them took from the same batch and were fine, so there wasn't anything bad in it," he reported. "Her friend Renee said it took them an hour and a half to get back to campus from the concert, and that Kelly was fine when she put her to bed. So even if Kelly had found and taken more drugs from someone else at the concert, which I find hard to believe, it would have kicked in while she was in the car and Renee would have noticed."

Charlie could feel his friend studying his face, trying to decide whether Charlie himself was being logical or was under the influence of his own desire to see his sister as pure.

"The toxicology report showed that there was more than one hit in her system," Johnny said carefully.

"I know. I think she must have taken it after Renee left."

"That doesn't make it murder."

"I found a water bottle in her stuff, and it has a powder residue in it that I think is Molly."

"That still doesn't make it murder."

"Why would my sister have woken up to sit in her room by herself and drink a water bottle laced with Molly?"

"Maybe it was suicide," Johnny said softly.

Charlie shook his head. "She was happy."

"How do you know?"

"I talked to her that day," he admitted. "She was upset with me, but she wasn't suicidal."

"But the drugs—the comedown—"

"Takes two days, not two hours."

"Do you know who she was sleeping with?"

"I think it was either this kid Luis, who gave her the drugs at the concert, or her RA."

Johnny waited. Charlie continued, knowing the impact his words would have.

"Renee said she locked the door when she left Kelly. The RA, Robby, was the only one with a key. And according to the doctor, he was still drunk in the morning when he brought her to the hospital, which means he must have been completely blacked out when she died."

"So you think he had something to do with it?"

"I think someone should ask."

"You can't get involved." Johnny shook his head. "Families getting involved never helps."

"I know."

"Are you asking me to write something?"

Charlie shrugged, looking down at his hands.

"You know this would make my career, right? Breaking a story like this?"

"I know you'll treat it fairly."

"But it'll make the attention that much worse. The punditry now will be nothing compared to—"

"I know," Charlie interrupted.

"Who else should I talk to?"

"I pulled some numbers from her phone." Charlie handed Johnny a piece of paper with the names and contact information he'd written down. "I'd start with Renee Schultz, Luis Guerrera and Robby Goodman."

Johnny checked his watch.

"Go," Charlie said, knowing he wanted to get working on the story.

"Are you sure you'll be okay?"

"Yeah," he said.

Johnny left and Charlie ordered another beer. It was the right thing to do, he reminded himself. If the media insisted on judging his sister, he was going to make sure she came out clean.

He pulled Kelly's phone out of his pocket and looked at the call log from the day she died for the dozenth time. He hadn't told Johnny about the other number—the 212 area code she'd called that afternoon. He held his breath and dialed it.

"L.Cecil, Tara Taylor's line," a woman said.

Charlie felt the flood of relief, laughing at his fear the number belonged to a drug dealer. "Oh, I must have the wrong—" he started, but changed his mind, suddenly curious who Kelly would have worked with. "Actually, yes, could I speak with Tara, please?"

"She's at a client event, but I can give you her e-mail?"

"Sure," Charlie said, "let me get a pen."

TARA

WEDNESDAY, MARCH 26; NEW YORK, NEW YORK

A man unhooked the red velvet rope as cameras flashed, and Tara lifted the skirt of her long purple gown, conscious of the curious gaze of the pedestrians who'd paused in the cold at the Frick's entrance to determine the cause of all the commotion.

Tara hadn't thought about anything other than Hook for the past three weeks. She got up at five, went for a run, was in the office by seven and stayed until midnight every day, only registering whether it was a weekday or the weekend by how crowded the twenty-seventh floor was when she left the conference room to go to the restroom. She'd been excused from all office- or team-wide meetings, and had finally put an Out of Office automated response on her personal e-mail so she could feel less guilty about being completely unresponsive to any of her friends. The country could have gone to war and she wasn't sure she'd have noticed.

But tonight, she was entering the world again: she was going to have a drink and be social and show Catherine that she wasn't just the kind of woman who could put her head down and work, she was also the kind of woman who could socialize with clients and sell them on the firm's merits.

She posed for a photograph with Beau, who was here as a benefactor rather than a corporate representative, and realized she'd forgotten to line her eyebrows. She chided herself for the neglect: how had she forgotten something so simple? She felt the anxiety that she *wasn't* in fact the woman who could work hard and do well at events start to swell and she pushed it away. She'd make a checklist when she got home of all the things she needed to remember to do when she got ready before these things, and then she wouldn't forget.

Tara followed the entrance lights through a mirrored hall, instinctively checking to be sure she didn't look fat. Her dress was cut on the bias, a swath of deep plum silk that crossed her right shoulder and gathered at her left hip, leaving a slit open for her leg to peek out when she walked. It was four years old, but it felt appropriately edgy for a gala supporting the currently-trending-on-Twitter artist George E.

She plucked a champagne flute off a passing silver tray and wandered through the Garden Court. Oversized party lights were strung around the ceiling, illuminating bouquets of rich burgundy roses and the glass panes of the roof and side wall, where white snow whirled and collected in the corners. She felt the bubbles from the champagne sweep up into her brain and she reminded herself to take it slow.

"Don't you look lovely." She turned at the voice and smiled when she saw Terrence.

"What are you doing here?" she said brightly, kissing him on either cheek. Another person she hadn't seen for weeks.

"Investor relating." He smiled. "One of the patrons is a rich gay, so L.Cecil sent me in to swoon him."

Tara laughed. "Do you feel used?"

"Not if it gets me a rich husband."

"I should learn to think more like you," she said.

"I trust the deal is going well?" Terrence asked.

"Yeah," Tara said. "We filed the S-1 today, which is a huge relief."

"That was quick," he said. "No wonder I haven't seen you."

"You know I literally have not been outside during daylight hours? It's terrifying," she said, "but I'm really happy." She added, "I feel like things are finally happening, you know?"

Terrence smiled and nodded. "I'm proud of you."

He clinked her glass and she felt the warmth of his honesty.

Dinner was announced and Tara and Terrence meandered with the crowd into the alcove where tables were set.

"Don't turn now, but there's a man over there staring at you," Terrence bent down and whispered to her.

"What?" Tara said, turning automatically. "Where?"

"By the staircase," he said, "next to the supermodel."

Tara's face went white when she saw Callum Rees. He lifted his champagne flute to say hello and she blinked, willing her jaw to close and blushing furiously as she smiled back and nodded her own hello.

"Shit," she said to Terrence.

"Who is that?"

"Callum Rees," she said. Now Terrence turned back to stare.

"*That's* Callum Rees?" he said. "Like billionaire investor Callum Rees?"

"Yeah," she said. "And I'm guessing that is his current squeeze," she added, hoping the disappointment didn't come through in her voice. The woman with Callum probably was an actual supermodel: tall and hyper-skinny, wearing some designer dress. She definitely hadn't forgotten to line her eyebrows.

"Why is he staring at you?" Terrence asked suspiciously.

"Because he's an investor in Hook and he wants me to sell his shares so that he can make a billion dollars," she said, knowing once and for all that that was the extent of it. He hadn't ever followed up after their drinks at the Crosby. Not that he needed to, but the absence of a note had made her confront the fact that she'd been expecting one.

"I love his date's dress," Terrence said, still looking back at them. "It's Valentino, right?"

"I don't know," Tara said, taking a gulp of her champagne, the four-years-ago-ness of her own dress burning her skin.

She found her table at the center front of the atrium and took a deep breath, running through the client bios Catherine's assistant had sent her. She was to be seated between Rick Frier, a self-made real estate developer famous for his conservative politics, and David Dwight, the CFO of Wyatt, one of the investment bank's largest clients, whose son was in rehab, making parenting an off-limits conversation topic.

She found her seat and checked her BlackBerry to look occupied while the table filled.

"You clean up nicely." She turned to Callum's voice as he pulled out the chair next to her and took a seat.

"What are you doing here?" she asked.

"I wanted to see you," he said, as if that were a perfectly good reason.

"Well that seat is for—"

"I got David to switch with me," Callum said without further explanation. "This is Katerina," he said, introducing his date.

"Tara," she said, careful not to crush Katerina's skinny hand.

"Tara is my favorite investment banker," Callum explained to the woman. Or was she a girl? She looked like she was barely legal, despite clearly being jaded by events like this one.

"I get the impression I'm beating a low bar," Tara said, trying to calm her racing heart and adjust to this new situation.

Callum plucked a glass of white wine off a waiter's tray and put it in front of Tara. "I know you're new to these things," he said, "but trust me, the best approach is to get very, very drunk."

"I'm representing L.Cecil," she said, wondering why he hadn't handed his date a glass of wine.

"And, as a major prospect of the firm, it is your duty to impress me, and I will be most impressed if you keep pace with my drinking," he said, lifting a glass. "And I intend to drink a lot."

She looked at him carefully. His hazel eyes were bright. She finally matched his grin, getting it: he wanted to be friends. He was giving her the chance to have the same friendly, drink-together, client/banker relationship that men like Todd had with their clients.

"Rick Frier," a fat, balding man announced himself at her opposite side.

Tara stood from her chair, startled. "Tara Taylor," she said. "It's so nice to meet you."

"Same," he said gruffly as he sat down. "Do you know Mr. Lewis?" he indicated the man at his side.

"Of course," the man answered for her. "Tara Taylor is in our investment bank." The man smiled broadly at Rick Frier, revealing a set of large and unnaturally whitened teeth. "The private bank works closely with the investment bank when our clients have capital needs for their businesses. It's another advantage of working with a large, integrated institution like L.Cecil."

Rick rolled his eyes. Tara bit her lip to hide a laugh. She'd never met John Lewis, but he fit the private-wealth-manager stereotype: charismatic, overly enthusiastic WASPs who enjoyed rubbing elbows with rich people enough to dedicate their careers to opening checking accounts for them.

Someone tapped a microphone and the crowd quieted, turning to the podium, where a young woman had taken the stage.

The girl at the podium could only be twenty, a clear product of the Upper East Side: her soft blonde hair was swept up into an intricate knot at her neck; her youthful skin glowed with professionally applied bronzer.

"Hi, everyone," she started nervously, batting her eyelashes in the light, clearly accustomed to attention but not the kind earned by speaking. "I want to thank you all for coming tonight. I am so excited you're here to celebrate our newest exhibit, featuring George E . . ."

"Catherine's daughter," Callum whispered to Tara.

"How do you know?"

"And Catherine's husband." Callum pointed across the room to a man in a tuxedo at the bar, taking a shot with the bartender, not paying attention to the stage. "I was a groomsman in their wedding."

Tara paused and turned. "You know Catherine?"

"Would be very strange if I'd been in her wedding and didn't, wouldn't it?"

"I didn't—" Her brain raced: Had she said anything foolish at the Crosby when they'd talked about it? Why hadn't he mentioned it then? "Do you know where she is?" Tara whispered, indicating the empty seat across the table.

"Guessing she's at work." Callum shrugged. "She usually finds an excuse."

Catherine's daughter approached the table.

"Well done," Callum told the girl, who was clearly happy to see him.

"I'm so glad it's over," the girl said, letting Callum kiss her on the cheek.

"Lauren, this is Katerina," Callum said, introducing the woman to his left. "And this is Tara—she works at L.Cecil, for your mother."

Lauren shook hands with the model but paused before taking Tara's, scanning her suspiciously. "Mom's still at work," Lauren finally said. "Why aren't you?"

"Oh, I've heard so much about this event," Tara lied. "There's no way I could miss it."

Lauren's jaw clenched and her thin throat swallowed without saying anything. She excused herself to make her hostess rounds.

"What did I do wrong?" Tara asked Callum.

"Don't worry about it." Callum brushed it away. "She's too old to not realize she isn't her mother's priority."

Tara watched Lauren smiling politely across the room and for a minute felt sorry for her.

"But Catherine clearly got Lauren up on that podium, and got L.Cecil to sponsor this event," Tara said, defending the mentor she'd never met. "I think all mothers love their daughters the best way they know how."

"Oh, Catherine certainly got the sponsorship, but not for Lauren. She did it for Phil Dalton." Callum took a sip of his drink.

"What?"

"George E is one of Phil Dalton's investments—he gets twenty percent of whatever George E creates. An event like this increases the value of the artist's work tenfold, maybe more. Catherine knew Phil had a bunch of companies in the Dalton Henley portfolio that could use an investment bank, so she orchestrated this event in exchange for throwing those deals to L.Cecil."

"Is that why we got Hook?" Tara squinted at Callum. "I thought Josh and Todd knew each other from—"

"There's always more to the story, Tara," Callum said, snapping at the waiter to get him to fill up their wineglasses and indicating her drink. "Keep up," he coached.

Tara let that sink in as the dinner was served.

"By the way, you might want to save your other prospect from that guy," Callum said, lifting his brow to John Lewis, who was talking rapidly at Rick Frier.

"And so with the premier checking account, you get *three* free wires every month and unlimited transfers to any other L.Cecil account, but you have to maintain—"

"Mind if I join in?" Tara turned and smiled pleasantly. The booze had her feeling surprisingly at ease.

"Please," Rick said, seeming to mean it.

"Is it true you grew up in California?" Tara asked the man, remembering the bio. "I went to school out there."

"Oakland," he said, pleased with the shift in topic. "Where'd you go to school?"

"Stanford," she said politely. John glared at her, offended that Rick was more interested in her than deposit rates.

"We've got a great presence in Silicon Valley," John interjected, shifting his tack. "In fact, we've been able to get our clients a lot of access to IPO shares for companies that—"

"That's where that girl went, right?" Rick ignored him. "The girl that died?"

"What girl?" Tara asked, taking a sip of her wine.

"Kelly something." Rick snapped his fingers.

"Jacobson," John filled in.

Tara felt her face drain. "Kelly Jacobson died?"

"Do you live in a cave?" Rick made a face. "She overdosed on drugs three weeks ago. Did I hear she was supposed to work for you guys? Better cover that one up."

Tara felt like her sternum was breaking. "I had just—" she started, lifting her hand to her mouth. "Oh my god, what a heartbreaking accident."

"Accident?" Rick scoffed. "You don't accidentally go to a concert and take a gram of drugs. She was at one of the fanciest schools in the country—she should have been making something of that, not squandering it by getting high."

"College kids experiment," Tara said, knowing she shouldn't say it but not liking the tone this man was taking about Kelly or girls like her. "It's how you learn who you are."

"How old are you?" Rick's brow furrowed at Tara.

"Twenty-eight," she said, unashamed.

"That's the problem with your generation. You"—he waved his hand in the air—"*millennials.*" He said it like a dirty word. "You have no sense of work ethic. You take an opportunity like a university education and squander it 'finding yourselves,' then come out with no useful skills and whine when your bosses don't make you feel good about yourselves."

"That's not fair." Tara's voice was firmer than she meant it to be, but she had been working her ass off for the past three weeks to make men like him money, and Kelly would have done exactly the same. How dare he accuse her generation of a bad work ethic. John Lewis glared at her from over Rick's shoulder but she went on. "We've worked hard our entire lives. To get into a school like Stanford? Kelly probably didn't have a childhood, she was under so much pressure—"

"Pressure?" Rick laughed. "Pressure to do what? Get good grades and participate in lots of extracurricular activities? You want pressure? Try having a draft number."

Tara glared at him. His face was rough and mean, and made her angry. "Every generation has experiences that shape it. You had Vietnam, we had 9/11—"

"No comparison," Rick interrupted. "I haven't got an ounce of sympathy for your generation, or some pretty sorority girl doing drugs and slutting around. I'm just glad I won't live long enough to witness you and Obama destroy this country."

"Speaking of which," John interrupted, flashing his fluorescent teeth. "Have you done much estate planning? We can help you set up a dynasty trust and—"

"Yours is the generation that destroyed this country," Tara heard herself announce.

"What did you say?" Rick turned to her, his jaw set.

"Nothing." John tried to pull his attention back. "She didn't say anything." John's eyes dared her to speak again.

"You exploited other nations and drove up spending to support your own short-term thinking. And now we're stuck with terrorists that hate us and debts we can't afford. And that perfect, happy life you told us we'd have if we just worked hard and took out student loans and went to good colleges: those dreams weren't real. We gave up our childhoods to become successful adults, and now that we're here we discover it was all a lie, that you've left us nothing but unsustainable policies to untangle. And you have the nerve to criticize us while you cash out and run? How dare you blame millennials for wanting to escape that burden sometimes, or for being drawn to a president that provides an ounce of hope in the midst of your bitter, selfish cynicism."

Rick Frier's jaw had come unhinged. John Lewis was fuming behind the man's shoulder.

"If you'll please excuse me," Tara said, putting her napkin on the table and standing up, focusing her eyes on the exit so she wouldn't feel the stares of Callum or the other guests who had paused in their meals to watch her.

"Oh my god, oh my god, oh my god," she repeated as she shut the door to the bathroom stall, letting her forehead fall against the door. "Oh my god. What did you just do?" she whispered, all the alcohol evaporating from her brain so she could see the situation with terrifying sobriety.

That was it. It was over. Just like that, she had ruined her career. She'd taken an opportunity people aspired to their entire lives and she had ruined it. Where had that come from? She hadn't even remembered to vote in the last election: why was she defending Obama to a notoriously conservative client? But something about his face—it had been so mean. And Kelly—fuck. Was Kelly Jacobson really dead?

She reached into her purse and found the Xanax she kept for emergencies, swallowing a pill as she heard someone enter the bathroom and lock the door.

The woman went into the stall next to hers and lifted the toilet seat. Tara held her breath, and waited for the vomiting to start. Tara had never been bulimic, but she'd tried the binge-and-purge thing a few times, as had every woman she knew, and she didn't judge the girl in the next stall for it. In fact, she kind of wished she could do it now: take a finger and punish herself, purge up the last hour and start over from empty.

The girl finally stopped with a gasp and a whimper and Tara slowly opened the stall door, taking a breath to collect herself. She washed her hands in the sink. Could she really go back out there? What was she going to say?

She looked at the closed stall door and called softly, "Are you okay?"

The door opened and Lauren Wiley emerged. "Fine," the girl said, unemotionally, avoiding Tara's eyes as she approached the sink.

Lauren rubbed soap deeply into her skin and rinsed her mouth, patting the corners of her lips dry. She kept her posture perfect as she opened her gold clutch and put a round mint on her tongue.

"What?" Lauren snapped, noticing Tara not moving.

"Nothing." Tara shook her head. "I just don't want to go back out there," she admitted. "Not that it isn't a lovely event," she added, remembering Lauren's position.

"You don't have to lie," Lauren said, turning back to the mirror and smoothing gloss across her lips. "It's awful. The art is weird and the company is dull."

"Well, I'm sure your mother would have been proud," Tara tried, checking her own reflection one last time.

"My mother can go fuck herself," Lauren said, testing the words like it was the first time she'd ever said them out loud. "Sorry," she added, "I don't mean that."

Tara didn't say anything.

"It's just—" Lauren started, neither of them sure why she was confiding in Tara, "I worked really hard on this." The girl laughed, looking up at the ceiling to blink the tears away. "And I know it wasn't hard like what she does, but it was hard for me, and I"—she shook her head—"I'm just never going to be enough."

Tara didn't know what to say.

The girl rolled her eyes at herself and leaned forward, using a finger to carefully nudge the tears back into her eyes so they wouldn't mess up her eyeliner. "Please don't say anything."

Tara shook her head. "I won't."

Tara left Lauren in the bathroom and went slowly back to the table, her legs heavy. That—what Lauren felt and felt like she couldn't show—was what Rick Frier didn't understand.

She saw her empty seat and changed her mind, heading for the coat check instead.

THE XANAX HAD STARTED to kick in by the time she got home, and she climbed the stairs to her apartment methodically. She plugged in her BlackBerry but didn't look at it, not ready to find an e-mail firing her for what she'd done. She took off her shoes and stepped out of the dress, placing it carefully back on the hanger. She wiped her eye makeup off, washed her face, took out her contacts, and rubbed under-eye cream on her lids and cold cream on her face. She unpinned her hair and brushed it carefully. She drank two glasses of water and took three milk thistle tablets and an Advil, and set her alarm for five a.m., giving her six hours to rest before everything changed.

5

TARA

"L.Cecil CEO Derek Strauss appears before Congress today to answer allegations of trading violations at the global investment bank in regards to . . ."

Tara hit the snooze button as memories from last night seeped into her consciousness: Rick Frier's fat face and her own stupid voice piercing the reverie of her Xanax-assisted sleep.

"Fuck."

She reached for her BlackBerry, which sat charging next to her iPhone, which sat charging next to her iPod, which sat charging next to her vibrator, which she left charging in the open because no one ever came in here anyway.

She scrolled through the new messages, looking for a note from HR saying she was fired, but not finding it. It was five a.m., though, so that didn't mean anything.

She got to the Printing House gym at five thirty, right as the doors were opening, and took the elevator to the top floor. She climbed on a treadmill that faced the window, looking out over the Hudson River to the glimmering lights of New Jersey still asleep.

She pressed the button to start the machine's belt, her legs reluctantly waking as the blood started to flow.

She couldn't drink, she realized: that was the problem. Alcohol was a depressant, and it made her think too much—or rather, think too much about the wrong things. Why had she kept accepting wine from Callum? He was clearly mocking her—the drunk nerd on his right getting wasted as the picture-perfect Russian model sat on his left eating lettuce.

She sped up the treadmill and watched the distance meter climb as the music reverberated in her ears and her chest started to burn with the effort. The pain felt good.

Maybe Rick Frier had been right: the kind of pressure millennials felt *wasn't* that important. Lauren's rich-girl problems were nothing compared to the rest of the world—who cared if she had an eating disorder, or felt unaccepted by her mother?

She pressed the speed up again, and again, to make the point stick.

And Kelly Jacobson *should* have known better than to do what she did. Tara had only tried drugs twice in college, and had always been responsible about it, only taking a little with people who knew what to do if something went wrong.

Tara watched the treadmill hit her normal six miles, but she didn't stop, pressing the speed up again and stretching her legs long as her pulse pounded.

The fact was, the world was a competitive place. If Lauren couldn't learn to get over her issues, she wasn't going to make it; and if girls like

Kelly couldn't figure out how to party responsibly, they weren't going to make it, either. It wasn't anybody's fault, it was just reality—a modern version of Darwin's survival of the fittest.

But Tara had made it through the tests of her early twenties, and now she had a place in the world. Now there were new tests, and to survive she had to stay competitive, stay focused, work harder. Tara pressed the speed up again, fueled by the thought. She watched the distance click to six and a half miles. She looked down and noticed her shoelace untied. *Don't stop*, she told herself, punching the speed up again. *Push it to seven. Almost there.*

Until last night, Tara had been a real competitor: the deal was going great, senior management was recognizing her talent, important people like Callum Rees were seeking out her company. She'd been doing well because she'd been keeping her head down, making her path without getting in anyone's way. She looked at the distance meter . . . 6.8 . . . 6.9 . . . the shoelace caught and Tara lurched forward, catching herself on the handrails as she jumped to the sides of the whirring belt. Her chest heaved as she watched the distance meter hit seven miles, still measuring the belt without her on it. She felt a surge of disappointment, as though it was a sign that she'd lost.

Who was she kidding? She wasn't in the race anymore: Rick Frier had been the test she couldn't pass.

Don't be ridiculous. She stopped the belt. *Signs are for children.*

Tara checked her BlackBerry on her way to the locker room: still nothing from HR. She showered and went downstairs, where one of L.Cecil's black cars waited for her.

Tara's phone rang and her heart jumped, anticipating a call from the office telling her not to bother coming in. She saw the screen, though, and rolled her eyes.

"You're up early," she told her mother as she answered the phone.

"Have you booked your ticket yet?" her mother asked without pleasantries.

"No, I haven't booked my ticket yet, Mom," Tara said.

"But prices are going to—"

"It actually doesn't make that much of a difference when you book," Tara cut her off. Her mother got on an airplane once every two years and still thought you had to go to a travel agent to book a flight. "And I don't know where I'm going to be flying from yet."

"I would just feel a lot better if you had the ticket," her mother said firmly.

"What are you afraid of, Mom?" Tara asked, exasperated. "It's my sister's wedding. I'm going to be there."

"I just—"

"I've got to go, Mom," she said. "I love you," she added before hanging up the phone. It's not that she didn't appreciate her mother's concern, but her family didn't understand Tara's life at all, and right now Tara had a hard time culling the patience to translate it into a values system they could understand.

She pulled out her BlackBerry and got to work on the e-mails. She responded to Neha's question about the syndicate list. Why could the girl not get it right? It was like Neha was intentionally defying her.

She opened an e-mail from Nick asking where they were having dinner the night they were in London for the road show. Why could he not just look at the schedule she'd sent? And did he not have more important things to think about right now, as CFO of an almost-public company? *Shoreditch House*, she responded.

She replied to an e-mail from a Charlie Jacobson at the Associated Press asking if they could meet. *Regulations prevent me from speaking directly to the press; please contact our Investor Relations department if you have questions.* Shouldn't someone from the AP know better?

Her chest clenched when she saw a new message with Catherine Wiley's name.

FROM: Catherine Wiley
SUBJECT: [none]
Are you in yet?

Her blood froze. This was it.

TO: Catherine Wiley
SUBJECT: Re: [none]
Good morning—Ten blocks away. Is everything okay?

She glared at the red light, willing it to start flashing with a response.

FROM: Catherine Wiley
SUBJECT: Re: [none]
Pls come to my office when you get in.

It was real: she was actually going to be fired. She felt a heat behind her eyeballs and swallowed hard to push it away.

"She's waiting," Catherine's assistant said without looking up when Tara arrived.

"Good morning," Tara said carefully as she entered the office.

Catherine turned to face her, the sun rising in the floor-to-ceiling window behind her desk.

"Good morning, Tara," the president said, her voice giving no indication of what was coming. "It's nice to finally meet you."

"And you," Tara said, shaking the woman's hand and praying hers wasn't noticeably clammy.

Catherine's hair was a perfectly coiffed brunette bob, and her skin had just enough lines to neither look her true age nor look like she was trying to hide it. She wore a Chanel suit that matched the one she was wearing on the "Power Women of Wall Street" cover of *Forbes* magazine that sat, framed, on the bookshelf beside her desk.

"Have a seat." Catherine indicated the chair and jumped to the point. "I heard what happened at the Frick last night."

Tara sat forward and started, "I can—"

"Lauren is very sick." Catherine cut her off. "We've sent her to all the best doctors, but at some point a girl has to help herself."

Tara paused, her mouth still open. "Lauren?" she asked. "You're talking about Lauren," she clarified.

"Yes," Catherine said. "My daughter."

"Right." Tara felt her blood pressure drop. "She did a really great—"

"I trust you haven't told anyone," Catherine interrupted. "And won't." She paused for effect. "I've got enough going on right now without being accused of being a bad mother because my daughter has a problem."

"Of course," Tara said. "I mean, of course I won't say anything. But I don't think you're a bad—"

"How is the Hook deal going?" Catherine changed the subject. Was she not going to mention Rick Frier?

"Oh." Tara adjusted. "Well. We filed the S-1 yesterday and the preliminary conversations have been extremely positive. I think we're going to be able to beat our initial price target without sacrificing investor quality."

"Good," the woman said. "I'm sure I don't need to tell you how important it is that it go well, for the firm's sake and your own."

"No," Tara agreed, feeling the weight again, "you don't."

"It's hard to find good women in this industry, but I've been told you have potential, and I hope to discover that's true."

"Thank you," she said, her heart in her throat. "I'll do everything I can to live up to that."

"Good," Catherine said. "Is there anything else?"

Tara felt her heart lift, like she'd been pardoned on the execution line. She was back in the race. "Do you have any advice?" she asked the woman.

Catherine paused, studying Tara's face, looking for what weakness the younger woman needed to correct. "Never stop improving," she said. "You can always work harder, go faster, be more. There's no such thing as too much discipline."

Tara nodded. Seven miles hadn't been so bad this morning—maybe she'd start doing that every day.

"How old are you?" Catherine asked.

"Twenty-eight."

"Boyfriend?" Catherine glanced at Tara's left hand.

"No."

"Don't get married until you're thirty-five," Catherine said, "but freeze your eggs at thirty so it isn't a distraction. I'll have Leslie send you the information for a good clinic."

"How old were you when you got married?"

"Twenty-five," Catherine said, turning back to her computer.

"Thank you." Tara started to stand, then stopped. She had to know. "Did John Lewis say anything about the event?"

"John Lewis is no longer with the firm," Catherine said without turning from her monitor.

"What? Why?"

"Rick Frier moved all his accounts from the bank," Catherine said. "When I heard about John's behavior I had no choice but to let him go."

"Rick moved his accounts because of John?"

"Were you there when John went on his pro-Obama rampage?" Catherine turned, lifting a brow. "Callum called me late last night to tell me about it—he said it was quite a scene."

"That must have been after I left," Tara said carefully, hoping it was a possibility, and not Callum covering up for her at John Lewis's expense.

She walked to the door before she had time to think about it.

"Oh, and Tara?"

Tara turned back, her heart racing again.

"The next time you go to an event, wear something less . . . edgy," Catherine said. "You've got enough working against you as a young woman without drawing extra opportunity for criticism."

Tara's cheeks burned as she thought about the purple gown. Had Callum told Catherine what she'd been wearing, too? "Yes," she said, nodding. "Yes, of course."

She walked carefully, feeling her anxiety still pulsing through her veins. *Calm down. Stay focused*, she coached herself as the elevator doors opened and she got to work.

TODD

MONDAY, APRIL 7; NEW YORK, NEW YORK

Todd was in a great mood and nothing was going to ruin it.

He'd been pissed as hell when Tara got Catherine's invite to the Frick event, but after some careful consideration, he realized anger was unproductive. Catherine was only in her position because the firm needed women leaders—she wasn't where the real power sat, and neither were the stodgy old clients who attended bank-hosted events like the one at the Frick. Tara could have them.

The real power, Todd realized, was in guys like him—the young, smart, driven future leaders of Wall Street. Which is why he'd corralled his crew to skip out of work this afternoon and convene at a bar downtown to watch the NCAA tournament finals and have a networking event of their own.

To top it all off, Todd was getting laid tonight. Louisa LeMay, his old fuck buddy, was in town from LA and had texted Todd to see if they could get together. Louisa was one of the few girls he'd slept with who could actually maintain a pure friends-with-benefits agreement, never asking to cuddle, never expecting him to pay for anything, never contacting him unless she wanted to hook up.

And so today, Todd was checking out of the office at four, watching the game with the guys, then spending the night having sex with Louisa.

All of which he deserved, he thought, as he took his seat in the conference room and read through the preliminary road show schedule. The deal was going great: he'd nailed it on the S-1 and funds were already calling to get in, which meant they'd be oversubscribed, which meant they could offer more shares at a higher price, which meant L.Cecil got a bigger fee and Todd got a bigger bonus and they both got great press.

"Is it just me, or are there no babes on this list?" Beau asked from his seat.

Todd looked up. "What are you looking at?"

"The list of employees who have shares in Hook. Jules is the only chick on here, and she has like ten percent of what the dudes who joined at the same time as her got."

"Who's Jules?"

"The receptionist," Beau said.

"Are you banging her?"

"Yes, but that's not the point," he said. "Like, I think she got screwed."

"She's a receptionist," Todd pointed out.

"Who cares. George E got twenty times the shares she got for painting those ugly mermen. No way he added more value than she does."

"She's still making five million dollars for answering phones for two years."

"Whatever," Beau said. "Doesn't change the fact she's the only chick on here."

"It's not like it's any different on Wall Street," Tara said without looking up from her computer.

"Yeah, but Wall Street's old-school. If you're a chick here, you know what you're signing up for. But out there? That's Silicon Valley. That's people our age making the decisions. You'd think they'd be more"—he looked for the word—"gender neutral or whatever."

"It's not Hook's fault. How many girls do you know who like computer programming?" Todd countered. "You can't always blame women making less than men on men."

"Oh, I blame women making less than men on the fact they don't eat."

"What?" Tara looked up and finally stopped typing.

Beau shrugged. "My girlfriends eat like nine hundred calories a day. And most of it's sugar-free, fat-free crap. How are you supposed to do good work when you're eating nine hundred calories a day? I'd be cranky and comatose."

Tara laughed. It was the first time Todd had seen her crack a smile since the S-1. Until the edits came back from the SEC, she was largely running the show, and she'd hardly looked up from her computer since last Wednesday. "You think that's going to set a girl back more than being fat? How many fat girls do you see in this office?"

"Eating real food doesn't make you fat," Beau said. "That's another problem: you're all so susceptible to these crazy get-skinny-quick marketing pitches that don't make any sense."

The phone rang and Tara picked it up. "Hey, Rachel."

Beau punched the speaker button. "Hey, Rach," he said. Tara reached for the console but Beau pulled it away. "Why do you think chicks are still behind men?"

"In business, you mean?" the PR director asked. Todd had only met her during their first visit to California, but she'd been helping Tara figure out how to position Josh and Nick during the road show.

"Yeah," Beau said. "Like, why haven't women really broken the glass ceiling?"

"Easy," Rachel said casually. "No orgasms."

Todd's face flushed and he leaned forward. Did she just say what he thought she said?

Beau laughed and lifted an eyebrow. "Do go on."

"Women don't masturbate as much as men, and half of them never have orgasms during sex." Her voice was calm, as though she were reporting data from the S-1. "So they don't think as clearly. Can you imagine how poorly you'd work if you hadn't jacked off in three days, much less a year, or your whole life?"

"That's ridiculous," Tara said unconvincingly.

"You know how women used to have hysteria?" Rachel's voice continued. Apparently she was an expert on this subject. "Like in the eighteen hundreds they'd be diagnosed with it? The 'treatment' was going into the doctor's office to get masturbated, until vibrators were invented and women could do it at home. Good for your heart, good for your brain, good for your nerves. I guarantee if you passed out vibrators in your office, female productivity would go through the roof. Men wouldn't stand a chance."

Tara reached over and pulled the console out of Beau's astonished grip, transferring the call back to her headset. "I promise I didn't start this."

Todd was definitely banging Rachel next time he was in California.

"Oh god," Tara sighed into the phone. "He hasn't changed his mind, has he? He told me a third was enough and he'd sell the others after the IPO."

Todd watched, assuming they were talking about Callum.

"What?" Tara asked the phone, listening. "That's ridiculous. He likes Russian supermodels. And I made such an ass of myself at the—" She listened. "Well, yes, I am, but—" She shook her head. "No, I'm not interested," she said resolutely. "But listen, we'll be out there next week—can we get some time on the calendar to run through this stuff in person?"

"What was that about?" Todd asked when she hung up.

"I just wanted her advice for how to coach Josh and Nick next week."

"No, the first part."

"What first part?" she said, falsely innocent.

"About Callum."

She shrugged. "I guess he wanted to know if I date older men."

Todd rolled his eyes. "I knew it."

"What?" she asked.

"That's why he wanted to meet with you and not me."

"I knew how to answer his question about selling shares," she said.

"But that's not why he asked you to meet."

"I can't help what men want."

"As a man, I most definitely disagree with that statement," he said firmly.

"You're right," she said. "Will you give me a minute? I'm just going to pop to the restroom and slip on my burka."

Todd felt his muscles tense. She was so full of shit—she knew exactly what she was doing. Which is why she sat in the office with her headphones on like a cold fish, hardly speaking to him or anyone else on the team, and then dressed up and turned on the charm when rich clients like Callum or senior management like Catherine came into the picture. She was such a fake.

Todd looked at his watch. He wasn't going to let this get to him. "I've gotta go."

"Where are you going?" Beau asked. Tara, apparently, didn't care.

"Catching up with a few fund managers," he said. "Probably won't be back tonight, but e-mail me if you need anything."

Todd let the door to the conference room slam and settled his mind with the thought of Louisa's naked body. He was going to get drunk and have fun and get laid and nothing was going to stop him.

NICK

There were going to be tears.

But Nick couldn't think about that. She'd understand in the long run that it was for the best.

Or would she? What was it like for girls who got dumped by guys just beginning their trajectory to success? Would she ever actually recover, or would she watch Nick gain in power and influence and wealth, his face on magazines and his name whispered in elite circles, and wince in pain, knowing how close she'd been to having a dream life? She would find someone else, of course—she was still pretty and smart—but no one in the same league as Nick. Because guys in Nick's league didn't need girls like Grace.

What was going to be hard was explaining that there was nothing she could have done. Of course, it might have lasted longer if she'd stopped crying in her sorority house over some slutty girl she hardly knew and come to San Francisco to support him. He lived in the nicest building in the entire city, after all; it's not like he'd been asking her to slum it.

But that wasn't worth bringing up: even if she had had sex with him, and she hadn't canceled dinner last week, she still wouldn't be right, and those things would only have delayed the inevitable. She wanted to start her own company, to wait until her thirties to have kids. And that, unfortunately, didn't fit in Nick's new world. He needed a woman who was going to focus on him, to put her own needs and ambitions aside to support his career and personal brand. Darrell Greene was right: not every guy could have that, but Nick could, as was clear by all the women drooling over him at the Rosewood last week. And why shouldn't he have all that? Wasn't this what he had worked so hard for through prep school and Stanford and McKinsey and Dalton Henley and Harvard Business School and two years of putting up with Josh Hart?

"Exactly," he said out loud. He zipped down 101 to Palo Alto, where he was stopping by Darrell's office to sign his loan documents before meeting Grace for coffee.

His phone rang and he answered it over Bluetooth. "This is Nick Winthrop."

"Did you take Juan off the Android update?" Josh's voice was irritated.

"I need him to focus all his energy on the IPO," Nick replied.

"He's our best programmer."

"We need to give the new guys opportunities, too," Nick said patiently.

"These aren't your decisions."

"The IPO has got to be our priority," Nick said. "For the next month it takes precedent. And I need Juan fully dedicated."

Nick knew Juan wasn't doing much, but he didn't like how much power the young programmer had accumulated in the office. All the employees looked up to Juan. They called him "Minister of Fun" and did whatever he said, like that time he'd led the sit-in when Nick had tried to cut back the bartender's hours. Having him work on the IPO, digging up statistics from the internal database, was Nick's way of isolating him for a bit, giving other programmers time to fill in the void and balance out Juan's power.

"I thought we hired L.Cecil to manage the IPO," Josh's voice said through the dashboard.

"We need someone internal to gather statistics for the securities filings. He's just pulling information from the database."

"You lifted his restrictions to the database?"

"He signed an NDA."

"You're a fucking moron." Josh hung up the phone.

Nick rolled his eyes, unbothered. Josh didn't know what he was talking about. He was a classic example of a great engineer who had no business leading a company.

He pulled off the freeway and parked outside Darrell's office.

"Hi, Nick," the busty blonde assistant in Darrell's office greeted him.

"Hi," he said, loving that she knew his name.

"Darrell had to run to a meeting, but I've got all your loan documents," she said. "Follow me and we can get them all signed?"

"Sure," Nick said, forcing himself to look straight ahead and not at her hourglass hips swaying back and forth as she led him to a small conference room.

A stack of papers was on the center table, along with a silver fountain pen and a notary pad.

"You're a notary?"

"Certified. Pass me your hand?" She bent over him to press his finger in the ink, and Nick was glad the room was dark enough to hide his blushing.

"So it's five percent interest, right?" he said, looking through the documents for the final terms they'd agreed to.

"I think it scales up after six months," she said, "to twenty-five percent." She smiled.

"Twenty-five?"

She shrugged. "You're going to sell as soon as the lockup expires, right?"

"Yeah, just enough to cover the loan."

"You've got nothing to worry about, then."

"Unless the share price drops," he corrected. Nick had 2.5 million share options. He'd need to sell three million dollars' worth to have enough, after taxes, to pay off the loan. That was fine if the price was thirty dollars a share—he'd only have to sell a hundred thousand of the 2.5 million—but if it dropped to, say, fifteen dollars a share, he'd have to abandon a lot more of his total position to pay off the loan.

"You're CFO of the company. If anyone knows that's not going to happen, it's you." Her red lips pursed together in a flirtatious pout.

"You're right." He laughed, shaking his head and going back to signing. "You're absolutely right."

"What's your name?" he asked, handing the forms over.

"Tiffany." She smiled.

"Well, Tiffany," he said confidently, "I've got to go to this coffee meeting right now, but it shouldn't take long. I was going to go back to the city, but I could stick around if you wanted to have a drink?"

"Oh, that's so sweet," she said, "but I've actually got a boyfriend." She still smiled, giving him the sense the boyfriend wasn't very serious.

"Well, if anything changes, let me know."

She laughed. "I will."

Nick left the office, his step light. He'd draw down the loan tomorrow and buy all of his options and officially be on his way to his eighty-five-million-dollar fortune.

GRACE WAS ALREADY at Coupa Café when he arrived, talking on her iPhone.

He took a deep breath as he approached the table.

"No, she and Luis had never hooked up. And he was definitely at SAE all night. We were beer pong partners, and that was going on until at least four thirty, maybe later. I would have known if he'd left." She lifted a finger to Nick and mouthed, *Sorry,* then turned back to the phone. "I didn't know Robby very well. I didn't really hang out with the rugby team. Yeah, of course. Let me know if you need anything else."

"Who was that?" Nick asked as she hung up the phone.

"A reporter from the *New York Times*." She looked up, her face serious. "He had a bunch of questions about Kelly."

"Oh," he said, uninterested. He hadn't come here to talk about Kelly Jacobson. "Do you want a coffee?"

"I'm okay." She indicated her cup already on the table.

He sat down across from her.

"You don't want anything?" she asked.

"No." He shook his head. "I can't stay long."

"Is everything okay?"

"Yeah." He nodded. "Great, actually. I just signed my loan documents."

"For what?"

"I took out a two-million-dollar loan to pay for my stock options." He knew he didn't have to say the number to impress her, but he couldn't help himself.

"What? Why?"

"It'll save me tens of millions in taxes," he said. She didn't look convinced. "I'm going to pay it all off as soon as I can sell my shares," he clarified.

"When is that?"

"I'm locked up for six months after the IPO, then I can sell whatever I want." Why did he feel like he was defending himself?

"But what if it doesn't happen?"

"What?"

"The IPO?" she said. "Then your shares aren't worth anything and you owe two million dollars."

"That isn't going to happen," he said, laughing.

She shrugged.

"Listen." He sat forward, irritated by how this had started. "I wanted to talk to you because I think you and I should—" he started, but something made him pause.

She sipped her coffee but kept looking at him calmly. She was so cute, so young and put together and exactly the kind of girl he'd always wanted to notice him in college. *But that was college, and this is real life, and you can do better now*, he reminded himself.

"I think you and I should break up," he said, sitting back in his chair.

Her chest lifted and fell, and she sighed, looking at her hands. "Yeah." She nodded. "I think you're right."

"What?" He sat forward again.

"I'm going to go to Europe for three months after graduation, and it doesn't make any sense to try to stay together for that." She shrugged. "I guess we might as well cut it off now."

"No." He shook his head. "No, Europe isn't the problem."

"I'm sorry?"

"We're breaking up because I need someone better," he explained.

"I'm sorry?" she repeated.

"I'm about to have eighty-five million dollars, Grace, and be the CFO of one of the most powerful companies in the world," he said. Her face was still confused: why wasn't she getting this? "I need someone who—"

She lifted her hands to stop him. "Right," she said. She reached for her bag and started to stand.

"Where are you going?" he asked.

"Home," she said, pulling on her jacket.

"But we're not finished."

"I thought you just said we were."

"But I—"

"Whatever you have to say, Nick, I don't want to hear it. Congratulations on your loan."

She picked up her coffee and swept to the door, leaving Nick alone. The guy at the next table looked up from his MacBook Air and laughed.

"Screw you," Nick said, pushing his chair back and leaving the café.

AMANDA

It took Amanda less than a week to find a place in San Francisco, albeit
with two random roommates from Craigslist, a guy and a girl who were
coworkers and shared a three-bedroom apartment in the Marina.

They'd said they were laid-back young professionals, which she knew
meant overachieving and well-paid, and the girl had seemed nice enough
on the phone. She'd gone to Stanford and he'd gone to Berkeley, so that
felt like a good vet. His name was Juan, which made her a little nervous—
a guy *and* a Mexican?—but whatever. She only had to commit to four
months, when their lease was up for renewal, and this was her great
West Coast adventure. Even if they were weird, it would be different,
and had to be better than New York.

Amanda had had a revelation the night of Harold Hammonds's
happy hour: New York was the problem. There was too big a pool of
women willing to be the meaningless hookups Todd thought he wanted.
This, coupled with the fact that people worked so much and visited the
same places so infrequently that running into someone often enough to
see them as something other than your initial impression was impossible. So long as he was in New York, Todd couldn't see her as more than
a Hook hookup until he decided he wanted to.

And Amanda didn't have time to sit back and wait for that.

San Francisco, though, would be different, she thought as she handed
her ticket to the gate agent and boarded the plane. It was smaller, for one
thing, and she'd read the stats: the pretty girls in California went to LA,
leaving SF full of tall, athletic men who started companies and ran mar-
athons and outnumbered their less-desirable female counterparts by 15

percent. Amanda would stand out there: she would be in men's minds, and dating quality men would be like shooting fish in a barrel.

Of course, she hadn't admitted that to anyone—she didn't want to jinx it. She'd told her mom it was a good professional opportunity, to experience Silicon Valley's booming start-up scene, and her mom had told her she thought it would be a good personal experience, despite the fact that it was as far from home as Amanda had ever been. Claudia and Cindy had been fine with it, too, not worrying about rent because Claudia's parents paid most of it anyway. She'd told them with confident independence that she was done with their city, ready for an adventure and to be around higher-quality men, and they hadn't disagreed.

That no one tried to stop her made Amanda self-conscious, as if she were telling people she had food stuck in her teeth without realizing they'd been staring at it the whole meal. Did they really believe the West Coast was better, or just that she didn't have what it took to cut it in New York?

Don't think about it, she told herself as the cabin doors shut. Who cared what other people thought? This was her life, and it was about to get a reboot.

Six hours later, she stepped out of the airport into the shining San Francisco sun. It was chilly out, but not like the negative-ten-with-windchill she'd left behind.

The cab was grungy and there was no Plexiglas between her and the driver, who was white, like her. She'd never seen a white cabdriver before. Was she supposed to talk to him? She asked him to turn on the radio.

She watched through the window as the car zipped down the highway, and felt her skin tingle when she saw the Bay Bridge stretching over the water. A real trolley car pulled down the middle of the street. She rolled down her window and when she smelled the fresh air, she knew this was right.

The driver continued through Fisherman's Wharf, and she grimaced at the tourists in T-shirts and tennis shoes eating chowder in sourdough bowls, already feeling like she knew more than them.

"You said 3373 Laguna?" the driver asked in an American accent. Were all cabdrivers in San Francisco like this?

"Yes," she said, looking up at her new home. It was gray-blue, with three layers of windows, all painted white to match the garage, tucked between two other houses, one yellow and one pale orange. She loved it already.

"Are you moving in?" the driver asked as he unloaded her very heavy bags.

"Yes," she said. "As a matter of fact, I am."

"You're going to want to ditch those heels." He gestured to her feet.

Amanda looked down. She wasn't wearing heels: she was wearing her most comfortable travel boots, which had a mere two-inch wedge.

She paid him, surprised the fare wasn't any cheaper than back in New York, and pressed the buzzer at the door.

"Hi!" her new roommate Julie exclaimed. Her toenails were painted bright blue and she was wearing a built-in-bra tank top and terrycloth shorts that were a size too small for her pudgy frame.

"It's nice to meet you," Amanda said, willing herself not to judge.

"Let me help you." Julie moved outside, blissfully ignorant of her half nudity, and pulled one of Amanda's bags into the door. A large open space with hardwood floors was divided between a dining room and a living area with oversized leather sofas and a big flat-screen TV. Amanda noticed the Wii and a PlayStation console and felt her heart clench. Video games? Who were these people?

"So your room is upstairs, next to mine," Julie said. "Juan lives downstairs. He has his own bathroom, but we kind of all share both."

The room upstairs was bigger than her room in New York and had a bay window and Ikea's classic Hemnes set with a Billy bookcase in oak.

"The boxes you shipped are downstairs in the garage. I can help you bring them up if you want?"

"Do you not have to be at work?" Amanda asked.

"No, it's cool. I'm working from home today so I could help you."

"What is it you do?"

"I work at Hook," Julie announced proudly.

"Like, the app?" Amanda squinted. *This* was the kind of person who was determining her love matches?

"Yeah!" she said. "It's awesome."

"Are you a programmer?"

"No, I'm the receptionist."

Didn't she go to Stanford? "How are you working from home, then?"

"Oh, they're not very strict." She smiled. "Besides, everything's so crazy since we filed the S-1 no one even notices when I'm gone."

"I'm sure," Amanda said. "I think my firm is representing you, actually."

"Seriously? I haven't worked with the lawyers, but I'm hooking up with one of the bankers when he's in town. He's totally hot and into art and a real gentleman. I guess you're used to guys like that, coming from New York, but *oh my god.*"

"Oh, I came out here for the guys," Amanda said.

"Oh." Julie's bottom lip pulled back as if she were saying *Eek.* "Well, the guys in SF are super *fun* but they're not like Beau."

Amanda smiled politely. Julie was a badly dressed, ten-pounds-too-heavy receptionist—there was no way they played in the same league. "Well, I better get to unpacking," she said.

"Are you sure you don't want me to help?"

Amanda declined.

But after two trips up the stairs from the garage, Julie insisted, and they spent the afternoon talking. Amanda's mind slowly started opening to Julie. Her carefree energy was embarrassing, but it was easy and comfortable, and if it was any indication of her single female competition in San Francisco, Amanda was set.

"Do you want some wine?" Julie asked, folding up the last of the cardboard boxes.

"Yeah," Amanda said, noticing the time. "Let me go out and buy us a bottle."

"Oh, don't worry about it," Julie said. "We've got some from the office."

Amanda followed her to the kitchen, where a cabinet was full of high-end booze. "Did you have a company party or something?"

"Oh, no, they keep the bar at Hook totally stocked, so Juan and I always take a bottle when we leave."

"You've got a bar? At your office?"

"Yeah, don't you?"

Amanda considered the floor of cubicles full of angry lawyers. "No."

"Really?" Julie considered it. "That sucks!"

TODD

It was happy hour on a Monday, but the bar was packed with testosterone, chicken wings and easy girls chugging cheap beer. Todd was holding center court at the round booth in the corner, his de facto position whenever he was out with the crew. It was quietly understood that he was the best looking in the group and should, therefore, take the most prominent position. Girls would never think this way: they'd get jealous and push the pretty girl to the side. But guys understood cooperation created a rising tide that lifted all ships.

And after ten years rolling together in New York, his crew was a well-oiled machine. Each guy had his role: Todd was the Looker; Tom, who ran his own hedge fund, was the Rich Guy; Kyle, a private equity partner who had studied Chinese history at Princeton, was the Intellectual; Jake, who worked at MTV, was the Creative; Max, a trader who spent most of his time working out and was always so amped up on steroids that he'd talk to anyone, was the Partier; Cameron, the founder of an insurance company no one understood, was the Entrepreneur; and Will, a hedge fund principal who was Southern and probably gay, served as the group's Good Guy. Whenever a girl came into their net, whoever brought her in knew where to put her, and did: so long as everyone kept to the rules and his role, everyone went home with someone.

The last time he'd been out with them was over a month ago, and being back in the mix felt good, even if work was still in the back of his mind. He sipped his beer and checked his phone. He was going to text Louisa at exactly seven fifteen. He knew her flight from LA had landed already, but there was no need to look desperate.

Todd scanned the room. They'd come to the East Village, where close proximity to NYU translated into younger, lower-maintenance female clientele.

"Dude, bummer you missed Sunday Funday yesterday," Max said. "We hit Bagatelle *hard*. It was epic."

"Yeah, this deal's a bitch." Todd shook his head. He hadn't had a weekend off since before the new year.

"It'll be worth it," Tom said, lifting his glass. "Everyone's already talking about it. Maybe you can finally start making some real money."

Todd rolled his eyes. He knew Tom was only partly kidding: hedge fund managers loved reminding bankers of their lower status in the financial services hierarchy.

"Gentlemen, get ready." Jake arrived from the bathroom, where he'd changed from his suit into a twelve-hundred-dollar Michael Jordan jersey he'd bought on eBay. He passed around neon orange sweatbands. "Trust me, these are chick magnets."

Jake and Todd had met at L.Cecil and lived in a three-bedroom loft in the Meatpacking District with Max until Jake had gone to Stanford Business School, where he'd picked up Cameron, Will, and a new image as a scruffy beard-wearing creative who loved organizing parties and sporting costumes.

"What are you doing, man?" Jake punched Cameron, who was engrossed in his iPhone and wasn't putting on his sweatband.

"Hold on a sec," he said. "Gotta send the daily texts."

"Are you doing your girl alerts?" Jake rolled his eyes and grabbed Cameron's phone to show the table. A spreadsheet was pulled up on the screen, with a hundred girls' names, color-coded and sorted into hot, warm and cold categories. A third column indicated "Nothing/Made Out/Sex," a fourth column was labeled "Date of Last Outreach," and a fifth "Total # Outreach."

"These are all the girls you're hooking up with?"

"You can't manage what you can't measure," Cameron said, taking the phone back. "I picked up a few things in business school."

"What do you do with it?" Todd asked, intrigued.

"The hot list gets a text every four days; warm once a week."

"You put in reminders?"

"Obviously. I can't remember all this shit."

"What about the cold list?"

"I've got my Outlook set to auto-e-mail them once every three weeks," he said. "Stay in their minds, just in case."

Todd nodded admiringly. "Too bad you can't link it with Hook," he mused aloud.

"*That's* what you should do instead of insurance," Kyle told Cameron.

Cameron lifted an eyebrow, considering, then went back to his texting.

AN HOUR LATER Todd and a blonde were both drunk and not watching the game. He had no idea what her name was, but she had enormous breasts and seemed like she didn't have a lot of STDs. He checked his phone: it was almost seven. Maybe he could hook up with this girl before he met Louisa, as a warm-up.

Todd felt his phone buzz.

> Louisa LeMay: Hey—Heading to Brooklyn to check out a new DJ. It's in the middle of nowhere so probably just crash out there. Sorry to bail!

Todd shook his head and blinked to adjust his tipsy eyes.

He read it again. And again. Was she serious?

Todd searched his brain for an explanation: were there cabs in Brooklyn? He typed back: *No worries. What's the address? I'll send a car.*

"Are you okay?" the girl asked, but he ignored her, watching his phone.

After a few minutes, he put the phone in his lap and reached for his BlackBerry, answering a few e-mails to distract himself. But when he looked at the phone again, there was still no text. He reached for the pitcher of beer. "Where'd that chick go?" he asked Kyle, realizing the blonde was no longer at his side.

"Think she left, dude," Tom said.

"I think we should make a move," Jake said. The game was finishing, and he hadn't found a girl. "Who's up for Houston Hall?"

———

"WILL YOU GO down on me?"

"No," Todd said simply, rolling the girl over onto her stomach.

"Why not?" she giggled, looking back over her shoulder as she arched her back and pressed herself up onto her hands and knees. "Pretty please?" She was raising her eyebrows flirtatiously.

"Maybe later." He smiled a fake smile, turning his eyes from her face to her ██ and jamming two fingers between her legs.

"Oh!" she giggled. "Oh, yes! Yes, yes that feels soooo good . . ." She turned her head back to the bed frame in front of her, and he positioned himself on his knees behind her.

He massaged her ██ long enough to get her ██, which wasn't difficult, and quickly unrolled a condom down his ████████. He gripped her ██ and pressed himself ████████ as she moaned. Her ██ was annoyingly bony. The skinny girls looked better in clothes, but it was less fun when they were naked. And given that he would never be seen in public with this girl, he'd just as soon she was twenty pounds heavier with some flesh on her ██. Maybe he should have gone for her friend instead. But that girl's face had been so beat. If only Louisa hadn't bailed. Fuck! The thought made him angry and he took it out on the girl, levering back and forth, pulling and pushing her ██ around his ████, looking down to admire his washboard abs. God bless Morgan. She wouldn't still be a lesbian if she caught a glimpse of this. And Louisa wouldn't have gone to Brooklyn. The girl in front of him groaned and moaned and made squeaking "Ohs!" which he tried to ignore. He was drunk and needed to concentrate.

Climaxing had been taking longer lately. Last week he'd been having sex with a girl he'd found on Hook and he hadn't been able to come at all. He'd tried every position he knew, but nothing worked. He thought it was a fluke, but he'd been behind this girl for like fifteen minutes now and nothing was happening. *Think about Morgan and her girlfriend*, he coached himself, imagining them here, in front of him, making out. Nothing. This girl's ███ felt like a watermelon. It was work, he concluded: he'd been working too hard, getting too stressed about the deal. Maybe she'd take it in the ██? He snuck a finger toward her ██ to test her reaction.

"Oooohh! You're so dirty!" she cooed.

"Do you want it there?" he leaned forward and whispered.

"I've never done it before."

Score.

"I want to be your first," he heard himself say soothingly.

"I don't know . . ."

"Relax. It'll be fun."

She bit her lip and closed her eyes. She was drunk, which would help. "Okay. There's some lube in the nightstand. We need lube, right?"

Todd kissed the girl's mouth. Screw Louisa: he didn't need her. He carefully pulled her ████████ apart and pushed slowly so she wouldn't tense up. She didn't. What a pro.

"That feels . . ." she started. "That feels . . . good. Oh yeah, that feels really"—she hiccupped as he pressed ████████—"really good," she stammered.

Yes, that was it. ████████. He ████████ and ██ and ██ ██, grunting, his brain melting into a blur as he sighed and fell over onto his back, hardly noticing as she curled her head into his shoulder and he passed out.

THE SUN WAS STARTING to rise when he woke up, and he shook his head to remember where he was. A blonde girl was drooling on his chest and he laughed as it came back to him. He pushed her away gently so he wouldn't wake her up.

He pulled on his jeans and slipped out of the apartment without a sound. It was seven a.m. and he wondered how far he was from the office. His head was pounding—they'd been at Houston Hall until at least three in the morning—but he'd made it a great night and he'd make it a great day, just like he always did.

JUAN

WEDNESDAY, APRIL 9; SAN FRANCISCO, CALIFORNIA

Are you seriously still at the office? Juan instant-messaged Neha when she responded to an e-mail he'd sent with the user demographics she'd requested. It was midnight in California, which meant it was three a.m. in New York, and the first e-mail she'd sent him that day had been time-stamped 7:15 a.m.

NEHA: Yes.
JUAN: Do you ever leave?
NEHA: Every few days.

He started to write *LOL*, then realized she wasn't kidding. He'd worked those late nights back when Hook started, but he'd been building something, not entering numbers into documents no one was ever going to read.

JUAN: Do you like it?
NEHA: What?
JUAN: Investment banking.

NEHA: Sure. I think I'm going to get a promotion soon.

JUAN: Nice! Will that make your hours better?

NEHA: Probably not.

JUAN: Then why do you want it?

NEHA: You do less grunt work as an associate.

JUAN: Is that what Beau is? An associate?

NEHA: Yeah.

JUAN: He seems to have better hours. He's usually hanging out with Julie when you guys are out here.

NEHA: That's because he's rich. He only got the job because his dad's a client of the firm.

JUAN: Oh.

NEHA: Ugh. I am so sick of Tara.

JUAN: Why?

NEHA: She's just so self-absorbed. She acts like her stuff is SO important and it isn't—Todd does all the models. All she does is make sales decks.

Juan really liked Tara. She was friendly.

JUAN: I guess I hadn't noticed.

NEHA: BRB.

Juan read the message and hoped he hadn't offended her. He liked Neha. She was anal and worked way too hard, but she had an underlying feistiness that Juan thought was funny. He and Brad had decided to try to get her drunk at the party they were planning for the day Hook went public, just to see what would happen.

Juan went back to the database where he was pulling statistics on how many active users there were in various parts of the world.

This database was one of several that stored all the connections,

ratings and private comments every user had made since downloading
the app. Juan hadn't looked at them since he and Josh had first developed
them, but doing so now made him realize the massive influence Hook
now had with its five hundred million users. He especially liked the map
of the world that had a dot for every user currently logged in, in their live
location. There were millions of dots, all over the world, and Juan's skin
prickled thinking about all those people using a product he helped create.

He zoomed into Europe and down into France and then Paris
and the Eiffel Tower and twenty-seven dots clustered around it. He
clicked on one of the dots to see where the account was registered: Ham-
burg, Germany. He watched more information load and marveled at
how cool it was that Henric Baumann was presently matching with
Amelia Guilb—

Wait: why could he see their names?

Juan blinked at the computer. Provided information, like a user's
name, was supposed to be separate from what they tracked, like user
location. He clicked on another dot: Benjamin Thibodeaux. He clicked
Benjamin's name and the computer prompted him to "Return to Database." He clicked the link, but it redirected him to a different database
than either of the two he'd been working in: this one cross-correlated
private and collected data.

"What?" Juan looked at this new database. It was a list of all users, with
columns of data indicating all prior history. There was a search field in the
upper right corner. The IM box appeared again on top of the database.

NEHA: Sorry. Just got harassed by this stupid analyst.
JUAN: All good.

"I wonder," he said out loud, then shook the thought away. He didn't
know where it had come from, but this database shouldn't be here, and
he definitely shouldn't pry.

Then again, it *was* here, and he should at least know how it worked. She probably didn't have a profile anyway.

But when he typed in her name, he found that Neha Patel, birthdate 12/03/92, zip code 10019 did, in fact, have a profile. He opened her information. She'd created an account two years ago and spent a month logging in around Manhattan. She'd swiped right for four guys but none had swiped right for her. She'd messaged one of them and then viewed his profile thirty-two times in four hours, but he'd never replied. She herself had only gotten thirty-six right-swipes, no reviews, and just one message, from a fat forty-two-year-old who looked like a serial killer.

Maybe they should use part of the funds from the IPO to create a service to help girls like Neha. They could develop an algorithm that would help her know what she needed to do to increase her likability, and that would increase her confidence, and then maybe she'd find someone, or at least feel less rejected.

As it was, he didn't blame her for not using it anymore.

Then again, Juan had stopped using Hook, too. And he had better stats than that. Didn't he?

Juan paused at the thought. Surely looking at his own information wasn't breaking any rules.

Juan typed in his name, and the user information started to load. He decided he should get a beer for this, and went to the fridge. The office was empty, leaving him alone with the view of the Bay lights sparkling outside the floor-to-ceiling windows at the end of the room.

It would be nice to have a girlfriend, he thought, at moments like this. To show her this office, and sit with beers watching the lights shoot back and forth across the water.

Juan had never had a girlfriend. It wasn't that he wasn't interested in girls, or that he didn't like a lot of them. And if he was being honest, he knew it wasn't that girls weren't interested in him. He'd just never really found one that was good enough. He needed someone smart and funny, sure, but he needed someone who got where he came from, too, and appreciated that he needed to take care of his mother back in East Palo Alto, and needed to not talk about his father's murdered body in Juárez. But the girls he met in San Francisco . . . their lives were just too uncomplicated for them to understand all of that.

Juan sipped his Pacifico and opened the summary page for his own profile. He had 12,012 right-swipes and 180 reviews that netted him an average score of 8.7 out of 10. He looked at the distribution: 75 percent were 10s or close to it; 25 percent were 1s and 2s. He choked on his beer and realized he'd been expecting all perfect scores.

He clicked a positive review first: it was from Isabel. His heart caught in his throat. He'd been in love with Isabel his entire childhood. But she was cool and he was a dweeb and when they got to middle school she dated Roberto, who was two years ahead. Juan got a scholarship to the Menlo School and left her, along with all his other friends, in the ghetto public schools in EPA.

Isabel had given Juan a perfect 10 in every category: looks, ambition, sex, humor, commitment and intelligence. She'd tagged #takehometomom and #bestguyever and written in: "This boy is a PRINCE; get him while he's HOTTTT <3."

Juan felt his cheeks burn and all his old feelings rush back like he was thirteen and in love for the only time.

Juan skipped to a bad review. It took him a minute to recognize the name, but when he saw the face he remembered Lydia Karr from Berkeley. They'd been in a Math 51 study group together and he'd had too much to drink once at a party and made out with her on the dance floor. He hadn't seen her since graduation in 2009, but the review was from six months ago. She'd given him 1s across the board, tagged #heartbreaker and #f*ck*gasshole and written: "Seems like a great guy until you realize he thinks he's better than everyone. What an asshole. Stay away."

Juan blinked. He didn't think he was better; he'd just been through more. And he hadn't been mean to her: they'd only made out once when they'd both had too much to drink. He closed the page. *This* is why he didn't use Hook, or hook up with girls.

A text message on his iPhone gave him an excuse to look away, and he clicked out of the database.

> Julie: New roommate is awesome!

He smiled at the phone. Julie thought everyone was awesome, but it was good to have her approval of their new roommate, Amanda.

> Juan: GREAT! Dinner party Friday? See if she's free and I'll make empanadas.

> Julie: Done!! Are you still at the office? We're at that Kelly Jacobson fundraiser in the Mission if you want to join?

> Juan: Still here. See you at home.

Everyone had been talking about the benefit to raise money for the dead girl's memorial fund. It's not that Juan didn't care, he just knew how the story was going to play out and wanted nothing to do with it. Stanford kids like Kelly got their drugs from the East Palo Alto kids he'd grown up with. With Carl Camp's war on drug dealers raging, Juan instinctively felt it was only a matter of time before his community got blamed for her death and the two sides of the track grew even more distant.

Juan clicked back into the database and typed to see if Julie had ever reviewed him. She had, giving him all 10s, except on commitment, where she'd given him a 1, #impossiblyhighstandards.

Did she really think that?

He had to stop.

He finished his beer and started to shut off his computer, but something made him turn back. What about Kelly?

He paused, staring at the screen, his fingers hovering above the keys. She was dead: how could it be violating her privacy when she was dead?

He typed in her name. There were over eighty million views since her death, with ratings ranging from 1, with tag #slut, to 10, with tag #victim. He filtered the results by date and scrolled to the beginning. She'd started using Hook last July, and met up with a few guys in New York. She'd used it again in New York on December 28 of last year. She'd logged in in California several times this year, but never rated anyone and only had one meet-up. Juan felt bad for her: she wasn't a slut like the media said, or if she was, there were about 459 million Hook users who were a lot worse.

He got up to go, then turned back to look at the date of her single meet-up this year: March 6. He stopped, feeling his palms start to sweat. When had she died?

Juan held his breath and Googled her name. He clicked on her Wikipedia article and blinked to make sure he was reading correctly. *Time of death recorded as 4:47 a.m., March 6, 2014.*

Juan clicked open the entry in the database. The time of meeting with the other user was 2:18 a.m. He clicked the map and scrolled into 558 Mayfield Avenue, Xanadu residence, Stanford University.

Despite all his attempts to not pay attention to the story over the past weeks, he knew Kelly's friend had dropped her off, alone, at one a.m. The news had never said anything about her being with someone else afterward.

He clicked the profile of the other user, bracing himself. But the profile wouldn't load. He refreshed. Nothing. Finally, a box popped up with the words PATH CORRUPTED.

"What the—" Juan blinked.

"You're still here?"

Juan jumped. Josh Hart was standing in front of his computer: where had he come from?

Juan willed the blood back into his face and quickly clicked out of the windows open on his screen. "Yeah, just finishing up some things for Nick," he said.

He could feel Josh's eyes peering into him from above the desk.

"Everything going okay with him?" Josh asked. His face twitched. Juan knew Josh well enough from their long nights programming together to know his face only twitched when he was nervous or angry.

"Yeah." Juan nodded, his heart still racing, wishing Josh would go away. "Everything's great."

"What are you looking at?" Josh said.

"Just some stats," Juan lied to cover. "It's crazy how much guys in New York flirt."

"They're like rabbits."

"Yeah."

Please go away, Juan screamed in his head. It felt like Josh was choking him with his gaze.

"Do you want to go to the symphony next week?" Josh asked. "I have a spare ticket. There's a group of us that always go. And I was thinking it's really been too long since you and I hung out." The cadence of his voice was different, like he'd rehearsed the line.

Juan looked up; Josh didn't seem like the symphony type.

"Sure," Juan said, "but you know I've never been to the symphony, so if you want to give it to someone who'll appreciate it more, I'd—"

"No, I'd like you to come," Josh said.

"Sure," Juan said. "Sounds good."

"Great. See you tomorrow." Josh turned to leave.

"Yep," Juan said, forcing a smile while he waited for the door to slam. As soon as it did, he collapsed back into his chair. Kelly Jacobson wasn't alone when she died: But who had she been with? And who did he have to tell?

6

CHARLIE

Charlie refreshed the browser on his laptop to watch the YouTube video of the chemical attack in Talmenes again, and felt heaviness hit from every direction. He was angry for the victims, but also for himself. If Kelly hadn't died, it would have been his story. If Raj had let him go back when he'd asked, Charlie might have written a story that prevented it. Or he might have been there and suffocated in the fumes. But at least if Kelly hadn't died, he'd have been doing something instead of sitting here in California, waiting.

There was no reason for him to be here, but he didn't know where else to go.

He couldn't stay in his parents' apartment, watching the twenty-four-hour news cycle. His mother barely moved from the sofa, just sat there getting upset every time another pundit passed judgment on his sister's morality, then got equally upset when an afternoon went by and no one mentioned her daughter, as if Kelly's life had been irrelevant.

He walked down University Avenue and found a table at a café, pulling the yellow notebook out of his bag. He'd decided to read Kelly's journal all the way through. He wasn't spying on her; he'd just realized that he'd missed certain details of her life, and he wanted to know she'd been okay.

September 23, 2010

> *Oh my god I love Stanford SO much. I can't believe I ever thought I knew happiness before college—nothing compares to this. We had this dorm meeting tonight—like an orientation meeting to tell us all the rules, except there really aren't any rules. Like our RAs basically told us we won't get in trouble for drinking, even though we're underage, because they'd rather we tell them when someone's had too much than have someone die because we're too afraid they'll get in trouble. I love that they trust us like that—it makes so much sense, right? Not that I'm planning to start drinking, but I just think that's totally the right attitude, to let people be responsible for themselves and their friends. Anyway! We're in this orientation meeting and then this whistle blows and all our RAs jump up and all of a sudden these people dressed all crazy with instruments come running into the lobby, playing music, and it's the Stanford Band. Oh My God they are CRAZY. Like, this one guy was totally naked, playing a saxophone. It was so gross, but I couldn't stop looking!! And the tree was dancing—I LOVE that our mascot is a tree!!!—and—*

"What can I get you?"

"What?" Charlie looked up, startled. The waitress indicated the menu. "Oh," he said, "just a coffee and the omelet."

The waitress left and he flipped forward in the journal.

November 5, 2010

> *So I lost my virginity tonight. Why did I think it would be a bigger deal than this? I don't love Jamie. I think that's why I did it: because I know I don't love him and won't love him and so I won't attach a lot of significance to his being my first. Like, I think it's a mistake when girls wait for true love to lose their virginity because then if it doesn't work out it's not just that you loved him, it's that you lost your virginity to him and then it becomes this really big deal. And it's not. Or it wasn't. It didn't hurt as much as I expected, but it definitely didn't feel good. Jamie said it gets better. He lost his virginity when he was fourteen. Can you believe that? That a guy that got into Stanford was having sex when he was fourteen? I guess that's what happens when you go to boarding school. Anyway, it didn't feel good, so I hope it gets better. It does make me think about how glad I am I didn't wait until marriage. Can you imagine if you did? If you had this magical, blissful wedding day and had been looking forward to this magical, blissful moment afterward, and then it felt like that? What a terrible way to start a marriage. And kind of weirdly male-dominating, right? Like starting a marriage with the man hurting you?*

"Here you go," the waitress said, sliding a plate of eggs in front of him, and Charlie stopped, grateful for the interruption.

"Thanks."

Charlie's phone rang as he cut into his eggs. "Hello?"

"Did you see the story?" Johnny asked through the phone.

"Is it out?" Charlie sat forward in his seat.

"Front page, above the fold." Johnny's voice was proud.

Johnny had already told him the narrative that had unfolded as he'd interviewed Kelly's friends about her death. Not only did Robby Goodman, as RA, have a key to her room, he'd had a crush on Kelly and been devastated that afternoon when he found out she was moving to New York after graduation. He'd started recklessly partying a few hours later for a rugby team reunion, an all-night debacle that he'd left, wasted, around two a.m. It wasn't hard to imagine that he'd wanted to see Kelly when he'd come home and had used his RA key to get into her room. From there, he'd given her the water laced with Molly, forced himself on her, passed out and, when he came to, panicked and taken her to the hospital.

"They've already got Robby in custody," Johnny said. "You'll probably want to get an attorney, if you haven't already."

"Yeah, that's a good idea," Charlie said, standing up to get the waitress's attention for the bill, grateful to Johnny for giving him something to do.

TARA

Friday, April 11; San Francisco, California

"So I slept with Todd last night," Rachel said with the nonchalance of reporting what she'd eaten for breakfast, her eyes on the wine list. "We'll have a bottle of the Trefethen Riesling, please."

"W-w-w-wait," Tara said. "You slept with Todd Kent? Like, my Todd Kent?" She felt her chest tighten: she and Todd had come back to the hotel from Hook's office at ten o'clock last night. Tara had worked until two a.m. in her room, bingeing on a pack of peanut M&M's from the minibar, which she'd run an extra mile for this morning to burn off. Had he really gone back out and had sex with their pseudo-client?

"Oh, have you two hooked up?" Rachel asked, unaffected by the probability that the two women had slept with the same man. Her silky hair was pinned back in a carefully constructed sloppy bun, and she had pristinely painted lines around her lids and lips.

"No." Tara shook her head. "Well, yes, I mean, back at Stanford. It was nothing," she lied.

"College hookup comes back around," Rachel said, smiling. "I love that story." She tasted the wine the bartender had poured and nodded with approval.

"I'll just have a sparkling water," Tara said. She hadn't had a drink since the Frick.

Rachel shot her a look. "You think Todd is out drinking water tonight?"

"The stakes are higher for me."

"One glass?" Rachel pushed.

"Sorry." Tara shrugged, declining.

"Suit yourself," Rachel said. "Anyway, it was *terrible*."

Tara coughed. "What?"

"Like, literally the worst sex I've ever had. Like having sex with a gorilla. Was he that bad in college?"

Tara felt her mouth drop and she laughed: if Rachel didn't think it was weird, she guessed she didn't have to, either. Tara had always thought she preferred working with men, but she really liked Rachel. She was confident and cool and didn't get distracted by gossip or take it as an insult to her own talent if Tara had a good idea.

"You know, I don't really remember," Tara answered Rachel's question honestly. She had never thought to consider whether Todd Kent had had any skill at sex. In fact, she had never thought about whether any of the men she'd slept with were good or bad at it, she'd just always focused on whether or not she was okay.

Rachel looked at her, confused. "I guess you were young," she rationalized. She took a sip of her wine. "Or maybe that's what New York does to guys," she said, thinking out loud. "Like, has Todd ever been in a relationship?"

Tara shrugged again. "Not since I've known him."

"So maybe he's never actually learned. I mean, he's had a lot of sex, but only one-off interactions, so he's never gotten any feedback."

Tara pressed her lips and took a sip of her water. "Do you think women know, though, if that's the case?"

"What?"

"Whether it's good or not?"

"Are you serious?"

"It's just that if a girl only ever has sex with guys like Todd," she said, "maybe that's what she thinks it's supposed to be like."

"No way. Girls have vibrators," she said. "They know what it's supposed to feel like."

"But a lot of women can't have orgasms from normal sex," Tara said. "There was that study—"

Rachel shook her head. "I don't buy it." She paused. "I think it's men like Todd doing the studies who want to justify their own inabilities," she said, then noticed Tara's face. "Oh my god, you've never had an orgasm with a man!"

Tara swallowed. "Yes, I have." Then she added, "Well, I think I have."

"You *think* you have?" Rachel glared at her, then punched her arm. "Oh my god, you poor thing! No wonder you're so miserable!"

"I'm not miserable," Tara corrected, sipping her water.

"I thought it was just your awful job, but that *and* no good sex? Jesus, I'd kill myself."

"A," Tara said, lifting a finger, "my job is not awful. And B, I just haven't found someone I'm really comfortable with. And C, I am not miserable."

"A, it is; C, you are; and B, you haven't gotten comfortable with yourself."

"I'm—"

"Drinking water on a Friday night. You're miserable."

Tara paused, looking at Rachel and taking the thought in. "Fine," she said. "Can I have a glass of wine, please?" she asked, turning to the bartender.

"Now, that' s a start." Rachel patted Tara's arm. "As for your orgasm problem, you have to go older," she coached. "Older men have been around long enough to know what else is out there and appreciate you, instead of comparing you to some fantasy they think exists because they watch a lot of YouPorn."

The guy at the bar looked over his shoulder to acknowledge he was listening to the whole thing, disgusted.

"What?" Rachel asked him pointedly. "Oh, hello!" Rachel exclaimed. "What about Callum? He'd be perfect."

Tara blushed. "I told you, he's a client."

"I'm more of a client than Callum is, and Todd slept with me."

"It's different for girls," Tara said. "You know that."

"Why does everyone say that?" Rachel said. "It's only different if you let it be."

Tara drank a sip of her wine. Rachel grinned. "You totally like him."

"I don't know him," Tara corrected.

"And you won't," Rachel said, "if you don't give him a chance. Come on, you're totally his type anyway."

"That's what Josh said, too," Tara confided.

"What?" Rachel's eyes got serious. "What did Josh say?"

"That Callum would like me because he likes girls with control issues." Tara rolled her eyes, remembering the first meeting. "That's what he made you all leave the fishbowl to tell me. Also to make sure I knew my sole purpose in the deal is to distract men with my appearance."

"Fuck Josh," Rachel said angrily. It was the first time Tara had seen Rachel look discomposed. "Josh is a misogynist prick."

Tara turned to look at Rachel, interested.

"I think the only reason he created Hook is to make women feel cheap."

"Why do you say that?" Tara asked carefully.

"I've seen the way he treats women. He's a total creep. He has no respect for other human beings, just treats them like objects or pawns. He's like a sociopathic robot."

"Why do you work for him, then?"

"Phil Dalton pays me an ungodly amount."

"To protect Josh's public image?"

"It's a big job."

"Do you use Hook?" Tara asked, suddenly curious.

"Absolutely not," Rachel said.

"But you're so—" Tara started, looking for words that wouldn't offend.

"Liberated?" Rachel helped her. "There's a difference between un-emotional sex that's respectful and transactional sex that's orchestrated by an app," she said, finishing her wine and looking at the empty bottle. "Which is a nuance Josh doesn't understand. Do you have dinner plans? I'm in the mood for Terzo."

"I should get back to work," Tara said.

"Have I taught you nothing tonight?"

Tara thought about Todd's night out yesterday. "Fine," she said. "Let's go."

AMANDA

FRIDAY, APRIL 11; SAN FRANCISCO, CALIFORNIA

Amanda handed Juan a beer and plopped down on the sofa beside him. She had an hour to kill before her first San Francisco date with a guy she'd met on Hook and she was in a great mood.

"Are you watching porn?" Amanda laughed at how glued he was to the TV, then bit her lip when she realized he was watching a story about Kelly Jacobson.

"No," Juan said but didn't smile.

She liked Juan a lot. Last Friday, she'd come home from her first day of work to a surprise dinner party that he and Julie had prepared to welcome her to the city. He'd cooked empanadas that were better than she'd ever had at a Mexican restaurant, and he'd asked questions in a way that made her feel like he genuinely wanted to get to know her.

"What's the news?" she asked, noting the headline, *Breaking News: Jacobson Death Ruled Suspicious; Suspect in Custody.*

"They think it was murder," Juan said. "They think her RA gave her drugs and made her overdose."

"What made them—"

"Shhh," he commanded, turning up the volume as the suspect came on the screen.

"Police today arrested Robby Goodman, a Stanford senior who was Kelly Jacobson's RA. An anonymous tip to a reporter at the *New York Times* led the university to open an investigation into the girl's death. The police have reason to believe the girl did not willingly take the drugs that killed her, as originally thought.

"We're still learning about Robby Goodman, but it appears he was actively involved in rugby, a sport that's been relegated to club status at most American universities owing to its extraordinary aggression. Here's Mr. Goodman's attorney."

"There is absolutely no basis for this accusation. Police have no information to prove my client was with Kelly that night. This is a witch hunt, trying to vindicate a girl's purity by vilifying an innocent man."

"Are you okay?" Amanda said softly. Juan's face was white.

"Yeah," he said.

"You're a lawyer, right?" he asked after a pause.

"A paralegal," she corrected. "I don't know whether I'm going to law school or not."

"So can I ask you a legal question, hypothetically?"

"Shoot."

"If someone had information that could help in a murder investigation, are they, like, legally, required to tell?"

"Legally, only if they're indicted. But ethically, they probably should."

"What if they aren't supposed to have the information?"

"Doesn't change the fact they have it and it could help."

"But what if they don't know if it could help?"

"What are you trying to get at?"

"I think Kelly was logged into Hook when she died and I think it might help the investigation if they knew," he blurted, then brought his hand to his mouth in surprise he'd let it out.

"How do you know?" She sat forward. "Can you look up people's histories?"

He bit his lip. "I can't tell you."

"Holy shit!" She punched him, excited. "Can you look up this guy I used to—"

"Please don't say anything." He cut her off. "It's super confidential."

"Well, yeah."

"So you think I should tell someone? About Kelly?"

"Only if you want to be responsible for ruining your IPO."

"What?"

"No one's going to invest in a company potentially wrapped up in a murder investigation."

"But Hook had nothing to do with it. She just happened to be logged in." He was getting defensive. "It's just a coincidence."

"Doesn't matter. The only thing that matters to public markets is perception. The minute investors hear 'Hook' in the same sentence as 'Kelly Jacobson,' they'll run."

Juan checked his watch. "Shit, I've got to go. Please, please, please don't say anything about this."

She lifted her hands. "I consider this client-attorney confidentiality."

"But you wouldn't say anything?" he asked. "If you were me?"

"Kelly was probably logged into Facebook, too," she said. "And Twitter and Spotify and a hundred other apps. It doesn't have anything to do with anything."

"Yeah, I guess you're right," he said, but he didn't look like he believed her. "Can you run out and tell Josh I'll be right there?"

"Who's Josh?" she asked on the way to the door.

"Josh Hart."

"Your CEO?"

"Yeah," he called. "We're going to the symphony."

Amanda opened the door and saw a bright blue Tesla roadster outside. "Sweet," she said. Maybe if tonight's date didn't work out she could date the CEO of Hook.

Josh rolled down the window. He was pasty white and his eyes were beady, like a reptile's, but he wasn't terrible looking. "Where's Juan?"

She stuck out her hand. "I'm Amanda, his roommate." She smiled and batted her lashes. He didn't respond. "He's on his way out, asked me to tell you."

Josh glared at Amanda in suggestion she leave.

"Have a good time," she said to Juan as he walked out the door.

Amanda went back inside, Josh's rebuff already forgotten by the time she got to the door. She turned on the radio and killed time putting on makeup while she waited for her date, Ben Loftis, to arrive.

San Francisco had been a great move. Her roommates were great, the weather was great, the profiles of men on Hook were great. Work still sucked, but her hours were better, and when she came home she had free booze, courtesy of Hook. It felt cool being in such close proximity to an app everyone used.

And to top it all off, Ben Loftis, who was now on his way to pick her up, was legitimately perfect. Not only had he messaged her, he'd asked her to dinner. When would that *ever* happen in New York? Guys there just used the app for easy sex, she now realized. Why had she ever wasted her time thinking she could fix Todd Kent? Guys here didn't need to be fixed, and they appreciated a woman like Amanda when they saw her.

As she curled her hair, Amanda thought through Ben Loftis's stats. He'd gone to Duke undergrad, then worked at Citigroup in investment banking in New York, then gone to Wharton for business school, and now he was starting the first-ever all-organic, locally sourced, sustainably manufactured craft beer hall in the country. *Plus* he'd run a marathon, visited *twenty* countries, was a certified scuba instructor, and had spent a summer teaching English to kids in China. *And* he had super-attractive photos.

The doorbell rang and Amanda took a deep breath, one last look in the mirror, and skipped down the stairs.

"Hi." Ben Loftis smiled, handing her a bouquet of flowers.

Oh my god, she thought, *should we just go up and sleep together right now?!*

"Hi," she said, containing herself. "This is so sweet of you."

"Here's the flower food." He handed her a small sachet. "It makes them last longer."

She opened her arms and gave him a hug, overcome. "Thank you so much. This is seriously so nice." His arms were stiff as he returned the hug and she blushed: maybe she'd been too effusive?

She put the flowers down on the table by the door. "Should we get going?"

He looked at the flowers, then smiled, closed-lipped, back at her. "Sure."

JUAN

Friday, April 11; San Francisco, California

Juan tried not to be nervous but he couldn't help it: everything was making him nervous since he'd discovered that Kelly was with another Hook user the night she died. Would it really derail the IPO if people found out?

"Who was that?" Josh asked as Juan plopped into the passenger seat of the sports car.

"My new roommate, Amanda," Juan said, trying to shake thoughts of Kelly. "She just moved here from New York."

"Why do you have a girl roommate?" Josh asked.

"I've got two, actually," Juan said. "I like living with girls."

"You should get your own place after the IPO."

"Nah—rent around here is crazy high," Juan said. "Didn't they only make like a thousand of these cars?"

"I don't know. Rachel suggested I get it," Josh said, apparently uninterested in the car everyone else was talking about.

"Can I ask you a question?" Juan asked.

"You just did."

"Do you use Hook?"

"Of course not."

"Why not?"

"Dealers should never use their own drug."

"Do you think it's safe?"

"In what sense?"

"Like, do you think people could get hurt using it. Like, a murderer could use it to kill people?"

"I think a murderer would be better off with a gun."

"But do you think Hook might"—Juan paused carefully—"facilitate it?"

"If a murderer drives to kill his victim, is the car guilty?"

Josh parked his Tesla around the corner from Davies Symphony Hall and Juan let the question go. Maybe he was right.

"Are you glad we're going public?" Juan asked, changing the subject as they got out of the car.

"I'm glad to get the VCs off my ass," Josh said. "You've got someone helping with your taxes, right?"

"No," Juan said. "Do I need to?"

"Yeah," Josh said, as if it were obvious, "if you don't want half of it going to the government, paying for unemployment for this guy the second you cash in." He lifted his chin to indicate a homeless man passed out at a bus stop.

"What do you mean?"

"Our tax bracket is like fifty-three percent. But a good accountant can help you reduce it by at least half, maybe more."

"Is that legal?"

"All tax loopholes are legal."

Juan shrugged. "I don't know that I've got enough to worry about it."

"What are you talking about?" Josh said.

"You know what I make," Juan said. He'd just gotten a raise to a hundred twenty thousand dollars a year, which was hardly rich in San Francisco.

Josh stopped and turned to look at him. "You do realize you own one and a half percent of the company?"

Juan felt his face cool when he saw the seriousness in Josh's eyes. "Is that a lot?" he asked carefully.

"If we get a fourteen-billion-dollar valuation, your shares are worth two hundred million," Josh said, then turned and kept walking. "But the government's going to take half if you don't get it sorted soon."

Juan stood, paralyzed. Had Josh just said two hundred million? As in two hundred million *dollars*?

Josh showed the ticket collector their passes and Juan followed him in a daze to their seats.

Juan was grateful when the lights went down and he could settle into his thoughts.

Two hundred million dollars? That was . . . that was actually more than Juan's brain could comprehend.

AMANDA

FRIDAY, APRIL 11; SAN FRANCISCO, CALIFORNIA

Amanda and Ben walked from her house down Union Street to Terzo, where the host greeted Ben. "The usual table, Mr. Loftis?"

"Please."

"So you come here often?" she asked.

"Yes." He smiled curtly. "It's the best restaurant in your neighborhood, although their beer selection is subpar. I've got a meeting with the owner next week to discuss a partnership for our craft beers."

"Oh, that's awesome," Amanda said. "I have so many questions about your business. It must be so cool having a start-up."

"It is. Not everyone's cut out for it—it's a lot of work, but I'm used to it from my years in investment banking." His brown eyes blinked rapidly when he talked. He wasn't as attractive as in the photos: he was fatter, for one thing. But Amanda gave him a pass. Starting a business must make it hard to keep up with his usual marathon routine.

"Oh, I've heard investment banking is brutal," she agreed. "I mean, I thought paralegal hours were long, but—"

"They're nothing in comparison," Ben interrupted. "Nothing is, except starting a company. Or at least starting a successful company, like mine."

"So it's going well?"

He lifted an eyebrow as if he didn't believe she was asking the question. "Did you not see *Forbes* this year? I was on the Thirty Under Thirty list."

"Seriously?" Amanda's jaw dropped. Was she really having dinner with a guy who was in *Forbes* magazine? "I don't read it, but that's amazing."

"You need to," he counseled. "If you're going to participate in the Valley you've got to stay on top of the *Forbes* Thirty Under Thirty list. It's pretty much what separates the good companies from the ones that are BS. What do you want to drink?"

"Wine?" she suggested.

"What do you like?"

"White, I guess?"

He studied her. "Dry or fruity?"

"Oh, I'm not picky."

"Interesting," he said, looking at the menu. "We'll have a bottle of the Napa chardonnay," he instructed the waiter, "and my usual order for food." He turned back to Amanda. "I'll order for both of us, just to get this going."

"Oh, sure," she said. "Do you know a lot about wine?"

"Yes. I'm certified."

"As a sommelier? Doesn't that take years?"

"I did a compressed course while I was in business school. It was thirty hours, but it's basically the same training."

The waiter came back with the wine and Ben tasted it before pouring her a glass. "Very good," he said.

"Delicious," she agreed, taking a sip.

He didn't say anything, so she asked another question. "So, did you like Wharton? I loved Penn as an undergrad."

"The business school is much different from undergrad. Much more competitive, for one thing." He was looking in the mirror behind her, studying the other people in the restaurant.

"It's annoying out here because everyone thinks Stanford Business School is the only place to go for entrepreneurship," he went on, "but statistically more companies come out of Wharton. And our average GMAT scores are higher than theirs. I met some girl from there the other day who got a 670. I couldn't believe it. Like, I know standards are lower for women because they need to keep numbers up, but that's absurd. They're clearly losing their edge."

Amanda took a deep breath and sipped her wine. Maybe she was asking the wrong questions.

"Will you hold on a second?" He stood up without waiting for her to respond and she watched him go to the table he'd been studying and confront a man and a woman on what looked like a date.

The waiter arrived with their food and she nibbled at the roasted eggplant, then finished it altogether, watching him stand and chuckle at the table.

Next she went for the meatballs, watching as Ben Loftis's perfection melted while he stood at the table, rocking on his heels with one hand in the pocket of his bright blue fleece vest. Who wore a fleece vest to a restaurant like this? His fat face got red as he laughed a fake laugh at something the seated guy said. He took a sip of the wine they were drinking and puckered, evidently using his thirty hours of wine training expertise to criticize whatever they'd ordered.

She watched and chewed without tasting. Had he asked her a single question this entire dinner? Oh yes, he asked what she wanted to drink. And Penn undergrad most definitely was as competitive as Wharton. And definitely more competitive than . . . Where had he gone? Duke?

But he gave you flowers, she defended him to herself.

"Here, babe." She turned to the voice. A woman at the table next to her slid a shot of tequila in front of her. "You need this more than Tara does."

Amanda looked up: the woman's face was Asian and flushed from drinking, and she smiled comically while the woman she sat with giggled helplessly.

Amanda felt herself puff up defensively, realizing the pair had been observing her date. She glanced at their fingers: no rings. How dare some bitter, older girls mock her when . . . she looked over at Ben, then back at the women.

The woman nodded, following Amanda's thoughts. "I'm telling you, honey, it's as good as it gets out here."

"But I came out here to find better men."

The woman shrugged but laughed, saying, "Didn't we all," then indicated the tequila shot. "Drink up."

Amanda downed the shot as Ben Loftis returned. "Sorry," he said. "Old girlfriend."

"Oh?" Amanda puckered her lips, swallowing the tequila taste.

"Poor girl ended up with that private equity loser. I have no respect for men who just make money off other people's work." He looked at the food. "Did you eat all the meatballs?"

"Yeah." She noticed the clear plate. "I was starving."

"Oh." His eyes darted back and forth, trying to decide what to do, then he gestured for the waiter. "Can we have more meatballs, Marc? Guess you won't need any dessert, then," he said, turning back to her.

The women at the next table paid the check and gave a good luck sign as they left the restaurant. Amanda chugged the wine in front of her while Ben continued to talk about himself and the things on his résumé.

She didn't even pretend to offer to pay when the bill came.

"I'm going to get a cab to Pac Heights," he said. "I can drop you off."

"That would be great," she said, and the gesture made her think maybe she should give him another chance.

He signed the bill and she followed him outside.

"You know, I've actually been thinking about starting my own company," she said as they got into the car. "Like, I've realized in law there isn't really a good system for people who aren't pro bono but can't pay the big legal fees for firms like Crowley—"

"Sorry." He put a finger up. "Do you mind if we watch this?" He gestured to the tiny TV screen in the cab. "I love this clip." He laughed as Jimmy Kimmel came on. She sat back and crossed her arms. The cab arrived at her door as the clip finished.

"Well, it's been fun." She opened the door.

"Hey, listen," he stopped her. "I'm sorry."

She turned, hopeful. "About what?" Maybe the ex-girlfriend had been serious, had broken his heart and made it difficult to sit through dinner.

"I should have cut this off before dinner," he said.

"Why?" she asked kindly, waiting for him to say he was still heartbroken, wasn't ready for a new relationship.

"The flowers," he said. "It was just so thoughtless the way you left them on the table. I bought those for you, and now they're probably dead, when all you had to do was take a minute to put them in water with the flower food I gave you instead of disrespecting my effort."

"What?" Her face squinted. Was he joking?

"J. C. Penney had this test that he wouldn't hire anyone who salted his food before tasting it. The flowers were my test. I can't be with a girl who treats my thoughtfulness so flippantly."

Amanda stared at him, mouth open, trying to figure out whether this was actually happening or she'd just had too much wine. "I understand," she finally said, getting out of the cab and shutting the door.

The cab drove off while she was still fumbling with the keys in the damp chill that had settled into the night. She shut the door behind her, picked up the flowers, and chucked them in the garbage.

JUAN

FRIDAY, APRIL 11; SAN FRANCISCO, CALIFORNIA

"Now you're thinking about it," Josh laughed at Juan when the concert ended and they followed the crowds down the stairs, his lips spread to reveal pink gums. Juan hadn't seen Josh smile without closed lips since the early days of Hook; it made him look younger, innocent and a bit naive. "Get trusts in place so you don't have to pay taxes," he coached.

"But who cares?" Juan said. "Even if they take half I still don't know what to do with a hundred million dollars."

"It's not about the money, it's about the principle. Why should guys like you and me, who fund the innovation that fuels this country, *also* be expected to prop up a bureaucratic government that's going to squander it all on inefficient programs that don't work?"

"But then who helps poor people?"

"Private foundations," Josh said, "which I'm sure you'll have."

Juan blushed: that was a great idea.

"Don't you think, though, that if all support switches to private foundations, only the causes rich people care about get any attention?" He'd use his to help kids in East Palo Alto, but all the rich guys he knew were programmers who only cared about video games, *Lord of the Rings* and the occasional rare turtle species.

"You think it isn't like that now? What do you think lobbyists are for? Private foundations are just more efficient."

"Are you Republican?" Juan didn't think he'd ever met a Republican before.

"Libertarian."

"What's that?"

"What you'll be as soon as you have money."

"Are you going to have a foundation?"

"No," he said. "I'm going to start another company. I'm using the money to pay for it myself so I don't have to deal with dickhead venture capitalists."

"You don't like Phil Dalton?"

"All he cares about is his return. He's watering down the vision."

"What's the vision?"

"Of Hook?" Josh's head twitched. "To make social interactions more efficient. Sex is a human necessity, and it's ridiculous how much time is wasted trying to fulfill the need. Hook uses technology to fix that. There are a million other applications of that logic, but Phil doesn't see them."

Juan didn't say anything. He was thinking about Kelly again. Making things more efficient wasn't a crime. Even if she had been killed, which they didn't even know for sure, at the very, very absolute worst Hook had only helped make it more efficient. It hadn't *caused* her to get killed. And that wasn't worth risking the IPO over, especially if the IPO meant he'd have money to maybe help transform East Palo Alto.

7

TARA

WEDNESDAY, APRIL 16; SAN FRANCISCO, CALIFORNIA

"Get in the car," Tara said sternly from the driver's seat.

Neha crossed her arms and didn't budge.

"Get in the *fucking* car or I'll get you fired so fast they won't buy your plane ticket home."

Neha relented, slamming the door behind her and keeping her arms folded as she stared out the window. Of all the things Tara had prepared for leading up to today's meeting with the sales syndicate, waking up to discover that Neha had never reformatted the sales deck she'd sent her four weeks ago was not one of them. The slides weren't in the order she'd asked for, the fonts were different between sections, and the margins were entirely inconsistent. The deck looked like a bad first draft by a bad summer intern.

And of all the things that could hold Tara back right now, an arrogant analyst who'd never met a hairbrush wasn't going to be it.

"It's not a big deal," Neha muttered.

"The fonts aren't even the same, Neha. We just spent twenty-five hundred dollars printing decks we can't use," Tara said as calmly as she could.

"Twenty-five hundred dollars is nothing for L.Cecil."

"That's not the point."

Tara drove down Mission Street from the St. Regis and turned onto the Embarcadero, without stopping at Hook's building.

"Where are we going?" Neha asked, sitting forward in the car seat.

"I need a manicure," Tara said, "and I'm assuming you do, too."

"But the syndicate meeting—"

"Starts at three o'clock."

"But I've got to reformat—"

"Juan's taking care of it."

"Juan?" Neha's face went white. "Does he know I messed up?"

"I told him the file got corrupted and your changes were erased," she said. Tara was furious, but there was no need to bad-mouth the girl to her only friend.

She pulled the car into a parking spot, and Neha followed her reluctantly into the nail salon, where Tara asked in Vietnamese for two manicures.

"You speak Chinese?" Neha asked, surprised.

"Vietnamese," she corrected. "They're Vietnamese."

"Why do you speak Vietnamese?"

"I spent two summers there teaching English when I was in college."

"What? Why?"

"I wanted to help people."

"I didn't know that," Neha said.

"There's a lot you don't know about me, Neha," Tara said, not caring how rude it sounded.

They took their seats and Tara picked a dark gray polish, then remembered the meeting today and exchanged it for a dull, neutral pink. Neha looked at the polishes, flustered, and selected the same.

"Why did you bring me here?" the analyst finally asked as the women put their hands in warm water. "You already fixed the problem."

"I wanted to ask why you never updated the presentation," Tara said evenly, watching the woman in front of her cut her cuticles.

"If you haven't noticed, I'm the only analyst on this deal," Neha said rudely. "I've got a lot going on, Tara, and frankly, I think making sure all the numbers are perfect is a lot more important than making sure the slides are perfectly formatted."

Tara turned to face the girl. Her skin was oily, her eyebrows were bushy, her glasses were outdated. She had the potential to be pretty; she just didn't make any effort.

"Unfortunately, that isn't true," Tara said. "No one will look at your numbers—no matter how perfect they are—if they aren't presented in an appealing way."

"Then people should know better," Neha said.

Tara studied the girl, wondering whether she recognized the weight of what she'd just said. "What's your goal, Neha?"

"To be the best." The girl didn't hesitate.

"The best what?"

"The best whatever-I-am."

"And you want to be an associate, right?"

"Yes." Neha sat up. "And I'm sure I'm going to get the promotion, especially after this deal. Everyone knows I'm the best analyst in the group."

"They're not promoting you," Tara said, turning her gaze back to her nails. She'd seen the list last week: Neha wasn't even up for consideration.

"What?" Neha asked uneasily, then said with more assertion, "Did you tell them something?"

"No," Tara replied. "I just know what they're looking for, and it isn't you."

"Bullshit. I've been on more deals and—"

"Gotten all the numbers right," she said. "At the expense of presentation, which is what matters to this firm."

"But Larry said I'm the best analyst he's ever seen."

"Exactly. Which is not the same thing as being good at anything else. Analysts sit in the back crunching numbers. Associates do some of that, but spend more time figuring out how to package it; by the time you get to VP your job is to work with people, and people care a lot more about what you're like to be around than how precise your numbers are."

"What are you saying?"

"That you're unpleasant to be around," Tara said bluntly.

"Are you saying I'm ugly?"

"No," Tara replied automatically, "I'm saying you're unpleasant to be around." But as she repeated the words, she got the feeling she was lying. Were the two synonymous? What was she trying to say? "I'm saying you need to pay more attention to presentation," she finally said, "if you want to grow in the firm."

The two women sat in silence as the women across painted their nails. Tara's brain felt heavy with the truth of what she'd just said. Was Wall Street really like that: more interested in appearances than fact? Were people really like that? Is that what Josh Hart had been saying?

"Why did you decide to work on Wall Street, Neha?" Tara asked, finally breaking the silence.

"To prove I could," the girl said without looking up.

"To who?"

"Parker Hughes."

"Who's Parker Hughes?"

"He went to my high school. He got dropped off in a black car every morning, all the way from the Upper East Side, and acted like he was doing us a favor by going to Brooklyn Latin instead of some boarding school." Neha's voice was bitter.

"Where did you grow up?"

"Astoria. I took the subway to school."

"And Parker's parents worked on Wall Street?"

"Both of them. And he acted like that made them special, like it made him better than me because my parents didn't. But I was smarter than him, and better than him at everything, and," she concluded, "I'm proving it."

"Where is Parker now?"

"At Goldman."

"Do you ever see him?"

"Not since we graduated from high school."

"Has it been worth it?"

"It will be."

"When?"

"When my kids are dropped off in black cars."

Tara thought about Lauren Wiley, puking in the bathroom at the Frick, her mother still at the office. She'd probably gotten dropped off at school in a black car.

"Do you really think I won't get promoted?" Neha's voice softened.

Tara didn't want to tell her, not now. "I don't know, Neha," she lied.

"So what should I do?" the girl asked.

Tara looked at her again: Was it really just that she needed to fix her appearance? And could Tara really tell her that? "I don't know," she repeated, quietly, then looked at her watch. "We better go."

"Are they dry?" Neha looked at her nails skeptically.

Tara lifted a brow. Was she serious? "It's shellac," she said. Didn't everyone know about shellac?

Tara paid and they drove back to Hook in silence.

"Why did you decide to work on Wall Street?" Neha asked after several moments of silence.

Tara was quiet for a long time, thinking about the question. "I don't know," she finally admitted. "I guess it seemed like the best option at the time."

They got to the parking lot and Tara pulled the car into the space.

"Hey, Tara," Neha said as they got out of the car, "I'm sorry about the presentation."

"It's okay," Tara said, and she meant it. "I know you're under a lot of pressure."

"Yeah, but," she said, "well, you can still trust me, you know? To take on more work?"

"I'll keep that in mind," Tara said. "Just promise to be honest with me about what your priorities are."

"Yeah, I will," Neha said, adding, "And you could maybe put in a good word for me, too, with the promotion committee?"

"Sure, Neha," Tara said, wondering if she actually had the heart to do it.

JUAN

WEDNESDAY, APRIL 16; SAN FRANCISCO, CALIFORNIA

"Is this seriously what you do all day and all night?" Juan asked as Neha took a seat next to him. "I actually think I want to kill myself."

Juan had been formatting a PowerPoint presentation for the past four hours, making sure the graphs were flush against gridlines and all the footnotes were in the same-sized font.

"You okay?" Juan asked when Neha didn't respond.

"Yeah," she said, shaking her head as if to get rid of whatever she was thinking about. "Sorry you have to do that."

"It's cool," he said. "It's kind of fun to see what you do. It makes me appreciate what I do a lot more." He smiled. "Hey! Nice nails!"

She blushed and clenched her fists.

"Don't hide them," he said. "They look really nice." He meant it. He liked that Neha had thought about what she looked like: it made her seem like a real girl instead of a human workhorse.

"Thanks," Neha said uncomfortably, uncurling her fingers.

"Okay," he said, looking at the screen. "I think we're all set."

"Did this put you totally behind?" Neha asked.

"Nah," he said jovially. "I was just working on my community center."

"What? What community center?"

"It's going to be called the Eduardo Ramirez Center, after my dad. It'll be like a hangout place for kids in my old neighborhood, to give them something to do instead of join gangs or deal drugs," he told her.

Juan smiled at her. He hadn't officially told anyone, but he'd spent the past week researching how to start a community center in East Palo Alto, which is what he was going to do with a third of his money as soon as the employee lockup expired six months after the IPO and he could sell his Hook shares. Focusing on what he could do with his wealth had made him realize how foolish he'd been to stress about Kelly Jacobson: he had no idea whether that database was even accurate, but he knew for sure that his money could help kids in EPA.

"You're building a community center?" Neha asked.

"Yeah." He loved the feeling of saying it. "It'll be a lot like Hook, actually—with free food and a basketball court and video game rooms and foosball tables. And every day there will be a different class, open to everyone. I already talked to our chef and he's going to come teach cooking classes, and Brad's going to do surf lessons."

"But how do you pay for it?" She lifted an eyebrow.

Juan shrugged. "Turns out I've got a lot of Hook shares."

"Are we ready?" Nick's voice asked, irritated, from behind his shoulder.

"Oh." Juan turned, startled to see the CFO standing beside him.

"Yep, just sent the presentations to the printer. They're delivering them to the St. Regis at two o'clock."

"Great," Nick said, jittery. "I don't want you to talk to anyone in the meeting," he instructed, "just sit in the back and I'll give you a signal." He paused, thinking. "I'll go like this"—he pinched his earlobe—"if I need you to bring me any statistics."

"Sure thing, boss," Juan said. "I've got it all right here." He indicated his laptop. Before the formatting fiasco, he had uploaded the Hook databases onto a laptop in order to calculate any user statistics if Nick got caught in a question he didn't know.

"Okay. Please be there forty-five minutes early," Nick said, moving on.

"Wow," Juan said, turning back to Neha. "He's even worse than normal."

"It is a pretty big presentation." Neha shrugged.

"Who is it with, again?" Juan asked. Nick hadn't bothered to explain any of it.

"It's with the sales syndicate," Neha said. "They're the ones who sell to institutional investors at whatever price we set at the pricing call."

"Who are institutional investors?"

"Big funds and certain individuals with enough money to buy a lot of shares."

"I thought anyone could buy stock."

"They can, but normal people buy from the institutional guys the day after the institutional guys buy from Hook. That's when the stock is listed on the NASDAQ exchange."

"Why would the institutional guys sell, right after they've bought them?"

"Because they expect the price to go up, in which case they make a profit," she said. "Of course if too many of them do that, there will be a huge supply when it gets listed and people will think that means it's not worth very much and then the price will drop, which is why we're spending all this time trying to get a 'good book' of institutional investors who won't flip it all immediately."

"So what you're saying is big funds and really rich people get the stock at a cheaper price than normal people?" he asked, stuck on the point.

"Yeah," Neha said. "We're trying to sell 1.8 billion dollars' worth of shares—it would be totally inefficient to bother with anyone who isn't in for at least a couple million."

Juan squinted at her. That didn't seem fair, but she didn't seem to mind, so he figured it was a dumb question. Instead he asked, "But Hook gets whatever the institutional guys buy—from the pricing call, right? So what does it matter if the price drops?"

"*You* don't get that price," Neha said, "the company does, but unless you get an exception to sell before the lockup, you personally don't care about the price until at least six months from now. All the same, though, it looks really bad for the company if the price drops."

"What do you think Hook's price will be in six months?"

Neha shrugged. "You know better than me."

"Why?"

"You know what's going on in the company. If it keeps doing well, the price should go up. If something happens and you don't ever become profitable, then I guess you're Zynga."

"What happened to Zynga?"

"They went from like fifteen dollars a share to two," she said. "But that's not as bad as companies during the bubble that went completely bust. All these guys who thought they had a hundred million dollars and then had nothing."

"Yeah, I remember," Juan said. "But I think it's different now, don't you?" Juan hadn't forgotten the dot-com bubble, he'd just gained some perspective. The guys who had lost millions and stopped paying his mom twelve years ago were betting on companies who didn't have real users. Hook had five hundred million of them—it wasn't the same.

"L.Cecil analysts don't think we're in a bubble," Neha said. "For Hook to collapse, something really bad would have to come out—like something criminal."

"You two need a ride?" Tara interrupted them.

"Sure," Neha answered for them, adding in a friendly tone, "did you get everything you need?"

"Yes," Tara said, smiling at the girl. "Thank you."

Juan looked at them suspiciously: didn't Neha hate Tara?

THE THREESOME got to the hotel and Juan sat in the back of the room and pushed the anxiety out of his mind—no one was going to find out what he knew about Kelly being on the app, and it wasn't criminal anyway.

When the meeting started, there were thirty-five people in the room, all men except for Tara and Neha and the girl checking people in. They were all wearing suits, had slick haircuts and sat in neatly arranged chairs in the stuffy banquet hall. The scene couldn't have been less like Hook.

He tried to pay attention, but Nick spoke in jargon that didn't seem to mean anything, so instead he researched rental spaces in East Palo Alto on his laptop. Maybe he would just buy a building. And a new house for his mom.

The Q&A finished without Nick ever pulling his earlobe, and Juan followed the crowd out into the bar area, which L.Cecil had rented for an after-meeting reception.

"Juan," a voice called.

Juan turned and saw the venture capitalist Phil Dalton lumbering down the hall. "Juan, can I speak with you, please?" he said, catching up to him.

"Sure," he told the man, following him to an empty conference room.

Phil shut the door, his face serious. "Is there a non-anonymous database?"

"What?" Juan asked carefully.

"Is there a database where individuals' histories on the app can be identified?" Phil's voice was hushed.

"Well, we collect everything separ—"

"Answer the question."

"Yes," Juan said quietly. He could feel his heart start to pound. Why did Phil look so upset? Had he found out about Kelly?

"Show it to me."

Juan hesitated. Dalton Henley owned the majority of the company: he couldn't say no.

"Is everything okay?" Juan tried to keep his voice calm as he opened his laptop and pulled up the combined database he'd discovered.

Phil didn't answer the question. He pulled the laptop toward him. "You can just type in anyone's name and find their whole history?"

"I don't—" Juan started to lie.

Phil stared at him, waiting.

"Yes. I don't know where it came from, though, I swear."

Phil typed a name into the database, and Juan braced himself for the fallout as he watched the man's face go white.

"We have to get rid of this," Phil said. He looked on the verge of panic.

"You don't think we should tell?" Juan asked.

"Tell who?" Phil glared at him.

"The police?" Juan asked, not sure what he wanted Phil's answer to be.

"What are you talking about?" Phil looked at him like he was crazy. "I have to talk to Josh." He slammed the laptop shut and left the room.

Juan looked at the closed computer and felt his heart sink. He opened the laptop to shut it down properly, but stopped when he saw the name the venture capitalist had entered in the database: it wasn't Kelly Jacobson, it was . . . *Phil Dalton.* Juan's jaw dropped as he scrolled through the married man's extensive history of Hook meet-ups across the globe.

AMANDA

WEDNESDAY, APRIL 16; SAN FRANCISCO, CALIFORNIA

"Finally he's gone," Andy Schaeffer, the frat-tastic paralegal who sat opposite Amanda's cubicle, sighed. He'd been working around the clock for a senior partner who had just left for a meeting, giving Andy a solid two hours without any nagging. "I'm still hungover from Saturday. But Chris Papadopoulos is just perky, perky, perky." Andy lifted his shoulders to imitate the enthusiastic Greek partner.

"What'd you do Saturday?" she asked. She'd spent her Saturday on a Marina bar crawl with Julie. She still wasn't sure what the occasion had been, but they'd donned two hundred dollars' worth of American Apparel gear and been drunk with other in-costume San Franciscans by ten a.m. It had made Amanda long for Lavo, and a nice sparkler in a magnum of champagne.

Between the beer crawl and her terrible date with Ben Loftis, Amanda's enthusiasm for San Francisco was starting to wane. It felt like going back to college, but without the cool kids.

"We hosted our Annual Schaeffer–Collins Beer Olympics," Andy said proudly. "We had twenty-two teams this year. Biggest turnout ever. It was epic."

"I take it you won?"

"Obviously. Even did a—wait for it—sixty-five-second keg stand."

Did he really just brag about a keg stand, at twenty-five years old? she thought, then coached herself to have more patience.

"Nice work." She smiled.

"Thanks." He leaned back in his chair and scratched his stomach. "Would be so much better if I could just revel in the glory instead of dealing with stupid Hook."

"You're working on the Hook deal?" She sat up in her chair. "Like the IPO?"

"Obviously."

"My roommates both work there," she said.

"Lucky bastards. They're going to make so much dough."

She lifted an eyebrow. "Like how much?"

"The early guys? Like the ones who joined in 2010 and 2011? Their options'll be worth like fifty mil, at least."

"What?" Amanda's jaw dropped. Were Juan and Julie making that much? Why were they living in a three-bedroom stealing booze from their company when they had that kind of money?

"Welcome to Silicon Valley." Andy lifted a brow. "I'm telling you, we picked the wrong profession."

"No kidding," Amanda said. Maybe she shouldn't go to law school after all, and should join a start-up instead.

"But yeah, deal's totally brutal. The CFO's a tool and their general counsel quit six months ago and the bankers are fucking idiots and Josh Hart is determined to get the whole thing done by May. It's a shit show."

"Who's the bank?"

"L.Cecil. But not San Francisco L.Cecil. Some team in New York, so I've gotta be up on their hours. It sucks balls."

Amanda felt her breath catch. A New York team from L.Cecil? Was it possible?

"Who are the bankers?" she asked quietly.

"What?"

"I knew a few people at L.Cecil in New York," she said. "Just wondering who you're working with."

"I mostly work with this girl Neha who's got a stupid stick up her ass," he said. "But the head of the team's this stud Todd Kent."

"What?"

"Yeah, some, like, big-shot banker. I bet he gets so much tail."

Amanda's face went white.

It was a sign.

It had to be.

Coincidences like that did not just happen.

"Are they here?" she asked, trying to control herself. "I mean, are the bankers in the building?"

"Why would they be here?" Andy made a face. "They're at the St. Regis for the meeting with the sales team. There's a cocktail hour after, too," he said, "which is why I'm going to curl up under my desk and go to sleep."

Amanda looked up the St. Regis on Google Maps. She checked her watch and, before she could overthink it, was on her way.

She got to the St. Regis just before five o'clock and went to the bathroom to fix her hair and her face, willing her heartbeat to calm. She'd been lying to herself: Todd *was* worth the effort. Much as she wanted something real, she wasn't ready to settle down if it meant settling for a guy like Ben Loftis or Andy Schaeffer or the other overgrown children who represented the men she'd encountered in San Francisco. The timing hadn't been right before, but now . . . this was the universe giving her another chance.

The elevator opened on the hotel bar: it was a closed cocktail party. She couldn't just pretend to be there. *Think fast*, she told herself. She dug in her bag and found a notepad, ripping out the marked pages and heading into the room to find Chris Papadopoulos.

She spotted Todd immediately, standing at the bar, talking to another guy and a pretty-but-not-that-pretty girl. Amanda's heart rose into her throat. He was even hotter than she remembered. It wasn't just his tall frame and his perfectly proportioned body, it was the way he stood, casually, with his hand in his pocket, the way his pants were tight enough around his butt to hang just so, the way he held his glass firmly with the same fingers he'd used to hold the back of her neck when he kissed her.

She felt her cheeks burn and watched him move. Where was he going? There! Toward Chris Papadopoulos! Her feet sprang into action without waiting for her brain.

"Chris," she said, tapping the lawyer's sleeve, not looking at Todd.

"Amanda?" He turned. She watched Todd behind Chris's shoulder. He hadn't noticed her yet. "The new paralegal, right?" Chris asked. "What are you doing here?"

She handed him the notepad. "Andy asked me to give this to you," she said. "He was working on some corrections and I needed to run an errand nearby, so—"

Chris opened the notepad onto its blank pages. "There's nothing here," he said.

"I'm not sure," she said, shrugging her shoulders. "He just asked me if I could bring it."

"Strange," the senior partner said. "Well, thanks. So long."

Shit. What now?

Just do it, she told herself. Now or never.

"Todd?" She walked up and touched his arm, remembering to bat her lashes.

Todd turned and squinted his eyes to place her.

"I thought that was you," she said, faking a laugh. "Amanda, Amanda Pfeffer," she said.

"Oh, yeah." He nodded. "Sorry, I—"

"Context, I know," she agreed. "So crazy to see you! What are you doing out here?"

"I'm working on the deal," he said, as if everyone here should know that.

"Oh, nice," she said. "I just dropped something off with Chris. I moved out here, actually," she continued. "Crowley Brown needed more people in San Francisco so I thought, why not, you know?"

"Sure." His smile was forced. "I'm sorry," he said, "I just need to get back to—" He tilted his head, indicating the conversation she'd interrupted.

"Yeah, of course," she said. "Well, give me a call if you're sticking around. I'm still learning the city, but it would be fun to catch up."

"Sure, will do." He smiled, turning his shoulders back.

She turned to leave, finally letting her breath go, but then turned back to make sure he still had her number.

"I—" she started as she reapproached, but paused when she heard him talking.

"Who was that?" the guy Todd was talking to asked.

"No fucking clue."

Amanda felt her face drain. Her legs moved her unconsciously to the hall, directing one foot in front of the other, until the elevator doors closed and she stopped and allowed the vacuum of disappointment to appear in her brain, then let it suck her down, down, down into its empty darkness.

TARA

WEDNESDAY, APRIL 16; SAN FRANCISCO, CALIFORNIA

"Hey, do you want to grab dinner tonight?" Todd caught Tara's sleeve as she turned to the elevator. "Please don't make me hang out with Nick."

"I'm having dinner with Rachel," she said, "then heading straight to the airport." Her brain was still spinning from her morning with Neha and she was looking forward to talking it through with Rachel, who she knew would have good perspective.

"Rachel Liu?" Todd's brow furrowed.

"Yeah," Tara said, watching his face, and concealing a smile as she imagined him as a gorilla having sex with the PR rep. "And I'm actually a little late, so—"

"Yeah, sure," Todd said. "Good job today, by the way."

"Thanks," she said, her smile changing from bemusement to genuine appreciation. It was the first time he'd ever complimented her, and it meant a lot.

AT THE RESTAURANT Tara sat down and checked her BlackBerry while she waited for Rachel. There was another e-mail from her mother asking if she'd bought her ticket to Maine for her sister's wedding. *I'll do it tomorrow*, she wrote back, irritated, but also not sure why she hadn't booked it yet. The road show started next week in London and would wrap up two weeks later, culminating with the pricing call and IPO on May 8. She could fly straight to Maine from New York and celebrate the deal closing along with her sister's wedding.

"Hello there." She looked up at the British accent. Callum Rees took off his black leather jacket and sat across from her at the table.

She tilted her head, surprised. "I'm sorry, I'm meeting—"

"Me," he finished her sentence. "Rachel had something come up, so I filled in."

"I don't—"

"Want to eat dinner alone."

"But—" she protested. She could feel her cheeks redden. Had Rachel also told him her theory that Tara should sleep with him?

"We'll have a bottle of the pinot noir," Callum told the waiter, ignoring Tara. "Then I'll have the duck, and the zucchini fritters to start. She'll have the winter salad, dressing on the side, to begin, followed by the salmon. And do you think you could do all vegetables instead of vegetables and potatoes?"

"You can't—" she started again, then shifted her tone. "You're not even going to let me order?"

"Did I get it wrong?"

It was exactly what she'd have chosen from the menu, except that she was too embarrassed to ask for no potatoes, so was planning to just eat around them. "That's not the point," she said. "What if someone—"

He watched her, sipping his water with an eyebrow cocked.

She paused, then relented. "Am I really that predictable?"

"Salad and fish? Yes."

"Why do you want to have dinner, then, if you know me already?"

"I think your clichés have been adopted," he said as the waiter returned with the wine. "And that there's more to you than the way you've been trained."

"Why do you think that?"

"Three reasons."

She waited.

"One: your outburst at the Frick. No good banker would have thought to stand up to a billionaire, even a shit like Rick Frier."

Tara blushed.

"Two: you turned down every single boy on Hook, even the really rich one. Most girls in New York would at least have gotten a dinner out of him."

"You were watching me?" She thought back to how she'd wasted time on Hook while she waited for Callum at the Crosby.

"Yes," he said without apology.

"And the third reason?"

"You had a hole in your sweater that evening."

"What?" Tara's jaw dropped.

Callum lifted his arm and pointed underneath it. "Right here. The seam had split and you kept moving your arm, oblivious, and I could see your turquoise bra," he said, then added, "Interesting color selection."

Tara's face burned. Was he making it up? Had she really not noticed a hole in her sweater? "I don't understand what that says about my character," she lied. She knew exactly what it said: that she was not at all put together enough to be a successful woman in business.

"It says that your perfectionist habits are not innate."

"I am so embarrassed."

"Why?" He furrowed his brow. "It was very sexy. You kept moving your arm, like a chicken"—he imitated—"yelling at me for my morals."

He took a sip of his wine and grinned as though he'd won a game.

"That's humiliating," she sighed.

"If that's your version of humiliation, you don't have a very interesting life."

"Thanks for making me feel better."

"Sorry," he said. "I heard you did a great job in the presentation today."

"Are you regretting wanting to sell your shares?" she said wryly.

"Not in the least."

"I'm sorry, why did you come here again?"

"To see you," he said.

Her cheeks burned: why?

"Where's Katerina?"

"In New York, I suspect?" Callum shrugged. "Don't really care, to be honest."

"Did you cover for me?" Tara asked. "With Catherine?"

"Yes," he said simply. "But only because it benefitted Catherine."

"What do you mean?" she asked carefully.

"Over the long term, you're more important to her than Rick Frier, but she wouldn't have seen it that way. Banks think too much in the short term."

"But John Lewis got fired, for something I—"

"John Lewis got fired because he wasn't a good banker. If he had been, my report wouldn't have been enough to get him canned."

"But—"

"You can just say 'thank you,'" Callum said. "You don't always have to make it more complicated."

"Thank you," she said.

"So what were you trying to say with Rick that night, about your generation?"

"Oh, I don't know," she demurred, "I think the wine had just gone to my head."

"Your generation really is a self-entitled lot, though. Incredibly absorbed in yourselves."

"See," she said, riling back up, "you say that like it's our own fault we're self-focused when we were raised the way we were."

"Gotcha." He smiled.

She blushed.

"Go on," he said, "I'm interested. Really."

"I just think your generation doesn't recognize how unsettling it was, to grow up in this world that was simultaneously hyper-competitive and committed to giving everyone a trophy. We signed up for everything in this effort to get ahead, but then everyone was too afraid of hurting our feelings to ever tell us whether we were actually good or not. We *did* everything, but had no idea whether we were actually *good* at anything."

"Forgive me for not having pity on a generation that had boundless opportunity and relentless encouragement."

"I'm not saying you should feel sorry for us, I'm just saying it's worth recognizing how incredibly destabilizing that is—to never know whether you're good or not, but always feel like you're being judged. It's a constant state of anxiety over not being good enough."

"Good enough for what?"

She shrugged. "Your job? Your parents? A man? The life you're supposed to want?"

The waiter returned again and set the plates in front of them.

Callum sat back. "Can I offer you a piece of advice?"

"Of course," she said.

"Figure out what you really want," he said, "as opposed to what you're supposed to want. It's worth the time."

"I could be happy doing a lot of different things," she said. "I think I'm very lucky in that regard."

"That," he said, "is the definition of settling. You may be able to make yourself happy doing a lot of things, but there is one life that you want more than other lives, and it is definitely not the one in which you wake up when you're fifty and figure out what you like after it's too late to do anything about it."

"Fine," she said. "Then I know what I want: it's to be on the path that I'm on, which, it turns out, is really starting to take off."

"Your path to being Catherine Wiley?"

"Yes."

"You want the life wherein you work all the time, never smile or laugh, have a drunk for a husband and daughters you never see?" He lifted a brow. "You haven't thought hard enough."

"You're her friend."

"That doesn't mean I think you should want what she has."

"She's achieved a huge amount," she said. "And that comes with trade-offs."

"There's more to life than achievement," he said. "You have to learn to enjoy things that aren't measurable."

She looked down at her salad. "How did you know what you wanted?" she asked.

"I didn't," he said. "But I knew I wanted to have an interesting life, and that sitting behind a desk a hundred hours a week like you do was never going to be interesting."

"That's not fair," she said defensively. "It's interesting learning about deals, and it's exciting to be a part of them."

"And I knew that if I took a high-paying corporate job, I'd be susceptible to convincing myself that it was interesting and never make time to think about what I actually wanted."

"But it is—"

"Interesting to some people," Callum agreed, "but not most of them, and certainly not you." He held out his fork with a bit of fried zucchini on the end. "Want some?"

She held up a hand to decline.

"Come on," he said, "quit being afraid."

She leaned forward, took the bite off the fork, and let it melt on her tongue.

"There we go." He smiled. "Small steps."

The waiter brought their entrées and refilled Tara's wine.

"The real thing to understand about your generation," Callum started in again, "is that the financial crisis is the greatest thing to ever happen to you."

"What?" she scoffed. "My bonus has hardly beaten inflation in the past four years, and taxes are going up."

"Exactly the point," he said. "The economic situation is so dire that it's pointless to do a job for the money anymore. And if you're not doing a job for the money, you're forced to ask yourself what you *are* doing it for. And, unlike your bosses, you're at an age when you can actually make a change."

"Are you telling me I should quit my job?" she finally asked.

"No," he said. "I'm telling you to be really sure it's what makes you happy, and if you determine the answer is no, you should quit and figure out what does."

"That's easy for you to say when you have a billion-dollar bank account."

"What is it with you and the money?" he said, exasperated. "I'm not saying it's *easy*, and I'm not saying there aren't a lot of things to work out, but you're never going to have fewer excuses. And it's frustrating, at my age, to see a lot of smart people sitting in their stuffy jobs, miserable, when there are so many problems in the world they have the brains and energy and access to solve *and* that would make them happier, if they'd just stop being so afraid of messing up their résumés."

He stopped to take a breath, then laughed lightly. "How's that for a soapbox?"

"Pretty good." She smiled.

He leaned forward so that his face was six inches from her own. She could smell his aftershave and see his laugh lines.

"Did it feel good?" he asked. "To say what you believed?"

"In the moment," she said.

"Listen to *that*," he said.

"What if it gets me fired?"

"Then you'll know you weren't in the right position."

"Why do you care so much about me?"

His hazel eyes searched hers, and their gazes darted back and forth together. He smiled, then pushed back in his seat and lifted his glass.

"I think you're interesting," he said, sipping his wine, then added, "and I'd like to sleep with you."

She laughed and bit her lip, not offended.

The alarm on her phone rang to remind her about her flight. "I have to go to the airport." She turned off the ringer and reached for her wallet.

He grimaced at her gesture. "I'm a billionaire."

"Right," she conceded, excusing herself to the restroom.

When she returned, Callum was on the street by a black car. "I ordered you an Uber," he said, opening the door. "But I'm taking this." He held up the *Self* magazine she'd had tucked in the pocket of her carry-on to read on the plane.

"You're taking my ten tips to a flatter stomach?"

"You don't need it," he said. "You're good enough."

"But—"

"And I know that makes you feel like I'm telling you you're not going to make it, but you are," he said.

She stood still, not sure what to say, but feeling like she'd like to kiss him.

"Go." He patted her hip to get moving. "You're going to be late."

"Will I—" she said. "I mean, do you—"

"Want to see you again? Yes," he said. "I'm visiting my niece in New York this weekend. Think you could escape for dinner Saturday?"

"Yes," she said, a bit too quickly. "I mean, Saturday should work."

"It's a date," he said.

"Great." She smiled. "It's a date."

She let her head fall back on the seat, watching the streetlights rush by and feeling her heartbeat light in her chest. *What are you doing?* she asked herself. She could feel her mind spinning but didn't want to stop it, just wanted to sit and spin.

Her head rolled back on the headrest and she noticed a box on the other seat, with a note on top.

I ordered you the berries, but threw in everything else on the
menu in case you were tempted to try. CR.

She opened the box: there were six desserts carefully arranged. She
dipped her finger into a caramel pudding and licked it off with her finger, laughing lightly at herself when a piece fell on her skirt.

NICK

WEDNESDAY, APRIL 16; SAN FRANCISCO, CALIFORNIA

"You have to erase the databases, immediately," Phil Dalton said, making an effort to keep his voice calm. "All *three* of them."

"What are you offering?" Josh Hart asked from across the table.

"This isn't a game, Josh!" Phil slammed his hand on the table angrily.

Nick's chest was tight, his eyes glancing from venture capitalist to
CEO. They were in the fishbowl. The shades were drawn, but the dampness from the bay outside was seeping through the windows, making the
room cold. Rachel Liu was next to him, tapping her pen lightly.

"What three databases?" Nick asked his mentor. "There are only two,
and we—"

"There is information in there that will ruin people's lives, Josh." Phil
tried to keep his voice steady, ignoring Nick.

"There is information that would ruin *your* life, Phil," Josh corrected,
"but maybe you should have thought of that before you started using
the app."

"What are you—" Nick started. Phil was married, with three daughters. Why would he ever use Hook?

"What do you want, Josh?" Rachel intervened.

"Buy me out," Josh said calmly, looking at Phil.

"Your shares are worth a billion dollars."

"Good thing you run a five-billion-dollar fund."

Phil rubbed his eyes. Was he actually considering this? "Even if I did, the road show starts next week. We'd have to disclose that, and then"— he shook his head—"it wouldn't work."

"You could fire him." Rachel turned to Phil.

"You can't fire the CEO right before an IPO," Nick jumped in. Who did she think she was?

But Rachel didn't turn, she kept her eyes on Phil. "Investors don't like him, anyway. We can say the syndicate meeting today made it clear he was no longer the person to be in charge, that the company has out-grown him. We pay him out and then resell those shares in a secondary offering."

Phil looked from Rachel to Josh, who sat back in his chair, waiting.

"Does that work for you?" Phil finally asked Josh.

Josh shrugged. "Fine by me."

"Wait, wait, wait." Nick's mouth was hanging open. "What the hell are we talking about here? You're going to fire Josh and pay him a billion dollars all because of some stupid database?" Nick stood up. "I'm going to call the rest of the board and—"

"Sit down, Nick," Phil commanded. "What's your problem?"

"Well . . ." Nick shook his head in disbelief. He'd just taken out a loan for two million dollars: nothing could jeopardize this IPO. "For one thing, who's going to be CEO? I mean, I'm going to have to work with someone entirely new, and—"

"You, Nick," Phil said, with exasperated patience. "You'll be CEO."

8

TODD

"Where have you been?" Todd snapped at Neha.

"I came straight from the airport," she tried to apologize. "I took the red-eye back—"

"Why weren't you answering your e-mail?" Todd was furious. "Do you seriously expect to get a promotion when you don't answer your fucking BlackBerry?"

The girl looked at the device in her hand, showing him the screen. "Nothing came through, Todd. I don't know what's wrong with it." She started to panic, letting her suitcase drop. "I'll call Tech right away."

"Don't," Todd snapped. "Get in the room. We have to redo everything."

"What? Why?"

"Josh Hart was fired."

"Is Beau here yet?"

"No, Neha!" Todd shouted. "Please just get to work."

This was not good. Not good at all. It was seven forty-five a.m. and Todd had been up since five fifteen. He'd gotten back to New York yesterday morning, feeling great about the syndicate meeting and their momentum heading into the road show.

And then he'd woken up this morning to a call from Tara. He'd ignored it, but picked up when she called again, his still-half-asleep brain imagining that she was booty-calling. But instead she'd asked him if he'd read the e-mail from Nick.

The little punk hadn't even had the balls to call: he'd sent a fucking e-mail at fucking two a.m. our time announcing that he was the new CEO of Hook and "could L.Cecil kindly work with Crowley Brown to revise the necessary documents."

What a fucking prick. Nick knew this fucked up everything. Not only would it be a PR nightmare, it meant they had to redo all the filings, all the marketing materials, all of— "Dammit!" Todd slammed his fist on the table.

"It's okay," Tara said seriously from the seat across from him. "We'll work it out."

She was typing away, calm and steady.

"I just don't understand—"

"Don't waste your energy trying," Tara said. "It is what it is."

"Why were you up at five a.m. anyway?"

"I run in the mornings," she said without looking up.

"At five a.m.?"

"Yes," she said as she typed, as if that weren't insane.

"Fuck. Every day?"

"Sundays I do yoga."

"Jesus. Why?"

"I can't think clearly otherwise," she said, then looked up and admitted, "and I don't want to get fat."

Neha came into the room with her laptop and printouts of all the documents that needed to be redone. "Hi, Tara," she said.

Todd looked at her: since when did she say hello to Tara?

"Hey, Neha." Tara smiled.

"Is Beau coming in?" Neha asked.

"I'm sure he's on his way," Todd said. Who cared about Beau? He was worthless for anything other than being a wingman anyway.

"What happened with Josh?" Neha directed the question to Tara.

What was going on? Todd looked at the girl: she was *his* analyst.

"It's not important, Neha," Todd said sternly. "We just need you to redo the filings, with Nick Winthrop as CEO and all of Josh Hart's holdings going to Dalton Henley, to be included in the initial offering."

"According to Nick," Tara said, ignoring Todd, "Phil Dalton decided Josh wasn't the right person to lead the company forward, and fired him. But Dalton Henley also bought all of his shares, which makes me think it was actually Josh's idea."

"Why? Why would Josh leave when the company's just about to go public?" Neha's brow was furrowed.

"It doesn't matter!" Todd yelled. "Can you please just get to work?"

The two girls finally acknowledged Todd and went back to their computers.

Jesus Christ, Todd thought. Was everyone going mad?

Todd's phone rang. "Hello?" he answered, exasperated.

"What's going on, Mr. Kent?" Harvey Tate's voice was irritated.

"Harvey!" Todd clenched his jaw. This was not what he needed. "Good morning, how are you?"

"Concerned. I heard there have been some changes at Hook."

"Yes," Todd said. How did Harvey Tate know? "But we've got it under control. I think it will be better, actually. Josh was a loose cannon. I think we can convince investors to see the change as a good stabilizer to take Hook to the next level."

"How long is it going to take to amend everything?"

"I don't know," Todd said.

"I don't pay you not to know." Harvey's voice was shifting to anger.

"Sunday," Todd said, confident. "That's my goal. But you know we have to submit everything to the SEC again, and that could take weeks."

"That can't happen," Harvey said. "We need this deal in May."

"I can't control the SEC, Harvey."

"Careful of your tone, Mr. Kent," Harvey said, and Todd felt his stomach churn. "We need to report this deal in our second-quarter earnings. If you can't figure out how to make that happen, I'll find someone who can. Don't think Phil Dalton is the only one with the authority to make personnel changes."

"I'll talk to Crowley Brown and see what we can do," Todd said. "I've got a call scheduled with them at eight."

"You better go, then," Harvey said. Todd looked at his computer: it was 8:02. *Fuck.*

He hung up the phone and dialed Chris Papadopoulos.

"Sorry I'm late," he told the lawyer. Harvey's threat repeated in his ear: he couldn't take him off the deal, could he?

"You're fine," the lawyer said. He sounded like he'd been up all night. "So this is going to put us back at least a month."

"Not possible," Todd said. "The deal has to be finished in Q2."

"It's not me, Todd, it's the SEC."

"You got the first pass filed quickly," Todd insisted, his heart starting to race as reality set in: Harvey *could* replace him. Larry would revel in the opportunity to take this over, and with Josh gone, there was no one at Hook interested in protecting Todd. "Surely there's someone over there you know," he half pleaded.

"Are you asking me to bribe someone at the SEC?"

"No," Todd lied, a second reality—that Chris wasn't going to budge—settling in. But desperation breeds ideas, and Todd suddenly had a thought. "Chris, I gotta go. Neha's working on the updates. Let's talk again end of day."

He hung up and checked his contact folder, his brain moving fast now. He'd slept with a girl at the SEC a few times: what was her name? Joan! Joan Hillier.

He scrambled to dial her number, collecting his breath as the phone rang.

"This is Joan."

"Joan! It's Todd Kent."

There was a pause.

"Joan?" he asked. "I'm sorry, maybe you don't remember me. We—"

"I remember you," she said. "What do you want?"

"Well"—his brain raced—"I know it's been a while, but I wanted to see if I could take you to dinner. I was going through such a shitty time when we met before, and I'm in a better place now, and I think it would be great to get reacquainted." He bit his lip, eyes tightly shut as he waited for her answer.

"What do you really want?"

Todd opened his eyes and hesitated before conceding: "I'm working on a deal and I need"—he paused—"your advice. Because I remember you worked at the SEC at one point, and—"

"I still do," she said. "Which I'm guessing you know since you called my office line."

"I did?" he asked, trying to sound surprised. "I thought it was your cell!"

"Don't bullshit me."

"Listen," he tried again, letting a little desperation seep into his voice, "I'm leading a deal and some things just changed and we're going to have to resubmit our filing and I need it to get through quickly."

There was another pause.

"Where is dinner?" she finally said.

Yes. "Gramercy Tavern?" he suggested. "Eight o'clock?" He needed a restaurant where no one he knew would see him.

"I'll see you then."

"Thank you, Joan." He punched his hand in the air. "I'll—" But she'd already hung up.

"What are you doing?" Tara was staring at him suspiciously.

"Saving this deal."

Tara sighed heavily, looking back at her computer. Was she upset that he was going out with another woman? He felt a wave of vindication, thinking about her drinks with Callum.

"What's wrong?" He couldn't help himself.

"It's not important."

"What?" he pressed. "Are you jealous?"

"My sister's wedding is May tenth," she said.

Todd scoffed, disappointed. "Guess you're off the hook for finding a date." The deal ought to have closed by then, but with the delay, they'd still be neck-deep in the road show that day. There was no way she'd be able to go.

"You're a jerk," she said, and actually seemed to mean it.

He let it go. He had more important things to worry about now.

JUAN

FRIDAY, APRIL 18; SAN FRANCISCO, CALIFORNIA

"I need you to erase the third database—the one that correlates private and collected information," Nick said from across his desk, then added, with a note of accusation, "Don't think I don't know about it."

Juan looked at him carefully. "Is everything okay?"

Nick had sent Juan an e-mail yesterday asking him to meet at seven thirty a.m., before the mandatory all-company town hall at nine. The e-mail had said there would be a sign-in sheet and any employee not in attendance would be fired. Juan was pretty sure half the company had never shown up to work before eleven, and he was cautiously anxious about what might be going on.

"Everything is great," Nick said, sitting back in his chair confidently. "Couldn't be better, actually."

"What is the town hall about?"

"You'll find out at the town hall."

"Why are you dressed up?" Juan asked.

"Some things are going to change around here, Juan." Nick sat up straighter as he said it. "And one of them is that we're going to start acting like professionals."

"Is Josh on board with that?"

"No more questions." Nick's voice dripped with condescension. "Please just erase the database and make sure that from now on any information the app collects from users which they do not provide directly is only stored for twenty-four hours so that statistics can be compiled and that it is then deleted from our servers. You're dismissed."

Juan started to say something, but changed his mind. He stood and returned to his desk, uneasy.

He logged into the third database and opened the code behind it.

It had to be because of Phil Dalton. He was probably afraid someone would find out about his affairs. It made Juan wonder how many of Hook's users were old men using the app to cheat on their wives, and suddenly he felt less proud of its prolific influence.

Juan stared at his screen. Whatever the reason, he should be relieved. If he erased the database, everything would go away: he would never have to worry about Kelly and the user she'd been with the night she died. It would be as if Hook had never collected the information in the first place, and then it would be like it had never even happened. He could just erase it, forget it, collect his two hundred million dollars, and move on.

He sat forward in his chair again and went to work.

WARNING: ACTION WILL PERMANENTLY ERASE DATA FROM SERVER. DO YOU WANT TO CONTINUE?

Juan's finger hovered above the mouse.

Just click it, he told himself.

"Brah, *what* is going on?" Juan jumped and turned to Brogrammer Brad, who put his bag on the seat beside Juan. "Nine freakin' a.m.? I haven't been up this early since, like, high school."

Juan looked at the time: 8:46. He clicked out of the database. It could wait until after the town hall, at least.

"Should we get down there?" Juan asked, standing.

"Totes," Brad said. They picked up breakfast burritos from the cafeteria and made their way to the tiki bar, which was the only room in the building big enough to seat the entire staff.

Someone had set up chairs in long rows, pushing all the palm tree decorations out of the way and installing a podium in place of the life-sized hula girl statue.

"What's going on?" one of the new programmers whispered to Juan.

"I'm not sure," he said, realizing that lots of eyes were on him, searching for a cue.

"Good morning, team." Nick stood behind the podium at precisely nine a.m. "Please make sure you all get your names on the sign-in sheet." He indicated the back door, which had been shut to keep out latecomers.

"I have some exciting news," Nick continued. "As you know, we are set to take Hook public in just a few weeks." He took a proud breath. He was beaming. "And as a public company we will be held to new standards of excellence."

Brad chewed his burrito loudly. "Dude, can I get some ketchup?" he whispered to Juan, indicating Juan's condiment puddle. Juan passed him his container, no longer hungry.

"And our company board, led by the esteemed Phil Dalton of Dalton Henley Venture Partners, has decided that more experienced leadership is necessary to take the company to the next level. Which is why"—he paused and took an audible breath—"they've appointed me as Hook's new CEO, to replace Josh Hart, effective immediately."

The room was still.

"We'll be rolling out some changes over the coming weeks," Nick continued, "some little things to help the company run more smoothly. It's going to be hard work, guys: I've literally got to play two roles now, until we can find a new CFO. But I'm happy to do it for you, and for this company, and for our shareholders. I haven't got time for Q and A," he went on, "but my new assistant, Tiffany"—he smiled across at a fake-tanned blonde, who waved and smiled—"has set up an e-mail account, questions-at-hook-dot-com, for any inquiries."

No one in the room moved.

"Okay," Nick said happily. "Back to work! Everyone have a great day!"

"I can't eat this." Brad dropped his burrito, looking down at the remnants of chorizo and sour cream as if it were the broken pieces of a shattered dream. "I'm so upset, Juan-dizzle."

Juan put his hand on his shoulder. "It's going to be okay, man," he coaxed. "Who cares about Nick? We're about to make a lot of money. We'll quit and start our own thing."

"I don't want to, bro." Brad looked up, his brow pinched, guacamole on the corner of his lip. "I don't want to start something else. I want things to be like they were, only with me and you multigazillionaires."

"Maybe it won't be so bad," Juan said.

"It will," Brad said gloomily, standing up with a pout like a six-foot-five child. "I'm going to the game room to play Halo. I need to be reminded of happier things."

Juan sighed and went back to his computer, but he couldn't work. He read the news about Kelly Jacobson again without reopening the database. The media had reestablished its loyalty to the girl, turning instead on Robby Goodman, the rugby player RA whom police had arrested on charges of her murder.

Just do it, he whispered to himself, closing his browser and navigating back to the server page. *Just do it, and then be done.*

He held his breath, his hands hovering over the keyboard.

He typed in Robby Goodman's name. The college student's profile came up and loaded. Eighty-two meet-ups. Juan scoffed: this guy got around. He sorted by date and clicked to March 6.

Logged In: Xanadu, Stanford University.

Juan zoomed into the map and transposed it with Kelly's. The two dots were close, but they weren't together, far enough apart to be next door from each other, as Robby had said he was that night. That didn't mean anything; he'd probably just left his phone in his room when he went to Kelly's. Still, Juan searched again to find all users within a one-hundred-meter radius of Kelly at three a.m. A dot appeared right on top of hers: the same corrupted profile Juan had found the first time he'd searched Kelly's activity log.

"Shit." Juan felt his heart beat in his throat. He shook his head and clicked out of the map. That didn't mean anything, either. Maybe Robby had gotten another phone to use to murder Kelly, and then hacked into the program to cover his tracks.

Robby didn't seem that clever.

Which meant he was innocent. He'd been in his room, asleep, when Kelly died, just like he'd said.

Juan closed his eyes and shook his head. "Why did you do that?" he whispered to himself.

TARA

FRIDAY, APRIL 18; NEW YORK, NEW YORK

"Will you tell me what's really going on?" Tara asked Rachel. She was in the corner of an empty conference room, talking on her cell phone. Since the latest round of investigations into L.Cecil, the regulators had started recording all the landlines in the firm, and management had responded by casually suggesting that bankers handle potentially delicate calls on their personal devices.

"It was the best choice we had," Rachel said, her voice tired.

"Best choice for what?"

"Do you really want to know?" Rachel asked. It sounded like she was asking whether Tara wanted to be told the details of a massacre.

"Yes," Tara said.

"You really can't ever say anything."

"What happened?" Tara looked down on Park Avenue. The gray sky was raining steadily, clouding the air so it was impossible to tell the time of day, adding to the sense she had that she was in some alternate universe.

"Phil Dalton is more than Hook's number-one investor," Rachel said.

Tara waited.

"He's also Hook's number-one user."

"Ugh." Tara shook her head. "His poor wife."

"Oh, she's fine with it," Rachel said. "Their contract runs out in four years and she gets a twenty-million-dollar payout."

"What?" Tara said. "They have a contract?"

"Phil's gay," Rachel said. "It's not just that he's on Hook: he's on Hook with younger men."

Tara's mouth fell open. "Phil Dalton is gay?" she asked. "Why doesn't he just come out?"

"I don't know," Rachel said, "but he's not the only one, and he's one of the more G-rated."

"Is that your business model?" Tara suddenly realized she'd never asked Rachel how she'd established herself at such a young age as the go-to PR rep for successful men in Silicon Valley. "To cover up private lifestyles of your clients?"

"There's a lot to cover up," Rachel said. "Take socially awkward men, plop them into San Francisco, the sexual fetish mecca of America, and give them billions of dollars to play with? Trust me, I deserve every penny I earn to have to see what I see. Anyway, I guess Josh somehow got a hold of Phil's entire history on the app. Every outreach, every location of every hookup. Phil freaked out and told Josh to delete all the databases, and Josh refused to do it. So Phil offered to buy him out, at which point he put Nick in as CEO, knowing Nick won't say no."

"I thought all the information Hook gathered was unidentifiable." Tara felt a pit in her stomach: that should be in the disclosures. "Can they look up anyone's history?"

"Not anymore," Rachel said. "Nick's erasing everything users don't directly provide."

"Did Josh not care?" Tara asked. "That he's getting pushed out?"

"No," Rachel said. "Josh doesn't care about the company, he just cares about power games. And he definitely established his power over Phil."

"Wow." Tara didn't know what else to say, thinking back on the first day in the fishbowl when Josh commented on her not using Hook. Had he looked up her history? Her skin crawled.

"Still, I'm sorry," Rachel said. "I know it's not ideal for you guys."

"It's okay," Tara said. She was trying not to worry about how she was going to get to her sister's wedding with the deal still going on.

"In other news," Rachel said, "Callum?"

Tara blushed. "I can't believe you did that."

"But you're glad I did?"

"Yeah," she admitted, thinking back on the dessert box. "We were supposed to go out here tomorrow but I had to cancel because of this."

"No!" Rachel said. "Ugh. How does Josh Hart always find a way to ruin everything?"

"It's okay," Tara said. "He's actually in London during the road show so we're going to get together then, assuming there aren't any more delays."

"Fine. Just promise you'll sleep with him and all my work hasn't been in vain," she said. "Oh shit."

"What?"

"Hold on a sec." Rachel switched to another line.

Tara looked back down at the street and watched a couple kiss on the corner, the woman tilting her umbrella out of the way and climbing under his long enough for a peck on the lips before they went their separate ways.

"Hey, Tara?" Rachel's voice came back to the line. "Can you do an interview on CNBC this afternoon?"

"What?"

"They got the news about Josh and need someone to answer a few questions. I can't do it, and I think putting Phil on is a bad idea. And I'm definitely not letting Nick on camera."

"I've never—"

"You'll be great," she said. "I'll give you what to say."

"Yeah, I guess, but I don't know if L.Cecil will let me. I mean, compliance is—"

"I know your head of PR. I'll get it approved."

"Okay," Tara said, acknowledging her excitement. Her? On CNBC?

"Okay. Be at their studios at three. I'll send you the info. I gotta run."

"Sure. Thanks, Rachel."

"No sweat," she said. "Talk to you soon."

TARA LEFT THE CONFERENCE ROOM and went straight to Terrence's desk, where she found her friend deep in concentration at his computer. He noticed her in his peripheral vision and held up a finger to indicate she should wait, without moving his eyes from the screen.

"Tom Ford on Gilt starting in five . . . four . . . three . . . two . . ." Terrence swung into action, clicking rapidly on the screen and typing in his credit card number with expert precision in a race against other buyers vying for the limited quantity of designer goods. "Come on, come on," he coached the screen, waiting for the transaction to go through. "Yes!"

He looked up at Tara and smiled proudly. "Got it."

"I am truly impressed," she said, laughing. "But I need a media tutorial—can you spare an hour?"

"Darling, clearly," Terrence said. "What's the occasion?"

"Me on CNBC—this afternoon."

"This might truly be the greatest day of my professional career," Terrence said, standing and grabbing his coat. "Come with me. We'll stop at Saks on the way."

"Saks?"

He put his finger to her lips to stop her speaking, then moved it to silently point out her undereye circles, un-done hair and wrinkled blouse.

"Yeah, yeah, yeah, I get it," she said, following him to the door.

CHARLIE

"They're going to have to exhume the body," Deb Stein, the attorney Charlie had hired to represent the family, said slowly but firmly.

"I know," he told her, looking at his hands.

"Is your mother prepared for that?" Deb asked.

"Yes," Charlie lied. How could a mother ever be prepared for any of this?

"They probably won't find anything new, but it's important to look at the body again with the lens of malintent."

"I understand."

"Semen will be lost, if there was any, but they'll check the body for signs of force and—"

"Yeah, I got it," Charlie cut her off, standing up. "Is that all?"

"It's going to be harder than this in there, Charlie," Deb said. Her brow was wrinkled with permanent exhaustion.

"I've seen worse," Charlie said.

"It's different when it's your family."

"I can handle it," he repeated.

"I've got a friend," Deb said softly. "She's really good at talking through this stuff. She works with people all the time who—"

"I don't need a shrink," he snapped.

"Right." She raised her hands apologetically, acknowledging she'd crossed the line.

He put on his jacket and walked to California Avenue. It was only four o'clock, but he went to Antonio's Nut House and ordered a beer, deciding it would be the first of many.

He took a seat in the corner and opened Kelly's journal again.

April 11, 2011

I can't believe I'm a Pi Phi. Like, how cool is that to say? Pledge week just started and it's amazing. I came out of class today and a really hot sophomore was waiting with a golf cart and a sign that had my name on it. He drove me home and gave me a candy basket and a Pi Beta Phi sweatshirt. I wore it all afternoon!! And now I'm getting ready to go to White Trash bowling. I was freaking out because I had no idea what to wear, but this other pledge, Emily, was on her way to Diddams so I went with her and we picked the most hilarious costumes. I know I said I'd never be in a sorority, but I think that was just because I didn't understand what they were. I was actually being hypocritical before—I thought sorority girls were shallow and judgmental, but really I was the one being judgmental of <u>them</u>. Sure, some of the girls I met at rush talked like valley girls and this one girl literally sticks her nose up in the air—I think it's like a medical condition—but most of them are <u>really nice</u>. This girl Jess gave me all her study notes when I told her I was stressed about this Chaucer midterm, and Emily and I stayed up until two a.m. yesterday to cheer up another pledge, Jennifer, when she texted to tell us she broke up with her boyfriend. That's <u>exactly</u> the kind of friends I want—people you can party with and who help you, not judge you, for studying, and who stay up late when you've hit a low point. Okay, maybe not all the girls are nice to everyone, but I don't know anyone who's nice to everyone. I think they're just more hated because they're more noticed. And they're more noticed because they're pretty. And that's not their fault. Wow—writing that . . . writing that and knowing that I'm one of them now . . . does that make me pretty? The kind of girl who gets noticed? I think I was the mistake. Or maybe they just picked me because I'm nice.

"Fuckin' hell," a voice called out. Charlie looked up. An older man with long, scraggly gray hair, wearing a worn sweater with a stain on the sleeve, was talking to the TV. If he'd been anywhere else, Charlie would have assumed he was homeless, but he didn't think they had homeless people in Palo Alto.

"See that?" The man pointed at the screen, talking to no one in particular. "These fucking idiot VCs are at it again."

Charlie turned to the TV screen, where the local news was running the headline:

JOSH HART FIRED WEEKS BEFORE HOOK'S IPO

"Hey, Hal, turn it up, would ya?" the man called to the bartender.

"Sure thing, Horace." The bartender climbed on a chair to turn up the volume. Charlie looked up to watch the story.

"Hook, the location-based dating app with headquarters in San Francisco, announced today that its board, led by venture capitalist Phil Dalton, has asked the company's founder, Josh Hart, to step down from his post as CEO, to be replaced by the company's current CFO, Nick Winthrop, just a week before the company was set to begin the road show for its initial public offering, which is expected to value the company at fourteen billion dollars. Neither Hook nor Dalton were available for comment, but Tara Taylor, a representative of L.Cecil, the bank underwriting the deal, has this to say."

Charlie felt his chest tighten as the camera cut to a woman whose name was written at the bottom of the screen; TARA TAYLOR, L.CECIL INVESTMENT BANK. *That* was Tara Taylor? She was attractive and spoke with the precise enunciation and smileless face that screamed alpha bitch. Charlie knew her type from college—the aggressive, feminist girls who sucked everything good out of what it meant to be a woman in pursuit of high-powered jobs. No wonder she hadn't responded to his e-mail. Was that who Kelly would have worked for?

Charlie looked back down at the journal, scanning the pages to see if Kelly had said anything about Tara Taylor, and landed on an entry from her internship last year.

July 21, 2013

I messed up. Like, really messed up. Oh my god I want to crawl in a hole and die. What if the recruiting team finds out? This is absolutely going to ruin my chances of an offer. I mean, no question. It's got to. What am I going to do? I have to find a new job. What if they fire me tomorrow? Then no one will ever hire me, ever. I'm supposed to start with ECM this week, with that girl Tara Taylor. I wanted her to like me so badly, but the minute she finds out about this it's game over. How did I get so drunk? A bunch of us went to dinner at Rosa Mexicano because it was our first weekend off all month. I was admittedly really tipsy—I had like three margaritas, I think. Maybe four. But then Chris ordered shots and I couldn't not do one—they were Patrón and probably cost like seventeen dollars apiece. Plus I guess it was cool to be one of the guys. It was just me and Lizzie Schuster at that point, with seven of the cool guys in our training class. And I was sitting there thinking, "What glass ceiling?" I can totally run with the guys. But then Lizzie ordered shots, too. I don't know what I was thinking, trying to keep up with her drinking: she's six feet tall and on the basketball team at Harvard. But I tried. And I puked in the bathroom after dinner and felt better.

But then we went to this club and they ordered bottle service—like, two entire bottles of vodka and three bottles of champagne for the nine of us—and then I don't know what happened. I just kept drinking and dancing and it all would have been okay if Beau Buckley hadn't shown up. Oh my god: of all the people! He's an associate for Harvey Tate. Like, super-wealthy associate to the senior vice chairman of all of L.Cecil. And he shows up and I'm sure I just flung myself at him and we're making out on the dance floor and the next thing I know I'm waking up in his bed this morning. I think we had sex. Okay, I know we had sex: there was a condom next to the bed this morning. And I can feel it. Like, between my legs, I can feel that I had sex and it makes me want to never leave this room. Why did I think I could do this? Why did I think I could work on Wall Street or live this life or—I don't even know how to get out of it. I wish I were back in Pi Phi—with someone who's been through something like this before and would understand. But none of the girls here would get it and how could I—

"Are you using that chair?" the homeless-looking man asked, gruffly. Charlie looked up at the chair across from him. "No."

"Can I have it?" the man asked. "Need to prop my leg up."

Charlie pushed the chair so the man could lift his leg. His shoe was held together with duct tape.

Charlie looked at his empty glass, then back at the journal, and decided he needed another before he went on. "Can I get you a drink?" he asked the man as he stood.

"Yeah," the man said. "Hirsch Reserve. They've got it behind the bar," he said, then tilted his head. "Help yourself, too. You look nice enough."

Charlie went to the bar and lifted his brow to the bartender. "Hirsch Reserve?"

"For Horace?" The bartender laughed at the man, pulling out a bottle from beneath the bar. "You want one?"

"I don't think so," Charlie said. It was probably moonshine.

"You sure? It's good shit."

"What is it?"

"Sixteen-year-old bourbon. Costs about three hundred a bottle."

"What?" Charlie's face was doubtful.

"Horace's favorite."

"Who is he?"

"You know when you send an e-mail secure? Like you hit that little button and it encrypts the message?"

"Yeah."

"Horace invented that."

"What?" Charlie looked back at the man.

"Swear to God." The bartender nodded. "He's worth about a billion dollars, which is why we're drinking his bourbon. Welcome to Silicon Valley."

Charlie took the glass of liquor back to Horace. "Thanks," Charlie said, indicating his own drink, then scanned the rest of the journal to see if there was anything else about Beau Buckley. He found his name on the last page and braced himself when he saw his own, and then noticed the date.

March 5, 2014

Charlie isn't coming to graduation. He hasn't said it, but I know he won't. And now that I write it, I realize how foolish it was for me to be expecting him to. I guess because he surprised me for high school graduation, I thought maybe he'd do the same for this one. But I thought he'd come visit me at Stanford, too, and he never has, so I should have understood before now that things have changed. It's so funny that he's worried I'll get sucked into L.Cecil and it will change me—as though he hasn't gotten sucked in and let his work change him. Not that I don't admire what he's doing—I just don't know where it ends. And I miss the old Charlie. Like the Charlie who used to roller-skate around New York in fluorescent spandex: is that Charlie even there anymore, or does that necessarily die when you spend all your time around tragedy?

He says they need him over there, but doesn't he realize I need him, too?

God, Kelly, that is so selfish. Syrians are dying and you're hanging out in California going to concerts and accepting a $90,000-a-year job. And I have other people watching out for me—I mean, Tara Taylor <u>wants to be my mentor.</u> She is so amazing—pretty and smart but still totally down to earth. Like that time last summer when she got drunk with us at the closing dinner Beau organized and did all of her impressions of the bosses at L.Cecil—she's smart and driven but still knows how to have fun, you know? Anyway— point is, I don't NEED Charlie anymore, I just WANT him—the old him—back. I feel like that Charlie would have understood why I'm going to L.Cecil and not been so grim about it all.

The world stopped. Charlie stared at the words on the page until they blurred from tears he had forgotten he had the ability to form. His brain raced back to the roller-skating incident: it was a few years after he'd graduated and he was in New York working on a story when his mother called to tell him Kelly had been cut from the high school dance team auditions. He'd called Stuyvesant and said they'd had a family emergency and she needed to be excused from class, then showed up with 1980s costumes and roller skates and taken Kelly to the West Side Highway, where they'd made a scene skating and laughing, finally ending up in Central Park with the hardcore roller skater dancers who were kind enough to let them join despite their novice skills. They didn't ever talk about the dance team, but he knew he'd made her feel better, and that made him feel as good as he'd ever felt.

He hadn't lost that part of himself. But the seriousness . . . the *world* had gotten more serious—between terrorism and technology and religious conflict and greed. Or maybe it had always been that serious, he just hadn't realized it before, safe in his privileged American cocoon.

He felt his defenses rise against the pain of Kelly's words: what was he supposed to do?

"Now this shit," Horace said to no one in particular, "this shit's sad."

Charlie looked up. The news had switched to Robby's trial and the final jury selection going on right now.

"Don't you think?" Horace asked Charlie.

Charlie nodded silently and left the bar.

TODD

Friday, April 18; New York, New York

Todd spotted Joan at the Gramercy Tavern bar, sipping a martini. Her blonde hair was swept into a tight twist and her suit jacket hung on the back of the chair, her arms bare in a silk blouse. She shouldn't have been wearing a sleeveless top, at least not in Manhattan. It wasn't that her arms were fat, their lack of definition just looked grossly out of place on an island of Pilates-toned limbs.

Todd took a breath: he could do this. He had to. His job depended on it.

"Can I help you?" the hostess asked.

"Reservation for two, under Todd Kent," he told her. It had taken him an hour of calls, three personal favors, and one lie (that his dying-from-cancer cousin was in town) to get the reservation. "My dining partner's right over there."

He tapped Joan's shoulder lightly and smiled. "Don't you look lovely," he said.

"Todd Kent," Joan said, sounding practiced. "It's really nice to see you."

"And you." His grin was set. It wasn't just her arms: her face had gotten pudgier, too.

"So how have you been?" he asked as they sat at a table in the back. "You look really wonderful."

"You're lying, but I'll take it."

"I'm not," he lied. "You know I always found you sexy."

Her eyes paused on him for a second before looking down at the menu. Todd could feel his palms sweat. What if this didn't work? He thought about the deal, his bonus, his reputation. It had to work.

"Could we have a bottle of champagne, please?" he asked the waiter.

"We've got the list right here." The man handed him a thick leather-bound notebook. "Sparkling wines start on page twenty-one."

"Why don't you bring your favorite? We're celebrating."

"Your tastes have matured," Joan said.

"So have I. I'm really sorry about how things ended," he said, trying to remember how, exactly, things had ended.

"Let's not talk about it," she suggested.

The waiter arrived and showed him the bottle of champagne and Todd approved it. Once the glasses were filled, he toasted Joan: "To fresh starts."

"To fresh starts," she said.

They ordered dinner and another bottle of wine and Todd searched for things to talk about.

"So how is working at the SEC?"

"Awful," she said. "It's gotten even worse since the crisis, as you can imagine."

"Why?" He'd never thought about it. The SEC was where people who couldn't cut it on Wall Street went to work. There was no point in going to the trouble of understanding the financial markets in order to collect a government salary when, if you had half a brain, you could make ten times as much at a real firm. It was why the whole idea of government regulation was so absurd: as if the government would *ever* attract talented enough employees to regulate what the more sophisticated talent on Wall Street was doing.

"Way too much work, not enough staff," Joan said. "Even if it were easy, there's no way we could ever do a thorough job. And it's not easy, as I'm sure you can also imagine."

"I'm sure." He tried to sound sensitive but didn't really care.

"So what's going on with Hook?"

"How did you know I'm working on Hook?"

"I approved the first S-1."

"You did?" he asked. "Thanks for getting it through so quickly." He relaxed: she was on his side, so long as he didn't fuck tonight up.

"It's fine," she said, taking a bite of her duck. What woman ordered duck? Especially at her weight?

"Well, I'm sure you heard that Josh Hart is leaving," he said, "and Dalton Henley is buying him out."

"So he'll have no ownership in Hook at all?"

"None," he said.

"Is he upset?"

"No." Todd shook his head. "Everyone agrees it's for the best."

She looked skeptical. "What happened?"

Todd shrugged. "I think everyone just realized Josh is a programmer, not a CEO."

"Yeah, right."

"What?" Todd asked honestly. After spending a day convincing other people of the story, he felt confident in it.

"Nothing," she said. "When are you submitting your new docs?"

"Sunday."

"I'll take a look on Monday," she said. "Unless there's anything really wrong, you should be able to start the road show the following week. You said you need it done by end of Q2, right? That should keep you on schedule."

"You are seriously the greatest." Todd clinked her glass, his chest melting with relief.

The waiter came back with the dessert menu. Todd ordered an espresso martini, deciding the best course of action now was to get very, very drunk. Or maybe he could get her very, very drunk, and then she'd pass out before they had to have sex?

He sipped his martini and ordered a cheese plate.

She polished off a chocolate torte and ate the petits fours.

She excused herself to the bathroom as he gave the waiter his corporate card.

"Todd?" He looked up at the familiar voice. Louisa LeMay, his old fuck buddy, stood slim beside the table. Her tight black dress clung to her tiny waist at his eye level, and her face glowed in a slightly tipsy smile.

"Louisa?" His heart caught. "What are you doing here?"

She turned her gaze toward the bar, where an old man was sipping a scotch, grinning at her. She smiled back at him. "Too many martinis," she laughed, lifting her fingers to indicate she was on her third.

"How long are you in town? Can I take you out?" he asked, the memory of her body against his making him forget how much work he had to do before Sunday.

"I go back tomorrow," she said, then added, "And it probably wouldn't be appropriate anyway."

"Why not?"

She bit her lip and blushed. "I think I might be in love," she said, lifting her shoulders. "Can you believe it? Me?"

Todd's jaw dropped. He looked back at the man at the bar. He was old and not even attractive. "What?" he snapped, not comprehending.

She shrugged. "I don't know. Something just happened. I didn't think I'd ever want to settle down, but this guy is just so . . ."

Joan came back to the table, looking at Louisa, who turned. "Hi, I'm Louisa."

"Joan." The two women shook hands.

"Anyway," Louisa said to Todd, "I'll let you get back to each other, but really nice to see you, Todd, and great to meet you, Joan." Her happiness made him want to vomit.

Joan's eyes followed her back to the bar, studying her jealously.

"Is that Callum Rees?" she asked, and Todd realized she was looking at the man, not Louisa.

He turned. "What?"

"Callum Rees. The billionaire who started all those companies."

"No way." Todd turned. "Is it?"

"I think so." She lifted her brow. "Good for Louisa."

The waiter returned with Todd's credit card before he could process Louisa falling in love with Callum Rees. He looked at the receipt, then coughed: the bill was $3,618. "Shit." He looked up at the champagne: it was $2,600, and didn't even taste good.

"Everything okay?" Joan asked.

"Absolutely." He smiled. The normal expense limit for client dinners was three hundred dollars a head, but he'd get the bill approved once he explained the reason: keeping the deal from getting delayed was worth a lot more to L.Cecil than thirty-six hundred.

He helped her out of her chair and tested his willpower, putting his arm on the small of her back as they left the restaurant. He hoped Louisa wasn't looking. Ordinarily, he'd try to make her jealous, but being with a woman like Joan just made him feel foolish. But when he glanced back at her, she was laughing with Callum, absorbed in their conversation and oblivious to Todd. It would have been more comfortable if she'd just slapped him in the face.

"Are you going uptown?" Joan interrupted his disappointment.

"Just across," he said. "It's a nice night—do you want to walk?" He needed more time. She was not attractive and had just eaten more than a linebacker, and seeing her side by side with Louisa had made it all even worse.

"I'm on Eighty-seventh and York," she said. "It'd be a bit of a hike."

"Oh, I'll get us a cab, then," he said, reaching out his hand and praying she didn't have cats.

A car arrived and he opened the door for her. "It was good to see you, Todd," she said, climbing in and putting her hand on the door to close it. "Congratulations on your continued rise."

"Wha—" He stared at her extended arm. "I—"

"What?" she asked, pausing.

He looked up, shaking his head, dumbfounded. Was she leaving? Without him?

"What kind of person do you think I am, Todd?" She laughed.

"I thought you—" he started, his brain trying to compute: she *didn't* want to sleep with him?

"Wanted to get a good dinner," she finished his sentence. "We never get this shit in government. Have a good night, Todd." She laughed again, pulling the cab door shut.

"Yeah, you too," he said to the already closed door. "And thanks," he called after the cab.

He started walking west, his heart emptying with drunken relief that the deal was saved and he didn't have to sleep with Joan, and disappointment that someone else was going to sleep with Louisa. *Whatever:* she wasn't who he thought she was—just another shallow girl who wanted to lock a man down. And Todd didn't want to be locked down any more than he wanted to sleep with Joan Hillier.

Still: Why *didn't* Joan Hillier want to sleep with him? And why *didn't* Louisa want to lock him down?

Todd paused on the corner and logged into Hook. He sent a message to a cute blonde:

> You have to forgive me if this is forward, but I find you so
> stunning . . . do you want to have a drink with me?

He copy-pasted the message to six other girls who were within a mile radius. Four wrote back before he got to Fifth Avenue. He picked the one closest to his apartment and met her at the door.

9

AMANDA

Amanda opened a bottle of wine and poured an oversized glass. She sat on the edge of the sofa, taking a deep breath, opening the LSAT study book.

She stared at the words, but didn't read them. San Francisco sucked.

The weather sucked, which no one had bothered to mention, blatantly lying with their *"Oh, lucky you to be going to California and escaping East Coast cold"* farewells when she'd left New York. But here she was, trapped in microclimate arctic hell, the damp rain chilling her bones and ruining her shoes. Shoes she wasn't even sure why she bothered to wear: no one wore heels in this city, or dressed up at all. She could let herself go entirely and would *still* be the most attractive person for miles and it would *still* suck because the guys here were all so arrogant. But not like New York guys were arrogant: New York guys at least had fashion and taste to show for their egos. Here the guys derived their inflated sense of self-worth from knowledge of which start-ups had funding and who had been in TechCrunch and which farmers' market had the best locally sourced raw organic gluten-free sustainable kale chips with biodegradable packaging.

Which is why Amanda was going to law school. It hadn't been a mistake, coming to California, because now she had more confidence that grad school was the right move. There would be great men in law school, men who were smart in a not-computer-programmer way and—oh, fuck, what did she know? She pushed the books off the table and sat back on the couch, taking a gulp of her wine.

Maybe the problem was her: maybe she expected too much. At the end of the day she hadn't done anything particularly noteworthy. Sure, she'd gone to a good university and worked at a good law firm, but she'd never led a deal or started a company. She'd never even had a boyfriend. Maybe she didn't deserve to be remembered by a guy like Todd Kent, or respected by a guy like Ben Loftis.

She finished the glass of wine and poured another, then reached for the remote. The TV came on to CNBC.

They were reporting on the Kelly Jacobson case again. The police had found a water bottle with Molly residue on it and arrested Robby Goodman, accusing him of lacing the water bottle and giving it to the girl so he could have sex with her.

"Do you think he did it?" Julie asked.

Amanda jumped, startled to find Julie standing behind her. She turned back to the TV and shrugged. "Does it matter?"

"Of course it matters," Julie said seriously.

"Not really. I mean, his life is over either way."

"But what if he's innocent?"

"Even if he's innocent of the murder, they'll dig up enough to prove he's a douchebag."

"That's not a crime," Julie said. "Everyone gets drunk in college."

"And a lot of people try drugs like Kelly did," Amanda said. "But once the media decides to portray someone as a villain, no one is going to risk his own reputation to identify with him. It's why the media basically runs the legal system now. It's so fucked up," she said.

"Is that why you want to be a lawyer? To fix it?"

"Don't be naive." She rolled her eyes. Why did everyone in San Francisco think their purpose in life was to change the world? "It's human nature to create heroes and villains. You can't fix that."

The TV shut off and Amanda turned to Julie, who held the remote in her hand but was looking at Amanda, her jaw set.

"What did you do that for?"

"Get a jacket," Julie commanded.

"What?"

"You're being a bitch," she said. "Now get a jacket. We're leaving."

"But I've got to—"

Julie cut her off with a glare.

"Fine," she said, standing from the couch and picking up her fleece.

She followed Julie out the door onto the street, walking quickly to keep up with the girl's irritated clip. She'd never seen Julie in a less than deliriously exuberant state and wasn't sure what to make of it.

THEY GOT TO THE TIPSY PIG and Julie led Amanda to a table on the patio in the back, where a heat lamp warded off the damp evening air. The patio was pretty, strung with flowers and arching trees above the wooden picnic tables where groups and couples dined.

"I'll have a Kentucky mule and she'll start with water. We'll share a mac and cheese," Julie told the waitress, before turning to Amanda. "Now," she said, "what's the matter?"

"What?" Amanda said defensively.

"You've been moping for the past two weeks, and it's getting annoying

to be around," she said bluntly. "So why don't we talk about whatever set
you off, so you can start to get over it and put us all out of your misery."

Amanda's jaw dropped. Where had this Julie come from? "I—"
Amanda started.

Julie waited.

"There's a guy," Amanda finally said. "Todd Kent. One of the bankers working on your IPO. We used to date. When I was in New York."

"Did you really date?"

"What do you mean?"

"I mean, did you actually go on dates."

"Not exactly. But it's different in New York. Men don't—"

"So you used to hook up with Todd Kent," Julie corrected. "You did
not date him, although you wanted to."

"Yes," Amanda conceded. She made it seem so . . . uncomplicated.

"Then what happened?"

"Then I moved here, and I saw him," Amanda said, then corrected,
"I mean, I heard he was here, and I went to see him, and he didn't"—
she'd never said it, even to herself—"remember me."

"So he's an asshole," Julie said.

"No"—Amanda shook her head—"he's just—"

"Conceited, self-centered, thoughtless and rude."

"But he could be—"

"But he isn't," Julie corrected.

"I think guys like that can change, when they meet the right girl."

"Which you clearly are not, given he didn't remember you after you
slept with him."

Amanda looked at her hands. Was it really that simple? And that
obvious?

"If it makes you feel any better, Beau was exactly the same way," Julie
said. "You know he hasn't texted in two weeks? We finally had sex and
then, poof! Gone! Just leaving me to wonder whether I wasn't good or

something." She rolled her eyes. "What a waste. I've probably spent ten hours thinking about it this past week—can you imagine how much happier I'd have been if I spent that time on something productive? I think I'll take a year off of men."

"You're twenty-six." Amanda made a face. "You can't do that."

"Why not?"

"You'll miss your window."

Julie looked straight at her, her eyes full of pity that made Amanda feel vulnerable and exposed. "Please don't tell me you actually believe your value has an expiration date," she said.

"I—" she started, caught off guard. "I guess I'm just afraid of ending up alone," Amanda finally admitted. "My mother," she added, "is alone. And she's . . . pathetic."

"Are you like your mother?" Julie asked softly.

"God, no." Amanda recoiled at the thought. Her mother had dropped out of a tiny college in Florida to marry her father. She'd lived off alimony since the divorce, always too much of a snob from her decade of marriage to a doctor to get any of the jobs her modest education made available.

"So how could you end up like her?"

"If a man—" Amanda started, then stopped. She'd never thought about it that way before.

"Even if you did end up alone—and you won't because you're gorgeous and smart and nice when you're not all up in your own head—you still wouldn't have to have your mother's life."

Amanda sat for a long moment considering the thought.

"Here you go," the waitress said, delivering their mac and cheese with two forks.

"She can have a drink now," Julie told the waitress.

The girls ate the mac and cheese and drank another round. They talked about how jealous they both were that Juan got to go to London for the Hook road show, and Julie opened up about how she had started

Stanford as a computer science major, but could never get anyone to take her seriously. She'd taken the job at Hook as a receptionist so she could see all parts of the business. And she had: no one paid attention to the receptionist, so she'd quietly become privy to how things got done in the organization, and which employees were set to bounce after the IPO.

Two guys came up and asked if they could join and Julie said "yes" before Amanda could say "no" and after fifteen minutes they actually weren't so bad, even though all they talked about was the company they were starting that made no sense but had apparently gotten one million dollars in funding.

The bar closed at one o'clock and the girls said good night to the guys and walked home in the fog that no longer seemed so grim. It was late and Amanda had had a lot to drink, but her mind was clear and energized, and she was happy in a way that felt real.

"What if we started a company together?" she mused.

"What?" Julie asked.

"We're way smarter than those guys we just met, and they got one million . . ." Amanda said, the idea feeling like one of the more reasonable ones she'd ever had. "And with all the extra time we'll have if we both take a year off men . . ."

Julie's lips curled into a smile and Amanda felt her heart flutter, seeing a new—better—path unfold before her.

NICK

THURSDAY, MAY 1; LONDON, ENGLAND

This was how life was supposed to be, Nick thought as the plane touched down in London. He was meant to be taking international trips on

private jets, heading to meetings where the most important fund managers in the world gathered to listen to him speak about his company's
potential, while guys like Todd and girls like Tara catered to his needs.
Finally, the universe was recognizing his importance within it.

A black limousine was waiting to drive them to the hotel, a Four Seasons on Park Lane.

"I thought I asked that we stay at a Starwood property?" He turned
to Tara in the car.

"You're going to spend all of three hours in your room, Nick," she
said.

"All the more reason to stay somewhere I can collect points." He'd
made a firm commitment that no matter how rich he got, he was never
going to be the kind of person who threw away money by disregarding
loyalty programs. "Can you make sure that we're properly booked for
other cities?"

"I'll see what we can do," she conceded.

"Next time, please don't make me ask twice," he pressed. "Tiffany,
can you make sure she follows up?" he said, turning to his new assistant.

"Sure thing, Nick." Tiffany smiled warmly.

Snatching up Tiffany, the assistant at Darrell Greene's office, had
been Nick's first move as CEO. She'd been expensive—$275,000 a
year—but it was worth it to have someone you could trust. Plus she was
a certified notary.

Nick wasn't trying to be difficult by asking about the hotel, he just
knew it was critical, in this early stage as leader, to set the right prece-
dents. All eyes were on him, watching to see how he'd handle his new
responsibility, making judgments based on every little move. People
were going to test him, and if he let them get away with the slightest
mediocrity, they'd think he was weak.

And Tara Taylor was at the top of that list. She'd snuck her way onto
CNBC to talk about the changes at the company—a privilege and

responsibility that clearly belonged to Nick. She'd said it was Rachel's idea, but he sensed she was behind it. Tara was more clever than he'd originally thought: she hid behind her nice, pretty, play-dumb-girl persona, but she knew exactly what she was doing going on CNBC, and he was not about to let her steal any more of his moments to boost her own career.

THE FIRST PRESENTATION went off without a hitch. As did the second, and the third. All the fund managers loved Silicon Valley and wanted to be part of the world Nick was creating. At six o'clock, the black cars whisked them across London to Shoreditch House, the members-only club where they were having dinner with an exclusive list of British fund managers. Everything else had just been a warm-up for these guys.

Nick checked his phone for Facebook "Likes" on his job status change to CEO: only three. Maybe he had accidentally disabled something? He checked his settings, then went to his own news feed.

Grace had posted on her wall: *Kelly Jacobson Memorial Fund Hits $2 Million!!!!*

There were 328 "Likes" and 200 comments on Grace's post, the first of which was from some guy named James: *Awesome work, Grace. You are such a Rockstar!*

Nick's stomach turned. He clicked on James's profile. SAE, on the golf team, last job: summer intern, J.P. Morgan. He clicked on his photos and found a whole set from some formal he went to with Grace, both of them obviously drunk and having a good time.

Nick fumed, shutting off the phone. Screw her.

The cars stopped.

"This is it?" Nick glanced out the window: the sidewalks were grimy, intersecting with concrete walls covered in graffiti. Grungy pedestrians passed by without noticing the black cars, save a girl in a flannel shirt and hat who spat on the car ahead of Nick's.

"Welcome to East London," Beau said as the driver opened the door. Nick hesitated before getting out. "Is it safe?"

"So long as you leave the Timbuk2 bag in the car, you should be fine," Beau said, pointing to Nick's Hook-monogrammed briefcase. "It kinda screams 'I'm packing Apple devices.'" The associate grinned playfully and Nick glared back. How dare he mock the CEO of Hook?

But Nick left the bag as a precaution, after pulling out his hand sanitizer, and moved quickly to follow Beau inside.

Once they got in the door, things were better, but still not to Nick's taste. They followed the hostess through the bar. The people there looked ridiculous. They wore clothes that tried too hard. Why couldn't people just wear suits, like he was?

Calm down, Nick told himself, feeling the dampness under his arms and admitting he was nervous. They got to a private room in the back, where he took the seat at the center of the table and greeted the fund managers as they entered, relieved that they were all wearing suits.

"What is it you do?" Nick asked one of them.

"I'm at Clyde Capital," the man said in an English accent.

Which one was Clyde Capital? Nick was losing track. He needed one of those earpieces like the president wore, so someone could feed him information and he'd always look smart.

They sat for dinner but Nick remained standing, coughing to indicate he was ready to deliver his remarks. "Juan, can you please pass out the presentations?"

Tara shook her head, but he ignored her. She'd said they shouldn't give the full presentation at this meeting, but Nick knew she was just trying to keep the attention on her. He could read the crowd, and they wanted to hear from him.

TARA

Tara sat back in her seat and sipped her second glass of wine, careful not to drink too much even though she wanted nothing more than to be drunk enough to find this all amusing.

Nick might actually be the most annoying guy on the planet. She hadn't thought he could get any more arrogant, but man, oh man, was she wrong. The CEO title had taken his ego to astronomical heights, without lending any degree of self-awareness or sociability or skill. He'd spoken for *twenty-five* minutes at this dinner, as if any of these men cared at all about the presentation. As she'd told Nick a dozen times, they were already buying shares: she'd gotten verbal commitments from all of them, and she offered this dinner as a thank-you to stroke their egos and meet them all in person. Now she worried that seeing Nick would make them change their minds.

Rachel had been right: Shoreditch House was the perfect choice for the dinner. It was edgy enough to make the investors feel young and give them a sense of the crowd that used Hook, but the private members' club still had the kind of overpriced menu and designer hand soap in the bathrooms that made them feel comfortable. And now that the men—it was all men, of course—had had six cocktails apiece and Todd had taken center court from Nick, they seemed to be plenty comfortable.

"So there I am in Bagatelle. It's three in the afternoon and the shades are down, the music pumping, two waitresses in tight spandex dresses assigned exclusively to our table. And I'm standing up on the sofa, so I can see the talent on the floor," Todd said, his grin broad, "and the champagne is just flowing, you know—sparklers in every bottle and all the girls just going totally nuts every time they bring a new bottle out.

And Manimal is in the bathroom banging some chick—that's totally his move—and all of a sudden these two girls show up and climb on the table in front of me, but they're pissed, holding their phones in my face and showing me the identical messages I'd just sent them on Hook."

"Shit," a balding man with pink cheeks and a gap between his teeth said. "What'd you do?"

Todd paused and grinned. "Gave them each a sparkler and told them there was enough of me to go around."

"You had a threesome?"

"I'm nothing if not a great problem solver," Todd said proudly. "Though I'm sorry to say by the end of it I think they were more into each other than me."

A short, squat man with a big nose shook his head in envy. "Hell. If I'd had Hook when I was single . . ." he mused.

"You've gotta come to Ibiza with me next year," the American expat seated next to Todd said. "The two of us together would *crush* it. The babes there . . ." He kissed his fingers and waved them in the air. American expats in London were the worst.

"Miss Taylor?" The waitress entered the room and the men catcalled to acknowledge their approval of her physique.

Tara looked up. The waitress gave a tired smile. "Mr. Rees is here," she said to Tara.

Tara checked her watch. It was eleven thirty. How was it already eleven thirty? "Thank you," she said. "Gentlemen, you'll have to excuse me." Tara smiled as she stood from the table.

"Oh, don't leave," the pink-faced, gap-toothed man said. "You were the only thing worth looking at at this table."

"Don't be silly," Tara said without a hitch. "Todd's far prettier than me." She winked at her colleague and the table laughed merrily at her willingness to play along.

"At least you were keeping us in control: no telling where this night will end now," another man said, reaching around to grab her hand as she passed behind his chair.

She gritted her teeth and forced a smile. "So long as you buy lots of Hook shares, and have these boys on the plane tomorrow"—she pointed to Todd and Nick—"I genuinely don't care what you do tonight."

"At last, the perfect woman," the balding man joked to the rest of the men, who all nodded in agreement.

"Good night." She waved and turned to the door.

"You scored with that one," she heard someone tell Todd.

"I'd rather be the one scoring with her now," another said.

She closed the door and rolled her eyes. Had it always been this bad? She sighed and let it go, allowing herself to be happy about the night ahead.

She checked her e-mail as she walked to the elevator: fifty-eight new messages during dinner. She scrolled through, looking for urgent flags, and stopped when she saw the subject line: "KELLY JACOBSON."

She opened the e-mail and read:

Tara—I'm Kelly Jacobson's brother, and I'm writing to you
because . . .

"Tara," Todd interrupted, touching her shoulder. "What's wrong?"

"Oh, I—" She looked up, then quickly put the BlackBerry away. "Nothing. What's up?"

"Where are you going?"

"To meet a friend," she said, pressing the button for the elevator.

"Why don't you bring your friend to the club with us? Be a team player?"

Beau had organized bottle service at a club in South Kensington for Nick and the team after the Shoreditch House meeting. No one ever slept on road shows. When there were only five hours between when the last meeting ended and the car left for the airport to head to the next city, it was easy to think there wasn't much difference between two hours' sleep and four.

"I think I'll pass," she said. "Though watching Nick try to pick up foreign women does sound terribly amusing."

"Who's your friend?" Todd pressed, stepping to face her so their bodies were close in the narrow hallway. She could smell the scotch on his breath and see the laugh lines starting to show on his cheeks and forehead. They made him look less like a Ken doll and more like a man.

His blue eyes stared into hers, the way they had when they'd slept together so many years ago, asking silently if she was okay as he pressed inside of her.

What had happened to make him the guy who bragged to investors about threesomes at boozy Meatpacking clubs? Did he really still think that was impressive?

"I'm meeting Callum," she said, taking her eyes away from his.

"What are you doing, Tara?"

"It's none of your business."

The elevator doors opened and Tara stepped inside.

"Don't you think you deserve better?" he said, putting his hand out to block the doors from closing.

She searched his eyes for meaning. *Better?* she thought. *Like your one-night stands, or Mr. Catherine Wiley's public drunkenness, or Phil Dalton's homosexual affairs?*

"There is nothing better, Todd," she said. "I'll see you in the morning."

He stared at her for a moment before moving his hand. She let the doors close, grateful for the few moments alone.

She was going to sleep with Callum, she'd decided. It had been almost a year since she'd had sex—a drunken night out at a bar where she ran into a guy she knew in undergrad and let loose for a night—or, rather, two hours, after which she'd taken a cab home to sleep in her own bed. But she was a grown, single woman, and it was normal for people in her position to have sex with people they found attractive. And she did find Callum attractive, and so she was going to sleep with him, like a normal person, and not worry about what people might say if they ever suspected it.

"How was it?" Callum greeted her as she stepped off the elevator, standing by the front desk in his jeans-and-leather-jacket uniform.

"How do you think?"

He kissed her cheek, letting his hand reach lightly to her waist, inside her open suit jacket. "Full of drunk Englishmen hitting on you?"

"They were more in love with Todd."

He held her hand and led her outside, where a black Aston Martin coupe was waiting.

The car zipped through East London, silencing the sounds outside. It was the closest she'd ever felt to feeling invisible, in a superhero kind of way: looking out the window at the busy streets and traffic and knowing they ought to be accompanied by noise and bad odor and the tenseness of keeping your purse close, none of which existed behind the steady purr of the performance engine.

"So what'd you have to miss to hang out with me?"

"Bottle service at Boujis."

"Of course they're going to Boujis." He laughed, bemused.

"Where are we going instead?" she asked.

"What are you in the mood for?"

"Oh, I don't know."

"Liar."

"What?" she asked innocently.

"I'm not so dumb as to believe a woman like you hasn't thought this night out."

"I don't know what you're talking about."

"If you knew you had one more hour to live, but you had to spend it with me, and you could be absolutely certain I'd say yes, what would you propose?"

"I—"

"Be honest."

"I can't say it." She laughed.

"I'm going to make you."

"Fine. If I could have anything, I guess I'd want to . . ." She rolled her eyes, blushing furiously. Why was it so hard? "Be . . ." She emphasized the word—that was the right word, right? ". . . with you."

Callum grinned and his eyes darted coyly. She laughed, relieved. "Back to mine, then?" he asked.

"Sure." She nodded. He shifted the gear and placed his hand casually on her leg, and her skin tingled.

They circled back toward Shoreditch and he pulled into the garage under a large block warehouse, where he helped her out of the car.

"Where are you taking me?"

"Scared?" He lifted a brow.

The elevator shaft was naked, a series of exposed beams in the corner of the garage that clanked and screeched as they rode it to the top floor. But the doors opened onto a spotless, spacious loft enclosed by floor-to-ceiling windows that looked out on the London skyline and the twinkling lights of cars on the street below.

"Wow," she said, stepping into the room.

"Views are one of my indulgences," he said. "Can I get you a glass of wine?"

"Sure," she said, moving to the window. She'd thought the view from Shoreditch House was nice, but this was another level. The Gherkin twinkled like a diamond egg, glistening against the dark night sky, mocking the ordinariness of the other buildings.

"My dear." Callum handed her a glass of red wine and stood by her side, taking in the view. He pulled a stool from the aluminum bar and perched on its edge.

"Do you worry it'll get old?" she asked, imagining what it was like waking up to this view, day in and day out.

"If it does, I'll move," he said simply.

"Do you think there's anything that doesn't get old, after a while?"

"I think that fear is not a good reason to avoid things that are novel to you."

"But what if—"

"Shhh . . ." He put his finger gently on her lips. "Stop talking."

He pulled her hand up to his and kissed her fingers, keeping his eyes smiling on hers, before putting her hand behind his neck and moving his own to the small of her back.

Their lips pressed together and her body melted.

He lifted her onto the stool so their faces were on the same level. She hooked her heels on the crossbeam and let her skirt slide up so his torso rested between her legs. His lips moved to her neck and a shiver ran down her spine. She'd forgotten how good it felt to be kissed, and knew it had never felt like this.

Her hands played with his hair as his lips moved down her neck and she reached to pull off her blouse. She caught the reflection in the window: this man kissing her chest, mingled with the city's lights and bustle, and she realized this was what women meant when they talked about feeling sexy.

He stopped and put his hand to her cheek. "Are you okay?" he asked gently.

She nodded, smiling, and let her forehead fall on his. He smiled back, and picked her up to carry her to the bedroom.

He pushed her onto the bed and she arched her back as his lips resumed their kisses. He slid his hand to unsnap her bra in a single movement, and she hesitated with the ease of his motion, remembering his playboy reputation. *Don't think about it,* she told herself. He took his own shirt off and slid his forearm behind her arched waist and pulled her effortlessly up so that her head was on the pillow. She willed her brain to stop thinking about why he wasn't at all clumsy: *Who cares? Just appreciate that he knows what he's doing.*

His lips continued their trajectory to her navel and the top of her lace underwear as he unzipped her skirt and pushed it down over her ankles. *How many girls have been in this bed?* She felt her body tense as he moved his lips between her legs and she became conscious of her stubble: it had been four days since she'd shaved. *How did you forget to shave?* she screamed at herself. *Katerina wouldn't have forgotten to shave.*

She ran her fingers through his hair and whispered, "It's okay," coaxing him back toward her face. He batted her hand away as he gently kissed her inner thigh. His warm breath gave her chills and she closed her eyes, willing herself to relax. But she couldn't now. Not with him *there*, comparing her to all the others, who had remembered to get waxed and lasered and trimmed—all those women who knew what to do when a man was doing *this*.

She moaned with pleasure so he wouldn't think she was rude. "Yes, there," she said in as sexy a voice as she could muster. It feels good, she told herself, his tongue moving here and there and right *there* and "Oh," she caught herself. How long had he been down there? Too long. She put both hands in his hair and gently pulled his head up. "Come on," she said. "Let's do this together." He looked at her and cocked his eyebrow skeptically. "I just started," he countered. "Relax." And he resumed his efforts.

"Come on," she whispered again, more firmly this time. "I just want to feel you inside of me."

"Do you mean it?" He slid his body back upward so he was on his hands and knees over her, his eyes not believing her.

"Yes," she insisted, brushing his hair back behind his ear.

"I wish you would let me," he said.

She shook her head. "I'm sorry. I'm not good at this."

"That isn't true; just relax," he whispered, reaching for a condom while he unbuckled his pants.

He pressed himself inside of her and the feeling made her forget the other women.

"Yes," she said, meaning it this time.

His hands were firm on her body, directing her with the same masculine authority as they'd directed the car's gearshift. A thin film of perspiration formed on his body, mingling with her own, and the stickiness made her feel alive, connected, like there was pleasure in the imperfect.

"I'm almost there," she whispered, knowing she wasn't, and he moved faster.

"Come."

"You first," he said.

She hesitated again. "Okay," she breathed more heavily.

"Don't fake it," he said.

"I—" she started.

"Don't," he said.

"I'm not going to," she admitted.

But he was already there, and grunted, his muscles relaxing around her body. She tried not to move, letting him have his moment while her own heartbeat slowed.

He rolled over onto his back, breathing heavily. "Wow," he finally said.

"That was great," she agreed, rolling onto her side to face him.

"You didn't come," he said without opening his eyes.

"I never do," she admitted. "Don't take it personally." Then she added, "Not that I do this often."

He laughed, still catching his breath. "We'll get you there."

She smiled, comforted by the thought he didn't want this to be the only time.

A noise rang from the other room.

"What's that?" he asked when it didn't stop.

"My phone alarm," she realized. She'd set it for nine a.m. and nine p.m. to remind her to take her Celexa, which she'd upped to twice a day. But they were in London, so the alarm was five hours ahead.

She pulled her legs out of bed and found her underwear in the sheets, then pulled on her blouse.

"Stay naked," he said from his pillow. "Why can't you accept how hot you are?"

She laughed at his compliment—didn't he realize he'd already gotten laid?—and went to the other room, turning off her phone and digging for her pills. She saw her BlackBerry light flashing but ignored it: whatever it was could wait three hours. She poured a glass of water and came back to bed, swallowing her Celexa, half a Xanax and a handful of vitamins.

"You take drugs?" he asked. He'd sat up in bed and was typing something on his BlackBerry.

"Yes, I'm an addict."

"Of what?"

"Birth control, vitamin B, ginkgo, calcium, Celexa," she said, leaving out the Xanax, which she worried would give the impression she had issues.

"Celexa?" He looked up from his BlackBerry and made a face. "Are you depressed?"

"I've been on it for a long time," she said.

"How long?"

"Since I was fourteen."

"Bloody hell, no wonder you can't have orgasms."

"What?"

"It's a libido suppressant. So is birth control," he said, returning to his device.

Was that true? Her doctor had never mentioned that.

"Why are you depressed?" he continued without looking up.

"I'm not depressed," she said defensively, crawling back into bed and taking her blouse off again.

"Then why do you take an antidepressant?"

"I just use it as a precaution, I guess, so I don't get overly emotional about things. No reason not to."

"It keeps you from feeling," he said.

"No," she corrected. "It keeps me from letting too many feelings cloud my judgment and my ability to evaluate their roots." She repeated the explanation her doctor had given her when she'd made the same protest half her life ago.

He lifted a judgmental eyebrow.

"I *was* depressed," she said, "and it was really bad, okay? I don't want to go back to that—ever."

He pursed his lips. "What can possibly make a fourteen-year-old depressed?"

"My youngest sister died," she said.

"Shit," Callum said. "How?"

"Leukemia."

"They couldn't find a donor?"

"They did, but the transplant didn't work," she said, looking away.

"Babe, I'm so sorry." He reached a hand over to hers.

"It's not your fault."

"Do you have other siblings?"

"Another sister," she said. "She's getting married next week, actually."

"Where's the wedding?"

"Maine," she said. "My grandparents had a house there, so we'd go up in the summer."

"That'll be nice."

"Oh, I can't go." She forced a smile so he'd know she didn't need to be comforted. She had called her mother on the way to the airport to tell her she wasn't coming, and sent a long e-mail to Lisbeth on the flight explaining why. "We'll be in the middle of the road show."

"What?" he said. "It's your sister's wedding."

"It's the biggest IPO of the year," she countered with the mantra she'd been telling herself.

"Shit." Callum leaned over to turn out the light. "No wonder you're depressed."

"I'm not depressed," she said firmly, offended by his tone.

"Right," he said sarcastically, "you're just on antidepressants as a precaution."

"You have no idea what it was like," she said, allowing herself to remember fourteen just long enough to prove her point. "I didn't want to do anything," she said. "I just wanted to sit there and be numb. And it was my sophomore year—do you have any idea how important sophomore year is in America? I had to take the PSAT, I had to do AP classes. I couldn't afford to lie in bed being sad: it would legitimately have ruined all my opportunities, just like getting overly emotional now would derail everything I've been working toward."

Callum looked at her again, but his hazel eyes had gotten sad.

"Don't pity me," she said firmly, moving her legs from under the covers.

"What are you doing?"

"I don't know why I did this," she said, shaking her head as she stood and looked around for her bra.

"Let yourself almost feel something?" he replied without sitting up. "Get back in bed."

"No," she said. "I'm going back to the hotel."

"Tara, don't be absurd. I didn't mean—"

"You don't know what you're talking about, okay?" she said sternly. "I don't have the options you do."

"To feel?"

"To risk losing control."

It was suddenly so clear: she couldn't take advice from him—he had already had his success—he had money and power and he was a man; he could afford to be casual and relaxed in a way she couldn't. He was totally untrustworthy.

He laughed.

"What?" she snapped.

"Don't you see?" he asked. "That you already have?"

"What are you talking about?" she said, angry.

"You've given all your control over to L.Cecil," he said gently. "You're not in control, and you like it that way because it means you don't ever have to make any decisions for yourself. All that independence of yours, and you're terrified of the responsibility of owning your own path. You're afraid you might decide wrong."

"I've got to go," she said, her voice quiet.

"Tara, wait!" he called, but she was already out the door.

JUAN

FRIDAY, MAY 2; LONDON, ENGLAND

He should be in bed. It was two thirty in the morning and they were leaving the hotel at seven thirty to go to Geneva. They should all be in bed.

But Juan wasn't tired, and he wouldn't be able to sleep even if he were. Every time he closed his eyes he thought about Kelly and Robby and what he was going to do if Robby actually went to jail. So he'd gone with Todd, Nick and Beau to a club somewhere in London where he now sat, by himself, on a long sofa at their table, guarding the magnum of champagne and still thinking about Kelly and Robby.

Think about the fact you're in London, he told himself. *Think about how cool that is, and how cool your life is going to be from here on out.* But this club was not cool: it was just a bunch of drunk people in nice clothes showing off for each other while the music pounded too loudly to hear what anyone was saying.

"Let me get you a drink," Todd said to Nick as he led him back to the table and poured a glass of champagne from the enormous bottle.

"I'm being serious, Todd," Nick slurred, holding on to a chair to maintain his balance. He was wasted. "*I'm* CEO," he said, pointing to his chest. "I get to be center of attention, not you."

"I know, man." Todd was drunk, too, but not like Nick. "I'm your wingman, buddy. I was just playing backup today. This is all your show. Why don't you sit down for a little bit?" Todd laughed, unbothered, and ushered Nick to the couch, where the CEO promptly let his head fall back and his eyes close.

"He had a good night." Todd smiled at Juan. "You doing okay?"

"Great," Juan said. "Just taking it all in."

"Sure," Todd said. "Awesome club, right? They do it so well over here."

"Definitely," Juan lied.

"There you are." A girl who looked like a model tapped Todd's shoulder and he pulled her toward him, kissing her mouth with the same casual ritual with which he'd shaken investors' hands at dinner.

Juan scanned the room for Beau. Juan always felt responsible for making sure everyone was okay. He saw the associate by the bar, talking to a girl in short shorts and tall heels that made her skinny legs look freakishly long. Their faces were close, glowing in the purple-blue lights beaming from the ceiling.

Juan sipped his beer and watched. His roommate Julie had hooked up with Beau the last time he was in San Francisco, which Juan only knew because he'd come downstairs the next morning to find the banking associate in their kitchen using Juan's laptop to recharge his phone.

Juan didn't get it. Julie was smart: what did she see in a guy like Beau? He and Todd treated women terribly. Maybe if this was the track Robby Goodman, with his eighty-two Hook meet-ups, was on, it was just as well he got locked away and the world was saved from one more asshole.

Juan watched Beau hand the girl a shot and they each took one, squinting at the taste, before she fell into him, pressing her open mouth on his.

Beau led the girl back to the couch and they started making out. Juan shifted uncomfortably in his seat.

It was three o'clock now. *Screw it*, he decided, standing to leave.

He looked around for Todd to see if he wanted him to take Nick out.

"Yo, Juan," Beau called from the couch. "You know if those cars are still here?"

The girl smiled flirtatiously at Juan, her eyelids barely open. She was wasted.

"Yeah," Juan said. "I was just going to go back to the hotel. Do you know her address? I'm sure one of them would take her home."

Beau laughed. "Why would she go home?" He looked at the girl. "The party's just getting started, right, babe?"

The girl nodded. Juan stared at Beau: he couldn't be serious. She was totally gone.

"You're joking, right?" Juan said.

"What?" Beau tapped his ear and shouted, "Sorry—the music's really loud."

Juan sat down next to the girl, opposite Beau. "What's your name?"

"Fiona." The girl smiled. She fell forward and kissed Juan. He pushed her back upright. "Where do you live, Fiona?"

"Stop," Beau said, pushing Juan out of the way. His friendly blue eyes had changed with the booze. "She's coming with me." Beau pulled the girl up and they went out the door.

"What are you doing?" Juan said, following him outside.

"Quit being such a Boy Scout." Beau turned, returning to his confident ease. "Have you never gone out before?"

"She's drunk, Beau," Juan said, calm but firm. "She has no idea what's going on."

"Of course she does." Beau brushed it off. "She's been into it all night."

Juan held the girl's shoulders. "Fiona, are you okay?"

"Yeah!" she said, slapping his shoulder playfully. "I'm greeeeat!"

"See? Chill out," Beau said, pushing him away.

"Does this seriously get you off?"

"Mind your own business, man." Beau laughed at him, stumbling, drunk himself, as he opened the car door and Fiona fell inside.

"You think because you're rich you're just entitled to everything, don't you?" Juan felt anger boiling up, and knew it wasn't just because of Fiona. It was anger at Beau's casual attitude. At the casual attitude of the rich white men at dinner, the rich white men in the club, the rich white men like Todd and Nick and Beau, who dicked over girls like Fiona and Julie while they lived on the backs of those who couldn't afford to be so unconcerned.

"Says the guy about to make two hundred million bucks," Beau retorted, looking around for the driver.

"I'm not like that," Juan said. "I'm not like you."

"You will be." Beau smiled.

"I've worked my ass off. You've never done anything," Juan said.

"You don't know that."

"You only got where you are because of your parents," Juan pressed.

"And you only got where you are because of affirmative action."

"What did you say?" Juan felt his face drain, the blood rushing to his flexing muscles.

"Your education, your job—it's not because you worked hard any more than my having a job at L.Cecil is because I worked hard. It's because you're a poor Mexican from the projects and everyone felt sorry for you. They gave you shit to clear their own conscience, just like people gave me shit to win favors with my dad," Beau said. "I'm not saying it's your fault, I'm just saying that's what happened to you, and to me. We're not that different, Juan."

Juan's fist curled and shot out, landing squarely on Beau's jaw. Beau lifted his hand to his lip, looked at the blood on his finger, and then laughed. "Except you've still got that Latino temper, don't you?"

The driver emerged. "You boys okay?"

"Fine," Beau said, his eyes still on Juan. "I was just heading back inside." He brushed past, patting Juan on the shoulder. "I'll let you have her if you really want. Easy to find another, thanks to your fine app. See you in the morning, buddy."

Juan stood for a moment, fuming.

"You okay?" the driver asked.

His voice brought Juan back to reality. "Yeah," he said. "We need to take this girl home," Juan told him, "and then go back to the hotel."

"You sure you want to leave her alone?" The driver looked at Fiona, passed out in the backseat.

Juan hesitated, then shook his head. "Back to the Four Seasons, then," he said. "She can stay with me."

It started to drizzle as the car crossed London's empty streets and Juan looked out the window, aware of his separation from the world outside. He hadn't seen the city, hadn't gotten to know anyone here: did it even count to say he'd been to London?

They got back to the hotel and Juan helped Fiona out of the car, wrapping her arm around him and guiding her long legs to the elevator.

"Almost there," he told the girl, who nodded and smiled.

"Suuuuuuch a fun night," she slurred, rocking on her feet. "Where did—" she started, then closed her eyes again, dropping her head on Juan's shoulder.

The elevator doors opened on 4 and Juan blinked when he saw Neha, in sweatpants and a T-shirt, getting on.

"Oh," the analyst said. "I'll—" She looked down at the floor. "I'll wait for the next one."

"No." Juan put his hand out to keep the doors from closing. "It's not what it looks like. She . . ." He looked at the girl on his arm. "It's a long story. I'm just putting her to bed."

"Right," Neha said, unconvinced, but she stepped onto the elevator.

"What are you doing up?" he asked.

"Couldn't sleep," she said. "There's a lounge on four. I've just been doing some work."

The doors opened and they both got off.

"Can I help?" Neha looked at the girl.

"I think I've got it," Juan said, then added, realizing it was true, "but I'd love the company."

"Sure," she said. "Not like I'm going to sleep anyway."

They went back to Juan's room and he sat Fiona on the bed, where she fell sideways onto the pillow. Juan pulled her up and made her drink water before she slid under the covers.

"Guess I'm on the couch," he said to Neha with a shrug. He'd been looking forward to that bed—he'd never stayed in a hotel remotely this nice before.

"What happened?"

"Beau just kept giving her shots."

"Yikes," Neha said.

"Do you trust Beau?" Juan asked.

"He's not so bad," Neha said. "I mean, he doesn't work much, but I think he means well."

Juan studied Neha. How did a girl like her stand being around guys like Beau and Todd all the time? How did they treat her?

"Do you ever wonder whether we're contributing to something bad?" he asked her.

"What do you mean?"

"Just," he said, "tonight." He hesitated. "All those men we're working to make rich. It just made me wonder whether we're not feeding into a bad system."

"You just have to remember that wealth trickles down," Neha said. "You may not like those men, but they invest, and that grows the economy, and a bigger economy helps everyone. It gives people like you and me opportunities like this." She gestured around to remind him where they were: two kids of immigrants who'd grown up poor, now in a Four Seasons in London.

"But do you think maybe there are other consequences," he said, "besides the money?"

"I think capital markets are efficient, so they'll address any consequences over time."

"What does that even mean?" Juan asked, no longer feigning to understand the financial lingo.

"It means that markets always move to address supply and demand. So if a consequence emerges, eventually, if demand is sufficient to confront it, someone will move to take advantage of that opportunity and profit from correcting the inefficiency."

"Where does morality fit in?" Juan asked.

"If there's enough demand for what's right, the market will create an opportunity that actually rewards the person who does it."

"I don't think that happens," he said, shaking his head. "Doing what's right is so small, and so individual, it'll never create enough collective demand to force action. I mean, there is no reward to me for bringing this girl home, and Beau isn't going to have any consequences for not giving a damn." Juan felt his cheeks burn. "Do you know he actually had the nerve to say we're the same? Like I would ever just leave someone out to fend for themselves when I—"

Juan stopped. Robby Goodman's face flashed in front of him. "Fuck," he whispered.

"What?"

"I have to show you something," he heard himself say, moving to his computer. *What are you doing?* his brain screamed at him. *You decided not to say anything to anyone.*

"What is this?" Her cheeks paled when she saw the screen, where line after line of user information loaded from the database Juan had never erased.

"I found a database that matches users' private information with the activity we collect. It's all here—everyone's data from the moment they signed up."

"You're not supposed to do that," Neha said. "Per the privacy policy, you have to keep identities masked and—"

"I know, but that's not the point," Juan said, typing in Kelly's name. "You know that girl Kelly Jacobson?"

"Yes," Neha said cautiously.

"She was on it when she died." He pointed to her profile on the screen. "And Robby Goodman," he said, pointing to the three dots on the map of their dorm from the night Kelly overdosed, "was on it, too. But he wasn't with her. He was next door."

Neha's chest rose and fell, and she turned her face from the screen to look at Juan.

His brow relaxed for the first time in weeks, the confession lifting a weight from his brain. He wasn't like Beau: he cared about what happened to people.

"Why did you show me this?" Neha suddenly snapped. Her voice was angry and hurt.

"I thought—" he started, caught off guard by her reaction.

She started to back away from the computer, shaking her head at it as if she could make it go away. "You have to delete it," she said decisively. "No one can know. You shouldn't have told me."

"But—"

"It'll ruin everything, Juan. You've got to delete it," she said with more conviction.

"But what about Robby?" Juan said. "What if he—"

"What about *you*?" she interrupted. "If this comes out and the IPO doesn't go through, you're back to being a nobody."

"But I'm not the only one who—"

"There are too many people depending on this, Juan," Neha said. "Let the legal system work out whether Robby's guilty: it isn't worth the deal."

"Neha," Juan said, "we have information that could—"

"Ruin you," she said. "And you"—she looked for the words—"you have to make it," she said with determination. "If you make two hundred million and build a community center, you'll change so many lives, Juan. That's an opportunity you have that no one else does."

She searched his eyes and he knew she was right, but it felt wrong.

"But Robby—"

"It's him or you, Juan. And unlike Robby, if you make it, then you've won over guys like Beau and Todd and Nick and all those men at dinner," she said. "I know you don't like this system, but you can't change it by saving Robby. Just play it a little longer, and then you'll be in a position to set new rules."

10

TODD

What the fuck was Callum Rees doing here?

The lunch meeting was by invite only, and Callum had definitely not been invited. It made Todd sick the way men like Callum acted like they were above the rules.

Todd was working his ass off for this deal, and Callum was just using it as some platform to get laid. What a loser. Callum was a billionaire. If he was going to cheat on Louisa LeMay, he could at least be doing it with supermodels on a beach in Ibiza instead of following a girl like Tara across the Atlantic to an investor meeting. It made Todd angry: he would make so much better use of Callum's wealth and status if he had the chance.

When he had the chance, Todd coached himself. The European road show had been a runaway success. They'd flown back from Geneva last night to begin the American tour, which meant they had one more week before Hook went public and Todd solidified his status as a Big Fucking Deal.

Antony van Leeuwen interrupted Todd's drifting. Antony was a big-A Analyst, meaning he researched companies and issued opinions about whether or not investors should buy their stock. Unlike little-a analysts like Neha, who were entry-level data monkeys, big-A Analysts' opinions mattered, especially if they had a reputation for being right, like Antony did.

"Nick, can we be serious for a second about the risks on this thing?" Antony's brow was furrowed and his voice arrogant. Todd shifted in his chair.

"Sure," Nick said, flipping through the PowerPoint projected on the screen. "As you'll remember from slide seventeen, the greatest risks to our business are—"

"I'm not talking about the business risks, I'm talking about the security risks," Antony said. "One thing I've never understood about these companies is why there's not more discussion about the location tracking ability. Your servers must have an incredible amount of personal information—where people have been and with whom. What do you do with that data?"

"First of all, we track activity in an unidentifiable manner so that users can feel secure in their privacy. Even so, we erase all activity logs after collecting what analytics we deem necessary for the improvement of the app's functionality and overall user experience."

"It's got to be tempting to keep it, though," Antony said. "That information would be valuable to advertisers, vendors, the government, a lot of people with deep pockets. Your privacy policy is fairly ambiguous: How are users to feel confident that their actions remain unidentifiable? How do they know you won't start selling that data, especially after this deal, when your still-unprofitable model is under the pressure of public earnings expectations?"

Todd's jaw unhinged. What was Antony doing? Showing off?

"I'm perfectly capable of handling pressure without—" Nick started.

"Don't be hypocritical, Antony," Tara interrupted from where she sat next to Todd at the table. Her voice was disparaging. "You're bullish on Facebook and they have exactly the same capacity. Every app does— Uber and Foursquare and Google Maps could all do the same thing, and that hasn't kept users from downloading them or investors from buying their stock."

"Do you not think it's different for Hook, given the extremely personal nature of the information you have?"

"How many men do you know thinking about privacy policies when they're trying to get laid?" Tara asked. The room smirked. "If anything, I think people are willing to risk far more in their pursuit of the opposite sex."

Todd glanced at Callum, whose lips curled into a proud smile, but Tara's eyes were serious and locked on Antony's, putting him in his place.

"I'll keep that in mind," the Analyst said sternly, his nostrils flaring just slightly.

Nick fielded a few more questions before the men in the room started to clear back to their offices. They had a three-hour break before a cocktail reception and another dinner meeting with more of New York's top investors. From there, it was back to the office to catch up on e-mails and make updates to the model before tomorrow's flight to Boston, followed by more of the same in Philadelphia, Chicago, San Francisco and Palo Alto.

"You ready to go?" Tara said, picking up her things.

"You're not going to flirt with your boyfriend?" Todd mocked.

"No," she said, and walked to the door.

Todd glanced over at Callum, in conversation with another investor, then back at Tara, but she was already gone.

"He told you?" he asked as they stepped onto the elevator, suddenly realizing she might know about Louisa.

"What?" She looked at him and shook her head. "I don't want to talk about it."

They rode the elevator in silence.

"Why didn't we ever date?" he asked, not sure why.

"What?" She looked up.

The surprise on her face made him recognize his own, and he felt his cheeks burn. "I really liked you," he said, adding quickly, "back in college, I mean."

"That was a long time ago," she said. "And it never would have worked."

Todd felt his spine straighten defensively. "It could have."

"Yeah, right." She rolled her eyes as the elevator doors opened.

"I mean it," he said, walking quickly to keep up with her pace as they pushed outside to Fifth Avenue. "I would have been a great boyfriend."

"In what sense?" She laughed.

"Tara!" Callum's voice interrupted. "Tara, wait."

She kept walking. Callum followed quickly and grabbed her arm.

"What?" she snapped, stopping in the middle of the sidewalk.

"Can we please talk?"

"There's nothing to talk about."

"Oh, I very much disagree with that," his British voice demanded. Todd saw a cab pull up to let a passenger off and lifted his hand to hail it.

"If you haven't noticed, I'm a little busy," she said.

"Tara, you ready?" Todd interrupted, holding the cab door open for her.

"I flew all the way here. Can we just talk?"

"Tara?" Todd asked, ignoring Callum. What a prick.

Tara kept her attention on the older man, looking at him with a mix of anger and affection.

"Tara?" Todd repeated.

"I'll meet you at the office," she said, finally acknowledging him.

"But we've got—"

"I'll meet you at the office," she repeated firmly.

Todd's jaw opened to protest, but he scoffed instead, ducking into the cab. "Whatever."

HE GOT BACK to L.Cecil, but he couldn't concentrate. "Fuck it," he finally said to his Excel spreadsheet.

Ten minutes later Todd opened the doors at Equinox, but for once he didn't look at the people watching him go up the stairs.

"I thought you'd found someone new," Morgan said, greeting him at the reception desk. She sighed when Todd didn't respond to the joke. "What's wrong?"

"What?" he asked. "Oh, nothing. Are you free?"

She checked her watch. "I've got an hour."

"Me too," he said, heading to the locker room to change.

She put him on the treadmill and he ran hard, the sweat coming quickly to his brow.

He attacked the bench, pressing twenty pounds more than usual as if it was nothing, grunting with each press as Morgan encouraged him.

"Do you want to talk about it?" Morgan finally asked.

"About what?"

"Whatever's bothering you."

"Why do you think something's bothering me?"

"You're not counting how many girls are checking you out."

Todd held the bar up and grimaced. "I don't do that." Had she really noticed him doing that before?

"Right," she said. "Just like nothing's bothering you."

"Why are you a lesbian?" He wasn't sure why he asked.

"Because I love my girlfriend."

"Do you seriously not like men at all?"

"No, I like men a lot. I'm bisexual."

"Why a girlfriend then? If you're attracted to both, wouldn't it make life easier to be with a guy?"

"Societally easier, sure," she said. "But easier to live with?" She shook her head. "I couldn't find any guys who had what I needed."

"Which was?"

"I guess I wanted someone to take care of me," she said carefully.

"You're hot. You could find a man to take care of you."

"I don't mean money," she said. "I mean emotionally. I wanted to feel emotionally secure, and I never found that with a guy in New York."

"Did you date a lot?"

"Yeah," she said. "And everything always came back to sex, back to status, back to work. And all of it had to do with this constant wondering whether there was something better," she said, "which I get—I was there for a while, too—but there comes a point where you just want"—she looked for the word—"a real partner."

Todd followed her to the mat and sat, seriously considering it. Morgan picked up a medicine ball and tossed it to Todd, who crunched up to catch it.

"I could be a good partner," he said, crunching back, then forward, and throwing the ball to her. He took care of all the women he slept with; he didn't lie to them, or pretend he was something he wasn't. He was always honest, and bought their drinks, and made sure they got home the next day. Except the ones he met drunk in bars, but that was different.

Morgan laughed, throwing the ball back to him.

"What?" He caught the ball. Why were she and Tara so dismissive of him?

"You'd make it about a week," she said.

"How do you know?"

"Because I know guys like you."

"And what are guys like me like?"

"You're obsessed with one muscle group," she said. "You're like the guy at the gym who falls in love with his abs so he just does crunches until he gets a six-pack."

"Thank you." Todd stopped mid-crunch, grinning at the compliment as he tossed her back the ball.

"Except that it's the only muscle group you ever work." She threw the ball back toward him. "You let every other muscle get weak, and one day you realize your shoelaces are untied, but you don't have the necessary muscles to bend over and tie them because all you've ever done is work your abs. And then you trip and get hurt and think it's because you shouldn't have bent over, when really it's just that you need to stop spending all your time on crunches and stretch a little."

Todd looked at her, studying her face.

"Sorry," she said, "long analogy."

"But what you're trying to say is that I'm too obsessed with my job. That I just work all the time and miss relationships."

"No," she said. "You're obsessed with your sexual dominance."

"Go on," he said proudly.

"You're obsessed with your own ability to attract and have sex with women," she said. "So it's all you do, just play that game, working that muscle over and over and over again without ever developing any of the strengths or flexibility it takes to be a good partner. They're different sports."

"That's just biology," Todd said. "Humans are sexual creatures. I can't help how I'm wired."

"Then you're not evolved enough for a relationship," she said firmly.

He shrugged. "Does it matter? If I'm not evolved to do it, maybe I'm not evolved to need it. I can just be happy doing my crunches." He threw the ball back at her.

"Nah, at some point your muscles will become so desensitized you won't get any satisfaction out of crunching," she said.

"You're going to have to put that one in English."

"You won't be able to climax," she said casually. "No sex will be gratifying."

"What?" Todd caught the ball, his face flushed.

"First you'll think it's because you get bored with the same woman, so you'll only sleep with each one once." She caught the ball and returned it. "Then you'll start thinking about porn during sex so you can come"—throw-catch-crunch—"then you'll try threesomes, and then anal sex, and then it'll all stop working and you'll be lying on the mat, watching everyone else working out and you'll think maybe you should do what they're doing, but you won't know how. And then you'll either swallow your pride and start building your other muscles, or you'll just get really bitter." She shrugged. "Whatever girl is rejecting you is grown up enough to recognize that: she either doesn't think you have the stamina it takes to develop those new muscles, or doesn't have the patience to watch you try." She threw the ball and he caught it without throwing it back.

He could feel his abs burning as he gripped the medicine ball in his hands. "I didn't say anything about a girl."

"But clearly there is one."

He inhaled sharply. He didn't give a shit about Tara.

They finished the workout in silence and Todd went to the locker room to shower. Morgan was waiting when he came back out in his suit and tie.

"I'm sorry," she said. "I got carried away."

"Don't worry about it," he said. "You're just wrong."

"You're right," she said. "I mean, I don't know you at all. It wasn't fair for me to assume just because . . ." She paused. "I'm sorry."

"Apology accepted," he said without smiling. He handed her a check for two hundred dollars and walked out the door. He didn't give a shit about her, either.

TARA

FRIDAY, MAY 9; NEW YORK, NEW YORK

"I really don't have time for this," Tara said.

"Your next meeting isn't until six," Callum reminded her.

He leaned in as he said it, putting a hand on her arm.

"Then I don't have the energy," she said, moving away from his touch. "I'm exhausted." She hadn't slept more than three hours in the past four days, hadn't had a full eight since before the deal began. She'd been holding it together just fine until London, but now their night together was dragging her down, like someone had given her a hundred-pound weight to carry on the last mile of a marathon.

"My hotel is right here," he said, pointing to the Peninsula behind them.

"I don't want to sleep with you," she said quickly.

"I don't want to sleep with you, either," he rebuffed. "I want you to take my key and have a nap."

"Why?"

"Because you said you're exhausted."

She hesitated, considering.

"Fine," she said. He was right: a nap would do more for her now than anything else, and a plush bed at the Peninsula was a better option than a cot in a closet at L.Cecil.

But when he followed her into the bedroom of the hotel suite her anxiety returned. "What are you doing?"

"Getting you a T-shirt," he said, pulling one from the closet and handing it to her. "Calm down."

"Thanks," she said, taking it from him.

"What time do you want me to wake you?"

"I'll set my phone alarm."

"Okay. Sleep well," he said, shutting the door.

Tara blinked at the closed door, willing her heart to stop beating so quickly. "Chill out," she whispered to herself. She'd spent the past two days trying to block out what he'd said about her path: he was wrong, of course. She was in control, and was headed exactly where she wanted to be. The life she had now might not be perfect, but at least she was in charge of it.

She undressed and hung her suit in the closet. She felt the pleasure of the sheets, cool and crisp against her skin, before she dropped into a deep sleep.

She was on the plane to Boston, wearing a suit and sleeping with her head against the window. Her youngest sister, Abigail, still eight years old, sat next to her, wearing her favorite yellow pajamas with her teddy bear propped on her lap. Abigail pulled at Tara's sleeve to wake her. She indicated the Barbie coloring book open in her lap, and handed Tara a crayon.

Abigail pointed to a picture of Bride Barbie, whose dress she'd colored a light pink. "That's Lisbeth," Abigail said, and Tara agreed, remembering her sister's wedding the next day and ignoring the fact she was missing it. She nodded at Abigail and stroked her baby soft hair, running her finger along the barrette she'd affixed on the side.

"That's me," Abigail said, pointing to Soccer Team Barbie, and Tara nodded, remembering Abby running around the house in the soccer jersey she insisted on wearing every day the summer before she died.

Tara looked at the opposite page in the coloring book and pointed to Business Executive Barbie. "And that's me," she told Abigail.

But Abigail shook her head and flipped through the pages looking for another picture. Tara patiently took the girl's small hand in her own and directed her back to the picture, but Abigail got angry, shaking her head and turning the pages faster. "Stop," Tara said softly, but the girl kept flipping the pages, faster and faster so that they started to rip. "Stop it," Tara said more firmly, feeling herself get angry. But Abigail refused to stop. Tara took hold of her wrists, and held them tight to make her still. But then Tara kept squeezing, squeezing and squeezing until she felt the girl's tiny bones break in her palms.

"Tara?"

She jolted awake, blinking fast. "Wha—" she started, remembering that she was in the Peninsula hotel, taking a nap between meetings, and the man shaking her awake was Callum, whose room this was, whose T-shirt she was wearing.

"It's almost six," he said. "I thought I should wake you."

"Oh," she said, pushing herself up, and registering what had happened. "I forgot to set my alarm."

"Are you okay?"

"Yeah"—she could feel her heart pounding—"I just had a bad dream."

"Do you want to talk about it?"

She shook her head.

"I'll let you change, then," he said, turning back to the door.

Her brain was spinning: she didn't want to be alone.

"It's my fault my sister died," she blurted.

Callum turned back. She didn't know why she said it.

"What?"

"I was a match. For her bone marrow."

She looked at her manicured hands against the thousand-count sheets on the thousand-dollar bed in the thousand-dollar-a-night suite she'd done nothing to deserve.

"What happened?"

She shook her head, as if it would keep out the flooding images of the hospital and the needles and the doctor announcing that the transplant hadn't worked and her mother starting to cry because Tara, the daughter they had had so much hope in, had let them all down.

She saw Abigail looking over from her bed to Tara's, clinging to her teddy bear and telling her big sister it was okay, and felt all the weakness of knowing that it wasn't.

Callum moved to the bed and she sank into his arms, letting the sobs come in heaving waves. His chest supported her as she cried and cried for the first time in as long as she could remember. He didn't say anything: didn't tell her not to cry, didn't try to convince her it wasn't her fault. He just held her. And when she stopped they just sat there, saying nothing.

She finally broke the silence. "I've got to go."

He nodded, lifting her face to him and tracing a finger under her eye. "You're going to need to re-do your mascara."

"Shit," she forced a laugh at herself. "How bad is it?" She was conscious of how horrible she must look.

"You'd make a very pretty raccoon." He smiled. "Get changed. I'll order you a car," he said, and moved to the door.

TARA SLIPPED OUT of the dinner meeting before the meals were served so she could get back to the office and reply to all the requests that had come in that afternoon. She'd bummed an Adderall off of Neha to help her push Abigail out of her mind and focus on the cocktail presentation, and thanks to the dim lighting in Del Frisco's, no one had noticed her bloodshot eyes. Todd was pissed at her, but she didn't care: he could think whatever he wanted.

Her phone buzzed with a text.

> Wish you were here. Hope it's going well. Love you so much.

Tara felt her heart catch. The message had a photo attached, of her sister, Lisbeth, and her husband-to-be, smiling at the rehearsal dinner Tara was currently missing, offering a piece of cake to the camera, with a sign that said FOR TARA.

She paused on the street and swallowed hard. What must Lisbeth think of her? And Callum, now that he'd seen her at her worst? Tara suddenly saw herself from the outside, and missing her sister's wedding for the deal didn't make Tara seem incredibly important, it just made her seem . . . pathetic.

She put the phone back in her pocket and shook her head to refocus. *Work*, she told herself. If she was going to make these sacrifices for her ambitious career path, she was sure as hell going to do it well.

"How's it going?"

Tara looked up at the voice. Lillian Dumas, the gorgeous senior colleague who she'd been avoiding since she'd accused Tara of stealing the Hook deal, was standing over her desk, her thin lips smiling.

"Hi, Lillian," Tara said, turning her attention back to her computer, hoping she would take the hint to go away.

"It's not that easy, is it?" the woman's voice pressed. "Being under the pressure to deliver a big deal?"

"It's fine," Tara said.

"Especially with Todd leaving you with all the work." Lillian clicked her tongue. "Guess we know now who was using who."

"What are you still doing here?" Tara tried to keep her voice steady.

"I'm waiting for Lucas to finish at the office. He had a call with Asia. We're going to Le Bernardin. It's our anniversary."

"Congratulations," Tara said without looking up from her screen.

"You should really get a boyfriend, Tara," Lillian said.

"Maybe after the deal."

"I mean, at your age, you really don't want to be that girl working late on Friday nights."

Tara's brain snapped, shooting the words to her mouth before she could keep them from coming out: "Because I'd rather be the one killing time at the office while my fiancé finishes a call with Asia?" she heard herself say. "Which is probably code for screwing his secretary." She watched Lillian's cheeks redden but didn't stop. "All so that I can brag to a junior colleague who doesn't give a shit that I'm going to a Michelin restaurant, where I order a salad with dressing on the side, which I throw up afterward so I can maintain my double-zero dress size that he doesn't even enjoy fucking?"

Lillian's jaw dropped, her face pale. "What?" she squealed. "Would you like to apologize before I—"

"You know, Lillian, I really don't want to apologize? And now that I think about it, I don't really want to spend my Friday night here at all."

She grabbed the suitcase that she hadn't had a chance to take home since landing that morning. She left, neither fully conscious nor unaware of what she was doing or the ramifications it might have, just trying to preserve the feeling of freedom she felt pulsing through her veins as she exited the building and hailed a cab.

"I need to get to Kennebunkport," she told the agent at the airport ticket counter, "by noon tomorrow."

"My last direct flight to Portland was at 9:50, but I could get you on the 11:05 tomorrow morning."

"That's too late," she said. "What about Boston? I'll rent a car."

"There's a flight leaving in thirty minutes." The agent looked up at Tara. "Do you have anything to check?"

"No." Tara indicated her carry-on, handing the agent her credit card. "I'll take it."

JUAN

FRIDAY, MAY 9; NEW YORK, NEW YORK

Beau hadn't apologized after their fight in London. Nick hadn't remembered anything from the night, and Todd had only acknowledged it by playfully teasing Beau about his failed conquest of Fiona. Juan couldn't believe it.

He didn't know why he'd shown Neha the database in London, or why he'd expected her to think they ought to tell. She was just like the men in the other room: all she cared about was the deal going well so she could collect her promotion and her paycheck. Her line about him being some kind of hero was just that, a line, like all the other lines the bankers used to make people believe what they wanted them to believe so they'd do what they wanted them to do.

Juan came out of the restaurant's restroom and found Neha waiting for him.

"Did you erase it?" she whispered.

"No, Neha," he said, annoyed, "I didn't."

"But you heard the man in the lunch meeting," she said, skipping to catch up with him. "What if—"

"He's not going to find out, okay?"

"No," she said, "what if he's right? What if Nick sells the data?"

Juan stopped and turned to face her. Her eyelids were puffy behind her glasses, and the bags underneath weighed them down. Her skin had cleared, though, and she'd gotten a new suit for the road show that looked less like something she'd borrowed from her grandmother.

"He won't," he said. "He thinks it's gone. And you heard Tara: every app has this kind of information. It's not a big deal."

"Can you at least find out who the other user was? The one who was with Kelly?"

"Why do you suddenly care? What about supporting the rich men so you can keep your job and climb up the ladder?"

"I didn't get the promotion," she said.

"What?"

"They sent the e-mail announcement today. I didn't get it."

"That's bullshit. There's no way anyone works as hard as you."

"It doesn't matter. You have to find out who the other user was."

"The path is corrupted," he said. "It's a moot point."

"You're the best programmer for the best tech company in Silicon Valley. You're telling me you can't figure that out?"

"I don't want to know, Neha, and I don't want to tell," he said. "I just want this to be done so I can get my money and not have to deal with any of these people anymore."

"I don't believe you."

"Why not?"

"Because if you meant that you would have deleted the database."

"We need to get back in there," he said, moving past her to the dining room, ignoring her point.

NICK

American investors were proving more difficult than the Europeans. It was past midnight now, after a day of meetings in New York that had been full of serious questions about the long-term health of the app market, sparked with speculation that the entire thing was a bubble.

That was New York, though, Nick reminded himself. New York investors got caught up in things like revenue and profitability. They didn't recognize that the number of users was the new currency, and that once a company had that piece worked out, like Hook did, the rest was cake.

Todd was talking on the phone, his voice serious. "You know what'll happen if he does this. You have to talk him out of it."

What's going on? Nick mouthed to Todd, who held up a finger.

"Fuck you, Tom. I've got to go." Todd hung up the phone. "Fuck!" he said to the car.

"What's going on?"

"Antony van Leeuwen's issuing a negative report."

"What?"

"He's setting a price target of two dollars a share, and issuing it ahead of the IPO."

"Two dollars?" Nick's chest tightened. "Is that a joke?"

"He's trying to get attention for himself," Todd said. "It's bullshit."

"Who told you?"

"My friend Tom. He runs a fund that just got the tip from Antony and is now thinking of taking a short position," Todd said. "Fuck him— he's trying to build his career by fucking up my deal."

"*Your* deal?" Nick's jaw dropped. "Todd, this is *my* company. If he puts out that report and people listen to him . . ." Nick blinked his eyes, his head spinning. Their target was twenty-six dollars. If the price went to two dollars, he wouldn't even have enough to pay back the loan he'd taken to exercise his options.

"They won't," Todd said. "He's got nothing to back it up. Just his stupid conspiracy theory that location-based apps are going to go bust. The problem is that if guys like Tom take his side, it doesn't matter whether he's right or not. Which means we just have to do a better job convincing them of our view. Jesus fucking Christ, I do not need this."

The car stopped at the hotel.

"I'm going back to the office," Todd told the driver. He turned to Nick and took a deep breath. "Don't worry," he said, calming his voice for Nick's benefit. "We'll figure this out."

"You better," Nick said angrily, getting out of the car and slamming the door behind him.

This couldn't possibly be happening. Two dollars a share? And a hedge fund shorting the stock? Nick wasn't having a good time anymore. The questions were intense and he was hungover from all the drinking and Tiffany still hadn't tried to make out with him and no one was "liking" his Instagram posts. He needed something he could control.

He spotted Juan in the lobby and grabbed the programmer's arm. "Can I talk to you?"

Juan frowned but followed him to a corner in the hotel bar.

"It's gone, right?" Nick said sternly.

"What?"

"What do you mean, 'what'?" Nick whispered angrily. "The third database."

Juan looked down.

"You erased it, like I told you to do?" Nick said, getting angry again. How was he supposed to operate a company if his lead engineer didn't follow directions?

Juan shook his head. "I found something."

"What?"

"Kelly Jacobson was on it when she died."

Nick's throat tightened. That didn't matter. Lots of famous people were on Hook. "You've been looking up user information?"

Juan nodded.

"Do you have any idea what would happen if people found out that a Hook engineer is looking at individual users' information?" Nick's voice got angrier as he said the words. If Antony van Leeuwen was threatening a bad report on conspiracy theories, what would he say if he knew programmers were stalking users?

"I didn't know what to do," Juan said. "I think Kelly—"

Nick could feel his chest start to constrict. He couldn't breathe. He'd taken out a loan. He'd launched a public reputation. He'd broken up with Grace. Juan's lips were moving, talking frantically, but Nick couldn't make out what he was saying.

". . . and so I think Robby Goodman is . . ."

"You're fired," Nick heard himself say.

Juan paused, his mouth ajar. "What?"

"You're fired," Nick repeated more confidently, his nerves starting to resettle.

"What are you talking about?" Juan asked, as if Nick were crazy.

But Nick wasn't crazy. He was back in control, rebalanced, and the engineer's flippancy gave him even more certainty in his decision. "You signed a nondisclosure agreement, saying you'd keep the data you saw to yourself, which you violated when you showed Phil Dalton. That was strike one. Now you're violating user privacy by looking at their information."

"Nick, I—"

"I can't have people like that working for me."

"But what I found . . ." Juan's eyes were wide. "It means—"

"I'll have Tiffany book you a ticket back to California, and we'll pay you out through the end of the year. You can keep any options that you've exercised."

"I haven't exercised any options." Juan's face was white, panicked.

Nick lifted an eyebrow. "You're joking."

"I was going to wait for the IPO and sell enough to . . ."

Nick shook his head, laughing in disbelief. "You should have been more responsible."

"I—"

Nick looked down at the laptop case Juan was carrying and grabbed it. "I'll need that."

"Are you seriously firing me?" Juan asked in disbelief.

Nick straightened his spine. This was good, actually. If Juan hadn't exercised, that meant two hundred million worth of shares back in the pot.

He stuck out his hand, remembering the etiquette he'd learned at Harvard Business School about how to behave when you fired people. "It's been a pleasure working with you, Juan. I'm sorry it had to end like this, but I wish you all the best."

JUAN

SATURDAY, MAY 10; NEW YORK, NEW YORK

"Juan!" Neha called. "Juan, wait!" She grabbed his arm. "Juan, what's going on?"

Juan shook his head and kept walking, quickly, away from the hotel.

"Juan, stop! Where are you going?"

Juan didn't stop.

"What were you talking to Nick about? Did you tell him?" She scrambled to keep up.

"Yes," he said.

"And? What'd he say?"

"He fired me."

"What?" Neha stopped. Juan walked another step, then he stopped, too, closing his eyes and feeling his chest rise and fall. "Nick fired you?" Neha repeated softly.

Juan let his head drop. "Shit, Neha."

The community center would never happen now. His mother wouldn't get her new house. And who else would hire him? Nick would get rich and Todd would get rich and all those guys in suits in the meetings would get even richer and he would go back to being nothing, like Neha said. They'd won.

Neha caught up and stood in front of him, looking straight into his eyes. "What are you going to do?" she asked softly.

"Can you get me onto one of L.Cecil's computers?" he asked. "Nick took mine."

She nodded.

Neha used her security badge and passed it back to him while she checked the elevators to make sure no one was there.

"Only employees are allowed up here," she explained.

"I don't want you to get in trouble."

She shrugged. "Let's not think about it."

The elevator doors opened and Neha led him to a corner conference room. Beau and another analyst were at their computers, but neither noticed. She pulled her laptop out of her bag and logged in, then passed it over to him.

Juan sat forward and started typing. Neha sat by his side at the desk while he worked, hacking through layers and layers of code to figure out where the corruption in the mystery user's profile had happened.

"This doesn't make any sense," Juan said after half an hour.

"What?"

"Kelly never matched this user," he said, squinting at the screen. "But he was able to see her full profile anyway," he said. "That's not supposed to happen."

"What do you mean?"

Juan stopped, remembering Neha hadn't used Hook since the first version. "The way it normally works is the app gives you people nearby and you 'match' who you like, and if they match you back then you can communicate with them. You can search for people to see their ratings, but you can't see their full profile, or their location, unless they allow it by matching you."

Juan looked more closely at the screen and went on, "But the system thinks they matched at midnight, even though there was no communication from Kelly's device." He looked back at Neha. "I think it was manually entered," he concluded. "I think someone hacked in so they could find out where she was."

Neha's face went white and she sat forward. "Find out who."

Juan kept typing. Neha's phone rang but she ignored it. It rang again and she left the room to answer it.

He sat back and stared at the screen: why couldn't he figure this out? *Think!* he screamed at his brain.

SYSTEM SHUTTING DOWN.

Juan sat forward: what had he done? He felt his heart rate speed as he tapped the keys to stop the reboot, but the screen went black. He felt the panic rise as he pressed the restart button again and again.

At last the familiar bell of the computer starting sounded and he waited for the Hook database to reload, still holding his breath. He exhaled, everything was still there. He navigated back to Kelly and her matches. But this time when he clicked to the corrupted profile of the user that matched her on March 6, he found an IP address and his heart caught again: how had he not seen that before?

If he could figure out who owned that IP address, he could figure out who set up the account. He hacked into several banks' servers and felt his head go light when he found an account with an IP address that matched his mystery user. He scrolled to the name registered to the bank's account: *Jorge Menendez.*

He went back to the Hook database and typed in Jorge's name, then backed into the IP address for his uncorrupted account: it was the same. He clicked on Jorge's history. A list of matches loaded, until they stopped where March 6 would have been: PATH CORRUPTED.

He'd found his guy.

"Did you find it?" Neha asked, returning to the room.

"Wait," Juan said, his heart starting to panic as he read Jorge's other matches: they were all in East Palo Alto.

He Googled Jorge Menendez. His mug shot came up on the screen, a young, round face with worn brown eyes. Juan read the public criminal record:

NAME: JORGE MENENDEZ

AGE: 26

OFFENSES: DRUG POSSESSION (3/14/03); DRUG POSSESSION (10/12/07)

RESIDENCE: EAST PALO ALTO, CALIFORNIA

Juan stared at the screen, his hands hovering over the keys.

"What?" Neha sat up, noticing his stillness. "What did you find?"

"Nothing," he said, clicking to another screen.

"What did you find?" she asked, leaning over him. He forced her away. "Nothing," he said. "The file's corrupted, I can't see anything."

She sat back in her chair. "You're lying."

"No I'm not," he lied. "It's ruined. I can't do it."

"What did you find?" she repeated.

"I told you, there's nothing there. Whoever this guy is, he's smarter than me."

"Bullshit," she spat.

"What the fuck are you two doing in here?" Todd Kent was at the door, his face red. "Jesus fucking Christ, has everyone lost their minds? Get to work, Neha. And where the fuck is Tara?"

Juan's blood froze. He expected Todd to say something about him being there, but he didn't, storming off instead.

Neha didn't move, she just kept her eyes on him.

"What?" Juan snapped.

She shook her head, disappointed, and stood up to leave.

She left the room and Juan sat alone with the computer. He'd never met Jorge Menendez, but he knew of him: he wasn't a bad guy. He was just a guy from East Palo Alto who'd never gotten any breaks, who'd joined a gang because he didn't have any other community and started dealing drugs because he didn't have any other options. Even if they didn't pin him with the murder, if he got one more possession charge they'd lock him away.

But the media *would* pin him for the murder. People would freak. They'd put up walls blocking East Palo Alto from regular Palo Alto, and the rich families that hired Juan's mom to clean their mansions would start looking at her even more suspiciously than they already did. And he wouldn't be able to do anything to protect her, not now that he was a has-been engineer fired for violating user privacy.

He shut the laptop with calm certainty that he was doing the right thing and took the elevator down to the street, eerily aware of the quiet as he walked back to the hotel. Even though he'd left to try to be something else, it was clearer now more than ever before that this new world was not his people: East Palo Alto was his people.

The least he could do was keep their secrets safe.

TARA

SUNDAY, MAY 11; BOSTON, MASSACHUSETTS

The almost-full moon hung bright against a clear sky as Tara drove south on I-95 from Kennebunkport to Boston. It was almost two in the morning and she was still in the tight cocktail dress she'd borrowed from one of Lisbeth's friends to wear to yesterday's ceremony, which she now replayed in her mind as the car zipped down the empty interstate.

Everyone had been in bed by the time Tara arrived at the hotel Friday night, and she'd indulged in six hours' sleep before making her way to the bridal suite Saturday morning. Lisbeth had been laughing at something one of her bridesmaids had said when she opened the door, her face radiant with happiness. She'd stopped, though, when she saw her sister in the doorway, and Tara's heart stopped, too, worried that coming had been a mistake as she watched Lisbeth's eyes fill with tears.

But Lisbeth had cut Tara's apologies off with a tight embrace and they'd held each other, laughing and crying with the overpowering sensation of sisterhood.

The wedding had been everything a young bride could hope for—the sunset red over the ocean just as the groom kissed the bride. Tara had watched Lisbeth and her new husband spin on the dance floor and been keenly aware of the extent to which her sister's joy held a mirror to Tara's own lack of it. She'd sipped her wine and, before she could stop it, felt the truth of what she really wanted begin to articulate itself in her mind, seeping down to her heart and forcing her lips open in a silent vow to change.

And so now she was driving to Boston to rejoin the Hook road show with a surreal peace that she didn't quite understand but trusted to lead her down the right path.

When the car radio lost its signal, she plugged her iPhone into the auxiliary system and turned it on for the first time since she'd left New York. Before her Spotify could load, a notification of six new voicemails filled the phone's screen. She braced herself for messages from Todd yelling at her for leaving, but found that all six were from Neha, frantically asking Tara to call her back. It was almost two-thirty now but Tara knew the analyst would still be up.

"Tara!" Neha answered on the second ring. "Where are you? I've been trying to—"

"I went to my sister's wedding," Tara cut her off without apology. "What's going on?"

"You know that guy's question in the road show on Friday, about Hook keeping identifiable information?" Neha asked.

"Yeah, Antony van Leeuwen," Tara said, switching her brain back into work mode. "Why?"

"They do," Neha said. "They do keep it."

"They *did*," Tara corrected, remembering what Rachel had told her. "They stopped, though, and erased everything. That's why Josh left."

"No they didn't," Neha said.

Tara felt her throat tighten. "How do you know?"

"Juan showed me," she said. "And he found this third database that links all the private information and collected activity so you can see everyone's history. But that's not all."

Tara gripped the steering wheel.

"Juan looked up Kelly Jacobson, and she was on Hook when she died, and she was with someone, but that user's profile was corrupted, and so Juan broke into it after the dinner on Friday, and found out that the person that was with her wasn't Robby Goodman, it's someone who hacked into Hook and I think he's the one who killed her, not Robby, and—"

"Wait, wait, wait, Neha," Tara interrupted, her brain racing to keep up with the girl's voice as she looked out at the empty road before her. "Wait, Neha, start from the beginning."

11

NICK

"Is this why Josh really quit?" Tara snapped in a hushed voice, her long neck tense.

"What are you talking about?" Nick spat back.

She'd caught Nick on his way to breakfast and pulled him into her hotel room, where the sheets were crumpled back in the unmade bed. She'd been absent yesterday and missed the flight from New York, but apparently that hadn't kept her from sleeping just fine whenever she'd shown up in Boston.

"Why didn't you tell us about the third database, Nick?" she demanded.

"I don't know what you're referring to," he said.

"Do not lie to me, Nick," she growled, pronouncing one word at a time.

"As you told Antony in Friday's meeting, all apps can collect user information. And as I told Antony, we use that information responsibly."

Nick hadn't told anyone, but he'd decided not to erase the third database, or delete user activity after twenty-four hours like Phil had suggested and Juan had failed to do. Antony was right: it was a gold mine of information. Companies and advertisers and the government would pay huge money for it, which would not only provide a revenue stream to ease Wall Street concern over earnings, it would catapult Hook beyond a simple dating app and into the realm of big data.

The same way Palantir helped banks catch fraudsters and the government catch terrorists, Hook could develop algorithms that mined their data sets to find patterns that . . . well, meant something . . . to someone. He hadn't figured out the details yet, but that's what the engineers were for; he was just the visionary.

"I want to see what you have," Tara demanded.

"That's against our policy," he said.

"I am underwriting this IPO, Nick." Her eyes were wide, exasperated. "We are legally required to include something like this in our disclosures. I am not going to keep this up if I think you're hiding something."

"First, underwriting an IPO is very different from leading a company that makes important decisions—"

"Do not lecture me on how your job is more important than mine, Nick," she said. "I will go to the police, with or without you."

"What? Why would you go to the police?"

"Because a girl died, and an innocent kid is about to go to jail, and you know who the real killer is," she said, emphasizing the words with her manicured hands.

"What are you talking about?"

"Are you seriously going to deny it?" she yelled. "Jesus Christ, Nick!"

"Tara, I honestly don't know what you're talking about," he said, his tone shifting. "All Juan found was that the girl happened to be on Hook, like a hundred million other active users that night. It doesn't make Hook responsible."

"No." Tara shook her head, a lock of hair falling in front of her face. "But the fact that another user was with her, and hacked into your system in order to find her, might be cause for concern, don't you think?"

"What?" Nick felt the blood in his cheeks drain. "That isn't possible."

"It is," she said, "and it happened, and we have to do something about it."

"You have no way of knowing that happened," he said, calming himself with reason. "How could you possibly? You're not an engineer."

"Juan found it," she said, "via the database you said you had erased."

"When?"

"Friday night," she said. "Neha told me. She was with him."

Nick relaxed: that explained it. "Juan is no longer an employee of this company," he said. "He's trying to make trouble."

"What?"

"I let him go on Friday." Nick shrugged. "He's trying to get back at me. It isn't real."

This was why women were never going to be as good as men in business, Nick thought. They were too dramatic. They always jumped to the most exciting story of something, like Juan finding ludicrous information, instead of taking a minute to see the logical reason behind things.

"Why did you fire him?" Tara asked sternly. "He's your top engineer."

"I can't trust him," Nick said. "As is especially clear now."

"Why would he lie about something like that?"

"Because he didn't exercise any of his stock options." Nick guffawed. "So he loses them. He's bitter and he's lashing out."

Tara looked like she'd just witnessed a shooting.

"Come on." He laughed gently to lighten the mood, putting a hand on her arm. "This is good news! Juan was making it all up. There's nothing wrong with Hook."

Tara pulled her arm away from his grip. "You're seriously taking away all his shares." She said it as a statement, not a question.

"He violated his NDA," Nick said innocently. "I can't have people like that working for me, Tara, not with all the scrutiny going on."

"Bullshit," Tara snapped. "What the fuck is wrong with you? That kid worked his tail off for three years while you were collecting Starwood points at your cushy—"

"I can't help the past, Tara," he said. "All I can do is draw conclusions from the facts of the situation, and the fact is that he used the database in a way that he shouldn't have, violating users' privacy as well as my trust. And the conclusion is that whatever he's telling you is not to be relied upon."

Tara's jaw was clenched, her eyes glassy. "He's poured his life into this and you're hanging him out to dry."

"The money he's made at Hook is still miles beyond what others in his community—"

"You elitist prick!" she spat. "Jesus Christ, he built the entire program, and you—"

"—are the only reason it's going to be a viable business," he said, calmly and firmly, "so long as you keep your mouth shut about whatever you're inventing in that pretty little head of yours."

"How dare you accuse me of inventing when—"

"You have no proof. Just the words of an angry former employee with questionable values."

"Then look in the database yourself," she said. "Let's see if it's true."

"Are you suggesting I hack into our users' private information?"

He made a face. "That's entirely unethical. It goes against all our stated principles."

"Are you kidding me?" Tara threw her hands in the air. She didn't have the stamina for this.

But how could she, really? All she'd ever done was work in an investment bank, she'd never had to deal with real business problems, like employee difficulties and product errors and ethically challenging situations. She thought the world was black and white, right or wrong, but it wasn't.

"Listen, Tara," he coaxed, "you're tired. I know you've been working really hard, and I understand why you might not be seeing things clearly, but I promise, this is not a big deal."

"An innocent kid might go to jail," she said.

"That isn't true." He shook his head. "If Robby Goodman is innocent, our judicial system will find that out. It's not our right or responsibility to step out of our own expertise." He reached out and squeezed her arm. "Which is why you need to go back to what you know, which is how to make this the biggest IPO in history."

Her eyes held his, big and brown and moist with recognition that he was right. Her chest started to heave less and he could feel her pulse slow through the grip on her arm. A rush of warmth spread over him: this is the kind of thing great leaders did.

"Go to hell, Nick," she spat at him, shrugging her arm away and turning to the door.

"Don't you even think about repeating this to anyone."

She glared at him. He wanted to grab her neck, to strangle her or maybe fuck her: something to put her in her place. "Do you understand?" he repeated, angry.

She moved to the door but he grabbed her wrist, hard. "I said, do you understand?"

"Yes," she hissed between gritted teeth.

He held her a moment longer, then released his grip and took a deep breath, readjusting his suit coat. "Good." He nodded. "I'll see you at the meeting, then."

Tara calmly opened the door and left, letting it slam shut behind her.

Nick felt the panic start in his toes, creeping up his legs and into the pit of his stomach. First Antony's report, and now this?

The deal had to go through. There was no room to consider any alternative, even if Hook were somehow responsible for Kelly Jacobson, which it wasn't. And he had had to fire Juan: the engineer had broken the rules, and he'd become a threat to Nick's efficacy as a leader.

Nick might not have built the program, but he had worked hard for this. He'd worked hard his whole life, since he was five years old, multitasking piano lessons and T-ball and accelerated reading classes after school. He'd put every moment of his time toward building a perfect résumé, then risked it all for Hook. And he'd dumped Grace. *And he'd borrowed two million dollars.*

He sobbed involuntarily, his chest heaving from the pressure. He could already see the headlines: *Promising Harvard Business School Graduate Goes from $80 Million to Bankrupt Overnight.*

"No, no, no!" he said, steadying himself on the hotel desk and addressing his reflection in the mirror above it. "You haven't done anything wrong. Everything you believe is right according to the facts that you have."

Nick repeated the mantras he used to calm himself:

1. You went to Stanford and graduated from the hardest major magna cum laude.
2. You worked at McKinsey, the best consulting firm in the world, and got promoted to engagement manager in *three* years.

3. You worked at Dalton Henley, the world's best venture capital firm, under Phil Dalton, the most important VC in the Valley.

4. You went to Harvard Business School, the best business school in the world, where you were a Baker Scholar.

5. You are CEO of the most important social media company on the planet.

6. You can attract any girl you want at the bar at Rosewood.

7. Todd Kent works for you now. And Tara Taylor. And Tiffany.

He felt his brain start to relax as he went through the list: not only had he done nothing wrong, he'd done everything right. Tara didn't know what she was talking about. Guys like him didn't make mistakes.

TARA

SUNDAY, MAY 11; BOSTON, MASSACHUSETTS

"Do you care to explain what's going on?" Catherine Wiley asked.

"What?" Tara looked up, startled. "What are you doing here?" She glanced around the hotel lobby. She was still in shock from what had just happened with Nick.

"I'm speaking at a Women in Business conference at Harvard tonight," Catherine said. "I was on my way to Cambridge when I got a concerned call from Harvey Tate asking if I'd drop by to find out what's happening with our biggest deal." She was at least three inches shorter than Tara, but her posture was so straight that she seemed taller. "Shall we speak in private?"

Tara followed Catherine into an empty conference room, where the two women sat across from each other at the long, empty table.

"You know?" Tara asked. She wasn't sure whether she was more relieved or afraid that Catherine had found out about Juan and Hook's link to the Kelly Jacobson trial.

"Of course I know," Catherine said.

"Who told you?"

"Todd Kent," she said.

"Todd knows?"

"Of course he knows." The woman's brow furrowed. "Tara, you were gone for an entire day."

"What?" Tara's brain searched. What did that have to do with Kelly?

"Jesus Christ, Tara." Catherine flexed her hands in the air. Her wedding band was gone, replaced by what looked like a golden finger brace. "You let one of Wall Street's top tech analysts leave a meeting ready to issue a negative report, then skipped town in the middle of the road show? What the hell were you thinking?"

"That's what you're upset about? Me leaving?" Her head felt hazy. Did Catherine *not* know about Kelly?

"Yes." Catherine nodded in bewilderment. "*That* is what I'm upset about. Where were you?"

"It was my sister's wedding," Tara answered, remembering it as if it were an eternity ago. "My sister got married in Maine and I flew up to be there."

Catherine's chest rose and fell. "Why?"

"Because she's my sister," Tara said.

"Let me tell you something, Tara," Catherine said, angry, "your sister is always going to be there—that's what families are for—but deals like this? Opportunities like the one that I have entrusted in you? They aren't always there, and they certainly aren't there for people who treat them casually."

"I only missed one day and it was Satur—"

"No excuses, Tara," Catherine snapped. "You do not get ahead in this business by making excuses."

"I'm not making—"

"Stop!" she yelled, putting her hands up again. "Stop talking. We all have to make sacrifices. And your unwillingness to do that is why Antony van Leeuwen is issuing a comically negative view on the IPO. You know this IPO is the only good thing this firm has going for it, and now, because of you, it's going to be one more bad piece of press."

Tara looked up at the ceiling. "How bad is Antony's report?" she asked.

"He's setting a price target of two dollars a share. Did you seriously miss that?" Catherine guffawed. "This is completely unacceptable, Tara. I was told you were worth watching," she said. "I was trying to help you." Her voice got more and more angry. "I put *my name* behind you."

Tara waited for the feeling of guilt, for the terror of being in trouble to push its way through the sand in her brain and propel her into action. She waited for it, but nothing came.

"What if he's right?" she said softly, shifting her gaze back to Catherine.

"What did you say?"

"I said, what if Antony's right?" Tara said more firmly, her eyes steady now. "What if these apps really aren't worth anything?"

"You were hired to sell this IPO, Tara," she said. "Nothing less and nothing more."

Tara nodded. "So I've heard," she mumbled. Her eyes dropped back to Catherine's hands. Her fingers were folded together, but her ring finger was extended, held straight by the golden contraption that went where the wedding ring ought to be.

"What happened to your finger?" Tara said.

"What?" Catherine asked, irritated.

"Your finger." Tara lifted her chin toward it.

"Don't change the subject."

"Did you hurt it?"

Catherine took a sharp breath in, stretching out her hand and looking at it over her glasses. "It's a new ring," she said, lifting it to Tara. "It's to remind me of my own strength, and not to get sentimental." She looked back at Tara. "Advice you ought to heed."

"Does your husband not mind?" Tara said carefully.

"We're separated," Catherine answered, sitting up even straighter. "He was never able to handle the fact that my success exceeded his."

Tara looked at Catherine for a long time. Her hair was perfectly in place, her outfit perfectly pressed, her skin just made-up enough, her teeth just white enough, her body just thin enough to escape criticism from any view.

"I'm sorry that I left in the middle of the road show," Tara finally said, standing. "It won't happen again."

"There aren't many strong women in this world, Tara." Catherine's voice softened. "But I think you've got it in you, if you just apply yourself."

Tara searched Catherine's eyes for understanding, but found none. "I hope you're wrong," Tara said quietly, turning to leave the room.

She went to the bathroom, locked the door and lifted the lid to the toilet seat. She opened her bottle of Xanax and poured out the pills. She did the same with the Celexa, watching them drop one by one into the toilet bowl, before she flushed them all away. She washed her hands in the sink and looked, satisfied, at her reflection, confidently deciding what she was going to do.

AMANDA

Amanda couldn't sleep. It was three thirty in the morning, but all she could think about was the as-yet-to-be-named company she was going to start with Julie.

She turned on the light and reached for *Venture Deals*, the book by Brad Feld that had become her bible for learning the ins and outs of becoming an entrepreneur.

Amanda's thoughts hadn't been so consumed by anything since Todd Kent. Julie was right: giving that time to something more useful was exhilarating. She couldn't believe how much she'd underestimated her roommate.

She looked at the clock: four a.m. Screw it, she wasn't going to go back to sleep anyway. She got out of bed and showered and dressed and headed into the office to do a few hours of trademark research before the rest of Crowley Brown got in.

When the elevators opened on her floor, the light was already on, and she saw Andy Schaeffer tapping away at his computer.

"What are you doing here?" she asked, taking a seat at her cubicle.

"Hook is fucked. The road show's about to explode."

"What?" Amanda asked. She hadn't heard from Juan in three days—she'd figured he was busy but maybe this was why. "What happened?"

"This analyst issued a two-dollar-a-share price target," Andy said. "Now everyone's freaking out that investors are going to pull out and make the price plummet."

"Do you think they will?"

"No clue."

"So what are you doing?"

"Preparing everything in case the IPO doesn't happen." Andy looked up at her. "If this deal doesn't go off and I've spent all my time . . ."

Amanda didn't hear the rest: she'd already started Googling "Hook IPO" for the latest news.

Amanda read the first search result, which had been posted twenty minutes before: *Scathing Analyst Report Values Hook at $2 a Share.*

Antony van Leeuwen, top tech research analyst at Credit Suisse, issued coverage in advance of the location-based dating app's NASDAQ debut, setting a price target of two dollars a share in an aggressive statement against what he called "farcically unrealistic pricing of social media applications." Unlike many naysayers who speculate the social media bubble will burst because of failed revenue models, van Leeuwen's predicted downfall is predicated on a thesis of user backlash if and when they catch on to how much information these apps are capable of collecting, and the safety risks associated with the storing of that data. L.Cecil, the IPO's lead underwriter, is reeling from the news, desperately trying to restore investor confidence in the twenty-five- to thirty-five-dollar price range it's been quoting for the IPO later this week.

Amanda's face went white: if the price dropped to two dollars a share, Juan wouldn't be able to build his community center, and Julie would walk away with practically nothing. All their new plans would go up in smoke.

"No way," Amanda said out loud, shaking her head at the screen. They'd worked too hard for this: she wasn't going to stand by while her friends got screwed.

TODD

"Wall Street is buzzing again today with speculations over the fate of Hook after a scathing report from Credit Suisse research analyst Antony van Leeuwen. In a nonstandard move, van Leeuwen initiated coverage before the deal is finalized, at a low two-dollar price target that is sparking others to ask whether Hook's anticipated twenty-six- to thirty-two-dollar public debut might be a scam for public investors."

Todd had always like Lucy Lowe, CNBC's hottest anchor, but right now he wanted to punch her. He watched the report as he tied his tie in the hotel room at the Rosewood in Menlo Park, where they'd arrived last night for the final two days of the road show.

"In other news, closing arguments in the Kelly Jacobson trial will be heard today in Palo Alto. The girl's RA, Robby Goodman, stands accused of sexual assault and involuntary manslaughter after allegedly giving the girl a lethal dose of the drug MDMA, or 'Molly,' which caused her to have a heart—"

Todd turned off the TV, pausing to take a deep breath and collect himself. Today was going to be difficult; there was no way around that. But with challenge came opportunity: van Leeuwen had raised the stakes, but that only meant Todd had more to gain if he won. He just had to get investors back on his side, and then he'd be even more of a hero than he'd been set up to be before.

His phone rang and he answered it as he picked up his briefcase and headed to the hotel lobby.

"Hello?"

"You need to fix this." Harvey's voice was angry.

"Antony isn't going to withdraw the report," Todd said. "You know he's trying to—"

"Then you'll have to find another way to fix it, won't you?"

"If it were a twenty-two-dollar price tag," Todd said as confidently as he could, "I'd be worried, but at two dollars? People will see through—"

"People respect third-party opinions," Harvey interrupted.

"I know," Todd said. "But—"

"You're not going to win the match if you don't get in the pool," Harvey said. "I have to go."

The phone clicked off and Todd shut his eyes, defeated. Would it be so difficult for senior management to give a little positive encouragement from time to time?

He spotted Tara in the lobby and went to join her. "Good morning," he said.

"Morning." She glanced up from her laptop, then went immediately back to typing. She'd been a bitch this entire road show. It was Callum's fault: he's where it had all started. Whatever had gone down with him in London, it had changed her, and gotten even worse after she went to his hotel last week for some midday quickie. She hadn't even apologized for skipping town for her sister's wedding, and now had the nerve to be pissed at him for ratting her out to Catherine.

"I had to tell her, you know," he said.

"What?" Tara stopped typing and looked up.

"Catherine," he said. "She showed up and asked where you were. I couldn't lie for you."

"I know," she said, going back to her computer.

"Then why are you being so pissy?"

"Am I?" she asked, still typing.

"This whole thing is your fault," Todd said.

"Antony's report, you mean?"

"Yes."

"He told me it was because he didn't trust Nick," she said, still typing.

"You talked to him?" Todd's jaw jutted forward.

"Of course," she said, glancing up, as if it were nothing. "I wanted to see if I could do anything to address his concerns."

"Which you obviously failed to do."

She shrugged, looking back at her computer screen. "I guess he has a right to his opinion." She kept typing.

"Will you stop typing?" he shouted.

She did.

"What did he say?" Todd asked more calmly.

"We had a long conversation about user information and data security. He doesn't disagree with the collection in principle, but thinks that without a clear company statement on how it's used, consumers will get nervous, especially if they don't like the CEO, and consequently stop using the app as soon as there's a viable alternative," she said, her voice casual. "I thought it was an interesting point."

She resumed her typing. She thought it was an interesting point? How could she be so flippant?

"Louisa says they're really in love, you know," Todd said, his voice full of spite.

"Who is Louisa?"

"The woman Callum's cheating on you with."

Tara's fingers stopped typing. Got her.

"Oh, you didn't know?" he asked. "Yeah, I ran into them canoodling at the bar at Gramercy Tavern weeks ago."

"Why are you telling me?" she asked without looking up, her voice weak.

"Because I'm a good guy," he said.

Tara looked up at Todd, her eyes glassy, hurt, as they connected to his. She looked innocent and vulnerable and sad, and for once Todd didn't like the feeling of his power over her.

"Tara, I'd love a coffee if you're not doing anything." Nick Winthrop appeared beside them.

"I am actually doing something, Nick," she said firmly as she broke Todd's gaze. "But I'm sure one of the thirty-five staff at this hotel could get you a coffee."

"What did you—" Nick started.

"If you'll excuse me," she cut him off, getting up to leave.

Nick's pink face turned red. "Where's an analyst to get me a coffee?"

AMANDA

Tuesday, May 13; Menlo Park, California

Amanda pulled the car onto the 280 freeway heading south to Menlo Park. She'd been up for over twenty-four hours but didn't feel tired: she was amped up with determination to save Juan's and Julie's fortunes, and the thrill of having found the evidence that would do it.

She'd started by reading Antony van Leeuwen's report, looking for errors in his logic and trying to think of a way to counter his points. But, finding nothing, she'd turned to Antony himself. It took several calls to the SEC and European Securities Committee, but eventually her prying revealed that Antony had a large stake in a fund that held a short position on L.Cecil shares. His negative report had nothing to do with debunking the social media company, and everything to do with putting another nail in the bank's coffin: one that would send *its* share price to hell, and Antony's personal returns soaring.

Whether or not Antony's points were worthwhile was irrelevant. His personal position made his opinions unreliable, and could be the key to restoring investor confidence in Hook.

She'd waited for Chris Papadopoulos to come in this morning, only to discover he was going straight to the road show breakfast at the Rosewood. Which is where she was heading now, to tell him what she'd found and save the deal, along with her friends' rightful millions, and her and Julie's plan for their company.

The parking lot was packed, but Amanda found a spot and steered the car carefully into it, taking a deep breath as she shut off the engine. She knew Todd was here and it scared her: What if seeing him made her fall for him again? What if she got sucked back under his spell and started to doubt her new path? *Just find Chris*, she told herself, getting out of the car.

JUAN

TUESDAY, MAY 13; EAST PALO ALTO, CALIFORNIA

Juan closed the door quietly behind him as he slipped out of his mother's house in East Palo Alto. It was still early, but it didn't matter: he'd been up all night agonizing over whether or not he should do it.

Juan had taken the Saturday morning flight back to San Francisco but come straight here instead of his apartment: he wasn't ready to tell anyone what had happened with Nick, not even Julie or Amanda. They'd feel sorry for him, and try to comfort him, and that would only make it worse. Juan didn't feel sorry for himself—he'd been stupid to get wrapped up in Stanford kids' problems and white people's multi-million-dollar dreams. They weren't his people, and he didn't need them or their pity.

But he did need to know what had happened.

He walked up University Avenue toward the Shell station next to the

101 overpass that separated the university part of Palo Alto from the part where he'd grown up. The area had cleaned up since the Ikea moved in on Bayshore Road, but something told Juan she'd still be there.

The sky was still gray in predawn light when he got there and saw her through the glass, bent over reading a magazine.

"Izzy." He tapped on the window, teenage butterflies reawakening in his stomach. She was still beautiful.

Isabel jumped, startled, and peered through the glass at his face. When she recognized him, she unlocked the door and threw her arms around his neck.

"Juan, Juan, Juan," she said. *"Cuánto tiempo ha pasado?"*

"Too long," he said, pressing his nose into her hair.

She let go. "What are you doing here?" she asked, glancing back at the station.

"I need your help," he said, getting to the point. "Do you know Jorge Menendez?"

Isabel's eyes got wide, then disappointed, and she shook her head. "No, Juan, not you," she said softly.

"What?" he asked. "What 'not me'?"

"Jorge's a dealer, Juan. You don't want anything from him."

"Do you know if he sells Molly?"

"I'm sure," she said. "It's what all the college kids want now. Juan, what's going on?"

"I think he killed Kelly Jacobson."

"What?" Her face paled. "Why?"

"I found something," he said, "when I was working at Hook. He was with her when she died."

She shook her head. "It isn't possible. Jorge's a sweet guy. He'd never hurt anyone."

"But if he was high, maybe?"

"He's never done drugs. You know better than to think dealers use."

"Do you know where he is?"

"Probably on his way to work," she said, pulling out her phone. "I'll call him."

TODD

Tuesday, May 13; Menlo Park, California

Every seat was taken and two dozen more men stood in the back. It was the biggest turnout they'd had the whole road show, all the invitees curious about how the team would handle Antony van Leeuwen's report. Todd took his seat and watched the presentation for the hundredth time.

As he listened to the familiar words, he felt like a point guard running down the clock, his heartbeat powered by steady anxiety as the moments ticked by. They'd retaken possession of the ball, and now they just needed to play smart and keep investors' minds focused on the positive.

He looked at his watch: nine thirty a.m., just fourteen hours until the road show was over and they flew back to New York; which meant twenty-five and a half hours until the pricing call, where they'd determine the final share price. Another twenty-four hours after that the stock would be out, trading publicly, and his part would be done. That was fifty-one hours from now. He could do this.

"Now, I want to address one more point before we switch to Q and A," Nick said.

Please don't fuck this up, Todd prayed. They'd rehearsed it over and over last night, but Todd still held his breath.

"Hook is deeply committed to maintaining individual users' privacy," he said. "While we do collect certain data in order to understand user behavior and improve our service—like all apps do—we would never share that information in any way that is identifiable or incriminating to individuals' privacy."

Good. Todd let his breath go. Nick left out the part about erasing the data immediately, but it was good enough to make the point.

Tara rose to host the Q&A. "We've got time for two questions," she said. They had planted both those questions in the audience: one from an L.Cecil analyst and one from a private bank client who was happy to ask a softball question in exchange for a guarantee he'd get Hook shares at the institutional price.

Tara called on the private bank client and he asked the question they'd prepared about projected growth rates. Tara answered as planned. The man thanked her and returned to his seat.

"Abishek?" Tara pointed to a man in a linen suit toward the front of the room. Todd's head snapped back to Tara. The L.Cecil analyst's name was Jeremy. Who was this guy? Tara kept her eyes calmly on the man named Abishek as he stood. What was she doing? This wasn't the plan.

"Has anyone ever hacked in?" the man asked casually.

Nick's face drained onstage.

"Just, with all these hackers making headlines," the man continued nonchalantly, "I wonder if you've ever had any problems?"

Tara passed the microphone to Nick and stepped away from the podium.

"Well," Nick said. "That's a risk everyone has."

"And how do you—Hook—mitigate that risk?" Abishek pressed.

"We attract the best engineering talent in the country," Nick said.

"And you're confident that talent pool will stay at the company, even with Josh Hart and Juan Ramirez gone?"

Todd looked at Nick. Since when was Juan Ramirez gone?

"How did you know we fired Juan?" the CEO asked. The crowd took a collective breath, suddenly intrigued by Juan Ramirez and why he was fired.

Todd looked back at Tara. She just stood there, doing nothing. Was she smiling?

Phil Dalton stood in the audience. "Gentlemen, in all my time in the Valley, I've never seen a company I believe in as much as Hook. So long as I'm on the board, talent is never going to be an issue and neither is security. I assure you, there is no one as dedicated as I am to making sure user information is safe. Now let's let these guys get on to their next meeting."

The crowd murmured in reluctant agreement and Tara left the stage with Nick close at her heels. Todd stood and followed them into the back hall.

"Do not touch me," Tara's voice snapped, and she shrugged her arm from Nick's grip.

"What the fuck is going on?" Todd demanded in a hushed voice.

"She planted that question," Nick said. "She's trying to sabotage me."

"Why didn't you call on Jeremy, like we planned?" Todd turned to her.

"It would have looked biased if I'd called on someone from L.Cecil."

"Liar," Nick spat. "She's pissed because of Juan. She's going to ruin everything. She's just trying to get ahead. But you're not going to," he snarled at her. "I'll stop you from ever getting anywhere."

"Did you really fire Juan?" Todd asked, stepping between Nick and Tara.

"He was in the way," Nick said.

"I cannot deal with this right now," Todd said firmly, looking between them both. He felt like he was with children. "We've got one more day of this and then it's over. Can you two please just hold it together for three more meetings?"

Nick's chest was heaving. Tara's eyes were annoyed.

"Fine," Tara said, pushing past him.

"You need to do something about her," Nick said.

"*She* is not the problem here, Nick," Todd snapped. "Now hold it together."

Todd left the room and looked around for Tara. He spotted her hurrying down the hall toward her hotel room.

"Tara, wait," he called.

She didn't stop. Todd raced down the hall, feeling the adrenaline in his legs.

He caught up with her as she reached her room. "Tara, wait," he repeated more softly. "Can we just talk about this?"

"I'm sorry, Todd," she said, pausing and looking at him for a suspended moment, without offering further explanation, then pushed the door open and let it slam behind her.

He banged his fist into the door. "Don't do this to me, Tara!"

He let his head fall into the door and closed his eyes, feeling like he was on an amusement park ride that wouldn't stop and had long ago ceased to be fun. What was he going to do? His brain raced: Harvey was going to find out about the meeting—if he hadn't already—and then he was going to call Todd and yell again with more useless lectures about third-party opinions and getting in the pool. What the fuck did that even mean?

Todd's head snapped up.

Todd had to *get in the pool*: people trusted Antony's opinion because it wasn't biased, which meant Todd had to find an Antony for his own team—a third-party analyst who investors would think wasn't biased—to write a report countering Antony's. But who?

Todd's brain searched through his Rolodex of analyst friends.

Rich! Rich Baker! Todd remembered. Rich was one of the most respected analysts in Silicon Valley, covering tech for Morgan Stanley. He and Todd had been little-a analysts together at L.Cecil ten years ago, when Rich had come out of the closet and confessed his crush on

Todd. Rich was *exactly* who Todd needed, and exactly who Todd knew
he could get.

Todd turned and headed back to the meeting room, praying it hadn't
yet cleared.

AMANDA

TUESDAY, MAY 13; MENLO PARK, CALIFORNIA

Amanda scanned the emptying conference room for Chris Papadopoulos, spotting him in the back tapping furiously at his laptop.

"Chris," she said, "I'm so glad I found you. I have something I
need to—"

He looked up. "What are you doing here?" he snapped. "This is a
closed meeting. You cannot be here."

"I know, but I found something out about that guy who wrote—"

"Do you have any idea how much I'm dealing with right now,
Amanda?" he said. "I do not need more criticism because an insubordi-
nate paralegal snuck into the road show."

"But I—"

"Leave, or I will fire you," Chris said, and she saw he was serious.

She felt her face go white and turned carefully, her legs starting to go
weak. Chris never lost his temper: for him to be that anxious, things
must be looking really bad. She felt her heartbeat race again. What was
she going to do if Chris wouldn't listen? She had to save the deal or Juan
and Julie and her company would . . .

Todd.

She had to talk to Todd.

She looked around the conference room again and felt her chest burn when she saw him come through the door, scanning the room. Why did he have to be so hot?

She took a deep breath to refocus and followed his gaze to the object of his search, then watched him beeline for a short man in a tight pink shirt and skinny purple tie.

The two men shook hands as Todd's best smile shone and the other man—clearly gay—accepted his flattery. But then Todd leaned in and said something that made the man's brow furrow.

"Excuse me," she said, interrupting two men in conversation beside her. "Do you know who that gentleman is over there, in the pink shirt?"

"That's Rich Baker," one of the men said, turning to look. "He's a tech analyst at Morgan Stanley. Probably their best. Wonder what he has to say about van Leeuwen's stance." He lifted a brow at the other man and turned back to the conversation.

Amanda's brain clicked: she knew Todd, and she knew exactly what he was doing. And if Rich Baker decided not to play ball, and to report Todd instead, he was going to screw up the deal—and her friends' fortunes—even more.

Before she could stop herself, her legs were carrying her to them.

". . . it's just a favor," Todd was saying to Rich.

"Todd"—she touched his arm—"Todd, can I talk to you?"

Rich turned to acknowledge Amanda.

"What?" Todd snapped.

"I have something to tell you," she said. "It's important."

"I'm in the middle of something," Todd guffawed. "Whatever it is, just put it on the bill," he said.

"No, I—" Amanda paused, processing his words: did he think she was staff? She looked down at the simple black dress she was wearing: he totally thought she was hotel staff.

"I don't think we should talk about this here, anyway," Rich said.

"Agreed," Todd said, and the two men went outside, leaving her standing alone, her brain reeling.

"Oh, no," she whispered, shaking her head. "No *fucking* way." She lurched out the door, feeling all her disappointment and hurt switch to anger that overwhelmed everything else. She'd figure out a way to make sure Julie and Juan got their cash, but for right now all she cared about was making sure Todd got a much overdue piece of her mind.

She spotted them by the pool, near a rose-covered trellis. She walked deliberately toward them, her inner voice reeling with the ugly words she was going to spit at his stupid perfect jawline and his stupid deep blue eyes that didn't even know who she . . . Amanda stopped. Yelling at Todd wasn't going to make him remember her. But she suddenly knew exactly what would.

Ducking behind the trellis, she pulled out her iPhone and cleared a space for the camera lens to peek through the roses, careful to avoid the thorns, then pressed RECORD.

"He's trying to make a name for himself," Todd said. "You know his report is bogus, but you also know how much these reports matter. It's going to destroy the deal."

"What do you want me to do?" Rich asked. "Antony won't listen to me."

"Can you write a good report?" Todd asked. "And send it out today?"

"You mean, something to counter his position?"

"Yes."

Rich hesitated.

"I can get you whatever information you need," Todd said. "Just name it."

Amanda held her breath: he was really doing it—cajoling an analyst from a rival firm to write a positive report about his deal. Jesus Christ.

"Please?" Todd asked.

"My report's already written, Todd, and it's good. I'm bullish on this, I really am. But I'm initiating coverage Thursday, with everyone else," he said.

"What difference will two days make?" Todd pressed him. "And a tiny boost to whatever you were planning to price it at?"

"Why me?" the man asked.

"Because you're the best," Todd said, "and I know I can trust you."

Amanda knew that voice, the charming, flattering Todd Kent voice he employed when he was using someone to get what he wanted. Amanda rolled her eyes. She no longer cared why Todd was the way he was: he was an asshole, and that's all that mattered.

"You know I've always had so much respect for you, Rich," Todd went on, flirting. "I was so bummed when you moved to SF and we couldn't hang out anymore."

"Fine," Rich finally said. "But I'm only doing this for you and Dalton."

"Thank you," Todd said gleefully. "I always knew we'd do great things together."

"I've gotta go," Rich said. "I'll let you know when it's ready."

Amanda pulled the phone back through the flowers and looked at the video: 3 minutes 47 seconds. Done. She let out a deep breath and emerged from behind her cover, then jumped back when she saw Todd still standing by the pool.

"Rachel?" she heard him say, and realized he was talking on the phone. She slid her iPhone carefully back through the flowers and pressed RECORD again.

"Rachel, how are you? // Listen, I need your help with something. // You know people at CNBC, right? // Could you get them to run a story tonight? Rich Baker is going to issue a positive report on Hook, and I want to make sure everyone sees it ASAP. // Yes, Rich Baker—he's a top tech analyst at— // Yeah, the craziest thing: he thinks Antony is full of shit, too, and wants to do us all a favor. // What? Twenty thousand dollars?" Todd's voice was angry.

Amanda realized she was holding her breath: was he bribing someone to get press coverage for the report he'd just solicited?

"But you work for Hook! // It's not a freelance project, it's a critical project to the success of— // Fine. I'll wire you the money, but the contract will be with me, personally."

Yes, Amanda silently laughed. *Yes, he was.* And from his personal account, which was 100 percent against the rules.

Amanda waited for Todd to pass, which he did with a satisfied lightness in his step. She emerged from her hideout and sat on one of the pool chairs, letting out a deep exhale before she replayed the video. The sound wasn't great, but the message was clear: Todd had just saved the deal, and brought himself down in the process.

TODD

WEDNESDAY, MAY 14; NEW YORK, NEW YORK

"Another twist in the Hook IPO came yesterday afternoon, when Rich Baker, Morgan Stanley's top tech research analyst, initiated coverage on Hook two days in advance of the company's IPO, setting a thirty-eight-dollar price target. The analyst said he decided to publish his report early in order to offer a counterargument to Antony van Leeuwen's earlier note, which set the price at a farcical two dollars per share based on fears about information privacy."

Todd liked Lucy Lowe again, watching her on the airplane screen as their plane was descending toward New York.

"For reactions to the divergent reports, we turn now to Business Day's senior correspondent Norm Naylor. Norm, what's the vibe from the investment community on all of this?"

"Thanks, Lucy. The drama is certainly high, but the consensus opinion seems to be landing in favor of Rich Baker. The fact is, Lucy, he's on the ground in Silicon Valley: he lives and breathes with the engineers who build these products and the consumers who adopt them early and, largely, indicate where the rest of the market is headed. It's really another case of New York versus Silicon Valley, and who you trust to evaluate the positive benefits of technological innovation versus their potentially negative side effects—"

"Sir, I'm going to need you to stow away the television," the stewardess politely commanded Todd. He rolled his eyes: returning to commercial travel was such a drag after two weeks flying private, even if he was in first class.

Todd exited the plane with Tara, Beau, and Neha and followed the stream of passengers to the airport exit. He'd hardly slept on the overnight flight back from the final day of the road show, but he wasn't tired. Lots of guys needed coke to keep going at this point in the deal, but not Todd: he got more energy from Rich Baker's report and CNBC's coverage and the self-satisfaction of knowing he'd made it all happen.

Rachel's story had been worth the twenty grand. The New York versus Silicon Valley spin was brilliant.

"CNBC was running the story again this morning," Todd told Tara proudly.

She looked up from her BlackBerry with a forced smile.

"Cheer up," he said, wanting someone to share his good mood. "You never have to talk to Nick again after this pricing call."

"Thank God," she said.

"We should really grab drinks sometime," he said. "After this is over and we're both rested."

She looked up from her BlackBerry again and studied his face.

"I mean," he said. Had that been too much? "It'll just be weird to go from seeing you twenty-four/seven to not at all."

"Yeah," she said. "It will be strange."

"JP Morgan thinks Hook's good up to thirty dollars," Beau announced, turning his BlackBerry to Todd so he could read the e-mail from Beau's private banker recommending he purchase the stock if it came out in the twenty-six- to thirty-dollar range they were predicting.

"Yes!" Todd high-fived Beau. Another great sign. They were so golden.

"SOUNDS LIKE you did okay in California," Harvey Tate said as he entered the conference room on the forty-second floor and took a seat next to Tara. Neha brought in copies of the final model, which suggested a price of twenty-eight dollars, with a willingness to go to thirty-one.

"Thank you." Todd accepted Harvey's compliment.

"Not over yet," the old man cautioned.

Whatever, Todd thought. Everyone knew pricing calls were nothing more than a formality, a negotiation ritual that gave the investment bank one last chance to show off and company management one more opportunity to pretend they had real power before they agreed to a price they all, after two weeks on the road together, already knew.

Todd dialed the number and the phone rang on the speaker console in the middle of the table.

"Good morning, Nick," Todd leaned forward and said into the speakerphone. "Ready to make this thing real?"

"Yes." Nick's voice failed to meet Todd's enthusiasm. "What is your proposal?"

Okay, Todd thought, no pleasantries, then.

"Well," Todd said, "as you know, there's been a huge amount of demand, which has only trended upward since Rich Baker's fantastic approval of the stock and CNBC's nonstop coverage of it. And that puts us in an even better position than we'd originally hoped."

"What's your proposal?" Nick's voice repeated bluntly.

"Twenty-eight dollars," Todd announced proudly. "It gets us a beautiful book and puts us two dollars ahead of our initial target."

"Can you hold, please?"

The line muted. "Isn't Nick alone?" Todd said to Tara. She returned the confused look.

"I'd prefer thirty-six," Nick's voice came back through the phone.

Todd coughed. "Thirty-six dollars?" he repeated. That was above any price range they'd ever considered. "Nick, at that price I don't know if you'll be able to sell all the shares."

"You mean L.Cecil won't be able to sell the shares. Isn't our contract a firm commitment?"

Todd stared at the phone. The firm commitment contract Harvey had approved at the beginning of the deal meant L.Cecil had to take on any shares they couldn't sell or walk away from the deal. "Nick, going out at that price practically guarantees a drop when it hits the market, and that won't look good for anyone."

"I don't think that's necessarily true," Nick said. "Rich Baker thinks it's worth thirty-eight dollars."

Todd hesitated. Why hadn't he told Rich to keep it more reasonable?

"Thirty," he proposed.

"Thirty-six," Nick said. "Or I think I might reconsider."

Todd muted the phone.

"No way." Tara shook her head. "He's got a two-million-dollar loan to repay. He won't pull the deal."

"What does it look like at thirty-two?" he asked Tara.

"I don't know if you'll be able to sell everything," she said. She looked up at Harvey and added, "We'd have to take a lot on as a firm."

Todd unmuted the phone. "Nick, as your advisor, I think going above thirty-one dollars is a terrible idea," he said. "You do not want your personal legacy to start as the CEO who let the price plummet on the first day of trading."

"Thirty-four fifty," Nick said. "Final offer."

Todd could feel his heart racing. Harvey's eyes bored into him. JP Morgan was capping their recommendation at thirty dollars. There was no way L.Cecil could sell all the shares at thirty-four. The bank would get hit with the loss and Todd would be held responsible. But no deal at all would be even worse. Todd watched his vision of himself crumble: he was fucked.

Harvey leaned forward to the console. "Thirty-four dollars, and we're done," he said.

"Who's that?" Nick said.

"Harvey Tate," the senior vice chairman said. "I've been in this business a lot longer than you, Nick, and I can assure you this is your best option."

Nick's breathing was heavy on the other end. "Fine," he finally said. "Thirty-four."

"Thirty-four dollars," Harvey confirmed. "We'll see you at the opening bell tomorrow."

They hung up and Harvey stood. "Thirty-four dollars," he repeated to Todd. "There you go."

"But—" It was all Todd could muster. "What if we can't sell the shares?"

"This firm can afford a loss more than it can afford this deal not going through," Harvey said.

"But my bonus! My reputation—" Todd protested, his mind racing. "All the sales guys are going to be furious—they're going to blame *me*. *You're* the one who negotiated the firm commitment. You can't just—"

Harvey's eyes were like a hawk's on Todd's face, but his voice was calm. "Since when do you think any of this is about you?" he asked.

"I—" Todd started, but couldn't find any other words.

Harvey left the room, letting the door slam shut behind him.

"Dammit!" Todd slammed his fist on the table, his brain flooding with all the ways the past half hour should have gone and didn't. "We could have kept going. Nick was bluffing. He wasn't ever going to walk away."

"Nothing you can do now," Tara said, folding her notebook. "We better get to work."

She and Neha left the room, but Todd stayed seated, looking down at his hands on the table, processing.

This entire deal happened because of him: he brought it in by impressing Josh Hart, he worked his ass off for over two months, he saved the deal—twice—at his own personal risk and financial expense. And now everyone was getting what they wanted—Josh had cashed out for massive sums, Nick got the fame and fortune he'd been pining for since college, Harvey got his deal in the headlines, and Todd . . . Todd was going to go down as the sucker who took the fall for everyone else's benefit.

Todd looked up. Had he been used? Had all of them been fucking using him?

CHARLIE

Charlie didn't know why he was here.

He'd read her e-mail two dozen times over the course of the four days he'd waited to respond. Why should he feel any urgency, when she'd taken almost two weeks to reply to his?

But something—curiosity about this woman who had had so much influence on his sister's thinking, perhaps, or maybe just the desperate need for distraction amidst the intolerably slow pace of the trial— compelled him to agree to meet her.

Charlie surfaced from the subway and his heart skipped as the hallways opened onto the empty main concourse of Grand Central Terminal. The moon shone through the high windows, merging with the orange glow of the century-old lights, waking the gold shimmer of the central clock, just before five in the morning.

"You came."

He turned at the sound of Tara Taylor's voice and was surprised. He hadn't expected to find her pretty, but she looked different than when he'd seen her on the news. "Can I buy you a coffee?" she asked.

The Starbucks in Grand Central was the only place open, but it didn't have any seats, so they walked back to the main concourse and sat on the stairs.

They sipped their coffees in silence for a moment, looking down at the empty room. His heart was beating fast, and he wasn't sure why.

"I love this time of day," she finally said.

He wasn't sure how to respond, so he didn't.

"It just feels so untarnished, doesn't it? Like anything is possible? And it's all in your hands for this one fleeting moment before everyone else wakes up and makes their mark."

"I've never known how to feel about the stars," he said, gesturing up to the building's painted ceiling.

"You don't like them?"

"I don't know whether they're nice or it's sad that someone had to pay an artist to paint stars on a ceiling in order for New Yorkers to see them."

Tara studied the ceiling through her glasses, giving it thought. "How did you know about me?" she finally asked.

"Kelly wrote about you in her journal," he said.

Tara's lips parted in surprise. "What did she say?"

"She wanted to be like you," he said, then turned his eyes away from her and added, "I don't know why." It was mean and he knew it, but it felt good to have someone to be angry with.

"You don't like me," she observed.

"Working on Wall Street would have been a waste of Kelly's talent," he said. "Anyone who really cared about her could see that."

Tara sipped her coffee but didn't respond.

"I have something to tell you," she finally said. "About Kelly."

He inhaled sharply. "Okay."

"She was logged into Hook when she died," Tara said.

"Hook the dating app?"

She nodded. "They have a database that stores information about users—where they've been, who they've been with, all their ratings. It stores all the history, from the time an account is created."

Charlie felt his throat constrict, not ready to see his sister as the kind of girl who hooked up with guys she met on an app.

"One of the programmers looked up Kelly after the news came out and found out she was logged in when she died, and that there was another user with her."

Charlie was silent.

"And apparently Kelly had never matched that user, so this engineer looked further into it, and found out that user hacked into the app's servers to find out where Kelly was that night."

Charlie felt his blood drain. "Was it Robby?" he asked carefully.

Tara shook her head. "No," she said. "I think Robby's innocent."

"Then who was it?" he asked softly, looking at his hands.

"I don't know."

"You must be able to find out."

"The programmer who found it—his name is Juan—could, I think, but he was fired."

"For finding this?"

"I think so," she said.

"You think Hook is trying to hide it?"

"It could ruin the company, if it came out."

"How do you know all this?"

"I was on the team that underwrote the IPO," she said. "Hook goes public in four hours."

"Why are you telling me this?"

"Because I think you're the one who should get to decide what to do," she said, turning her head toward him, her eyes peering into his.

Charlie could feel his chest rise and fall, looking into her eyes as if they held the key to what all of this meant. "What will you do?" he asked her.

"Whatever you ask me to," she said.

"This would ruin your deal," he said. "And probably get you fired."

"Yes."

"What if I tell you I want to do nothing," he tested her. "And just let Robby go to jail?"

"You won't do that," she said.

"How do you know?"

"I read your writing. You care too much about the truth."

Something slammed into Charlie's arm and a man in a suit paused two steps down, looking back up at the pair, whom he'd tripped over as he read his BlackBerry while descending the stairs. "Get the fuck off the staircase!" he yelled.

Charlie turned back to Tara. "Will you come somewhere with me?"

She nodded.

She hailed a taxi while he called Johnny Walker, who met them at the *New York Times* building. They sat in his new corner office as the sun began to rise and Tara recounted everything she knew.

Johnny took a deep breath. "Jesus Christ," he said, looking up at the both of them. "You're sure you want to do this?"

Charlie nodded.

"I gotta get writing," he said.

Charlie stood, but Tara hesitated. "One more thing."

Johnny turned. "What is it?"

"Do you have recording equipment?" she asked. "I mean, to record a telephone call?"

"Yeah, why?"

"Can we use it?"

Johnny left the room and came back with a recorder, plugging it into her iPhone. Tara sat up straight in her seat and dialed a number, placing the phone on speaker as it started to ring.

A chipper man's voice answered. "Good morning, Tara! Everybody ready for the big day?"

She looked at Charlie as if for courage, then closed her eyes, directing a forcibly upbeat voice to the device. "We sure are, Nick. I trust you had a good flight in?"

"It was fine," the voice said, "though my NetJets account is still being approved so I had to fly commercial one last time."

"That's a bummer," Tara said. "But over soon enough."

"Indeed."

"Listen, Nick, I just had one quick question."

"Shoot."

"You erased the database, right? The one that had that information about Kelly Jacobson and the user who was with her the night she died?"

Nick hesitated on the other end and Tara pressed her eyes tight, holding her breath as she waited for his answer.

"I told you, Tara, I can be trusted to use that information properly, but there is no need to get rid of it right now."

Tara's lips spread into a relieved smile. "Of course, Nick." She nodded. "I just wanted to double-check."

"And Tara?"

"Yes, Nick?"

"If you say one word about what you think you know about any of this I will get you fired so fast you won't know what hit you."

"That won't be necessary, Nick."

"Good." His voice relaxed. "See you in a few hours."

Tara hung up the phone, and Johnny grinned broadly, looking at Charlie, then back at Tara, who was looking at her hands, tapping her fingers on the table as if to collect herself.

At last she looked up, laughing, as tears started to form in her eyes and she wiped them away. "Just wanted to make sure he didn't get away with it."

12

TODD

Todd sipped his coffee and watched Nick attempt to flirt with the NAS-DAQ event coordinator who was giving him instructions. He couldn't wait to never see Nick Winthrop again.

Todd had been at the office until four a.m., then gone home to sleep for an hour and shower in time to be in Times Square at seven to meet Nick and support him when he rang the NASDAQ opening bell.

He looked around for Tara but she was nowhere to be seen. When his e-mail to her bounced back, he checked to make sure he'd typed the right address, then called her. When she didn't answer, he texted.

Todd: You coming?

She'd still been at the office when he left this morning. She'd said she had one more thing to do after they'd finished the calls to confirm the orders for Hook's thirty-four-dollar-a-pop shares.

They'd managed to sell all but eighty million dollars' worth, thanks to L.Cecil's private bank, which took a one-hundred-million-dollar chunk to dole out to their "new money" clients in Asia, who were so eager to get in on Silicon Valley deals they'd probably have paid even more. The book was still full of low-quality investors, though, and Todd had left the office bracing for a day of sell-offs and a commensurate drop in share price that took L.Cecil's eighty-million-dollar Hook holding into the red.

But spring was in full force outside and Todd's hope had been steadily rebounding since he'd gotten out of bed. It was possible that the price would go up, and that the eighty million would turn into a profit, not a loss, and make him a hero with foresight, not a failed banker who couldn't manage his client. It was his last hope, but in the morning sunshine it didn't seem entirely impossible.

He checked his phone. Where was Tara? He'd realized that what he'd said at the airport was true: he did want to have drinks with her after the deal, because he was genuinely going to miss seeing her all the time. Unlike everyone else, she had never been using him. She might only be a seven, but she was real.

His phone rang and Todd picked it up. "Where are you?" he asked, assuming it was her.

"Get to my office, now." The voice on the phone was Harvey's, not Tara's, and it was angry.

Harvey hung up and Todd put the phone away. "Fuck you," he said out loud. Whatever he had to say could wait.

But when he called again and Tara still didn't pick up, Todd realized that whatever Harvey wanted him to come to the office for might be related to her.

"Nick, I'm just going to pop back to the office for two seconds," he said, trying to hide his rising concern. "I'll be back in time."

"It's cool." Nick grinned broadly. "Christy and I have got this, don't we, Christy?" he said to the event coordinator, who forced a smile as she affixed a microphone onto Nick's lapel.

Todd felt his heartbeat escalate as he sat in the cab, cursing the traffic. They hadn't made a mistake in their work last night, had they?

"Can you please go?" Todd snapped as the driver slammed on the brakes again.

"What you want me to do?" the driver said, pointing at a delivery truck backing into the street at a glacial pace.

"Fuck it, I'll walk," Todd said, throwing a ten-dollar bill at the driver.

HE WAITED FOR THE ELEVATOR, ignoring all the people who congratulated him on his big day, punching the button again and again as if it would help.

"What'd you do to Tara?" Lillian Dumas smirked as she strolled up, standing beside him and watching the floor numbers above the elevator tick by.

"What are you talking about, Lillian?" Todd said, exasperated. He didn't have time for Lillian's bullshit.

"Do you not know? She quit."

"What?" Todd's jaw dropped as the elevator doors opened.

"Yo! Todd! Good luck today, man." Someone punched his arm, but Todd ignored him, his gaze set on Lillian. "Tara quit?"

Lillian stepped onto the elevator and Todd followed. "She sent an e-mail to the team this morning, thanking us for the pleasure of working together. You didn't get it?" Lillian asked smugly. "I guess she didn't have as good of a time working with you."

"Did she get an offer somewhere else?" Todd asked, not caring that his face revealed his shock.

"No." Lillian shook her head. "Her e-mail said she was taking time to figure things out."

The elevator doors opened and she stepped out, fluttering her fingers in a wave. "Have a good day, Todd!" What a bitch.

Had Tara seriously quit? Why? And why hadn't she e-mailed him or talked to him about it? Weren't they friends? And what was she doing if she wasn't going to a competitor?

He got to the forty-second floor and caught the silhouette of a pretty blonde girl standing at the window of one of the conference rooms next to Harvey's office. He wished he were meeting with her.

"You can go on in," Harvey's assistant told Todd, looking nervous for him.

The senior vice chairman stood with his arms crossed over his chest, looking out the window.

"Would you like to tell me what you've done?" he asked when he heard Todd enter, not bothering to turn around.

Todd shut the door behind him. "We closed the book last night," he said cautiously. "We were able to sell all but eighty million, which I think is pretty good given the circumstances. I've been over at NASDAQ with—"

"When was the last time you spoke to Rich Baker?" Harvey asked, his back still toward Todd.

Todd's stomach dropped. "Why?" he asked, careful.

"And Rachel Liu?" Harvey asked, finally turning around. "When was the last time you spoke with her?"

"Is something the matter?" Todd asked.

Harvey pounded his fist on the table. "Yes, something is the fucking matter," he said, his voice losing control. "You asked a research analyst to write a favorable report and then paid out of pocket for a PR firm to bribe CNBC to run a story about it."

"Who told you that?" Todd's defenses shot up. He wasn't admitting to anything.

"You did, Todd," Harvey said. "I just saw a video of the whole thing, which was conveniently recorded by a Crowley Brown paralegal at the pool of the Rosewood Hotel after your meeting there. Luckily, she's decided not to go public with the information which, I'm sure you know, would ruin the deal and this firm."

"What? How?" he asked, trying to piece it together as the room started to spin. "Who?"

"She's here." Harvey tilted his head to the conference room. "Shall we go talk to her?"

Todd's legs were uneasy as he followed Harvey to the conference room where the blonde woman turned from the window. She looked familiar.

"Mr. Kent," Harvey said. "This is Miss Pfeffer."

Pfeffer? Did Todd know anyone named Pfeffer?

She reached out her hand and smiled. "Amanda," she said. "We've met a few times before, I believe."

Todd studied her face, stripping away the neatly done hair and fitted suit and professional smirk until he saw the girl he'd . . .

Holy shit.

NICK

Thursday, May 15; New York, New York

Nick sat with his hot assistant, Tiffany, at a table by the window in the lobby of the Mandarin Oriental.

"A bottle of champagne, please," he asked the waiter. "Your finest."

"I personally would recommend the 1995 Salon Grand Cru." The waiter pointed to the menu.

"Sounds excellent," Nick said, not even flinching at the twenty-five hundred price tag. At thirty-four dollars a share, he was worth $111 million, not a measly $85. Any figure that was in the single thousands was practically pocket change.

Of course, he couldn't sell any of his shares until the lockup expired six months from now, but by then the price would be even higher, boosted by his strategic leadership.

Nick smiled out the window at the sweeping view of Central Park. He'd turned down several interviews following the opening bell on the NASDAQ, which he'd rung this morning when the markets opened. Everything would still take an hour or two to settle and for the share to start actively trading, and rather than have the cameras watching his reaction, he'd decided to come here, with Tiffany, to celebrate. There would be plenty of interviews in the coming weeks and months and years, but how often did a man get to experience his first IPO, with a bottle of champagne and a beautiful woman, looking out over Central Park from one of the most luxurious hotels in the world?

The waiter returned and popped the champagne, and Nick toasted Tiffany, who smiled sweetly. He hadn't asked whether she'd broken up with her boyfriend yet, but he wasn't concerned. No woman could resist what he now had to offer.

He sipped the champagne and looked at his iPad, which streamed a Notorious B.I.G. playlist into his headphones while he toggled between Yahoo Finance and CNBC, reading for news about himself.

He felt Tiffany's hand on his arm and looked up. She'd put down her champagne and her face was concerned.

Nick took out one of his earbuds. "What?"

"Nick, you need to look at this," she said.

"Just a second." He held up a finger while he refreshed Yahoo Finance. Nothing new yet.

"Nick," she insisted.

"What is it?" he said, annoyed.

"The *New York Times*." She handed him her iPad.

"Who reads the *New York Times*?" he said as he took the device from her. Everything that mattered was on TechCrunch and Forbes.

Nick read the headline:

SECURITY BREACH AT HOOK LINKED TO JACOBSON MURDER CASE

He felt his heart stop.

The Times has learned that Hook, the location-based dating app company scheduled to go public this morning, had a security breach last March, when an unidentified user hacked into the app's system to locate Kelly Jacobson the night of her murder. While the user has not been identified, the source confirmed the user was with Kelly in the hours leading up to her death, and that it was an account linked to someone other than Robby Goodman, the Stanford senior who stands accused of her murder. The same source revealed that the company stores information in a way that makes users' histories identifiable, in contrast to statements made by—

Nick's phone rang in his pocket. He felt sweat burst from his pores when he saw the number.

"Phil," he said into the phone, trying to sound casual.

"What's going on, Nick?"

"What do you mean?" Nick asked, deciding to feign ignorance until he had all the facts.

"Why, with all that education of yours, did you not think it prudent to tell me someone had hacked into our systems?" Phil's voice was not friendly. "And then have the nerve to let me stand before all my peers and vouch for our security?"

"I didn't think—"

"Please tell me you deleted the database," Phil said, "per the agreement we made wherein I installed you as CEO, and that this reporter in the *New York Times* is mistaken."

Nick's face drained.

"Juan was supposed to do it," Nick said. "I'll call the team right now and have them make sure—"

"Federal investigators are already at the office, Nick. They're at my office, too, collecting files and making sure no one touches anything."

"They can't do that." Nick shook his head.

"They can do whatever they damn well please," Phil snapped. "Call L.Cecil and have them stop the IPO immediately. We have to take back all the shares until we figure this out. And I swear to God, Nick, if the information from that database gets leaked, I'll see to it that you never work again as long as I live."

The phone clicked off.

Nick's heart was pounding so fast he couldn't breathe.

"What's going on?" Tiffany asked, but she was far away, shrouded in glass.

"Water," he said, reaching a hand out to the waiter, then trying to stand, collapsing back into the chair.

"Here." Tiffany passed him a glass of champagne. "Drink this."

"I can't drink that!" he shouted at her. Was she stupid? "We can't afford that!"

The other guests started to turn and stare, but he couldn't see them.

"Tara!" he shouted. "Call Tara now!"

The girl took her phone out and dialed the number carefully. "She's not picking up," Tiffany reported. "Let me try your phone." She reached across to his phone while he sat, gripping the chair, willing his heart to slow.

"She isn't there." Tiffany shook her head. "I'll try Todd." She dialed the number, but to the same effect.

Nick swallowed, closing his eyes as the room started to spin. *Stay calm,* he told himself, but the world went dark and his forehead hit the floor with a thud.

Tiffany's enormous breasts were the first thing Nick saw when he came to. "What happened?" he grunted, as she dabbed a towel on his forehead.

"You fainted, Nick," she said. "Do you remember?"

He shook his head, but then Phil's voice came back and he closed his eyes again. "How long was I out?"

"Twenty minutes."

"Is the stock trading yet?"

She shook her head. "Do you feel okay?" she asked.

"Yes," he said. His heartbeat felt manageable and his brain was starting to clear.

"I've been trying to call Todd and Tara but neither is answering."

"It's okay," he said. "We can't cancel the IPO anyway."

"But the news about—"

"We can't cancel the IPO, Tiffany," he said more firmly.

Nick had a two-million-dollar loan. If they canceled the IPO, that loan became a two-million-dollar debt that would start compounding at 25 percent annual interest six months from now, which he had no way to repay. But if the deal went through, his two and a half million shares would have some value, and the price would have to drop down to a dollar for him to not have enough to repay the loan and start clean. Even with the information about the database, surely there were enough investors out there who saw potential in a rebound to keep the price above a dollar.

"What about Phil?" Tiffany asked carefully.

"Let Phil think it was too late."

He climbed into his chair and carefully read the *New York Times* article, start to finish.

It must have been Juan who told. Which was good, because no one would believe him once they found out he'd been fired for violating users' private information. Rachel could write a story explaining how Juan was nothing more than an angry programmer trying to blame his former employer for his own misconduct.

The thought made his brain resettle. Everything was going to be fine. And if Phil couldn't see that, then Phil wasn't the hero Nick thought he was.

Nick refreshed his Yahoo Finance browser and the stock information loaded. The ticker symbol HOOK appeared, priced at $33.25.

"Okay," he said, reaching for the champagne again, "here we go."

A seventy-five-cent loss wasn't the end of the world. He had six months to make it back, after all.

He waited fifteen seconds, the time it took for Yahoo to refresh its tickers, and refreshed the screen.

$33.08

He swallowed while he waited another fifteen seconds.

$31.17

Another fifteen seconds.

$29.12

Another fifteen seconds.

ERR.

Nick looked at the screen, pulling it closer to his face. "What?" He refreshed the screen, but got ERR again.

"Where is Todd?" he screamed at Tiffany, his pulse shooting up again. "What does ERR mean?"

"I don't know," Tiffany said helplessly, calling Todd again, but still unable to reach him. What good was she?

He looked at the screen: ERR. Refresh. ERR. Refresh. ERR.

"Here," Tiffany said, turning her iPad toward him, where she was streaming CNBC's coverage.

"Trading has halted on the NASDAQ for shares of Hook, which hit the exchange about twenty minutes ago, and we're getting reports it's because of a computer glitch . . ." The female reporter stopped to listen to something coming in through her earpiece.

"Yes, it seems the computers that are trading Hook have actually crashed as a result of an unprecedented number of sell requests. A story posted on the *New York Times* website this morning reported on a security breach in Hook's systems that appears to be linked to the Kelly Jacobson murder, and the market seems to be having a literally catastrophic reaction."

Nick swallowed, clenching his jaw. He could feel the tears start to form in his eyes. *Don't cry, don't cry, don't cry,* he willed himself, repeating the mantra he used to repeat when he was eight and the kids at school were being mean.

"This is good." Tiffany's hand was on his.

"How?" Nick shook his head as he felt the wetness work its way past his lids.

"It's good," Tiffany insisted. "Great, actually."

"What do you know," he spat, like an angry toddler. "You're a secretary."

"Nick," she said, ignoring his jab, "if trading's stopped, it'll give the market time to settle down. People will start to gain perspective, and they'll see this isn't worth panicking over."

"But—"

"But, nothing," she interrupted. "This gives you time," she said, "which is exactly what you need."

Nick felt the tears retract and he took a deep breath in, nodding silently.

"They're halting trading for the rest of the day," she reported from the iPad she was watching. "They think it might take up to two days to get the system up and running again."

"Two days?"

"Yes." She smiled, leaning forward. "That gives you two whole days to straighten this out."

"You're right." He nodded, sitting up straighter. "Get Rachel Liu on the phone."

"It's going to cost you," Rachel answered without any pleasantries, as if she'd been waiting for the phone to ring.

"How much?" he asked.

"Two million a day," she said. "Cash, obviously."

"You know I can't give you that right now," he said. "Come on, Rachel, after all the business I've given you, you're really going to—"

"Call me when you change your mind." She hung up the phone.

Nick took a breath and dialed her number back. "Fine," he said. The price today didn't matter to Hook: the company itself raised over two billion dollars last night. He might as well spend it on this.

"Okay," she answered. "Here's my proposal: We deny it entirely. Say we knew nothing about the database or the hacker and force whoever told to come forward and hang themselves," she explained. "And then we say we'll cooperate with officials so long as they see fit, but it's our preference to shut down the database entirely and preserve user security."

"Okay," he said.

"I'll send a statement to you by end of day to have your lawyers review."

"Okay," he said again.

"Just one thing," Rachel said, her voice turning more serious. "Nick, you have to promise me there's no way it can ever come out that you knew."

"There's nothing."

"Are you absolutely sure?" she asked. "No e-mails, no voice messages, no texts? If we do this and they found out you knew, you're a hell of a lot worse off than you are right now."

"There's nothing," he repeated.

"Okay," she said. "I'll get started, then."

He hung up the phone and looked at Tiffany. "Can you call Phil and tell him it's under control?"

"Where are you going?" she asked as he stood up from the chair.

"I need to be alone for a little bit."

TARA

THURSDAY, MAY 15; NEW YORK, NEW YORK

Tara woke up to nothing.

She rolled onto her back and let the events replay. She recounted the pricing call and the long night calming angry brokers and her confession to Charlie and her call to Nick and her final e-mail announcing her resignation. She waited for her stomach to get queasy about what it all meant, but it didn't, and she realized she wasn't scared.

Her head ached, a dull pain pushing against her temples, which she'd read was a side effect of going off the Celexa. She didn't mind it. She got up without checking her e-mail and took a shower without going for a run, letting the water fall longer on her body than she needed it to.

She pulled on jeans, a T-shirt and flats and left the apartment without putting on makeup.

She walked down Charles Street and turned onto Hudson and went to the bagel shop she'd heard was delicious but had never gone to because bagels were full of empty calories. She walked north, stopping to buy a coffee at one of the street carts to see if it really came in a blue cup and only cost a dollar. It did.

She climbed the steps from Gansevoort up to the High Line and sat on a bench. The cream cheese had melted on the toasted bagel and she chewed it slowly, watching a man take a picture of his wife, who wore a fanny pack and an "I was on the Today Show!" sticker on her David Letterman T-shirt.

"Can I get one of you together?" Tara asked the man, who turned at her voice, pulling his camera closer toward him the way tourists do in New York, automatically suspicious when someone offers to help.

But he looked at her and the melted cream cheese on her fingers and relaxed. "Sure," he said in a Texan drawl, "that'd be great."

She put down the bagel and took several photos, including one of them kissing, which she decided was sweet, not gross or annoying.

"See," Tara heard the woman say to her husband as they walked away, "I told you not all New Yorkers are mean."

Tara finished her bagel and continued walking north.

When she got to midtown she watched the suits hurry back and forth, like ants scurrying, each carrying his speck of sand with blind faith in the seriousness of his mission, all working together to build a sand empire, without worrying what would happen if the rains came.

That's what people who hated Wall Street didn't understand. They thought bankers and brokers were malicious—that they were purposefully lying to make a profit for themselves. It wasn't true: in reality, everyone on Wall Street was just too focused on his piece of sand to see the bigger picture. However much subprime mortgage brokers had deceived the people they sold bad products to in the years leading up to the crash, they'd deceived themselves just as much. Not into thinking what they were doing was *good*, but into thinking it's *the way things were*. Their crime wasn't that they'd been evil, it was that they'd settled for a shitty system.

Her mind drifted to Charlie and she thought she'd like to talk to him about it—talk to him about anything, really, if she ever saw him again. She'd searched her in-box for his e-mail after her meeting with Catherine on Sunday, and replied asking to meet, then, noticing he was with the Associated Press, looked up his reports. She'd blushed two hours later when she realized how engrossed she'd become in his writing.

They had nothing in common, save Kelly—she understood why he didn't like her, but she still wanted him to. He was different from the men she knew: all his reporting was infused with a passionate need for justice that had nothing to do with money. She respected that kind of courage, even though it made her feel foolish for ever thinking that quitting a cushy banking job was a risk.

She took out her iPhone to listen to music and saw fifty-eight missed calls. She scrolled the list to see if there were any that were important, but they were all from Todd or Nick or Catherine or the 212.464 extension she knew meant L.Cecil. There was, though, a text message from Callum, which she opened.

> Callum: Was I right or what??? Jesus Christ. You turned out to be an expensive date. Are you surviving all this? When am I seeing you again? Xxx

Her throat burned as she reread the message. How could he be so casual when he was in love with someone else? *Because* he was in love with someone else, that's how. She cringed, knowing he'd never had real feelings for her—from the very first meeting he'd treated her as a project: a grown man giving advice to a young woman who needed perspective.

But in the process she'd become putty in his hands. He'd made her feel supported and appreciated and secure—to the point where she'd cried like a child in his arms, letting all her emotions spill out at his feet.

And as much as she wanted to hate him now—now that she knew he'd been cheating the whole time, letting her be vulnerable while he kept his own secrets separate—she couldn't. Because he'd been right: she had needed perspective, and he had given it to her. He may not be everything that she wanted him to be or hoped he was, but he'd been the only one in the world, including herself, who had ever made her feel . . . not judged.

She felt the tears well up but forced them away. She'd learned a lot, she'd gained a lot, she was a better person for it. And that was enough. It had to be enough.

She read the message one more time, then deleted it, along with Callum's contact information, and put in her headphones, letting James Blake's velvety voice fill her ears and make a soundtrack to the city's movements and her new start.

The text alert beeped in her headphones and she felt her heart clench as she looked back down at the phone, but smiled when she saw it was from Terrence:

> Heard the news. So happy for you, so sad for me. Drinks soon? Xo

Her friendships: that was another thing she was resolved to start giving the attention they deserved, along with her family and her dating life and her happiness.

She wandered to Columbus Circle and through Central Park to the Frick, where she decided to see the art she'd missed at the L.Cecil event.

George E's portraits were all photographs that he'd painted over to mimic Instagram filters. She read the commentary about social media, obfuscation of truth and the new world of self-invention, wondering where the real reason for the exhibit—that the Frick needed to attract a younger audience if it had any hope of surviving—was recorded.

She wandered to the West Gallery and her breath caught when she stood before the Turner canvas, mesmerized by the blues and yellows.

"This one's dusk."

"What?" Tara turned, startled, at the voice of an old woman beside her.

"This one's dusk," the woman repeated, "and that one is dawn." She pointed across the room to the other Turner. "Isn't it funny how hard it is to tell the difference?" the woman mused.

Tara turned to look at the painting of dawn, just as a tour group cleared, leaving behind a single man standing before it.

Tara blinked her eyes to see if it was true. "Charlie?" she whispered.

He turned and laughed, surprised, when he saw her. "What are you doing here?" he asked.

"I'm not really sure. I just decided I wanted to come," she said, forgetting what had propelled her uptown, but suddenly grateful that it had.

There was a pause, but neither of them moved.

"I haven't watched the news today," she said, breaking the silence before he could leave. "Is it bad?"

"No." He shook his head. "They let Robby Goodman go home, on bail, and are reopening the case."

"What about Hook?"

"They're saying it'll be up to the Supreme Court to decide whether information from the app should be admissible in court," he said. "It'll take years, I imagine."

"How about the IPO?" she asked.

"NASDAQ shut it down twenty minutes after it opened. The system crashed because too many people were trying to sell."

"Yikes," she said.

There was another pause.

"So did they give you the day off?" he asked cautiously.

"I didn't get fired," she said, knowing what he was asking. "I quit."

His eyes smiled. "Good for you."

"Yeah, it is good for me."

There was another pause, but neither of them moved.

"This is my favorite painting," he said, gesturing to the one of dawn. "I like mornings, too," he added.

"And here I thought we didn't have anything in common." She smiled.

"Oh, I bet we could find some. I mean, I'd give us at least . . . four."

She laughed and bit her lip.

"Where are you headed next?" he asked.

"Oh, I've got to—" she said automatically, then stopped. "Do nothing." She laughed. "So I have no idea where I'm headed."

"Do you like Central Park?" he asked. "That would bring us up to two."

"That doesn't count: everyone likes Central Park."

"Yeah, but I bet you're a Sheep Meadow person," he said, making a face.

"No," she corrected. "My favorite spot is by the Alice in Wonderland statue."

"Not as good as Balto."

"You're such a boy."

"Balto definitely transcends gender."

He winked as he pushed open the door for her and her heart skipped a beat, realizing it was an invitation.

They stopped at an ice cream truck as they walked into the park and debated the merits of chocolate (his favorite) over vanilla (hers) and by the time they stopped to decide which statue to visit first, the sun was settling in and they'd already passed them both.

JUAN

A car pulled up and Jorge Menendez kissed Isabel's cheek before saying hello to Juan. He was shorter and rounder than Juan expected from his mug shot, with jovial cheeks and curly hair, dressed neatly in jeans and a flannel shirt.

"What can I do for you?" he asked, trusting Juan because Isabel did.

It was dusk on Thursday, back in the Shell station parking lot. Juan knew Hook's IPO had happened today but he hadn't looked online to see the results. It didn't matter: he had other things to focus on. Namely, this meeting Isabel had set up with Jorge Menendez.

"Do you remember where you were the night of March fifth?"

"That's pretty specific," he said. "What are you getting at?"

"Why were you with Kelly Jacobson?" Juan said.

"That girl that died?" he asked. "I wasn't. Never seen her in my life."

Juan felt his heart sink. How could Jorge lie to his face like this?

"Are you sure?" he pushed.

Jorge took a breath in, puffing his chest. "What have you got to say?"

"I'm an engineer at Hook—or I used to be—and we can see where users have been, and our database shows that you were in Kelly's room the night she died."

"Your database doesn't know shit," Jorge said.

Jorge's macho voice made Juan feel ridiculous saying he was an engineer at some app company, but he pressed on. "She never matched with you, so I also know that you hacked into our system and—"

"Bro, you seriously think I know how to hack into some computer app? You outta your mind?"

Juan felt his cheeks blush. "But there's no other—"

"What day did you say she died?" Jorge cut him off, pulling a notepad out of his back pocket.

"March fifth," Juan said, "or technically the sixth, between two and four a.m."

Jorge flipped through the notepad, where, evidently, he kept his deliveries. He laughed. "Nah, I was definitely not at Stanford that night. We went down to the Gold Club. I got six brothers and three strippers who can all vouch for me."

"What were you doing at a strip club?" Isabel said scornfully.

"Celebrating"—he grinned, lifting his notebook so she could see—"I made two grand that day."

"Selling what?" Isabel's eyes got wide.

"Some rich kid from out of town bought my whole supply of Molly. Paid me double to deliver it to his fancy-pants hotel, then tipped me an extra hundred to use my phone."

Isabel punched his arm. "What is wrong with you? He could have been a cop."

"It was two grand." Jorge shrugged. "What are you gonna do?"

"You said he was from out of town?" Juan asked.

"Yeah. New York, I think. Said he got my number from some frat boy at Stanford."

"Do you know his name?" Juan asked carefully.

"Got it right here." Jorge lifted the notepad so Juan could see. "Beau Buckley," he read. "What a fucking name, eh?"

Juan's mouth went dry. "What?" he finally croaked.

"Beau Buckley," Jorge repeated, looking down at the paper again. "I guess that's how you pronounce it."

"Have you seen him since?" Juan finally got it out.

"Nope," he said. "Hope I never do, either. That wasn't the finest batch, if I'm being honest."

"I've gotta go," Juan said.

Isabel stood up. "Is everything okay? When will I see you again?"

"I'll call you," Juan said, rushing back to his car. His brain was spinning.

Juan's phone rang, interrupting the thought, and he looked down at the unknown caller. He sat in the driver's seat and locked the door before answering.

"Hello?"

"Is this Juan Ramirez?"

"Yes, this is Juan."

"Juan, my name is Dennis Cameron. I'm an attorney in New York who has been engaged to make you an offer."

"I'm sorry, what?"

"I've got all the paperwork ready to create a charitable foundation in which you'll be sole operator, in charge of all donations and financial decisions subject to the legal requirements of a private foundation structure. The foundation will be established in East Palo Alto and funded with a twenty-five-million-dollar check from an anonymous benefactor," the man said. His voice was kind, but professional.

"I don't think I—" Juan started. "What anonymous benefactor?"

"I just wanted to check, though, that I've got the spelling right on the form—it's the Eduardo Ramirez Community Foundation, correct? That's E-D-U-A-R-D-O?"

"Yes," Juan said softly, "my father. That was my father's name." How did this man know that? Did someone really want to fund his foundation?

"Great," the man said. "So all I need is your signature and then we'll be good to set up a bank account for you and transfer the money."

Juan's brain raced through the list of people who knew about the community center—would someone really back him? Maybe someone had taken pity on what had happened—wanted to throw him a bone after making millions in today's IPO. It must have been Josh Hart, or Phil Dalton, or—

"In addition," the man interrupted Juan's thought, "we'll need you to sign a confidentiality agreement and contract for your silence in matters related to information you might have encountered while working at Hook."

Juan's bubble popped. "What?"

"I've been informed that you may have seen information that might lead you to certain conclusions about individuals and their activity on the app," he said. "We need you to agree that you won't ever speak about anything you saw."

"You're bribing me?"

"We're asking for your cooperation."

"You're using the foundation as a bribe so I won't go public with what I know about—"

"The use of information that was gathered in violation of privacy laws for the purposes of a criminal investigation is a question for the Supreme Court," the man said, "and one that will, I assure you, be in court for a long, long time. We're asking you to not interfere with that process by making public statements about information you obtained in what might be deemed an illegal manner."

"I'm sorry," Juan said, "but I'm done cooperating. I know what happened."

"I would urge you to consider your options, Mr. Ramirez. I'll give you forty-eight hours to make up your mind."

Juan heard the phone click off and let it drop with his hand into his lap. He looked through the car window at Isabel, back in her booth, making change for a man, as if she might possess the answer, but once again she felt a million miles away.

NICK

THURSDAY, MAY 15; NEW YORK, NEW YORK

Nick Winthrop took the elevator up to his hotel room and locked all the locks on the door. He carefully removed the comforter on the king-size bed—even at nice hotels, he knew, they were covered in all sorts of human filth—and went to the bathroom to wash his hands. He straightened all the toiletries on the counter where the maid hadn't gotten them exactly right and did the same for the minibar.

He undressed and hung up the favorite fleece vest he'd worn today and lay down on the sheets, taking deep breaths, repeating his self-worth mantras until things felt okay again. He'd raised over two billion dollars yesterday. And as bad as today had been, he had survived. And given it really couldn't get any worse, he would continue to survive until he once again thrived. He liked how that sounded and repeated it again to himself, closing his eyes and letting it carry him into a deep, dreamless sleep.

It was pitch-dark when he awoke to a sound he didn't recognize, and it took him a moment to remember where he was, giving him a brief hiatus before the flood of his current reality hit him.

The sound went off again and he realized it was coming from his iPhone on the nightstand. He rolled over and looked at the device. There was an alert from SnapChat, the temporary photo app he'd downloaded but never used after he found out it was mostly for seventeen-year-olds.

He looked at the message quizzically and pressed the VIEW button.

His body went still when he saw the image, and then the thirty-six-dollar soup he'd had for dinner gurgled in his stomach and spewed over the bed, the floor, the phone and its Snapchat:

The body of a naked girl that looked like his ex-girlfriend, Grace, was splayed on a twin dorm-room bed. She had a tie around her neck, and her eyes were heavily made up, staring, dead, at the camera. Words had been printed at the bottom of the photo that read:

I'm Hooked, how about you?

The image was from an unidentified user and hung for another fifteen seconds on the vomit-splattered screen before it disappeared.

ACKNOWLEDGMENTS

The first version of *The Underwriting* appeared in the spring of 2014 as a twelve-part weekly serial on www.theunderwriting.com, accompanied by music, photography and various other experiments in digital presentation. Above all, I want to thank the readers of that original incarnation—you were the most patient critics and the most uplifting friends, and your e-mails, tweets and participation meant more than you will ever know.

I'd also like to thank those who made the original work what it was, in particular Brooke Botsford, John Crepezzi, Justin Shenkarow, Meredith Flynn, Si Domone, Hayden Wood, Dom Hammond, Alexandra Warder and Jarrett McGovern. It's hard to describe how powerful it was to work with you to bring the story to life through your own media. I remain humbled and inspired by your talents and your willingness to share them with me.

For taking the story and making it a bona fide novel I am indebted to my agent, Sloan Harris (and Heather Karpas). Your understanding and articulation of my work and your belief in this project are the greatest motivators.

If I had written down everything I hoped for in an editor, it wouldn't have skimmed the surface of what I've found in Tara Singh Carlson. Your notes in every way elevated the text, and your belief in and commitment to its publication have been the cause of much skin-tingling. I am so deeply thankful, and excited to think that this is the first of many journeys together.

Very broadly, I'd like to thank Wall Street and the Silicon Valley for supplying a steady stream of content that fed the development of this book. You were the grand affair of my twenties: I loved you fanatically and hated you with equal fervor. I'm still not sure who broke up with whom, or if we'll ever really be able to be friends, but I'll defend you to the death, and hope I've done you justice here.

I also want to thank Harriet Clark, Tom Kealey and the Stanford undergrads who let me—a *very sketchy* business school student—crash their Intro to Creative Writing seminars in 2010/11. You were all so rad, and I hope you never forget it.

For keeping the story straight, I am indebted to Henry Davis and Grace Sterritt for their IPO tutorials; Jon Levy and Bill Guttentag for their early notes; the baristas at The Smile and Euphorium Bakery for the endless coffee refills; and the various unsuspecting men on Tinder who enlightened me on the dynamics of app dating by flirting with my (super-hot) avatars.

As much as I'd like to deny it, there is a lot of me in this book, and a lot of the clumsy, raw emotion of leaping from one path to another. There are no words to describe my gratitude to the friends who held my hand and had my back during that jump, but I want to publicly thank them here: Eli Berlin, Carey Albertine, Cristina Alger Wang, Jessica Balboni, Panio Gianopolus, Dan Kessler, Adam Ross, Daniel and Cheryl Lilienstein, Jay Backstrand, Laura Davis, Nick Hungerford, Asif Qasim, Jim Mellon, Ross Lavery, the Sete crew, Matthew Murray, Molly Barton, Bruce Rosenblum, Richard Villiers, Stephen Hartley, Ashleigh Pattee, Noah and Elizabeth Lang, Jessie Borowick, Elisabeth Gray, Emily Cherry Bentley, Karlygash Burkitbayeva, Artem Fokin, Eric Kinariwala, Jessica Burdon, Tom Lee, Olaolu Agana, Moudy Youssef and Julio de Pietro. If any of you are ever having a bad day, please call me so I can remind you what a difference you've made, and how deeply grateful I am for your presence in my life.

Not at all least, I want to thank my godmother, Mary Ann Rice, my sister, Stephanie, and my mom and dad. Any words wouldn't do it justice: I am just so very glad you are you, and thankful for the ways you are always there for me. I love you so very much.

THE UNDERWRITING

MICHELLE MILLER

———

A Letter from the Author

———

Discussion Guide

———

A Conversation with Michelle Miller

———

BOOK
ENDS

PUTNAM

A Letter from the Author

FEBRUARY 2011
STANFORD GRADUATE SCHOOL OF BUSINESS
CLASS OB 388: LEADERSHIP IN THE
ENTERTAINMENT INDUSTRY

Neal Baer, creator of *ER*, is speaking. I'm in the second row, and I'm not listening.

This is what is happening in my brain:

Ohmygodohmygodohmygod. Michelle! Holy shit! You're graduating in five months and still have no clue what you're going to do with your life or how you're going to pay back that $140,000 in student debt. What the fuck were you thinking coming to business school? The only class you've even enjoyed was the freshman creative writing seminar you crashed last fall (could I submit that story to The New Yorker? *It was good. Are you kidding? It's* The New Yorker! *Yeah, but wouldn't it feel so good to show all these b-school people who think you're just a dumb blonde that you . . . Michelle!* The New Yorker! *No!).*

You should have taken the Bain offer: London would be an amazing place to live and then maybe you and Henry would get together. Is it weird that he never tried to sleep with you? Or is that sweet? Is he gay? Whatever: it's too late. Maybe this J.P. Morgan Private Bank gig wouldn't be so bad, Michelle: you could pay back your loans in two years. WHAT are you talking about? Do you *seriously want to go open checking accounts for rich people, like your freshman-year boyfriend who went to work at Facebook because he couldn't get a real job and is now going to make $80 million on the IPO? It is so totally unfair. Or is it unfair? It's actually kind of amazing, if you take the personal out of it: the way all of us with our fancy 3.9 GPAs back in 2006 were clamoring for jobs at Lehman Brothers, snubbing our noses at Zuckerberg trying to get us to work for equity. Someone should write a television show about that.*

Television's great, isn't it? Why, though? Because it has such good characters. Yes: that's why. Can you imagine creating empathy for a mobster? But David Fincher went and did it and people ate it up. I wonder if it's possible to create empathy for investment bankers. Like, would anyone ever really care about any of the people in this room being stressed? It's so pathetically privileged, isn't it: the way we're sitting here right now at one of the best business schools in the country having existential crises over what we're going to do with our lives and our excessive opportunities. But what ARE you going to do with your life? Michelle! Stop! Pay attention!

I look up at the slides, and tune into Neal Baer saying something about showrunning *ER.*

I try to concentrate but fall quickly back into my own head:

See? That's a cool job. Holy crap: what would that be like? Controlling a story and creating a show people watch, and characters they care about? Shit. I have screwed everything up, haven't I? Me and my insecure need to keep my résumé pretty, and now I'm twenty-six, sinking money I don't have into a degree I don't even like. Oh my god: our generation is so messed up.

Class ends. I have never gone up to a professor, ever. But I go up to Neal Baer.

"I think I should have gotten my MFA, not my MBA," I confess to this man who doesn't know me and won't remember.

"Why?" He is gracious.

"Because I want to write," I say, and saying it is liberating, and feels weirdly honest.

"Then write. You'll know within two seconds whether or not you're any good," Neal Baer says, turning away. But then he turns back to add, "The question is whether you have anything to write *about*. The best thing I ever did for *ER* was go to Harvard Medical School."

Neal Baer leaves. I stand, dumbfounded, letting the pieces fall into place.

Two weeks later I took the J.P. Morgan gig in Palo Alto. During my training, I was applauded for "taking the most diligent notes of anyone in the associate program" (they never looked at my notebook). Almost four years later, I hand you *The Underwriting*, as a culmination of truths I found when I dug into Silicon Valley and Wall Street, as a portrait of the generation those two worlds have shaped, and as an attempt to unpack some modern stereotypes (Todd the playboy, Nick the wannabe, Tara the alpha female, Juan the do-gooder, Amanda the ditz, Charlie the activist) and create empathy for those who don't always seem deserving.

As for me and my brain: I've got nothing left but conviction that the world works in some awfully funny ways, and the sincerest gratitude to you for spending a little time with the product of it all.

All my very best,
MM

Discussion Guide

1. How are the worlds of San Francisco and New York City similar in the novel, and how are they different? Do you agree with the author's portrayal of each? Do these cities shape the narrators that live in each city?

2. While many women in the novel hold vital positions at L.Cecil and other companies, they seem to come up against a very different set of expectations than the male characters. How is the world of finance different for women than for men? What about the world of tech? Do the women in *The Underwriting* confront or conform to these different standards? Do the characters' experiences reflect your own?

3. Has reading *The Underwriting* changed your views on privilege, its benefits and potential drawbacks? As a reader, do you respond differently to each of the six narrators because of their different levels of privilege? Why or why not?

4. How did you feel about the portrayal of the finance and tech industries in the novel? Does it seem accurate? In what ways have these two industries shaped the Millennials that Miller depicts?

5. When Rachel and Tara get drinks in San Francisco, Rachel claims "there's a difference between unemotional sex that's respectful and transactional sex that's orchestrated by an app. . . . Which is a nuance Josh doesn't understand" (p. 184). Rachel argues that Josh created Hook to

make women feel cheap. Do you think the women in the novel experience Hook differently than the men? How do Hook and online dating shape the way the characters interact? Has technology changed the nature of dating?

6. Have you faced challenges similar to those that Tara faces in *The Underwriting*? Do you think that Tara made the right choices? Why or why not?

7. Miller's characters at first seem like stereotypes—Todd the playboy, Nick the wannabe, Tara the alpha female, Juan the do-gooder, Amanda the ditz, and Charlie the activist—but ultimately each is more than a stereotype. How does your understanding of these characters change throughout the novel? Do you think these stereotypes are challenged as the story progresses? Do you feel differently about each character at the end?

8. Michelle Miller has been called a "digital-age Edith Wharton" and lists Wharton, who was lauded in the early twentieth century for her incisive novels about the privileged classes of New York, among her influences. In what ways does *The Underwriting* comment on New York society?

9. At the end of the novel Charlie thinks that Tara "looked different than when he'd seen her on the news" (p. 341). Why and how has Tara changed? How did you respond to her relationship with Todd, and then her relationship with Callum? Do you think Tara will live her life differently moving forward?

A Conversation with Michelle Miller

Your novel starts as a sort of urban corporate portrait, then the killing happens. What made you decide to introduce this element of mystery?

When I started the book, Grindr was hugely popular with the gay community in San Francisco, where I was living at the time. One of my best friends was all over it, and I got so paranoid about his safety—this notion of an open community where gay men were meeting up with strangers nearby felt like a hate crime waiting to happen. Around the same time, I visited a friend who worked at a location-based app company that has since become prevalent, and he showed me a map that had a dot where everyone who was currently logged in was; when you scrolled over, you saw their name and account details. I was shocked by the happy-go-lucky attitude about location data that both users and employees of this new breed of app had (and I'm really not usually a nervous person about this stuff). With the death of a young character in *The Underwriting*, I wanted to raise the issue of the potential dangers of these things, and to show the attitudes of the people we entrust with our information.

You write about two rarefied worlds: Wall Street and Silicon Valley. How much of your personal experience did you bring to the novel?

I graduated from Stanford undergrad in 2006, a year when hyper-ambitious kids elbowed for jobs at Lehman Brothers and the less-alpha ones kicked it in Palo Alto after graduation, working for start-ups like Facebook. Fast-forward ten years, and nothing quite worked out the way anyone thought: the Lehman kids all got canned, and the Facebook kids are worth $50 million. I always found that twist to be delightfully karmic, and the lesson from it—that you can't count on things to work out as you plan—a really important underpinning to the Millennial ethos of doing what you love. As for me, I was a consultant to ad agencies in New York and Europe right out of undergrad, then returned to Stanford for business school where I dabbled in start-ups and eventually joined J.P. Morgan Private Bank in Palo Alto, managing relationships with Ultra High Net Worth individuals in the wake of the Facebook IPO (read: under thirty-five, hundred-millionaires). So I wasn't any of my characters, but I had personal and professional links to people like them, and learned a lot from seeing the challenges—sometimes really empathy-provoking, sometimes really eye-roll worthy—that they faced.

Any roman à clef aspects to the novel, or is it wholly fiction?

I definitely wrote it to be realistic, and a lot of the details are lifted from real life. As for the characters, I 100 percent believe that all of them *could* exist, but none of them are based on real people. Except for one, who shall remain nameless.

There are a lot of characters in the novel, and at least six that we follow closely. Was it hard to juggle the numerous intertwined plot lines?

Oh God, yes! When it comes to my process, I really relate to method actors—I very much step into the character when I write—I pretend to be them as I go about my day, trying to notice what they would notice on the subway, trying to feel what they would feel and think as they would think. To keep things straight, I structure my days based on characters—there are Amanda days when I'm super fun, Todd days when I'm uncharacteristically aggressive, and Tara days when I'm pretty philosophical. I know to clear my calendar on Nick days. . . . no one wants to be around me on a Nick day.

There is some questionable—at times heinous—behavior from the characters in your book. Are any of them redeemable in your view?

I think they all are! I deeply believe that, with very few exceptions, people are good, and capable of kindness and compassion and behavior that makes the world better. But I also think that people adapt to their surroundings, and that if you have structures and systems that are built without strong values in mind, people will not only default, but start to see as normal and permissible, behavior that is not good. I think business is exactly the same way: it can be good and compassionate and make the world better—and there are businesses that do. But business can also bring out the worst in people, and in an economy motivated purely by short-term thinking it often does, to the point where "their worst" becomes so natural that they can no longer see what is wrong about their behavior.

Do you have a favorite character—or least one to whom you most relate?

That's hard! I certainly relate the most to Tara—her experiences and the pressures she feels are most similar to my own, but I don't think she's my favorite. Rachel, maybe—she's such a badass. I definitely have a crush on Callum. And to be honest, I have a real soft spot for Todd—he's got so much to offer, but he's just so stuck—it's almost maternalistic the way I root for him.

Fans were first introduced to *The Underwriting* as a web serial when you released the story online in twelve episodes. What drew you to initially share your novel online, and in this way?

I'm really interested in serial fiction, and in using it as a starting point for stories that are later developed into novels and television/film. This is how Charles Dickens and Henry James wrote, and even Tom Wolfe initially published *The Bonfire of the Vanities* serially in *Rolling Stone* magazine. I'm not sure why it died, but I think the form is particularly suited for the modern reader: content comes in short, satisfying chunks, but still fosters a close, ongoing relationship with characters. On the business side, it's also a great way to build audience, since it gives you multiple touch-points with readers, and to test content before investing on a larger scale.

Would you call the book a satire or an accurate portrait of how we live now?

Compassionate satire. I wanted it to be real, and to poke fun, and to prompt consideration of real-world issues, but I didn't want people to leave the text feeling hopeless about the world or the people in it. I guess I hoped people would leave and look at the "real life" characters a little differently: a little more aware of their contexts and a little more open to understanding why they do what they do.